Love in the Lowcountry

A Winter Holiday Collection
Volume 2

Linda Joyce • Paula Gail Benson
Suzie Webster • HM Thomas
J. Lynn Rowan • Addie Bealer
Robin Hillyer Miles • Victoria Houseman
Elaine Reed • Victoria Benson
Danielle Gadow

LRWA

Love in the Lowcountry
A Winter Holiday Collection Volume 2

ISBN 979-8-9871057-0-2

Cover Art and Formatting by Elefont Books, elefontbooks.com

Editing by SJF Books

Contents

A Sunrise Christmas

By Linda Joyce

A Sunrise Christmas

Magical Realism

Portrait artist Lauren "sees" in others their heart's desire. She fled the Lowcountry after her father's death and only returns to Sunrise once a year to visit her great aunt at the beach house. Now she may inherit it, but only if she completes the two-weeks-before-Christmas task list. Can she bury the past and call the beach house her home? Justice, her aunt's estate attorney, seeks fairness in all he does, including falling in love. He fears Lauren doesn't remember him, but if he can get her to gaze into his eyes, he's certain she'll recognize true love.

Rated: G

Chapter 1

A thick gray mist blanketed the beach. Lauren walked closer to the lapping waves to keep an eye on her two canine boys. They raced and frolicked in the whitecap ripples of the Atlantic Ocean's changing tide. Seagulls cawed, flapping their wings to take flight when the dogs invaded their flock. The resort house on the island, a hundred yards inland, disappeared in the fog. She was alone—except for Jake and Max—on a deserted beach.

The choice had been hers. It was the way she liked it.

Christmastime in Sunrise, South Carolina, bore no resemblance to her Midwest ones. Here, when the sun shined, saltwater turned blue, sand glistened a silky beige, and palm trees waved green—the stark opposite of mostly flat, mostly brown, and very safe Kansas.

"You can't not go," her half-sister had insisted. "It's romantic there."

"As romantic as a bison caught in a carwash," Lauren muttered, remembering the argument. And yet, here she was.

Jake pranced toward her, kicking up sand, his tongue hanging out. "Where's Max?" She stopped to pet Jake. "Max!" She whistled twice. Her eyes searched the grayness and then caught a streak of black and white. "There you are. Here!"

"Hey there. Are you the one exercising these guys?"

A man jogged toward her. She rubbed salt spray from her eyes. It was as though he stepped through an opening in the fog. If she let her imagination run, this was an episode of *The Twilight Zone*. The old black-and-white ones on permanent rerun. Except for Jake's orange-and-white coat, the world, like the TV show, was a monotone black and white photo.

Max raced the man, heading toward her. Her boy was clearly winning.

"Max. Here!" She hoped her salt-and-pepper dog hadn't bothered the guy. Max put on his brakes, turned on a dime, and obeyed. "Showoff," she muttered.

The man's jog slowed to a walk. He did a skip-hop to avoid the incoming seawater. He was definitely real, unlike the legendary Gray Man of Pawleys Island—the ghost harbinger of hurricanes.

Lauren moved inward toward the soft sand. The dogs followed. So did the man. She turned partly, looking over her shoulder. "Yes, I'm with Max and Jake. Dog owner. Dog exerciser. Dog entertainer."

The blond man garbed in running wear walked closer. She guessed him to be about six feet tall. Thirty-something. Possibly younger than her thirty? Maybe. She'd been told while standing in line with her purchases at the grocery store that her selection of skincare products needed a more professional approach—Southerners, she'd remembered, were very friendly that way. The woman offered her business card. She owned a spa and had said the beach sun aged people more. High-quality products with a high level of SPF would ward off skin cancer.

So maybe he was younger than she imagined given his winter tan. Other than a quick glance, she avoided his hazel eyes.

"You're Lauren Davis, right? Nice to meet you. I'm Justice." He held out his hand.

She curved her hand for a fist bump instead. "Guilty."

He grinned. "You have a sense of humor."

She rolled her eyes. "A pitiful attempt."

He nodded. "It's not a crime. Look, I live next door. I'm very sorry for your loss. Your aunt was a wonderful woman. She told me you'd be coming. But I had expected you back before Halloween. There's not much time left."

"Oh, you're *that* Justice. Mr. Justice Heyward. Aunt Jessie's attorney." She'd thought from his many emails that he'd be older.

"My friends call me JD."

"As in Juris Doctor degree?"

"You *are* really funny. JD is for Justice Drayton. The other JD is only my professional title."

Lauren turned his words around in her head. How could Aunt Jessie have known she would agree to come? It had taken Chantilly, her half-sister, weeks of constant harassment to convince her to investigate her inheritance. The calendar added stress. The inheritance had an expiration date. Lauren had finally caved and hit the road in her Jeep when news of an ice storm threatened to shut down I-70 out of Kansas City.

She zipped up her jacket against the damp morning, all the while keeping her gaze lowered to avoid any direct eye contact. "Very impressive name, Mr. Heywood." She focused on his mouth, his chin, his jaw. Lips full. Chin solid. Jaw square. "It's nice to meet you. I need to get Jake and Max back."

Overhead, a few seagulls hovered. The sea breeze stiffened. It *popped* the edges of the flag she'd hoisted before dawn. Aunt Jessie had always stressed the flag must see dawn's early light. Besides, it was the only way she could identify the house from the beach. An anchoring landmark.

The ocean's salty-mist scent filled her senses. Clean. Calm. Cleansing. She walked in the direction of the house still hidden in the fog.

She stopped when Justice spoke in falsetto, mimicking a stereotypical female voice.

"Mr. Heywood, what else did my aunt tell you about me?"

She turned to have him in full view.

He crossed his arms over his chest. "Well, let's see." His voice dropped to a deep baritone. "She told me your middle name is Jessamine, you're named for her and for her sister, Lauren. She told me you are the perfect one to inherit the house. She told me she made the terms of the will tough because you're a tough cookie, a tough nut to crack—her words, not mine."

Lauren stared at his feet to avoid his eyes. Had Aunt Jessie told him the truth about her? People outside the family had called Auntie Jessie crazy, and it wasn't just because she wore stripes and plaids together. Did he think her aunt peculiar?

"I left several messages for you. We must go over all the terms of the will. This afternoon would be convenient for me. What about you?"

The truth rose brighter and quicker than a sun rising at dawn. Their meeting wasn't by chance. He'd known she was here, probably since she'd arrived. Known who she was. Known she exercised the dogs at dawn. She knew he knew. And now he'd turned all business and attorney on her.

"Well, Mr. Justice Drayton Heywood, if you know so much about me, then you know I'm not sure I'm going to accept my inheritance. And until I do, there's no reason to meet."

Avoiding his gaze, she walked away at a fast pace. Not fast enough to be a trot or a jog, not enough to hint she feared what he had to say, but fast enough to let him know their conversation was over.

"Hey!" he shouted. "Miss Lauren Jessamine Davis. It's exactly two weeks until Christmas. Your aunt was avant-garde. I'll expect to see some colored holiday lights on the house this evening. If you decide you want some help, I'm available."

"No thanks!" She waved him off. Lights on the house? Maybe. Help? Definitely not.

Jake and Max ran on ahead. They waited for her at the start of the long wooden walkway that crossed the dunes, leading to the house.

"Miss Davis."

Justice's sudden appearance behind her startled her. She turned. The wind, waves, waterfront symphony of bird cries had muffled his approach. However, he'd left deep tracks in the soft sand, indicating he'd jogged. She focused on those footprints. Not his face.

"In order to fulfill my obligation to my client, I'll expect you at my office at 2:30 p.m." His voice was full of attorney authoritativeness. "There are specific conditions of the will you must meet. If you're not at the appointment, you'll leave me no choice but to find you. Today."

Lauren simmered with resistance.

"If you don't cooperate, then I'll be forced to evict you from the property tomorrow."

What? So soon? She'd been there for forty-eight hours. Barely enough time to explore the large beach house. Not enough time to discover if she could be comfortable there . . . again.

She laced her fingers together, pressing her palms closed, and gazed at her feet. "Mr. Heywood. Compromise. Could we meet at the beach tomorrow morning at sunrise? We could go over things then. Are there any other specifics I *must* fulfill today to prevent eviction tomorrow? If I must display Christmas lights tonight, then I shall."

She could feel the heat of his gaze though she couldn't see his eyes.

"You're a curious woman, Miss Davis."

"Strange, you mean."

"No, I say what I mean. Curious. Therefore, yes. If you display Christmas lights tonight, I'll meet you tomorrow at sunrise."

That would buy her time to meditate with the house. Sit in each room and listen to its sounds. Feel its vibrations. Hopefully, by tomorrow, she'd *feel* whether or not her future was here.

Jake barked and ran further toward the house. Lauren kept him in her sight. "I'll see you tomorrow, Mr. Heywood." She walked to where Max waited.

"Miss Davis. Your aunt said you were also a peach. Pretty. Endearing. Attractive. Compassionate. Headstrong. I look forward to getting to know those sides of you too. At least I will, if you give Sunrise a chance."

Lauren smiled and lifted her gaze so it settled just above his head. "We shall see, Mr. Heywood." She waved to be polite when he departed.

"Over your salt-baked body at a Southern barbeque." She said it only once she was certain he was out of earshot.

Chapter 2

Lauren petted Jake and raced him to the house, a fifty-yard dash on wooden slats. Jake won. Max gave his "I want to eat!" bark from the deck.

"I know you want breakfast." She and Jake climbed the gray, weathered wooden stairs to the second-floor deck, choosing exercise over the elevator—a luxurious want for an able-bodied person, yet a crucial need for an elderly woman living alone. It had given Aunt Jessie independence until her final days.

On the deck, Lauren grabbed the water sprayer hooked on the wall and sprayed the sand from her waterproof boots. Max's bark grew insistent. He acted like Mr. Heywood's mini-me.

"I'm here. Be quiet." She opened the sliding door, sloughed off her boots next to a box of Christmas lights Aunt Jessie had left, and entered the living room. Her fur kids trotted behind when she crossed to the beachy white kitchen, updated only a year ago. She imagined making magical meals there while watching the pups on the deck and beachgoers at the water's edge. But only if she ran the fourteen-day gauntlet Aunt Jessie prescribed.

Lauren fed the hungry boys. They ate, and she grabbed a container of yogurt from the fridge, poured in a scoop of granola, and mixed it in.

Her sister called, but she ignored it. It would irritate Chantilly, who, in turn, had already irritated her. Her sister must have known about Aunt Jessie's plan and Mr. Justice Heywood—JD. Chantilly always meant well. Older sisters always do. She proffered advice on what career Lauren should have and where and how Lauren should live. She needed her sister to be a sister and stop mothering her.

The kettle whistled. Lauren made tea and took it, along with the yogurt, to the deck to eat. The morning breeze had lightened and shifted. The sound of the waves and the birds and a few barks from dogs on the beach soothed her mood. She had many good childhood memories of this place. Yet, sadly, she'd allowed recollections to be forever colored by a single event.

Sunrise was not only the town's name but also the name of the magical private island nestled off the coast of South Carolina. People often overlooked it. Years ago, a barge hit the single-lane bridge connecting it to the mainland. The wooden structure had never been rebuilt. The two hundred island-home properties had been in the same families for a century.

The houses along the beach rested on tall pilings, hoisting them into the air. Building codes had changed in modern times. Height protected the structures from flooding during storms. Trees, ones Aunt Jessie planted after a hurricane, had grown up and offered some protection from windy gusts. They added the extra benefit of creating a barrier between the houses, which reduced the opportunity of a nosy neighbor's prying eyes. Ones like Mr. Heywood.

What he didn't seem to know was that Aunt Jessie had provided her a copy of the will over a year ago. She was well aware of the time limitations and the tough requirements she must pass in order to legally inherit the house. As far as she knew, Mr. Heywood stood nothing to gain if she went or stayed. He'd been nothing but pushy in his emails. There *had* to be something in all of it for him. But what?

"Christmas lights by tonight," he'd said. Insistence should've been his middle name. Her father had possessed a similar demeanor, he'd been a Charleston attorney and died in a sailing accident when she was a senior in high school. The end of his life had brought the end of her life as she'd known it.

Her thoughts returned to the will. Rather than twelve days of Christmas, Aunt Jessie presented her with a fourteen-day to-do list. Each day she was required to perform a task. Nothing heroic or grandiose. Something most people would consider normal holiday preparations. But it sure felt like manipulation. "And Mr. Heywood is check-off-the-list monitor," she grumbled.

Lauren leaned on the railing, pausing to commit the beach view to memory in case she decided to leave before Christmas or failed her tasks in some way.

Maybe she could live here again . . .

"But that won't happen unless I comply. There are no rules about how *many* lights, so let's do this, boys." She grabbed the box of lights from inside the house and set it on the picnic table. The box held strings of neatly rolled lights waiting to adorn the house. When she was a kid, decorating for Christmas had been one of her favorite things to do. More good memories.

She threaded the lights horizontally through the deck rails for the entire length of the deck. Three strings, three stripes: white, red, and green. Once lit, the lit lights offered a soft glow, visible in daylight and vivid at night, all the way to the beach as long as it wasn't too foggy.

Her cell phone rang. Max barked at the ringtone and then went inside and curled up on his bed. He wanted no part of the conversation certain to take place.

"Hello, Tilly," Lauren answered stiffly, using the nickname her sister hated most.

"Hello, yourself. I know you have the lights up. What's next?"

Lauren laughed. "Of course, you know. You wouldn't be you if you didn't. *Why* am I doing any of this?"

There was silence from her sister.

"Chantilly, you still there?"

A deep sigh rang in Lauren's ear.

"Lauren, you do not listen. Do not. Listen. You know *why*."

"You said it was romantic here. That's a reason for a honeymoon, it's not a reason to uproot my entire life." There was something Tilly wasn't saying, she'd have to get her to confess.

"Hello?" A familiar voice called from the wooden walkway below.

She spotted JD. "Hey there."

He waved. She waved back.

"Tilly, I've got to go." At least her neighbor served a useful purpose this time.

"Yes, I know." Tilly's voice was smug. "Be nice to Mr. Heywood. I'll bet you haven't looked him in the eyes yet. Don't not look. I dare you."

Her sister consistently hit the sorest of her nerves.

"Later." Lauren ended the call and went to the edge of the deck. "Hello, Mr. Heywood. Is there something you need from me?"

"I brought a timer for the lights. On-off automatically."

"I planned to just leave them on. It's winter, it's not like they'll interfere with the sea turtle egg-laying season. That way, I'll have Christmas on all day every day . . . at least until the twenty-fifth of December."

"That's an interesting notion, Miss Davis." He continued closer and closer to the house. "I'll leave it on the table down here in case you change your mind. You can pick it up when you run the boys again."

He disappeared beneath the deck. "I can see the lights from my house. I hope you'll put up more."

"Thank you, Mr. Heywood. See you tomorrow morning." She didn't want to see him. Didn't want to deal with him. And especially didn't want him keeping an eye on her from his house.

Lauren sank into a lounge chair and closed her eyes. "If I could do anything today, what would I do?"

An image of the woman from the grocery store, Sophia Walker, popped into her head. Lauren searched for her purse in the house. After finding it, she pulled out a business card. "The Pearl. Relax. Refuel. Revitalize. Owner, Sophia Walker. Sounds like perfect self-care and a distraction."

Lauren made a call.

"Yes, I remember you. I've been booked solid. If you'd called ten minutes ago, I would've said no appointments until after the new year. However, someone just canceled their day of beauty. Massage. Hair. Nails. What would you like?"

A vibration zipped through Lauren. "All of it." As soon as the words left her lips, she understood that a spa day was exactly what she was supposed to do.

"Be here in an hour. Lunch is included. Champagne is a little extra charge and your choice."

"By all means, I want to champagne it up." Usually, she only afforded herself a day at a spa once a year. A birthday present.

Feeling lighter, feet of feathers, Lauren danced through the house, room to room, up the stairs to the family room, and three other bedrooms. She hummed and clapped, practiced her pirouettes, and performed jetés. The house shimmered. The energy sparkled. It was as though she was ten years old again with dreams of still being a ballerina.

The house welcomed her.

A flicker of hope blossomed. Maybe it had been waiting for her return.

Lauren checked her phone. She had to leave in ten minutes. "Max. Jake. Let's go outside." They pushed past her to scamper down the stairs to the carport and small yard below. She followed and found Mr. Heywood, eyes closed, lying on the wooden picnic table.

Jake did a hop to the picnic table bench. With the second hop, he landed squarely on the man's stomach, then began to lick his face.

"Ouhhhh!" JD sat up, pulling earbuds from his ears.

"Jake! Down." She ran to the dog, scooped him up, and set him on the ground. "I'm sorry. Are you okay? Jake has a tendency to be assertively affectionate."

"I'm fine. You're very devoted to your Brittany boys, Miss Davis." He turned and planted his feet on the bench.

"You must be psychic, Mr. Heywood. I'll see *you* tomorrow at sunrise. Boys, let's go for a ride." She pulled her keys from her purse. Jake ran to the Jeep. Max stood by her side, her Velcro boy.

"They say you can tell a lot about a person by the way they care for their dogs. I think that's part of your compassion. Certainly an endearing trait."

She liked that he noticed her commitment. Maybe she'd been too quick to judge Mr. Heywood harshly. "Dogs are creatures of habit. I can count on them to be consistent in their behaviors. I can't always count on humans in the same way. I'm sorry to run, but I have an appointment."

"See you later." He waved goodbye.

She wondered what kind of music Mr. Heywood preferred. She could ask him, but it would be easier to ask Chantilly. She was sure to know. Maybe he wouldn't be so bad as a neighbor. Her sister would know that too. But she would never ask.

Her sister already knew too much.

Chapter 3

Lauren pulled the Jeep into the only empty parking space at The Pearl. As though caught in a time-lapse film, the fog had burned away, sunlight brightened Sunrise, and Lauren soaked up island energy. Even the parking lot had 'Lowcountry' stamped on it. Large oaks with long, stretching branches, some dripping with Spanish moss. Full of shade. Lauren could feel the roots of her memories coming up through the soil, through the blacktop, to wrap around her ankles, claiming her as a daughter.

"Home." Everything whispered to her.

She wanted to curl into that welcome. Except she'd been run out of her home in humiliation before her eighteenth birthday. Why that event had produced an irrepressible ache, which refused to heal, she'd spent her adult life puzzling. Now, each breath the island offered came with an energizing spark. If she stayed, could enough sparks suture the festering wound closed? Could this truly be home?

She sighed, turned on a portable fan, and locked the vehicle, windows cracked for airflow. "Be good boys."

Relaxation, refueling, revitalization waited inside The Pearl's doors. Her ticket to temporary bliss. She'd take it.

Lauren walked into the sounds of a babbling brook, scents of the ocean, and shades of blue in a luxuriously decorated lobby. "Hello. I'm—"

"Miss Lauren!" Sophia clapped like an excited schoolgirl. "I'm so glad you came. In just a moment, Phoebe will take you back and get you acquainted with the spa. I need you to fill out this paperwork." She handed over a clipboard with several sheets of paper attached. "Have a seat right there. Would you like some mint tea?"

"I'm fine." Lauren took the offered clipboard and sank into a plush chair. The paperwork requested answers to routine questions.

Sophia took the seat next to her. "I got a dog. After we talked at the grocery store, I went straight over to Bluffton to the rescue. Walked in. Spotted a little cuddle bug. My heart swelled."

"Oh." Lauren had never had a person respond so quickly to information she'd shared.

"Little Calypso came home with me. You were right. What I needed most, what my life lacked was unconditional love." Sophia held up her phone. "Here's a picture of my sweet girl."

"She's precious." In the dog's eyes, Lauren could read Calypso needed Sophia. They were a perfect match. In Sophia's eyes—she'd read them at the grocery store—the forty-five-year-old woman needed love. Unconditionally. A dog could be woman's best friend.

"You have a gift, Miss Lauren. It's like you see into a person's soul and know what they need."

Lauren cast her glance downward at the paperwork.

"So, I'm thinking ahead, for next year's Halloween, I'd love to do a spa party." Sophia grasped Lauren's wrist. "Would you be interested in telling fortunes?"

Lauren lifted her gaze, her brows furrowed. "Miss Sophia. I'm not a fortune teller."

"It doesn't matter what name you give your gift. Your Aunt Jessie told me you were a gifted young woman."

Lauren's heartbeat rose. Pulsing sounded in her ears. Her cheeks warmed. Surely Aunt Jessie couldn't have told this woman about her. That would be a monumental betrayal.

"She said your artistic eye made your paintings sought-after works of art. And that you are a well-known portraitist. But now, I know there's something more because you looked at me. Looked me straight in the eye and asked me if I could recommend a place where you might volunteer to help dogs. That was all the sign I needed. It was like your magic sparkled inside me. You read me. That's what fortune tellers do, right?"

Lauren let a little breath escape. "Well, since I'm not a fortune teller, I can't say for sure. However, if you decide you'd like a portrait painted of you and Miss Calypso, please let me know."

"Excellent! That means you're staying."

Sophia had surprised her again.

"Wait. What? What do you mean?"

A young woman entered the lobby before Sophia could answer. "Miss Lauren, we're ready for you. This way, please."

Lauren rose.

Sophia stood, leaned in, and grasped Lauren's arm. "We are a small community. Word gets around . . . in the breezes, the calls of birds, the lapping of the waves. And Justice could be a special friend," she whispered, taking the clipboard with the uncompleted paperwork. "I'll fill this out for you, and what I don't know, you can fill out next time you come."

Was Sophia a fortune teller? She believed Lauren was staying, as in permanently becoming a resident of Sunrise? And what did she know about her encounters with Mr. Heywood? Unless of course, Sophia was indeed psychic. Or had her sister made a few calls?

Lauren pondered how to protect herself from the ethereal prying eyes of a person with mystical talents.

Phoebe ushered Lauren through the lobby doors and into a foyer with three doors. They entered the ladies' area. A breath of jasmine-scented air caressed Lauren's face. A cooling, relaxing entrance to a serene world. For a little while, she could sink into herself with the pampering, letting go of the world outside.

"We'll do the massage. However, Miss Sophia added a salt scrub before the massage as a gift to you. After that, you'll soak in the jasmine-scented water in the jetted tub. Then massage, shower, and your mani-pedi. Hair last."

"I'll be a completely new woman by then." Lauren smiled, her gaze rested just above Phoebe's head.

The young woman's smile faded. "Oh, I like you just the way you are. I wouldn't want you to become someone new. Just a relaxed you."

The young woman's seriousness humbled Lauren. "Phoebe, thank you. I think that's the nicest thing that anyone has said to me in a long time."

Phoebe's eyes grew wide. "I hardly doubt that, Miss Lauren. You're so pretty with your beautiful clear skin, auburn hair, and cupid lips. If I were a painter, I'd paint *you*."

Lauren was further humbled.

"Now, let's get you ready for that salt scrub."

Lauren zipped up her energy, it was her ritual for closing down her intuitive vision. Always avoiding eye contact could be entirely draining. This way, she could look at someone, but only their physical being, not see their deepest need. She didn't zip up often. She needed her visions to keep her safe in those cases where someone had nefarious intentions. However, the effects of the shutdown lasted about six hours. Long enough for her to indulge in one glass of bubbly, be spa refreshed, and then take the boys for a run on the beach at dusk.

Sophia didn't disappoint. The spa did everything it claimed and more. Lauren removed the plush robe and slid on her clothes. Her skin tingled. She was grounded and giddy.

At four-thirty, Lauren floated to her Jeep, drove to Aunt Jessie's house in the fading light, and parked. She grabbed leashes and opened the rear door, releasing Jake and Max. The boys took off across the yard, their feet clacking against the walkway's wooden slats. She jogged, but by the time she reached the beach's soft sand, the boys were a hundred yards away. She spied something with glowing lights next to the flagpole. Curiosity lured her for a closer look.

"Hello," a man called to her. "They went that way." He pointed to the left.

The jetty, in that direction, was the U-turn point for the boys. They'd head back shortly.

Lauren blinked. Someone had placed a lit Christmas tree in a large red planter next to the flagpole. The man who'd spoken lounged in a chair. She walked in front of him. While the tree and man were curious, a bothersome thought niggled at her mind. He looked familiar. About as tall as Justice. Medium-brown hair neatly cut above his ears. A khaki-pants-and-button-down-shirt kind of guy. Leather boat shoes. His wool blazer reeked of wealth. He probably belonged to the golf club, yacht club, and polo club. The way he took in the sight of her, she fully expected him to call her by name. She averted her gaze to avoid his eyes.

"Thanks for the locate on the boys. Do we know each other?"

"Yes, I suppose we do. Or rather did."

She studied him hard, but other than a vague familiarity, nothing came to mind. Her instincts plucked at her. Friend or foe? She turned her attention to the live tree. "Did you put the Christmas tree here?"

"Yes, I suppose I did."

"Why?" Who was he? What did he want?

"Oh, not that again." His annoyance popped like a blast from a tug-boat's horn.

"What do you mean *again*?" She bounced between being annoyed and slightly worried.

"Your sister told me you were in a *why* mood."

He knew my sister? As much as she wanted her sister out of her personal business, this would require a call—again.

Jake and Max dashed up, dripping cold water, and shook.

Two men and a woman, walking on the beach, moved from the water's edge and came toward her and the dogs.

"Hey! Nice tree." One man waved.

The woman smiled. "Miss Jessie always put one up every year."

"You're Lauren?" The other man lifted an eyebrow.

Lauren smiled. "I am." She smiled at the other two. "And this is . . . " She tried to get the wool-blazer man to reveal his name.

"Everyone knows Oliver. He lives there." The woman pointed to the house to the left of Aunt Jessie's. "He's the island poet."

"Oliver the Poet on one side. Justice on the other. Is this my poetic justice?" Lauren muttered.

"I supposed it could be." Oliver stood. "I came to let you know we'll be caroling tomorrow night. It qualifies as Christmas music, and you'll be able to cross it off your list."

The woman offered Lauren a bag. "These are handmade Christmas cards, this will help you with your list."

Lauren looked at each person standing around her. Did everyone on the island know her business? Had the fourteen-day list been published somewhere?

"I suppose you could say *thank you* for the support of the community rolling your way." Oliver tipped his imaginary hat and wandered toward his house.

The other people waved and continued on their walk, leaving her standing there alone with a lit Christmas tree and a bag of Christmas cards.

"Thank you!" Lauren waved. The people going on their way waved back.

"A chat with Justice Drayton Heywood is what I need, I suppose," she muttered to Jake and Max, then headed to the safety of the house. The thought of talking to Justice Heywood bothered her a whole lot less than it had that morning.

Chapter 4

Dusk turned to night. A close to a very long day. Diamonds twinkled in the blue-black sky. The red, green, and white Christmas lights sparkled through the darkness. Lauren fed Jake and Max dinner, then turned her attention to the ingredients on the counter. A peace-offering carrot cake for Mr. Heywood. He had answers. She needed answers. Cake was the key to unlocking answers . . . unless she could get him drunk.

But that would be unwise and possibly unsafe.

Thoughts of him kept rolling up, like an electronic billboard. The man's wit intrigued her. He clearly had brains—a very sexy attribute. His smile produced a warm flush inside her. And he was of an age to know what he wanted and say what he meant. She was smitten. But would never admit it to anyone.

Maybe that was a warning?

Either way, if she had any hope of making Sunrise her home, she required privacy. People didn't need to know her business. Back in Kansas, she rarely accepted clients there. Instead, she flew to meet them wherever they lived, did a basic sketch, took several photographs, then returned home to paint. The finished work shipped when completed. Home meant sanctuary. Alone. Except for Max and Jake.

"Focus on the cake." Her hand-grated carrots added a different texture than that from a food a processor. She doubled the amount of pecans. The batter glistened from the sunflower oil. Then it went into the tube pan and into the oven for an hour. Which would be about the amount of time she'd need to carefully consider what to say to Mr. Heywood.

Bzz. Bzz. Bzz.

"Hello, Chantilly. We haven't spoken in such a long while." Lauren didn't hold back the sarcasm.

"You are not unresponsive to the seduction of the island, little sister. It's where you belong. People are offering you support. They're welcoming you."

"Invading my privacy is *neither* welcoming nor supportive." She hated the truth of her sister's words, but until she'd made a one-hundred percent commitment to stay, she didn't dare let up on her battle of resistance with her sister.

"I beg you, please don't be stubborn for the wrong reason. The house has been in our family forever. No one has ever sold a property on the island. I want my children to come and visit you, like you and I visited Aunt Jessie."

"You're thirty-five and don't have any children."

"Well, I might. Sooner than you know."

Was she adopting? Chantilly's mother must be pitching a hissy fit. Her edict—only blood kin allowed. The woman had insisted Lauren was less-than because her mother had been the second Mrs. Davis, not the first, and Lauren was only a half-sister to her daughters. Half didn't count. Half was nothing.

"I'll think about it." Their family tree was as twisted as the windblown Southern live oaks on the island. Her mother had been her father's second wife. She died after childbirth. Her father and housekeepers had raised Lauren in Charleston. However, he allowed her to visit his aunt on the island now and again. Aunt Jessie convinced him Lauren would benefit from spending weekends and holidays there after her thirteenth birthday. Then he died in a boating accident.

Following the ugly incident at his funeral, she'd fled Charleston and the island, mostly cutting off family ties. Now there were other details her sister had omitted related to the island home. "Chantilly, who is Oliver? Oliver—what's his last name? And why have you been talking to him about *me*?" Her voice rose an octave.

"Little sister," Chantilly spoke in a hush. "Oliver was my first . . . crush." She sighed. "So romantic. But it was not to be."

How did Lauren know so little of her sister's past? Chantilly had loved Oliver?

Her sister had departed for college when Lauren was thirteen, only came home at Christmas, but never to the island. Home was at her mother's house south of Broad Street. However, despite their lack of childhood bonding, Chantilly had inserted herself into Lauren's life as a surrogate mother after their father's funeral—whether Lauren liked it or not.

"Chantilly, if I don't keep the house, does your mother benefit in some way?"

"Oh my! Lauren, it's not a consideration to be ignored. I must go. Say hello to Justice." Her sister ended the call.

"Arrrh!" Lauren clenched her fists. There was a thin line between love and hate, but no line between love and frustration when it came to her sister. Lauren paced from the dining room across to the living room and back again. Max lifted his head from the pillow on the couch, giving her stink eye for disturbing his sleep.

Jake jumped up from the other end of the couch and ran to the deck doors. His bark didn't drown out the footsteps thudding outside on the wooden stairs. Lauren flipped on the spotlight. The deck lit up.

"Hey, neighbor. I'm here to invite you to a party." Justice lifted a large paper sack and a bottle of wine.

Dilemma. Let him in? Drink wine until the cake was done? She'd be drunk! Maybe that was his plan. Maybe she had answers he wanted. Or maybe she'd crossed the line into untold suspiciousness.

"Jake, it's JD. Quiet." Lauren opened the doors. "Come in. I have a cake in the oven, so I can't really leave for a party."

"I brought the party here." He placed the wine bottle on the coffee table.

She kept her gaze on his mouth. His grin charmed her. How could her heart start a war with her brain?

"A party of two?" She walked to the kitchen to check the timer, but also to put more distance between them. The cake had another fifteen minutes to bake.

"For the moment." He lifted the paper sack. "These are decorations for the tree. People will arrive around seven o'clock to decorate. It's a tribute to Aunt Jessie."

The dilemma grew. How could she avoid people who wanted to honor her aunt? "I will meet you out there. When the cake's cool enough, I'll bring it to share."

Justice walked toward the kitchen, sniffing the aroma. "Carrot cake. My favorite!"

His desire for the cake reverberated, sending off little sparkles around her. How silly was that?

"It's my favorite too. What kind of wine?" She crossed the room and reached for the bottle. "A Boal Madeira from Portugal. Aged ten years."

Justice opened a drawer and a sommelier's key appeared on the counter. He opened a cabinet and brought out wine glasses. "I helped Aunt Jessie put her kitchen back in order after the remodel last year."

So that explained how he knew his way around.

"Lauren, will you bring it here?"

Had his voice turned seductive or was her heart trying to trick her brain?

Once the bottle was open and the amber liquid poured into goblets, he offered her a glass. To accept it, she had to move closer to him in the kitchen. The space shrank.

His fingers touched hers.

Frozen, she stopped when he leaned in.

Zuroom. Zuroom. Zuroom.

The oven timer shocked her into action. "You have to move."

He handed her potholders and opened the oven door.

A few minutes later, the cake checked and cooling on the counter—out of dog reach—she turned to find him smiling at her. She immediately dropped her gaze. "I need to make the orange glaze."

She felt the heat of his gaze as he studied her. "I'll take the wine and some plastic cups out to the gathering. If you don't come soon, I'll come looking for you. I promise."

Only after he'd gone, as she began to stir powdered sugar into melted butter, did her heart stop trying to break a rib. Max came and leaned against her leg. Jake stood watch at the door. Every time someone new joined the growing crowd on the beach, he barked.

Lauren added orange juice and zest to the saucepan, mixed it, then set it off to the side. "Boys, I'm going to meet everyone. I'll be back." There was no avoiding Justice, and she couldn't insult the memory of Aunt Jessie.

Lauren arrived at the party. The Christmas tree lights didn't offer much illumination. She could look at people and not worry about seeing too much.

"Lauren, let me introduce you to everyone. Everyone, this is Lauren." Justice handed her an ornament. "We saved the last ornament for you."

How like Aunt Jessie to think about the birds. The ornaments were birdseed cakes in the shape of bells. Lauren placed it on the tree. The group applauded.

"Tomorrow, we go caroling along the beach. You can bring Max and Jake," Justice said.

A woman with a red-and-green flannel shirt stepped forward. "I'm Zoe. I have a list of Christmas movies for you to watch. We could all come over and hangout and watch one on Friday night." She handed over an envelope.

"I'm Makayla. I'm going to help you make Christmas cookies."

"Me too," Oliver chimed in.

"That so?" Justice asked. "Or are you there to do quality-control sampling?"

Makayla laughed. "Oliver, you know better than to lie when Justice is around."

"He is the slayer of untruths," Zoe said.

"I'm collecting the RSVPs for the Christmas Eve dinner. All responses should be in within a week." A guy she hadn't been introduced to lifted his cup. "I'll help you with the menu. I'm Eustis."

"To Aunt Jessie." Justice lifted his cup in a toast.

Everyone followed suit. "To Aunt Jessie."

Tears filled Lauren's eyes. Aunt Jessie had tried to get her to come home for years. But she came annually for Aunt Jessie's birthday, always insisting the celebration be only the two of them. Her aunt had wanted her to meet these people who'd brought joy to her life, but Lauren had resisted.

Justice came beside her and squeezed her shoulder in support as though he'd sensed her pain. For a moment, she dropped her guard and accepted the comfort.

Maybe resistance had become a bad habit.

Or maybe it'd kept her safe from people leaving her. Like her mother, her father, even Chantilly when she'd gone to college . . . and now Aunt Jessie had left her too. While Lauren grieved Aunt Jessie's passing, her darling great aunt had offered a community.

Only if Lauren didn't resist.

Chapter 5

The next morning at dawn, Lauren made Jake and Max heel until they reached the beach. "Free!" she shouted. With bursts of energy, the boys took off like rockets down the beach. Max raced at the water's edge, his black-and-white coat stood out against the surf's white foam. Jake preferred hard-packed sand for better traction. Lauren walked closer to the water. A peace washed through her. The dawn whispered, "Welcome home."

"Good morning." Justice's voice carried above the cries of the seagulls.

Lauren waved, then jogged in his direction.

"Are you really a runner?" Lauren teased and jogged in place, still managing to avoid direct eye contact with him.

"Let's go!" Justice took off in the direction of the jetty.

Lauren chased after him with one eye on her boys. Max and Jake were already on their way back. "Let's go again, boys." She waved and pointed them back in the direction they'd come.

Justice had a solid five-yard lead. The boys beat him to the rocks. Lauren arrived minutes later out of breath. "I win"—she heaved a breath—"by proxy."

Justice laughed. "By what?"

"Jake . . . Max beat you. They're mine. I win."

"I wasn't wrong. Miss Davis, you are a curious woman."

The man wasn't winded at all.

She paced, trying to catch her breath while he petted the dogs. She could sprint a hundred yards, but never a mile. She walked around until her breath evened.

"I hope you enjoyed meeting everyone last night, Miss Davis."

"I did. And I've been consumed with guilt."

He chuckled. "That's a useful emotion."

She'd never considered that before. "I'll think on that, counselor. Aunt Jessie wanted me to meet all of you, but I kept making excuses."

"*I* know." He nodded, a nod of indictment.

"I arrived at the last minute for her funeral and left immediately when it was over."

"I *know.*"

"And now, I regret . . . "

"Lauren." Justice's voice softened. "I know."

A few seagulls soared overhead. Their cries admonished her. The sound carried on the light breeze, echoing her guilt. However, Justice's use of her first name held no reproach.

"And I know what I'm going to do about it." Lauren placed her hands on her hips.

"Actions speak louder than words." Justice jogged in place. "Race you to your house."

He was off like jet fuel powered him. Max and Jack raced beside him.

"Traitorous boys." She took off after them. She would honor Aunt Jessie by completing the fourteen-day list. Then the house would be hers. If she decided to leave, she could always rent the house and still keep it in the family. She had options.

Lauren ran downstairs when the doorbell rang. Every nerve in her body tingled with anticipation. Time had flown. Today, she welcomed others to Aunt Jessie's home for the holidays.

She opened the door, and someone held out a crystal vase with a bouquet of red roses that hid their face. "Delivery for Lauren Davis."

She smiled. Though she couldn't see the person, the voice gave it away. "Phoebe. For me?" Lauren opened the door wider.

The young woman lowered the vase. "They are for you. I read the card, but I'm not going to say anything. Here."

Tickled and more than a little excited, Lauren accepted them. She hadn't received flowers in a long time.

"The florist's van is here. They're setting up the centerpieces on the tables for tonight's Christmas Eve dinner. I came because I found a dress that's perfect for you. I need you to come with me and try it on."

"Oh, Phoebe, there's too much to do."

"Oh, Lauren, you can resist, but it's not what I came for. You have a small army of people at your beck and call."

Actually, she hadn't had to call. People began showing up and doing stuff for her, with her, despite her. They were all island folks. In the last eleven days, she'd completed every task: put up Christmas lights—thanks to Justice, gone caroling, sent Christmas cards, watched a Christmas movie every night—someone new arrived each night to watch with her, bought a special Christmas ornament—Sophia had taken her shopping. She'd hung mistletoe, baked cookies—Oliver was the quality control expert. Made three Christmas stockings—one for her, Jake, and Max, and put up a Christmas tree—about thirty people had shown up with ornaments and wine. She'd donated money, food, and toys to the animal shelter, and met the mail carrier, sanitation workers, lawn maintenance team, and the window washer—each received a fifty-dollar gift card.

And though they hadn't known, Lauren had gazed into each of their eyes to discover the ache in their hearts that needed filling. She's talked with them, asked questions, helping them discover clues for their healing.

Except for Oliver. He was the trickiest of the group. His ache came from unrequited love. Love of a woman he'd never told how he felt. But, Lauren believed, if that woman still walked the Earth, she deserved to know. He'd protested at first, then agreed a meeting with her would bring closure or possibly a new relationship.

She wondered if Chantilly knew the mystery woman and what barrier had kept her sister and Oliver apart.

And Justice baffled her too. Each evening, he appeared on the back deck and put a checkmark by another item on the list of actions Aunt Jessie demanded she complete before the house could be hers. However, he craftily dodged her gaze.

Had he learned of her gift? Or did he have a secret of his own, something he tried to protect?

The cat-and-mouse game had turned maddening. Whenever he was near, a magnetic energy pulled her toward him. Even when her feet remained rooted, her mind, her eyes, her heart sought him out.

"Lauren? Lauren? Did a tide take you away?" Phoebe waved. "We need to go now. In case the dress needs to be fitted."

"Lauren," Eustis called out when he exited the elevator. "The food and chef have arrived."

"What's the menu?" Phoebe asked. She tapped her watch and arched her eyebrows in Lauren's direction.

Eustis and Lauren spoke at the same time, "Pear and arugula salad, buttermilk biscuits, crab bisque, seafood pie, broccoli, deviled eggs, sweet potato pecan pie with Chantilly cream, and bourbon hot chocolate."

Phoebe's eye rounded. "Now I'm starving."

"But it's only ten in the morning. Where is this place we're going? Can we grab something to eat?"

"No time for food. I have protein bars in the car. We're going to Bluffton."

Lauren handed the flowers to Eustis, then plucked the card from the bouquet. "Please put them on the dining room table. I'll see you whenever Phoebe brings me back." She turned to the young woman. "Let's go. Just don't make me late for the only dinner party I've ever hosted."

Once buckled into the passenger seat, Lauren pulled the card that came with the flowers from inside the envelope.

Lauren, home isn't a location. Home is where the heart melds with another. Close your eyes. Open your heart. See with your heart. Hear with your heart.

I knew you could and would do it! Merry Christmas Eve, my darling niece.

Love, Aunt Jessie

How could she have missed all the signs all those years? Aunt Jessie had a gift too. She mended hearts, even the most broken of them.

Lauren sighed. "Phoebe, I already know the dress will be perfect. Let's go! I've got to get back as soon as possible. I must see a man about a heart."

Chapter 6

Minutes before five o'clock, the catering staff lined up on the deck. Everyone dressed in a white shirt, black pants, and a red Christmas tie. The evening sky provided a vivid backdrop of pink and orange and lavender clouds. The first star of the evening twinkled in the deepening navy sky. Mother Nature's perfect painting.

Giddy, Lauren floated from the house to the deck in the red, circular-skirt gown. She tingled head to toe. Aunt Jessie's ethereal presence made the special night all that more magical. Though Lauren's final decision to stay or leave Sunrise remained in neutral, the last two weeks had been the most exciting of her adult life. Tomorrow represented even more new possibilities.

"Good evening, everyone." Lauren offered a slight bow. "I appreciate all you've done to make this a special event for my guests. And thank you, Chef Eustis, for being such a good friend." She hugged him. The musical ensemble on the downstairs patio below them began to play. It had been set up as a dance floor with a bar. Eustis had helped her vision come alive.

The elevator bell sounded. "Excuse me." Lauren entered the house to greet guests. Sophia and Phoebe exited first. They gave her a quick hug, then headed for the deck with barely a hello. Then Oliver stepped into the room with a mystery woman, her face concealed by a gossamer scarf, her arm linked with his as though she needed him for support.

"Oliver, how nice of you to bring a guest." She smiled, hoping to make the woman feel welcomed. She had to let Chef Eustis know to set another place.

"It's a very special night, Lauren. If you don't mind, I want my date to see the last of the evening sky. We'll return in a few minutes to make introductions." Oliver blew her a kiss, stepping around her and guiding his guest to the deck. Lauren considered the glint in his eye and the smile on his face. The man—if men did such a thing—glowed. And the woman. THE woman. Oliver had reconnected with his heart's desire.

She had no further time to contemplate. The elevator doors opened again, and several more people arrived. She directed them to the bar and the hors d'oeuvres on the dining room table. "Dinner will be served on the upper deck at six o'clock."

Lauren mingled. A few more guests arrived, climbing the outside stairs. The waitstaff ferried drinks and appetizers. Jazzy Christmas tunes floated in the air. Chef Eustis lit evergreen scented candles on the tables decorated with freshly cut greenery for that holiday scent. Aunt Jessie's finest gold-rimmed china—handed down from Aunt Jessie's grandmother—glinted in the candlelight. Crystal stemware and polished silverware made the tablescape worthy of a magazine spread. Luxurious. Elegant. Perfect. All for her guests.

Sophia approached. "Lauren," she whispered. "This is a delightful treat." She leaned in close. "I'd never hurt Aunt Jessie's feelings, but you've outdone her."

She smiled. Sophia was being kind. Aunt Jessie was famous for her extravagant parties. "No one should ever be alone on Christmas Eve. It's a night for togetherness." Lauren told her friend the same words Aunt Jessie had instilled in her. Yet, she'd spent countless Christmas Eves alone since her father had died. It had been her choice. What she'd thought she wanted. Not any longer.

Six o'clock approached, and Chef Eustis directed the guests to the table. "Please find your name on the place card for your seat."

The guests seated themselves. Lauren glanced around. Justice hadn't arrived. His chair at the other end of the table remained empty. A thread of unease rippled through her. Lateness wasn't like him. Something had to have happened. She sat at the head of the table and checked her phone. No missed calls. No messages. Where was he?

"Good evening." Lauren raised a glass of wine in salute. "Thank you for coming. Thank you for honoring Aunt Jessie and for making me feel welcomed here. Chef Eustis has prepared a"—the mystery woman next to Oliver removed her scarf—"Chantilly?"

The guests chuckled.

"Hello, Lauren." She blew a kiss. "I was not prepared by Chef Eustis. Lauren, please continue."

Flustered, Lauren searched her mind for what to say next but it whirred with so many questions.

"If everyone will turn their place card over, tonight's menu is there." Chef Eustis stepped in to fill her gap.

Service started. The staff delivered the amuse-bouche. Lauren finished hers, then rose to speak with each of her guests. Justice's empty seat pushed Lauren's worry halfway to panic. She continued around the table to thank each guest for coming.

"Chantilly. I don't know what to say." She squeezed her sister's shoulder.

Her sister rose and kissed Lauren's cheek. "Merry Christmas Eve, little sister. You've given me the best Christmas present." She touched Oliver's arm.

"She's the one." His smile widened.

Lauren's heart surged with fullness.

"Let. Me. GO!" A woman's voice boomed like a cannon over the guests' murmurs, the music playing below, and the roar of the surf. Justice appeared from around the corner with a woman.

"Mrs. Davis, there's nothing you can gain by doing this." Justice's tight tone carried hints of anger.

"Do not, young man, deem to tell *me* what I can or cannot do!"

Baffled, Lauren stared at her half-sister's mother. The woman's hatred for Lauren shot like a laser. Hit Lauren in the gut. The pain grabbed her breath.

The woman lunged toward her.

She backed away. Justice moved to block Mrs. Davis from reaching Lauren.

"Mother!" Chantilly rose.

Oliver grabbed her wrist. "Don't go." He stood. "Mrs. Davis, either you leave now, quietly, or I'll call the police."

"Do what you want. But you can't have my daughter." Mrs. Davis spat the words. "Chantilly, you *can't* love this man. Ask him why. Ask him about his 'Mrs. Robinson experience.' Then you'll *see* how wrong it would be for you to have a relationship with him."

Chantilly gasped. She ran to Lauren, who opened her arms to embrace her. "What has she done? She's hateful and vindictive. I'm so sorry." Chantilly repeated over and over.

Lauren hugged her sister tighter. "You are not responsible for her actions."

"And you!" Mrs. Davis pointed to Lauren. "You and your mother ruined my life. I will never let you have this house. It should belong to *my* daughters. I will bankrupt you with legal fees defending your misguided notion that you could ever own this property."

Lauren closed her eyes and replayed the scene from long ago when Mrs. Davis insisted they meet before her father's funeral. The woman shoved her into the freshly dug grave, all the while spewing hate. Shocked, afraid, and humiliated, Lauren feared attending her father's service. She'd told no one about the incident. Instead, after the service, she ran away from everyone and everything she'd ever known.

Now, determination steeled Lauren. She let go of Chantilly and took a step forward. "You will leave here now!"

Mrs. Davis lunged.

Justice protected her. Lauren looked directly into his eyes. Gasped.

His greatest need blazed for her to see.

The power of emotion took her down. He caught her before she collapsed. Scooping her up, he carried her inside and laid her on the chaise by the fireplace. Jake and Max came bounding down the stairs and stood sentry.

Sounds of a siren drew closer.

Through the wall of glass, Lauren witnessed the police arrive and escort Mrs. Davis away. Chantilly cried into Oliver's chest. He stroked her hair, his other arm held her close.

Lauren hated the pain her sister felt. However, their love would overcome the darkness Mrs. Davis heaved at them.

"Are you okay?" Justice pulled a chair closer to her. His calm demeanor settled her shocked nerves.

"I'm more than a little surprised."

"About Mrs. Davis?

"There is that, but that's not what I'm referring to." Her heart beat with the rhythm of the waves rolling onto the beach.

In perfect cadence with his.

In perfect flow with him.

In perfect love with him.

"Justice, lean in." She crooked her finger, inviting him close.

31

He did as requested.

When he was near, Lauren leaned in, and her lips found his. His greatest need was her unconditional love. In his love, she'd found what she needed most—him and home.

Chapter 7

Christmas morning sunlight fanned across the sky when the sun crested the horizon. Jake and Max raced head toward the jetty, bursting through a flock of seagulls on the beach. The birds took flight, voicing their complaints. Lauren followed in the dogs' wake. Though her feet didn't have wings, her heart did, soaring higher than the flock of birds.

"Good morning." She waved at the group gathered in front of Justice's house. Unlike two weeks ago when the beach was desolate, gray, and encased in thick fog, this morning was crisp, bright, vibrating with joy. The bow on the package was seeing Chantilly with Oliver together and in love.

"Sister," Lauren called. "You were right. Sunrise is a romantic destination."

The group applauded when Oliver kissed Chantilly.

Justice left the group he'd invited beachside for breakfast at sunrise. "Hey there."

He grinned. His eyes danced. Sparkling sunlight glinting off the water couldn't be brighter. He walked a direct path to her, wrapping her in a hug.

She heaved a sigh of joyful contentment.

Last night, she saw his eyes, saw his greatest need, saw his heart's desire. Her heart lit up like a thousand candles and a choir of a thousand angels sang an aria.

"I love you," Justice whispered, then kissed her ear.

"I know."

"I've waited so long for *you*." Justice hugged her tighter.

"I *know*."

"I will never let you go." He stepped back and held her hands.

"*I* know." She smiled. "I had forgotten that we'd met, but I was just a child. Back then, my gift only extended to animals, dogs, and cats. I didn't know how to see into people."

Justice chuckled. "I've always heard 'the truth.' I know when people lie. As a little girl, you knew I was sad when my dog died. You told me it would be okay because you would always love me . . . and the little boy in me knew it was the truth. The man"—he paused and thumped his fist against his chest—"has been waiting for you ever since."

Lauren hugged him, pressing a kiss to his lips. "And Aunt Jessie knew all of this the whole time. Merry Christmas, Justice."

End

About Linda Joyce

Amazon Best Selling author and multiple RONE Award Finalist Linda Joyce writes contemporary romance, women's fiction, and coming soon, a cozy mystery series. She lives with her patient husband and three dogs in Atlanta. She's addicted to Cajun food and sushi. Linda hates yardwork, but loves growing veggies.

Find Linda online:
Website: http://www.linda-joyce.com
Newsletter: http://www.linda-joyce.com/newsletter/
Facebook: https://www.facebook.com/LindaJoyceAuthor
Twitter: https://twitter.com/LJWriter
Instagram: http://instagram.com/lindajoycewrites
Amazon: http://www.amazon.com/Linda-Joyce/e/B00BODDROS/
Goodreads: http://www.goodreads.com/author/show/6950241.Linda_Joyce
BookBub: https://www.bookbub.com/authors/linda-joyce

Candlemas

by Paula Gail Benson

Candlemas

Time Travel

By time traveling back to colonial Charleston, Amos practices medicine and marries. To save daughter Franny's life, he sends her and his wife Dorothy to the twentieth century. Marooned in the present, Franny fantasizes over an unknown eighteenth century man depicted in a miniature, while ignoring her classmate Chad, who adores her. After finding her way back in time, marrying the mysterious man, then becoming a widow, Franny's thoughts return to Chad. Meanwhile, in modern times, teacher Heidi continues to pine after restaurateur Payne while hoping for Dorothy and Franny. Can these three couples possibly be reunited by Valentine's Day?

Rated: G

Chapter One

Columbia, South Carolina, 2022

Heidi Runyon

In her fifty-plus years, Heidi had witnessed three types of romantic love: (1) enduring despite obstacles, (2) unrequited but hopeful, and (3) resistant yet not unyielding, which was what she personally had experienced and why she remained single. She admired the first, empathized with the second, and fought against the third, all the while remaining convinced that, like a candle lighting the way through darkness, true love remained resilient and found its own place and time, often under the most unusual circumstances.

She hoped she could count on that for Dorothy and Amos Morgan, Chad Howard and Franny Morgan, and Payne Liu and herself.

Chapter Two

Charles Town, South Carolina, 1770

Amos Morgan

Fear clutched at Amos's innards like the talons of a black vulture. He could not remember ever being this frightened before. Not as a boy, when his parents were tragically killed in a touring bus accident. Not as a teenager, when his sister struggled on her meager nurse's aide salary to provide food and shelter for them. Not even when at age twenty he foolishly stole the musty old volume from the community college library because it pricked his fingers with what felt like electric jolts when he opened its cover. From that volume, he learned how to get from the modern times to the past, where he felt most at home.

He never feared time traveling back to Charles Town. What terrified him was sending his colonial-born wife and child forward into a future completely foreign to them.

Dorothy, his wife and the daughter of an eighteenth-century physician, knew his secret—that he was a twentieth-century man. Somehow, she believed his impossible story and trusted him. Now she stood before him in Saint Michael's dark churchyard, holding a well-swaddled little Franny.

The baby had stopped crying.

Amos lifted the blanket from Franny's perfect face and hoped he had not overdosed her with laudanum. He could not risk the baby's cries alerting the watch to what they were about to do.

"You have the letter for my sister, Clara?" He almost said, "Like the nurse Clara Barton," before remembering Dorothy would not recognize Clara Barton's name or know the Continental Congress would employ women to serve as nurses. "Clara will know how to get Franny the medicine she needs to survive."

Dorothy's wide blue eyes gazed into his. "Why can't you come with us?"

A shudder replaced the gripping fear, as if a ghost passed through him, a phantom of what he might have been if he were a better man. He swallowed and placed his hands on Dorothy's shoulders, feeling them shiver beneath his fingers.

"When I came back in time, I changed another man's destiny," he said, keeping his voice steady and quiet. "That man would have prevented the spread of smallpox among the colonial troops. Now I must do what he would have done so that General Washington has the forces he needs to defeat the British."

Dorothy's face seemed paler in the moonlight. "General Washington?"

The stress added to Amos's confusion. Of course, Washington had not been appointed yet. There was no Continental Congress. "I mean . . ."

"The Boston massacre killings were a harbinger? War is coming? And you will be in it?"

Amos hoped his expression was more reassuring than it felt. "Don't worry about me, my love. Remember, I have the knowledge to avoid mishaps."

"Not to avoid changing that man's destiny." She looked down at their child. "Or escape disease."

He dug into his vest pocket, pulling out a locket containing a miniature portrait. "Look. I found this in my parents' belongings and brought it back with me as a good luck charm."

She looked at the man's painted face. "Who is it?"

"I do not know, but somehow, I feel this image is seeking its place in time just as I have been." He tucked the locket into the folds of Franny's blankets. "Now, are you ready?"

"Might we stay just a while longer?"

"No, my love. You must go before the first watch passes. Here, take the candle blessed at Candlemas." He lit the wick and handed it to her. "Hold it before you and concentrate on the flame."

"What am I trying to see?"

He remembered so well the last image he had focused upon: a poster on his bedroom wall of General Washington's battlefield standard. "Look for the elusive six-pointed star. As difficult as trying to find a four-leaf clover in a green pasture. Breathe steady and keep your focus. Tell me when you spot it."

She seemed mesmerized and began taking small steps. "I think I see it."

"Keep watching, my love. Let your vision expand. There will be a field of blue with thirteen six-pointed stars."

Her voice grew softer. "Like the colonies."

"Exactly."

He watched as she proceeded into the shadows, finally hearing her cry, "Thirteen stars on a field of blue!" before she disappeared completely.

A light breeze swirled around him, closing an unseen barrier.

"Time, be as good to them as you have been with me," he whispered.

Dorothy, Franny, and the wind were gone. He never felt so alone.

Chapter Three

Columbia, South Carolina, 1993

Dorothy Morgan

Standing in the center of the Windsor Elementary School library, Dorothy Morgan carefully turned the pages of a picture book telling the story of George Washington's life. She stopped at the page displaying the image of his battle standard: thirteen six-pointed stars on a field of blue. Her fingers lightly touched the image, and she remembered seeing it for the first time as a poster in a modern young man's bedroom. A strange place, with furniture made of materials Dorothy had never before encountered including a flat desk with a rectangle monitor and a board with keys that displayed letters, numbers, punctuation symbols, and seemingly unrelated words.

That had been eight years earlier, when Dorothy had walked out of one century and into another two hundred years later. She'd given Amos's sister Clara quite a start appearing in eighteenth-century garb and holding a tightly wrapped baby she feared might have already succumbed to the black canker. But, as Amos had promised, Clara had resources well suited for handling emergencies.

First, Clara assessed and got treatment for Franny's illness, which she called diphtheria. Then, she provided Dorothy with clothing that still felt too lightweight to be suitable in public.

Like her younger brother, Clara had a penchant for flouting authority and managed to acquire documentation that made Dorothy and Franny appear as if they had spent their entire existences during modern times. Clara found Dorothy had an aptitude for learning, and with Clara's help and support, Dorothy had attended college and graduate school, becoming a school librarian.

"If only Amos had the success with book learning that you have," Clara had once sighed.

"Why do you say that?" Dorothy had asked.

"Besides history, his greatest love was medicine. He always wanted to be a doctor, but he didn't have the grades to get into medical school."

Dorothy nodded, remembering in her own time that doctors were viewed as professionals needing a certain level of education. Amos's work as an orderly at a modern hospital gave him the experience and knowledge to convince the folks in Charles Town that Amos had the requisite training. But Clara's words about Amos's "greatest love" made Dorothy ponder something else.

"You said his greatest love was medicine?"

Clara had reached for Dorothy's hand. "Medicine and family. Why do you think he sent you and Franny to be with me?"

Dorothy had squeezed Clara's hand in return. No doubt Amos had wanted to send them where Franny's illness could be cured, but had he also wanted to rid them from his life so he might concentrate on medicine and history?

Hadn't they had a good life together, finding joy in each other's company and making plans for themselves and their children?

She had never imagined being separated from Amos.

Closing and reshelving the George Washington book, she locked the library and went to get her daughter from Ms. Runyon's third-grade class. Ms. Runyon had always asked Dorothy to call her Heidi, but Dorothy felt uncomfortable with such informality. Even saying "Ms." instead of "Miss" had proven to be a challenge.

Ms. Runyon stood at the door to the classroom, watching as Franny and her classmate Chad Howard worked at a table in the back of the room. She smiled at Dorothy, then nodded toward the two youngsters. "They're drawing a map of the Southern cities George Washington toured as president. An extra credit project that gives Chad some time to spend with Franny."

A few weeks ago, Ms. Runyon had confided in Dorothy that she noticed Chad had a crush on Franny. Dorothy dismissed it as the imaginings of a hopeless romantic, but as she watched the children working together, she saw Chad's acorn brown eyes glance up toward Franny while her daughter remained oblivious to his attention. Around her left pinky finger, Franny twisted the chain of the antique locket she always wore.

Dorothy should have insisted that Franny leave the valuable jewelry at home, but even as a baby, Franny clung to it like a talisman, and Dorothy hadn't the heart to take it from her. As much as she credited modern medicine for Franny's recovery, she couldn't dismiss that attachment to the locket might have somehow contributed to Franny's well-being.

Chad continued to watch as Franny leaned into the table, still fingering the locket with one hand while tracing Washington's Southern journey on a blank map with the other. Finally, he spoke. "I've seen Pew 43 in Saint Michael's Church in Charleston. Washington once sat there."

Franny shrugged. "I'd prefer to see Washington there in person."

Chad looked puzzled. "How?"

"By traveling back in time," Franny said, her focus remaining on marking the map.

Dorothy stepped forward. "Franny, we must be going now."

Within minutes, Franny gathered her things, and the two headed for the exit. Dorothy waited until they were out of earshot before continuing.

"It's important that you not talk to other people about time travel, Franny."

Her daughter looked up at her. "Why not?"

All the uncertainties flooded into Dorothy's mind. She had been so concerned about getting Franny to safety in the future that she wasn't sure she remembered all the time travel steps. Might it still be possible to return to Amos?

"It's best to share only with those you truly love and who truly love you." Dorothy looked deep into her daughter's eyes. "Promise me you'll do as I ask."

A stubborn frown remained on Franny's lips. Grudgingly, she gave her mother the promise, but she still held the locket chain curled around her hand.

Heidi Runyon

Within minutes, Chad joined Heidi at the classroom door to watch Mrs. Morgan and Franny head toward the exit.

"I hope Franny doesn't take to time traveling," he said.

Heidi looked down at him, putting her arm around his shoulders. "Why, Chad?"

"I would miss her." He didn't take his eyes off Franny and her mother as they walked down the hallway.

"Missing folks doesn't just happen when they go away," Heidi told him.

He turned his soulful brown eyes up to look at her face. "It doesn't?"

"No," she answered. "Sometimes it happens when they're too focused on something else to see that you're here."

Chapter Four

Columbia, South Carolina, 2007

Chad Howard

Weeks before college graduation, Chad opened his apartment door and couldn't believe who he saw.

"Franny? Franny Morgan?"

"In the flesh."

She twirled before him in vintage colonial garb. A cotton cap with lace edging. A joined bodice and skirt that revealed a stylish petticoat. Stomacher in place, emphasizing her slim waist. She wore no makeup, but she didn't need it. She glowed with happiness.

He couldn't help but reflect her joy. He felt as if he had just stepped into a dream, a wonderful one. "Wow. You look fabulous."

She curtsied, tipping her head slightly toward him. "You are most gallant, kind sir."

"I—I wish I had known you were coming. I'm expecting a client for a photo shoot."

She laughed. "I know you are, silly. The client is me. I disguised my voice to surprise you. May I come in?"

"Of course, of course." Chad smiled as he cleared the doorway, his eyes following her every flounce as she entered.

He watched her survey each aspect of his studio/home, from the clutter on the mantelpiece to the hastily made futon to the set up with his screens and cameras to his paper-piled desk with the framed photo of Sara Gibbons, who he had taken to the University's spring formal. Sara had been incandescent that evening in her body-clinging, silver-and-white gown. Today, Franny outshone her.

Chad felt like reaching to place Sara's photo face down on the desk, but it was too late. Franny had seen it.

She picked it up for closer inspection. "Sara's gorgeous. Are you guys dating now?"

Are we? Chad wondered. The spring formal had been the first time he remembered asking Sara out in advance. Chad shrugged. "We've had a lot of classes together. Both of us in the journalism school, though in different areas. She wants to be a reporter, and I'm determined to make a career in photography and graphics."

Franny looked back at him, her eyes glistening. "Planning on staying in Columbia?"

He nodded. "For the time being. We both have jobs after graduation."

Franny put the photo back on the desk. "It's a great place to raise kids."

"Oh, we're just casual . . . that is, you never know where you may have to travel for work. We haven't made any permanent plans."

She slid past him to take a seat on the bench in front of the screen. "Why not?"

Because I've never really gotten over my childish crush on you. He opened his mouth to tell Franny that, but nothing came out.

"You should tell Sara if you love her. Don't let time steal the opportunity away," she said.

Then, he noticed it. She wore the antique gold locket and still made a habit of twisting the chain around her pinky. She was lucky it hadn't broken apart.

"How about you?" he asked. "I've been hearing that you're doing all kinds of fascinating historical research at the College of Charleston."

She leaned back, cocking her head to one side. "You've been talking to my mother."

"Guilty. I took photos of the winter festival at Windsor Elementary."

"I know. That's how I heard about your photography business."

"Well, let's take a few shots."

As she posed, she talked about her research, which had considered the detailed social customs of early America. She knew exactly how she wanted to stand and sit to look the most authentic.

The last time he'd seen her was during his junior year at the University of South Carolina when he made a solo trip to the Gibbs Museum in Charleston.

He'd found her studying the miniature portrait collection there. She had been doing some research about Charles Fraser, a prolific artist during the late eighteenth and early nineteenth centuries who had produced over three hundred miniatures and more than one hundred landscapes.

When Chad had convinced her to leave the museum and go for coffee, she'd prattled on about the artist. "Can you believe after being orphaned and raised by his brother that Charles Fraser spent the first half of his life as a lawyer? Then, he stopped practicing and devoted himself to his art. Obviously, he was talented and had connections to other great artists, but to have that much faith in your own skill to change your entire existence—well, I think it's extraordinary."

"Yes," Chad had agreed before taking a sip of his coffee. It had been hard to get a word in edgewise. And, when offered the chance, he hadn't known how to respond.

"Could you ever do that?" she had asked him. "Walk away from everything you know to follow a path you've only dreamed about?"

Looking at her face in the light of that coffee shop, seeing her joy overflowing, he'd had no idea what to say.

Again, in the present, he realized he'd been so lost in thought, he hadn't registered Franny was asking him a question.

"I'm sorry. I was thinking about the shot. What did you say?"

"Remember in the third grade, Ms. Runyon's class, when we did the project on George Washington?" she asked.

"Yeah," he said as he adjusted his equipment. His thoughts were all garbled. He wanted to participate in a conversation but still wasn't sure how. Probably, he chose the wrong topic. "I didn't realize you were into reenacting," he said. "Your outfit looks like a genuine article from the time."

Her shoulders drooped. "It's a true replica, but I'm not into reenacting. I told you a long time ago that I wanted to make the journey back in time. I've learned everything I could about colonial and early United States days. Now, I'm ready to compare what I've studied to reality."

Taking his eye away from the lenses, he searched her face. "What are you saying?"

"I'm going back in time. My parents gave me this locket when I was just a child. They never knew the identity of the man in the portrait, but, through my research, I think I've found him. I have to go back to see who he was, what happened to him—"

He interrupted. "Because you've fallen in love. At best, with a ghost, and at worst, with the figment of some eighteenth-century painter's active imagination."

She stared at him. "I always thought you understood me."

"I always listened and couldn't believe what I heard. I knew you loved history and thought it was because your dad found it so fascinating, but when you started talking about time travel . . ." He shook his head. "I mean, even if such a thing were possible, your dad was a doctor. Surely, he told you about the hygiene, unsanitary conditions, and deadly diseases from that time period. How could you think about wanting to go there?"

"To find out—"

He couldn't take it. "Just stop."

"What?"

"Can't you see how talk like that affects your mom and those of us who love you? Why aren't we good enough for you to stay here?"

Franny stuck her chin out. "It's because of my parents that I want to go." She opened the locket and showed Chad the miniature portrait of a twenty-something man with dark curly hair and a sober face. "When I saw this portrait for the first time, I felt an immediate connection. I knew I had to find this man and I poured over every document until I did. You're right. I've always been a bit in love with him. Now, I want to find out if he could love me."

Chad began putting away his supplies. "That's crazy talk."

Franny wrinkled her nose. "Not exactly. Besides, why do you care where I go?" She pointed to the photo on his desk. "Obviously, Sara Gibbons adores you. Why don't you see if you could have a life with her?"

"Why not?" Chad didn't mean to be spiteful, but he couldn't help it. For years he'd yearned after Franny. Since they met in college, Sara had waited patiently for him to notice her. Maybe it was time he did. "You can send me a note from the eighteenth century. Goodbye, Franny Morgan."

Lifting her chin, Franny walked to the door of his apartment. Turning back to him, she said, "Goodbye," before exiting with a slam.

Franny Morgan

Even though she said goodbye, in her heart, she knew she would not forget him.

She had been foolish to cling to the hope that Chad understood her. From the third grade forward, she had done as her mother had asked and only talked about time travel with her mother and aunt. But even though she kept Chad at a distance, she always felt connected to him. More than just two history nerds obsessing over where George Washington stayed on his Southern tour.

Now, she realized she had been wrong. She rushed home without taking time to change her outfit. As soon as she reached the house, she secluded herself in her father's old room, lighting one of the candle stubs she found in his desk.

The candlelight soothed her. She gazed into the flame, amazed it seemed to take the shape of a six-pointed star, like the ones on the poster of George Washington's standard.

She was so focused on the image that it took her a moment to realize someone was speaking to her. Looking up, she was shocked to see the face of the man in the locket's portrait.

Glancing about, she saw she was no longer in the bedroom but in Saint Michael's churchyard. Not the modern place, but the location as it was more than two hundred years earlier.

"Who are you, miss?" the man asked her.

"Franny Morgan," she replied.

He smiled, and in that moment, she felt strength and comfort exude from his being, enveloping her with the assurance that she was where she needed to be.

"You are indeed a welcome sight," he told her, gently taking her arm. "Your father is receiving resistance for trying to inoculate the soldiers for smallpox. Seems there's a rumor he used that medicine to do away with his wife and baby daughter some time ago. He'll no doubt be very glad to demonstrate you're still alive. If you'll come with me, please?"

"And you are?"

"Edmund. Edmund Fraser."

Chapter Five

Charleston, South Carolina, 1790

Franny Morgan Fraser

"Seraphim, Cherubim, Thrones." Franny whispered the names of three of Saint Michael's bells as she dodged stepping on a break between the stones in the walkway. It was silly, really. A child's game, no longer suited to her age (thirty-six) or station (widow) in life. And, yet, this Sunday was one of those mornings when she longed to shed her current status and slip back into the romantic adventure of her recent past with Edmund or even further back in time to return to the possibilities in the future . . .

"Watch, Franny," her father, Dr. Amos Morgan, cautioned, taking her elbow to pull her toward him and away from the street. "There's a carriage trundling for us that will no doubt splatter what lingers of that soupy muck hole onto your good clothes. Save yourself some rinsing out on this cold morning."

She looked up at his face, lined from experience, yet showing a relaxed mien. He peered toward the murky sky, as if welcoming any inclement weather it might send. His words slipped off his tongue, naturally instead of thoughtfully, carefully spoken.

The time he was living in agreed with him.

"You love it, don't you?" she asked.

"What, dear?"

"Being here, now, in the Charleston you always dreamed of inhabiting."

He stopped, looking down at her, his eyes twinkling, yet also examining. She hated how he could see into her core so easily.

"Do you hate it?' he asked.

"No. Of course not." She had no regrets about following him back to this time. She had studied and prepared and arrived knowing what to expect, what she was leaving behind in the future.

He drew her hand around his elbow and began walking forward again. She kept pace with him.

"If you can't tell me, who can you tell?" he asked.

"Of course I would tell you, if there was anything to tell."

"You still miss Edmund."

She bit her lower lip. "Every day, but I've become more resigned."

He rubbed her cold fingertips that clutched his arm, warming them. "Life's not the kind of thing you want to become resigned to."

"I have no choice."

Looking at her, he said, "There are always choices."

She gazed into his hazel eyes. "Why did you decide not to come forward in time with Mama and me?"

He turned back to the overcast sky. "I thought perhaps your mother might have told you. In traveling back, I changed a man's destiny and felt obligated to do what he was meant to do."

"To inoculate the soldiers."

"Yes. And to be a doctor. I couldn't do that in modern times. I don't have the credentials." His eyes returned to hers. "Why did you come back?"

She gripped his arm. "I wanted to know you."

He laughed gently. "Very flattering. And I'm glad you did, but I suspect you had another interest as well."

She reached to touch the locket at her neck. "Yes."

"You made Edmund very happy, my dear. Together, you helped our country win its independence."

Franny hung her head and closed her eyes. "I don't regret that. I never will."

He squeezed her arm. "But something leaves you wanting."

She stared forward. How could she tell him? Everything that met his needs no longer fulfilled hers. Now that Edmund was gone, she didn't know what to expect for a future. "It's ridiculous to have based my life on loving and finding the subject of an unidentified portrait."

"Henry the Eighth did something similar in acquiring his fourth wife."

Franny shrugged. "At least she kept her head."

Together they shared a much-needed laugh.

"Sweetheart," her father continued. "You're still in mourning. Give yourself time to grieve."

"People in these times realize the importance of moving forward quickly," she said. "I know you've been approached by those who wonder when I'll be back on the marriage market."

He took her hand in his. "You are quite a catch, if I do say so myself."

She wondered what people thought. Even though she might be considered at mid-life, she was still a desirable widow. Like Martha Washington, she could have her pick of suitors. But each day mired in the past made her less certain she wanted to stay here. Each time she labored over picking feathers from a game bird and determining how to cook it so it remained tasty and tender, she had memories of stoves, refrigerators, and products packaged to be stored and prepared. She had adored Edmund and delighted in being a camp follower as his soldiers fought with the Swamp Fox, Francis Marion, through South Carolina's Lowcountry. But when she'd come back in time to meet and marry Edmund, she'd never imagined living in the past without him.

Now that he was gone and she was the widow of a respected war hero, she had lost her interest in building a new country. Each day, moments of her childhood and growing up in the twentieth and twenty-first centuries came back to her. In particular, the face of Chad Howard, whom she had too often taken for granted.

"How do you manage without Mother?" she asked.

She saw his right eye squint as if she'd jabbed it with a stick. It was his tell that he felt pain.

"Very badly, I'm afraid."

For a moment, they stood quietly in the brisk morning air, the crackling of stray leaves, pine needles, and palmetto fronds skipping past them, blown by the breeze. Two lost souls hidden away in time.

"I miss her," he said.

"So do I," she replied. "We would be celebrating Thanksgiving if we were together now."

"Ah yes." He chuckled. "Washington did issue a proclamation last year, didn't he? He said, 'It was the nation's duty to acknowledge God, obey His will, be grateful for his benefits, and humbly seek His protection and favor.' Then, he marked the occasion by fasting and taking food and beer to folks in debtors' prison. Such a remarkable gentleman. Sadly, I don't believe the holiday became permanent until Lincoln's time."

Franny shook her head. "How do you do that? Live in this time yet always keep mindful of the future?"

"I don't know." He shrugged. "It's all just a part of me."

She wanted to embrace him, but it would draw attention. "And Mother?"

He closed his eyes. "Oh yes. A very real part. I miss her every day."

Franny felt encouraged. "What's to keep us from returning to her?"

"Darling, in this century, I'm a doctor. Thanks to you and General Washington, I've been able to be useful and gain respect. If I returned to modern times, I'm sure there would be no place for me."

"There would always be a place for you with Mother."

He shook his head. "Not if I could not support her. I'd only embarrass her. Better for me to share a mug of ale with our president when he arrives to visit Charleston this spring." He paused and took a deep breath before continuing. "But you don't need to remain."

"Father, I won't leave you alone."

He gazed into her eyes. "I'd rather be alone than feel as if I deprived you of the life you were meant to live."

The bells rang out, filling the silence between them. She ticked the remaining bells' names off in her head. *Dominions. Virtues. Raphael. Gabriel. Michael.* She wished they had the answers she needed.

Chapter Six

Charleston, South Carolina, 1791

Amos Morgan

The ladies had insisted on their own meeting with the president. Amos wasn't surprised Washington graciously agreed to a tea where he would be the sole male in attendance. Sitting behind a secluded bush, Amos chuckled as he watched how smoothly Washington navigated the gaggle of females. His poise and unfailing courtesy kept them all enthralled.

Yes, modern politicians could learn a lot from this old campaigner, pun truly intended.

"If only they could see how he actually operates instead of relying on a scholar's speculated description," he said quietly.

He imagined a ghostly whisper in his ear. "Now, Amos, scholars spend hours reviewing primary sources to verify their descriptions are correct."

Despite the time and distance between them, he always imagined Dorothy being nearby, even if only as a voice in his head. Moisture gathered in his eyes. Franny had told him she became a librarian with a passion for preserving contemporaneous documents. "Oh, my dearest Dorothy. If only I had you here beside me to tease about your precious contemporaneous documents. What I wouldn't give to scheme with you on how to hide a particular relic away to save it for future generations. Maybe we could even convince our first president to contribute a set of his famous teeth."

"Father," Franny called as she led the president toward him.

How proud Amos was of her. If only Dorothy had been there; his chest would have been puffed out to bursting with sheer admiration.

"My good friend and colleague," the president greeted him. "How did you merit an invitation to this exclusive event?"

Amos bowed. "Mr. President, you know doctors are granted far too much leeway."

"I would say credit might be due to your lovely daughter serving as one of the hostesses."

Amos laughed. "As on the battlefield, your vigilance has led you to the accurate conclusion. And, because you are correct, I will gladly accept any indulgence on her behalf."

Franny shook her head. "Such excessive praise will leave me quite vain."

"Respectfully, I cannot agree," the president replied. "Your thoughtful kindness is always on display. Perhaps never more so than by this gift a young boy pressed upon me. When I tried to thank him, he insisted it was all your doing."

"I only suggested it as a gift for your wife. He produced it."

The president reached into his pocket and took out a miniature portrait that fit in the palm of his hand.

Amos leaned in to examine it and found the painted image was of the president himself. "So, Lady Washington is to be the beneficiary of an early work of our own Charles Fraser."

The president looked surprised. "I had not thought a child so young to have been the artist. I am regretful not to have asked his name." He turned to Franny. "He is a relative, then?"

"Distantly. Of Edmund's." She also examined the small treasure. "Charles's talent improves each year. I hope his family will encourage his endeavors as yours did."

The president smiled. "They knew better than to keep me indoors. Thankfully, surveying helped me to learn a craft while exploring the American landscape." He lowered his voice so that only Amos and Franny could hear. "It seems to me, Mistress Fraser, you similarly are out of your element being limited to garden parties and social occasions. I have always noticed in you an ability to lead, explore, and determine solutions that reminds me of the marvelous intellect displayed by Mistress Angelica Schuyler Church. That knowledge is most welcome in building a new country."

Franny curtsied. "Again, I find myself humbled at your comparing me to such a fine lady, Mr. President."

"Amos, convince her to heed my words and find the place where her talents may best be respected and appreciated. I know enough of women who have taken on monumental tasks with success. Do not have her stifled as a partner to one seeking only social advantage. I speak plainly, but out of the esteem with which I hold your daughter."

Feeling gratitude coursing through his veins that his commander in chief had spoken what he had been unable to express to Franny, Amos again bowed. "I take your words to heart, good sir, and promise to accomplish them to the best of my ability."

The president's large hand cuffed him on one shoulder. "Well said. Now, when I may take my leave, let us go in search of that ale you mentioned upon my arrival."

Chapter Seven

Columbia, South Carolina, 2021

Payne Liu

"Mr. Liu?"

Payne's most recent employee, a pudgy high schooler whose extra-long black bangs hung below the upper rims of her oversized glasses, came puffing up to him. He cringed as he saw her hand reach to brush the hair from her vision. How often did he need to preach hygiene for work in a restaurant? She saw his look, dropped her arm, and threw her head back to shift the bangs' position.

"Yes, Shani?" he tried to say patiently.

"We've discovered the missing bowl of fortune cookies."

"Good." He waited a moment, then realized she would have to be prompted. "Where did you find it?"

"On Ms. Runyon's table."

Inwardly, Payne smiled. Just as he had suspected. Each year, Heidi Runyon predicted ticket holders' futures at Windsor Elementary's winter festival, its chief fundraiser. Heidi always began her prep to serve as sooth-sayer by raiding Payne's bowl of fortune cookies.

He knew better than to share his amusement with Shani. "Did you tell Ms. Runyon the bowl needed to be returned to the entry table where it could be shared with all our guests?"

Shani's eyes widened behind her lenses. She shook her head. "Oh no, sir. I would never disturb Ms. Runyon when she's preparing for the winter festival."

"Now, Shani." He hated these correctional talks, particularly with young folks he'd hired as a favor to their parents to help them learn about the responsibility the parents should be teaching them. "You're well past elementary school. You can make a respectful request of Ms. Runyon without fearing consequences."

Shani's head shook more fiercely. "If I bother her, she might give me a bad fortune. I don't want to risk it."

Payne shut his eyes and counted silently to ten before opening them. "Then, I will."

Why, he wondered, did Heidi always begin her preparations so early? It wasn't Halloween yet, and the winter festival didn't occur until January.

He strode past Shani to the table where Heidi had set aside her sesame noodle salad so she could open fortune cookies one after the other from the bowl. She would read what was written on each slip of paper, decide whether to write it down on her pad, then toss it into an increasing pile at the center of the table.

"There are easier ways to predict the future," Payne told her. "Like those messages you get with Dove chocolate candies."

She looked up at him. "But none as succinct or pithy or containing less sugar. I need a message that will easily fit on a card. Besides, your cookies are less fattening than Dove chocolates."

He slid into the seat across from her. "And I need the cookies for my other paying customers."

Breaking another cookie in two, Heidi quickly read its message and tossed the paper into the pile. "Why don't you start your own fortune cookie business? I'm sure yours would taste better, and you would come up with much better fortunes than 'great happiness is yours this coming Tuesday.'"

"Actually, I personally would prefer that to over-rehashed Confucian quotes like," he paused, his long fingers pushing through the pile until he found one. "'Try to see the beauty in everything.'"

"Exactly," she agreed. "Those just open up a fortune-telling session to more questions. What is great happiness? Why should I try to see the beauty? You understand, Payne. That's why your product would be superior."

She gazed at him with such intensity. Her enthusiasm always made him nervous, particularly when she was praising his business acumen. He hadn't had her advantage. While she was away at college, he had taken over more and more of the workload at the restaurant, gradually becoming the managing owner, in hopes his father could have the luxury of rest.

"I haven't the skill with words that you learned in higher education."

"Don't be silly, Payne. You have an innate sense of knowing how to talk with people. You learned well on the job. Often that's more valuable than what a university can teach you."

She meant well, but he still would have rather had her experience. Going away to school. Dorm and campus life. Making friendships that would last a lifetime based on that time spent together. He'd been surprised when Heidi returned here to teach. She didn't have the large family depending upon her that he did. She could have spread her wings, flown . . . just as he wished he'd had the opportunity to do so.

Except he had always longed for a companion to fly away with him. Someone adventurous, compassionate, who understood him better than he did himself. If only he could have gone away with Heidi when she'd left for college.

He looked into Heidi's glistening eyes. If only she weren't deserving of someone who had so much more to offer.

"Mr. Liu?"

Shani had found him. He tried not to grimace as he looked up at her. "Yes, Shani?"

"The lady at the register wants to talk with you."

He glanced over to see Dorothy Morgan standing there.

"I ache inside to see how alone Dorothy is in the world," Heidi said. "She's always been sad that Amos didn't return with her from his mission trip. If only Franny had stayed and gotten together with Chad, then they could all be a family."

"But Chad married and had a son." Heidi's romantic notions always confused Payne.

"Yes, but Franny was Chad's first crush. After she left, Chad fell in love with and married his college girlfriend, Sara, who died shortly after giving birth to their little boy, Gibb. Now, Chad and Gibb are alone in the world too."

Just like you and I are alone, thought Payne. *Even though we might be so much happier together.*

"Should I tell the lady that you're busy?" Shani asked.

"Go see her, Payne," Heidi urged. She grabbed a handful of cookies. "Give her these to take home. I always feel like she needs some encouragement. Maybe she can find some in these messages."

Payne took the handful and placed them on Heidi's pad. "Wean yourself off the cookie fortunes. You can do better on your own." He picked up the bowl. "Shani, return this to the entry table. Now, ladies, please excuse me to deal with another customer."

Briskly, he walked to the register, feeling Heidi's eyes watch him and hearing Shani stutter an apology. He didn't look back.

As he reached the register, he bowed his head slightly and smiled. "How may I help you, Mrs. Morgan?"

Dorothy and Heidi were approximately the same age, yet he felt uncomfortable calling Dorothy by her first name. She always seemed much older than her years and wore such a mantle of sadness, Payne felt it disrespectful to address her more familiarly.

"I'm sorry to disturb you, Mr. Liu," she began.

Maybe that was it. Mrs. Morgan was very formal, and he felt the need to match her.

"Never a disturbance if I may be of help to you."

"I should just take my order and go."

"No, of course not. We want our customers to be satisfied. What is not to your liking?"

"I'm afraid I didn't get the hoisin sauce, but the other one. The one you serve with pot stickers. I checked the order in the car."

"Then you are more than justified in bringing it back. Shani," he called. Shani scooted forward quickly. "Go to the kitchen and get hoisin sauce for Mrs. Morgan's moo shu shrimp. Please bring it to me so I can check we have given her the correct order."

"Yes, Mr. Liu." Shani dashed off to the kitchen.

Payne would have to remind her to move speedily without calling attention to herself.

"I shouldn't cause you so much trouble," Mrs. Morgan said. "Particularly when you and Ms. Runyon are in conference. I know great things are coming when I see your two heads together."

Payne blushed. "You are very kind and no trouble at all. I remember when you used to eat in," he paused, "with your daughter."

The tiniest of smiles creased her lips. It almost looked painful instead of happy.

"Our favorite spot," she whispered. "Franny loved oolong tea."

"Please let me get you some tea bags to take with you."

She grabbed his wrist, more strongly than he expected. "No. No, thank you." She dropped her hand. "It wouldn't feel right to enjoy it without her."

Payne felt terrible. "I'm sorry. I didn't mean to be insensitive."

"You weren't. As so many have told me, I'm being overly sensitive."

Payne looked at her eyes, noticing their hopeless longing. "Don't listen to them. They have no appreciation or respect for loving those you are no longer with."

Mrs. Morgan smiled. This time, Payne sensed she felt relief from his understanding.

"Thank you. So many people expect me to move on. But Amos and Franny were my everything. If I had the chance to be with them again, I'd grasp it."

"Some of us only dream of a love like that," Payne said.

Mrs. Morgan looked toward where Heidi Runyon continued her search for fortunes. "It's not outside your reach."

Could Heidi have talked about him with Mrs. Morgan? For a moment, Payne felt a fleeting hope. Business dashed it quickly enough.

Shani arrived with the hoisin sauce and another take-out order as Chad Howard entered with his young son, Gibb.

"Mr. Liu," Chad greeted him. "Your food is exactly what I needed after a long week. Besides, Gibb's Revolutionary War costume for Halloween just arrived, and he's anxious to try it on. I told him he could check it out and take it off before we eat. I'm not sure an authentic colonial soldier would have a fried rice stain on his uniform."

"Shani, please ring up the Howards' order. Mrs. Morgan, here is your hoisin sauce."

Chad turned to Mrs. Morgan. "How are you? It's good to see you again."

Mrs. Morgan nodded, eyeing Gibb. "Your son has grown so much."

"I'm five," Gibb told her.

"Going on thirty," Chad said, waiting as Payne handed the sauce to Mrs. Morgan. She thanked him and turned to go, but Chad stopped her. "I just wondered. What do you hear from Franny?"

She paused. Payne wondered if she would reply or just leave. Finally, she looked at Chad and said, "I'm not in communication with her."

"I'm sorry." He seemed to genuinely regret the information.

"Don't be," Mrs. Morgan said. "I know you ask because you and Franny were good friends."

Chad shrugged. "I always hoped we were. Franny was not easy to know." He hesitated. "I kept a copy of the photo I took of her when we were graduating from college. She's in an authentic reenactor outfit. No zipper. All buttons."

Momentarily, Mrs. Morgan paused. Finally, she replied, "Franny wanted to replicate the eighteenth-century clothing."

"I wish I could have had her help in selecting Gibb's costume. The one I found is more looks than realism." He put his hand on his son's shoulder. "Gibb's as fascinated with history as Franny and I were. He loves looking at Franny's photo."

Mrs. Morgan nodded, and Gibb piped up, "I'm a Fire Monkey!"

"Fire monkey?" asked Shani. "What's that?"

Again, Payne sighed. He had hoped Shani had at least read over their paper place mats. "You know the Chinese zodiac identifies birth years with animals. Gibb was born under the sign of the Monkey in the year 2016. The years also are designated by the elements: metal, water, wood, fire, and earth. 2016 corresponds to fire, making Gibb a Fire Monkey. Also, the year of the American Revolution was a Fire Monkey year."

"Gibb likes that being a Fire Monkey connects him with the birth of the country," Chad explained. "I'll bring you a copy of Franny's photo, Mrs. Morgan."

"Thank you," she replied. "That would mean a lot to me."

Chapter Eight

Columbia, South Carolina, 2022

Dorothy Morgan

Another winter holiday season of Christmas and New Year's had passed with Dorothy wondering in what year Amos might still exist and if Franny had gone searching for him. Since Chad mentioned Franny's photo, she was more hopeful about seeing her daughter again.

Windsor Elementary's winter festival occurred on Saturday, January 29, preceding a break week for students. For her contribution, Dorothy organized a book sale with a trove of texts she had collected and library duplicates. Across from her table, Heidi Runyon's haphazard pup tent and makeshift booth offered customers a modicum of privacy to hear their fortunes. Just as Heidi went to the faculty restroom to change into costume, Chad and Gibb entered the decorated cafeteria/auditorium with Gibb wearing his colonial outfit and tricornered hat.

"Here's that photo of Franny I mentioned," Chad said, handing her a copy. "I hope you don't mind it's taken so long for me to bring it to you. Also, I hope you'll forgive me for keeping a copy."

"Of course." Dorothy clutched the photo, delighting in seeing her daughter's smiling face. Surely Franny must have gone in search of Amos.

When Heidi reappeared, she wore a long black dress with a belt that had a large gold buckle in the shape of a smiling cat's face. Standing at the open flap to her tent, she asked, "Who'll be the first to have their fortune told?"

"C'mon, Gibb," Chad encouraged. "Ms. Runyon is open for business. Don't you want to be her first customer?"

Gibb shook his head. He had found the book about George Washington on the sale table and was busy turning its pages.

Chad laughed. "A chip off the old block. Mrs. Morgan, why don't you go ahead? We'll watch your table while Ms. Runyon tells you your fortune."

Still holding the photo of Franny, Dorothy nodded and made her way to Heidi's tent. Inside, Heidi sat behind a small table a motioned toward a vacant chair.

"I hope you have some good news for me," Dorothy said as she took the seat.

"Certainly." Heidi pulled out her handwritten stack, fortunes face down, and held them so Dorothy could select. "I brought my best predictions. Take a card."

Dorothy scanned the array. A card in the center attracted her attention, compelling her to choose it. She did, turned it over, and read, *You'll soon see a person from your past.*

Looking from the card to the photo of her daughter, Dorothy a chill settled in her bones. "Is this a joke? Did you arrange for me to get this card?"

"I just hold the cards out. The selection is all random. What does it say?"

Dorothy let Heidi see the prediction and watched the color leave her face.

"Who does it mean? My husband? My daughter?"

Heidi looked stunned and shook her head. "I don't know."

Still clinging to the card and photo, Dorothy pushed her way out of the tent. Chad and Gibb waited expectantly.

"What's wrong?" Chad asked.

Dorothy tried to still her rapid breathing. "I . . ." She looked at Chad and Gibb and forced herself to smile. "Nothing. Sometimes fortunes take you by surprise."

"Good surprise?" asked Gibb.

Dorothy had to think for a moment. Wasn't that what she would want? To see Amos and Franny. And weren't they persons from her past? "Most definitely. So good, it's set my heart to racing."

Chad touched her arm. "Why don't you sit down? We'll get you something to drink."

"No, thank you." A mother and her children were at the book sale table. "I have customers, and Gibb needs to hear his fortune."

Nodding, Chad pulled the flap aside so Gibb could enter. Dorothy assisted her patrons while Chad waited for Gibb. After a few minutes, Gibb let out a whoop and ran out into the cafeteria. He circled the tent once before handing his card to his father and dashing off toward the refreshments table.

Heidi peeped out of the tent, watching Chad read the card. "I hope you're planning to get a pet."

"Actually, no," he replied. "My only plans were to take Gibb to see Saint Michael's Pew 43 next week during winter break. I remembered going with my parents and thought it would be neat to get some photos of him there wearing his colonial outfit." He looked toward Dorothy as she approached. "Since school will be closed on Groundhog Day, you'll have to let the children update the bulletin board when they return."

Dorothy smiled. She remembered Chad's enthusiasm for predicting the weather by pinning up either a cloud or the groundhog's shadow. "Why did Ms. Runyon ask if you were getting a pet?"

Chad held Gibb's card out for Dorothy to read: *Your family will soon have a new member.*

"Maybe I can distract Gibb with the trip to Charleston," Chad suggested.

"Don't count on it." Heidi emerged from the tent. "Look at the fortune I picked for myself."

She held out the card for them to see: *You'll be responsible for an amazing reconnection.*

It was all the encouragement Dorothy needed. "Could you use another model for the Charleston photos with Gibb? I have a colonial outfit I could wear."

Chad smiled. "The more the merrier!"

Chapter Nine

Charleston, South Carolina
1792 and 2022

Franny Morgan Fraser

Candlemas. The midpoint between winter and spring.

At home, Franny bundled the candles she had made to take to Saint Michael's for blessing. She was so focused on her task, she did not hear her father's approach.

"Do you know what we would be celebrating if we were with your mother today?"

Franny caught her breath. "You took me unaware."

"Please, forgive me, my dear. Usually, it is you and not me remembering the future, but today, I happened to meet John Bulow in the square, and he told me of the German legend about the badger seeing his shadow, which reminded me—today is Groundhog Day."

"So it is." The memories came flooding back for her now. A funny movie about a reporter covering Punxsutawney Phil and being forced to relive the day over and over. Not unlike how she felt. Trapped in the past.

"You told me your mother put up a bulletin board. The first child who heard General Beauregard Lee's prediction and made it to the library either got to pin up his shadow or a cloud with the happy message of an early spring."

Franny's eyes misted. "How could I have forgotten?" Her mother read the children stories about Georgia's groundhog mascot. Even though she heard the news on the radio on the way to school, her mother wouldn't let her complete the display. Chad dashed in just after they arrived at school and had the honor.

What was he doing today? Did he have a family? Had he forgotten her?

"Come, my dear. We'll be late for services."

She got her things and followed, but her mind couldn't stop contemplating the future. At this time of year, between the piercing cold of winter and the ever-rising temperatures of spring, might there be a chance to slip back through a rift in time? To light a Candlemas-blessed candle and search for the six-pointed stars in a field of blue? And, if she did, would she only be heartbroken again?

They arrived early at Saint Michael's and took their place in silence. Looking at her father as they sat in the pew, she noticed he also seemed preoccupied. "What is it?" she asked. "Are you ill?" She was quite certain she could not go on in this time without him. It made her anxious to think about him dying and leaving her alone.

"Your mother is much on my mind today. I feel as if she could be very near."

Franny's heart beat rapidly. Could it be? Might this in-between time, this day of speculation for the future, actually bring them in contact with it?

She felt a tugging at her sleeve and saw young Charles Fraser standing at her side.

"What is it, Charles?"

"There is a young boy in the churchyard. I have never seen him before. He said he came here with his father and Mistress Dorothy Morgan, but now he is lost."

"Dorothy?" Amos rose and moved passed her into the aisle, urging Charles to lead the way.

Franny followed as quickly as possible. She had been so young when she'd left with her mother that she didn't remember the process. She made her own journey back in a haze, guided by the lit candle stub while looking at the poster of Washington's standard, and feeling as if drawn to the churchyard by Edmund's presence.

Could it be her mother had found them? And who was the lost child?

In the churchyard, Charles took them to the child who sat on the ground crying. He lifted his tear-stained face as they approached. When he saw Franny, he looked surprised.

"You're the lady in Daddy's photo."

Franny bit her lip. The child had Chad's brown eyes.

"Can you stand, child?" Amos asked, taking the boy's hands and helping him rise. "Have you been hurt?"

"No, sir. Just lost."

"Can you tell us your name?"

Solemnly, the boy shook his head. "I'm not to talk to strangers."

"That's right, son, but these folks are not strangers to us."

Franny looked up. Chad stood before her holding the stub of a lighted candle. His hair had acquired a few strands of gray, but his smile was the same.

Her mother emerged from behind Chad, and her father immediately caught Dorothy in his embrace. Franny wrapped her arms around both.

Dorothy came to her senses first. "There is so much to say and so little time for choices. Let me try to make the way clearer. Ms. Runyon predicted reconnections at the winter festival. When I heard Chad and Gibb were coming to Saint Michael's, I asked to come with them and brought the Candlemas candles. We lit them when we couldn't find Gibb, and they led us to you. We're here because our hearts have brought us." She touched Franny's cheek. "I know, dearest, some of what has happened to you. I traced your research on Edmund further. Now is the time for you to see if your future lies in another direction. Chad can help you find out."

"But what about Father?"

Dorothy smiled and gazed into her husband's eyes. "Why do you think I've returned?"

Chad reached Franny's side. "If you'll come with me, I can promise we'll find a few adventures of our own."

Franny looked at her father who beamed his approval. Then, she said to Chad, "I will."

Chapter Ten

Columbia, South Carolina, 2022

Heidi Runyon

At Payne Liu's restaurant, Heidi had just tasted some of her sesame noodle salad when Payne slipped into the seat opposite.

"I take it all back," he said.

"What?"

"My disbelief in your predictive powers."

She nodded. "Thank you." She took another bite.

"I've just spoken with Chad, Gibb, and Franny." He glanced at the booth where the three sat sharing each other's dishes. "They seem incredibly happy together."

Heidi glanced in that direction even though she didn't need to. She had already observed two of her favorite students reconnect. "I told you they would be. Back when they were in third grade, if I remember correctly."

Payne lowered his head. "Yes. But then, I would be wasting our valuable time to simply grovel over my lengthy history of doubting you. Instead, I'd like to propose testing another prediction you had."

She never expected to hear Payne say "propose" in reference to herself. "Yes?"

"Might you be available for dinner? Valentine's Day is less than a week away. I need to make our reservation now to ensure we have a table. I might even be able to provide a bag of Dove candies for your future fortune-telling efforts."

Heidi didn't need Payne's Dove candies or fortune cookies to give him her answer.

End

About Paula Gail Benson

A legislative attorney and former law librarian, Paula Gail Benson's short stories have appeared online in the Bethlehem Writers Roundtable and Kings River Life as well as in the electronic and print anthologies: *Mystery Times Ten 2013*; *A Tall Ship, a Star, and Plunder*; *A Shaker of Margaritas: That Mysterious Woman*; *Let It Snow*; *Fish or Cut Bait: a Guppy Anthology*; *Love in the Lowcountry*; *Heartbreaks and Half-truths*; and *An Element of Mystery*. In *Killer Nashville Noir: Cold Blooded*, she co-authored "A Matter of Honor" with New York Times Bestselling thriller writer Robert Dugoni.

Her work appears in four of the Red Penguin Collection's publications: *The Empty Stage*; *Once Upon a Time*; *Stand Out: the Best of the Red Penguin Collection, Volume 2*; and *My Robot and Me*. Her short story "Reputation or Soul" is in Malice Domestic's *Mystery Most Diabolical*.

In addition to short stories, she writes and directs one act musicals for her church's drama ministry. She regularly blogs with others about writing mysteries and romances at the Stiletto Gang and Writers Who Kill.

Find Paula Online:
Website is http://paulagailbenson.com
Facebook: https://www.facebook.com/paula.benson.161
Twitter: https://twitter.com/PaulaGBenson
Instagram: https://www.instagram.com/pollygail/
Amazon: https://www.amazon.com/Paula-Gail-Benson/e/B001KCLXI0

CHASE
A Lowcountry Liaison's Short Story

By Suzie Webster

CHASE

A Lowcountry Liaison's Short Story

Contemporary

Chase Billings had watched all his friends fall in love and get engaged or married, but after Michael incinerated their relationship with his lies and betrayal, he knew that a life of domestic bliss was not in the cards for him. That was until he ran into the man whose kiss he'd never been able to forget.

Former college hockey star Dillon Peters never backed down from confrontation; in fact, he rarely missed a chance to jump into a fight. But after years of being conditioned by his homophobic father, Dillon knew he could never fall for a man, even one as tempting as Chase Billings.

Rated: R

Chapter 1

Chase

"Emmy! Get back in here, Daddy will be here in five minutes to pick you up!" Charlie, my business partner, yelled from her office.

I chuckled as a little blond head of tumbling curls appeared at the edge of my desk. "I see you. Your mommy is gonna be in here any second. Come hide under my desk." I scooted back to give her space to crawl at my feet.

With a burst of giggles, she tore around my desk, toddling toward me as fast as her chubby legs would carry her. Her bubbling laughter would give her away the minute Charlie walked into my office, but Emmy's wide smile was worth my friend's irritation with me for indulging her wild daughter.

Charlie came through my doorway, her red hair flying around her face and her lips pressed into a thin line.

"I told Luke this was a bad idea. He *promised* he would only need an hour to do his Christmas shopping and that Emmy didn't need a babysitter." She huffed. "Clearly, she listens to him better than she does me. I haven't done a lick of work since he dropped her off." An eruption of laughter drifted up from under my desk. Charlie raised an eyebrow.

"Seriously. *Why* do you encourage her, Chase? I'm about to lose my mind over these terrible twos. Emilia Rose, get your behind out here, or I'll make sure Daddy doesn't take you for ice cream."

I slid my chair back and leaned down, scooping up the bundle of energy and placing her in my lap. Her little arms reached and encircled my neck. She hid her face against me. Such sweetness.

"No, Mommy. Want to stay with Uncle Chase."

Charlie sighed, and I smiled. "It's fine. I've finished for today. Was going to North Charleston to check out the Park Circle project progress. She can hang with me until Luke gets here."

The minute the words were spoken, Charlie's handsome husband appeared in the doorway.

"Hey, Chase." He pulled Charlie into a hug. "So I'm guessing the inmate is running the asylum." He dropped a kiss on Charlie's lips.

The little firecracker lifted her head. In seconds, she wiggled off my lap, launching herself at Luke's legs. Squeals of excitement filled my office. Charlie rolled her eyes.

Luke grinned, scooping Emmy up into his arms.

She put her tiny hands on either side of his face to get his full attention. "Icequeem, Daddy? Can we get some chocwit iceqweem?"

He laughed and leaned down, kissing her nose. The adoration in his eyes melted my heart.

"If you tell Mommy you're sorry for being wild today, I'll consider your request for chocolate ice cream."

Emmy immediately turned to her mom, pouting. "I'm so so sowry, Mommy. Let's go, Daddy!"

Luke grabbed one chubby hand and brought it to his lips, kissing her tiny fingers.

"All right, my little demon, let's go." He strode to the door. Emmy waved both hands over his shoulders before they disappeared around the corner.

Charlie shook her head and released a long sigh. "I honestly don't know how single parents do it."

I laughed. I had known Charlie since tenth grade. She hardly resembled the girl from back then, but I had to admit, marriage and motherhood suited her.

"I think you handle it all beautifully. And Emmy may be a handful, but she is fucking adorable and smart as a whip."

Charlie bit her bottom lip. "Yes, well, I'd say that is part of the problem. I never thought I'd be outsmarted by a two year old." She dropped into the chair across from me. "I have so much work to do, and I can't muster up the energy to even get started. What are you doing tonight after work? I need to live vicariously through you, seeing that my Friday night will consist of fighting Emmy about going to bed and then falling asleep on the couch with Luke while attempting to Netflix and chill."

"If you're trying to make me feel sorry for you, it won't work, sweetheart. You have a charmed life with that hot husband of yours, not to mention that precocious bundle of deliciousness that you like to complain about, but I know is your entire world. As much fun as I have on my weekends, sometimes I'd like a little bit of what you've got. But I'm not sure I'm meant for monogamy. Or children."

Charlie flashed a sympathetic smile. "You sell yourself short, Chase. You and Michael. I saw something with the two of you . . ." Her voice trailed off.

She knew I detested any mention of my ex. I felt the telltale twinge of pain hearing his name.

"I wish you would tell me what happened between you guys. You both seemed so in love, and then it was just over."

His face flashed through my mind. Brown eyes twinkling, the tiny creases in the corners that made him look even more handsome. My stomach churned as I remembered how it'd felt to be with him. The way he looked at me like I was his everything. I had believed his words, believed his touches—sometimes gentle, sometimes firm. I had thought he was the one, so sure he loved me, and for the first time, I'd allowed myself to fall.

What Charlie had said was right. For a time, what we had was everything I thought I'd wanted. Until it wasn't. Until I discovered the truth and the shock and anguish over the depths of his lies made me lock up my heart and throw away the key. So many times I had the words hovering on my lips, wanting to share my pain with Charlie and Everleigh, my two best friends. But I was too embarrassed about how foolish I'd been and the idea of reliving those last moments with Michael by sharing what had happened hurt too much, so I'd just told them it hadn't worked out and didn't want to discuss it.

My voice was a whisper when I spoke, the jagged edge of pain scraping against my heart as I forced out the words. "I can't, Charlie. I just can't talk about him."

"But Chase," she protested, "it's been two years. Maybe it will help if you just get it off your chest. You know I would never judge you."

I shook my head, unable to say anymore. Charlie sighed, reading my expression, knowing the discussion would go no further.

"I hope you know I am here and available anytime."

"I'd rather talk about my Friday night plans," I said, forcing a smile and pushing any thoughts of my ex out of my head.

Charlie leaned forward, propping her elbows on my desk, and put her chin in her hands. "So spill. What's on the agenda?"

"I'm meeting up with Ethan and Everleigh and possibly a few other friends in Park Circle. Ethan and I are walking the new property, and then Ever is gonna meet us after at Madra Rua. We'll probably watch some soccer and then I'll see who shows up and go where the night takes me."

Charlie sighed again, but I could see the contentment in her expression and knew she didn't have an ounce of jealousy for my fly-by-night plans.

"Well, that does sound fun. Maybe next weekend Luke and I can get a sitter and we can all go out like we did in the old days."

"That would be amazing. It's been too long since we've all hung out. We can invite the whole gang. Well, except Darcy. I think she's still on tour."

"We could meet at Revival and pregame on the roof before we go out. The Christmas lights are up on the rooftop, and Luke said it looks amazing." Charlie had a dreamy look on her face and broke out into a big smile. "Yes, let's do it. I'll get a babysitter lined up and reach out to everyone. Ahhh, adult interaction to look forward to!" She stood from the chair and started toward the door, an extra spring in her step that hadn't been there when she'd entered. She turned back to me at the doorway. "Say hi to Ever and tell her I haven't forgotten I owe her lunch." She patted the doorframe and gave me a saucy grin. "Monday morning, I expect a full report on this evening's shenanigans. Or you can call me tomorrow if it's especially juicy."

"You got it, sassy. I'll take notes so I don't forget anything."

She giggled as she disappeared to head back to her office.

As I watched her red head disappear from view, my thoughts drifted back to Michael. I heard his low voice so clearly, it was as if he were right next to me whispering in my ear. The deep rumble of his words reverberated in my head, and my stomach lurched at the memory of the last thing he had said to me.

I wanted to tell you, Chase. This isn't how you were meant to find out. I never thought I would fall in love with you, but I can never be your everything. I'm so damn sorry.

Those words had erased all that had come before, the vowels and consonants grouped together to form a knife to my heart, the heart I had never expected to give away, and yet he had slid in there like a thief and stolen it.

Briefly, I wondered how far he would have let things go if I hadn't seen them together. The sight of their interlocked fingers, the lingering kiss they'd shared on the sidewalk before they'd disappeared inside the restaurant, had surged through me like an electric shock, instant and streaking through every cell of my body. The phantom pain had lingered for hours, days, and weeks afterward.

Even now, the memory of our confrontation the next day left me breathless with agony, all of my dreams of a future with my person dashed in one life-altering conversation. His words continued to echo in my ears years later. The excuses, the apologies, the promises that he was going to leave—all of it meant nothing in the face of his deception. And yet, after all this time, I still hadn't been able to move on, stunted by the aching wound that refused to heal. As I watched each of my friends find their soulmates, get engaged, marry, have children . . . I knew I was destined to be alone.

So I did what I had done every day since that fateful day: I pasted a smile on my face, buried the hurt, and headed out for another night of partying to numb the empty void that had once been a heart filled with love for a man who could never love me in return.

Chapter 2

Dillon

I knew it was ridiculous that my brain had stopped communicating with my legs, but the moment I saw him across the bar, I had been unable to keep moving. He was in the center of a small group of people, and I actually recognized a couple of them from the barbeque he and I had gone to together years ago. He hadn't noticed me; he was too caught up in whatever his friends were saying. My heart thundered in my chest as I took a deep breath, trying to calm down my frantic pulse. I watched him, his blond hair glinting under the bar's LED lights, as he threw his head back with a boisterous laugh. I remembered what it felt like to run my fingers through the fine hairs at his nape, what it felt like when his muscular arms encircled my waist as his lips brushed against mine.

It had been the first time I had experienced all the feelings I had read about in books or seen play out in the rom-coms I secretly enjoyed. A fluttering in my belly, a warmth spreading up my neck into my cheeks, my dick hardening in my jeans, just from one soft press of his lips on mine. Instantly, every girl or woman I had ever been with evaporated from my memories. Like a cloud of smoke, they were gone, replaced by over six feet of solid muscle and a rough cheek rubbing against my own as his large hands held me firmly, possessively. I had responded greedily, diving into his lips like a man starved for days who was getting his first taste of filet mignon. And everything about him had tasted oh so good. The way he'd moaned against my mouth when I'd stroked the back of his neck, my fingertips tangling with the ends of his hair, was everything I'd ever dreamed of in one short kiss.

I had wanted him as fiercely as I had wanted to win hockey championships in college, but that need that had surged up in me had also terrified me. It had sent me into a spiral of shame and fear, and I had reacted badly. Flashes of my father—red-faced, his eyes filled with disappointment and accusation—had clouded my brain, and I'd pulled away. Chase had known immediately, recognized the reaction for what it was: cold feet mixed with regret.

I hadn't been surprised not to hear from him again. I'd known from our earlier conversations during the few times we had been together he'd been hesitant to give me a chance because of my inexperience. He knew without my saying so that I wanted him, but he also knew I had never been with a man. I'd had crushes and many, many fantasies, but I had never crossed the line, always kept my feelings buried deep. Until I had met him, and he'd swept me off my feet with his singular smile; deep, booming laugh; and twinkling brown eyes.

He was so comfortable in his skin and everything I had wanted to be, but I'd spent my life denying who I really was. In high school and college, I'd played lacrosse and hockey. I had dated and fucked all the hottest girls; every step I'd taken had cemented my status as a confident jock, a real man's man. The perfect son for my college basketball coach of a father. The dark shadow of his homophobia hung over me like a storm cloud. His frequent comments and slurs reminded me he would never accept me loving a man—not to mention the thought of facing my true desires, pursuing a relationship with someone I had a real attraction to? I wouldn't have even known how to begin.

Though as I watched him now, nearly three years later, I realized the yearning I had felt for him had never gone away. It surged back to the surface, as if only days had passed instead of years. I was still firmly in the closet with just a few fumbling encounters—a blow job in my car, a hand job in the men's room of a club. Nothing meaningful and definitely no more passionate kisses. I just couldn't. Hell, I'd even had a couple of girlfriends. One of them had lasted for over a year, although she had finally ended it three months ago. Strangely, she never questioned my lack of passion in the bedroom, she seemed happy to just be my girlfriend, waiting for me to take the next step in our relationship.

Eventually, I guess she realized it was never going to happen and when she met someone else at work, she moved on. I found I wasn't even that upset, just sad not to have an excuse to go and see the latest rom-com in the theater with my girlfriend, pretending to sacrifice so she'd go and see an action movie the following week. In reality, I much preferred a good love story over the latest Marvel movie.

Our break up had made me realize how many years I had wasted trying to live up to my father's unrealistic expectations. All the years of unsatisfying relationships, which had nothing to do with the women I'd dated and everything to do with the fact that I was denying who I really was. A gay man, who had been in the closet his whole life.

Now here I was at thirty-three, standing in the middle of a crowded bar and mooning over a man who had taken me out on two dates before he had kissed me, and that had been years ago. But if I were honest, he was the one man who'd never quite left my head. I had daydreamed about that kiss more times than I'd cared to admit, and for the brief time his light had shone on me, I'd felt true happiness.

I had been so lost in my memories, that I hadn't noticed the man I had been thinking about was no longer at the bar. I jolted as warm breath tickled my ear, and a familiar voice made the hairs rise on the back of my neck. Even the smell of him, spicy and masculine, had me light-headed and hot.

"Fancy meeting you here, stranger." His voice had the slightest hint of a Southern accent, and his deep, sensual tone held a sprinkle of humor, just how I remembered it. I turned my head in surprise, and he was so close, we nearly bumped noses. He chuckled at my reaction, and I flushed, partly from embarrassment, but mostly from his proximity.

"Skittish as ever, I see," he said, taking a step back but smiling to soften the teasing reminder of how I had pulled away when he had kissed me.

"Hi, Chase," I said, feeling incredibly awkward as my voice cracked when I said his name.

His hands were in his front pockets as he leaned toward me to talk over the noise of the crowded bar. Again, the hair rose on my neck as his scent drifted under my nose, his breath ghosting across my skin.

"I never expected to run into you here. I thought you lived downtown. I'd expected to run across you at some of your old haunts down there," he said, his smile still lingering on his full lips.

"Yeah, I actually moved out here to Park Circle not long after we met. A buddy of mine was relocating to the West Coast and needed to sell his house quickly, so I bought it for a steal. This pub is one of my favorite spots in the Circle."

"Yeah, well, I should probably pick your brain then. Charlie and I are doing the design for a new community around the corner. We're doing the interiors for the different models along with helping with the landscape design and the finishes for the commercial buildings. It's an amazing project, but it'd be nice to get some perspective from a resident. Honestly, you're probably our target demographic, as far as your age and everything."

"Yeah, yeah, sure. I'd be happy to help." I wondered if I sounded as clumsy and insecure as I felt. I looked at him so relaxed and self-assured, not to mention sexy as hell; I wondered what he had ever seen in me in the first place.

He reached out and grabbed my bicep almost as if afraid I was going to bolt. "Hey, my friends are getting ready to leave. Do you wanna go somewhere a little quieter, maybe grab some dinner? I can tell you about the project, and you can fill me in on what you've been up to the last few years." He paused. " I mean, unless you already have plans with someone else."

My skin tingled at the feel of his fingers on my arm, and my head buzzed as I tried to decipher his words. *Fuck. He wants to have dinner with me? Me!*

Somehow, I managed to form words and not look like a complete fool.

"Umm, sure. That sounds great. No, I don't have plans, I just stopped in for a beer after work."

He smiled, and it nearly made my heart stop at how dazzling he was. His dimple popping out, his full lips stretching across white teeth, those chocolate eyes filled with the promise of so much trouble. *Oh God, I'm so screwed!*

He released my bicep and patted my shoulder.

"Okay, buddy, just hang here a minute and let me settle up my bill and say goodbye to my friends. I'll be right back."

I watched him walk away, my heart thudding so loudly in my chest, it nearly drowned out the bar noise. Damn, the view from the back was nearly as good as the front.

Fuck me.

Chapter 3

Chase

Dillon was quiet as we walked the couple blocks to Basil, where we had decided to eat. I could sense his nervousness; it practically radiated off of him. I decided to let the silence envelop us for now rather than fill it in with forced chatter. Besides, the quiet gave me a moment to examine my spontaneous decision to invite him to dinner. The moment I'd noticed him in the bar, the memory of our only kiss made my pulse thrum in my veins. I knew when I'd seen him that he'd noticed me first; I could tell by the way his jaw was clenched as he purposefully looked around the room, intentionally avoiding where I sat with my friends at the bar.

I remembered how hot he'd been when I kissed him, and I also remembered the moment he had freaked out and pulled away. I hadn't really been surprised. I'd known when I kissed him that could've happened. It was obvious he had wanted me, but it was also clear he was deeply in the closet and terrified to come out. At the time, I wasn't interested in navigating that minefield—even if that brief kiss had stayed with me for months afterward . . . and clearly now, three years later. Maybe that was what had made me leave my friends to approach him in the pub and ask him to dinner. The only other person who had rocked my world with just a kiss had been Michael six months later.

Dillon cleared his throat next to me, his voice tentative when he spoke. "So, umm, I assume you are still doing the decorating thing? With your friend, Charlie?"

His attempt at small talk amused me, but I held back my smile, not wanting him to feel like I was laughing at him.

"Yes, our business is booming in large part because Charlie married our biggest client, but honestly, that first job we did, the one I was working on when we met, really put us on the map. It's just that Charlie's husband's company keeps us so busy, it's difficult to accept other work. I'm here in Park Circle is to do some reconnaissance for that project I mentioned earlier."

He perked up. "Oh! Is it that big community with the condos and townhomes? It looks like it's going to be amazing," His enthusiasm changed his entire demeanor, as he smiled at me. Damn, he was even better looking than I remembered, his dark eyes sparkling in the dim light filtering from the businesses and restaurants we passed on the sidewalk.

"Yes, that's the one. It's a massive undertaking, but Charlie and I are a great team, and we're having a blast assembling all of the design ideas. Her husband and his partners are also easy to work with and basically give us free rein to do what we want, provided we work within their budget, of course.

"How about you? Are you still playing hockey?" I asked, returning his smile.

"Yeah, I play in a recreational league. I started a new job last year with a larger PR firm that keeps me busy, but I still play on the weekends."

We'd arrived at the restaurant and halted our conversation so I could ask the hostess about the availability of tables.

"Unfortunately, it's about a two-hour wait," she said in response to my inquiry.

Dillon and I looked at each other, and my heart sank. It was Friday night in the busy North Charleston neighborhood, and I was sure all the other restaurants would have long wait times too.

We walked outside and looked at each other, the early winter air making us both shiver. He tilted his head to the side, and his expression changed from uncertain to determined.

"Listen," he said, "if you still want to have dinner together, my house is a five-minute walk from here, and I have enough leftover spaghetti for the two of us. I'm not an amazing cook, but I do make a decent red sauce and I can also make us a salad to go with it." The uncertainty returned. "I mean, if you want to do that."

I regarded him for a moment. I could sense he was outside of his comfort zone, but I could also feel the chemistry sizzling between us, and I knew he wanted me to come. I watched a myriad of emotions flash across his face. His nervous expression should have had me running as fast as I could in the other direction. But I found I didn't want to leave him yet. I wanted to see where this night took us, and I had this incredible desire to pull him into my arms and hug him because he seemed so sad and lost. His loneliness called out to me, and this time, I didn't want to walk away.

"Yes, I'd like that," I responded carefully, hitting him with a reassuring smile.

He let out a breath, and I reached over and cuffed a hand on his shoulder. "Lead the way, Dillon; spaghetti sounds real good right now."

Thirty minutes later, I was sitting at the tiny island in Dillon's kitchen watching him plate our food. He'd insisted on making a salad, even though I'd told him it wasn't necessary. I had to admit, though, I'd enjoyed watching him chop vegetables and being all domestic. I could tell by the slight tremor in his hand he was still nervous, but somehow that made him even more endearing to me. The glances he kept sending my way were beginning to make my jeans feel a little tight across my lap, and when he smiled shyly at me as he set the plate of food in front of me, I wanted to wrap my hand around the back of his neck and press his lips against mine so I could see if he still tasted as good as I remembered.

Maybe he could read my thoughts—or more likely my expression gave me away—because when he finally sat down next to me, his face was flushed, and his hand shook more as he picked up his fork. I put my hand on his before he could lift the fork to his mouth, and his eyes snapped up to mine.

"Dillon, relax, it's okay. I don't expect anything to happen here. I truly just want to see how you're doing. I feel bad that I never called you after . . . after that night."

He set down his fork, and the look in his eyes caused goosebumps to break out across my skin like he had touched me. The yearning I saw there made me forget all about the food as I waited for his response.

His voice was hoarse when he spoke.

"Chase . . ."

I squeezed his hand underneath mine encouragingly, relieved when he continued.

"You have no idea how many times I've replayed that night over in my head. So often I've wished I could go back and change the way I reacted. But how you made me feel . . . it fucking terrified me."

I watched his throat bob as he swallowed slowly. His eyebrows drew together as he considered his words before continuing.

"I'd been attracted to men before. I knew that about myself, and I made the conscious choice to ignore my needs. Because being the man my father wanted me to be was so much easier. But when I met you, shit, the first time I saw you, that was no longer good enough. I wanted more for my life. You made me want to discover who I really was."

The look he gave me was heartbreaking and revelatory at the same time, and the urge to hug him rose in me again. But I stayed where I was, knowing he needed to finish. Hell, *I* needed him to finish. He didn't keep me waiting long, and the words he said next made my heart leap in my chest.

"That kiss . . . God, Chase, that kiss. I fucking dreamed about it for months. I know to you it was probably no big deal, but to me, it was everything I had never known I'd wanted. I could see it. I could see my life with someone like you, and I craved it, but the force of those emotions rocked me to my core, and I was so scared."

"I'm sorry," I whispered. "I had no idea."

He shook his head. "Of course you didn't. How could you? You know who you are. You've known your whole life, and you embrace it, own it, and don't care what anyone else thinks." His eyes glittered with emotion, and I was so thrown by his unexpected confession, I had no idea what to say.

"But my life is different. My father . . .'" He dropped his head, looking down at his lap. I pulled on his hand still under mine, trying to get him to look up at me.

"Tell me." It came out more forcefully than I'd intended, but he seemed to respond to the authority in my tone.

"You know who he is, but what you don't know is that he is homophobic to the extreme. As the basketball coach of Charleston University, he's respected, even revered, but the person he is at home in no way resembles that man. He's made it perfectly clear my whole life what was expected of his only son." He shrugged, almost in defeat. "And maybe he sensed something in me because he made sure I knew what he would not tolerate, and a gay son was at the top of the list."

"Why didn't you tell me this before?" I asked. "I would have been more patient; I could've helped you." I felt like a complete ass for ghosting him after that night.

He could read me so well, and a fissure of awareness bounced between us like a living thing. "Please, Chase. I'm not telling you this now to make you feel guilty about before. It's not your fault. And you're right; I should have said something. Probably from the first time we hung out together because I knew even then you were different." He took a deep breath and his hand moved under mine, flipping it over to clutch my fingers.

"I'm telling you now because I don't want to make the same mistake again. I'm telling you because ever since that day, three years ago, I've dreamed of having the chance to kiss you again. I've wondered what would have happened if I hadn't pushed you away."

Chapter 4

Dillon

I couldn't believe I'd said it out loud, but I didn't regret it even as Chase regarded me with a surprised expression.

I gestured to his plate. "I'm sorry I've distracted you from your food. Please, eat it before it gets cold."

I pulled my hand from his, hating the way my fingers suddenly felt empty and cold. I grabbed my fork and scooped a large bite into my mouth, but I was suddenly not hungry. My stomach was too filled with clenching nerves.

Chase picked up his own fork, still regarding me with a slight frown on his face. I hated the way he was looking at me, his eyes sympathetic. Suddenly, I felt a twinge of panic. *God, what if he had a boyfriend or a husband? Why had I assumed he was single just because he wanted to have dinner and catch up? How pathetic I must seem to him!*

We both ate in silence for a few minutes, and I forced myself to chew and swallow my food, yet every part of me wanted to fill the silence with words. But what could I say that wouldn't embarrass me further? No, no, it was better to let him pick up the conversation. I only hoped it wouldn't be to tell me about the wonderful man in his life. I mean, he *would* be wonderful to be with Chase. He had to be.

Chase wiped his mouth with his napkin. I tried not to stare as he performed that simple motion, but I was unable tear my gaze away, and his eyes caught mine. He smiled slightly, and I quickly looked down at my plate. He reached over and pushed on my shoulder, forcing my attention back on him.

"Stop that," he said, that smile turning into a smirk.

"Stop what?" I asked, knowing I sounded defensive.

"You're avoiding me, and I can tell you're regretting what you said to me."

I took in a breath, ready to deny it, but he beat me to it.

"Nope," he said, pushing away his plate and standing. He held out a hand. "That spaghetti was amazing—you totally undersold it—but we can talk about your culinary skills later. We need to have a conversation first."

He grabbed my hand and practically yanked me off my barstool. Damn, he was strong.

"What conversation?" I asked as I got clumsily to my feet.

He led me into my living room. It felt weird to have him dragging me around my own house, but I couldn't deny part of me liked his domineering ways. His hand felt rough in my own, and I marveled at the sensation, realizing I had never held hands with a man before. Not even my dad. He wasn't much of a hand holder. In fact, he rarely showed any affection.

Chase led us to the couch and sat, pulling me down next to him. The force of the motion caused me to land half on top of him, and I quickly moved away, feeling my skin flush from not only embarrassment but also from how good his hard thighs felt underneath me. When I looked up at him, his eyes glittered with mirth, and his wide smile made it clear he was delighted by how he affected me.

He scooted closer, and our legs pressed together, the warmth sending a jolt of heat to the pit of my stomach, reminding me of those brief moments when he'd kissed me.

"Maybe I should fix us both a drink." I hated how shaky my voice sounded.

Chase shook his head, still smiling. "Drinks can wait. I'd rather hear what you have to say while we're both sober." His voice softened, his eyes warm, and I started relaxing. "I want to know everything, Dillon. All the things you never told me those few times we went out. I'm sure I didn't misread your interest or your inexperience. And obviously, you're still interested, but I'm sensing you're still hesitant. I want to know what I can do to help you."

He paused, as if measuring his words carefully. A glimmer of hope filled me and wondered if I could trust him with the truth.

Almost as if he could read my mind, he put his hand on my knee, giving it a gentle squeeze. "I'm not here to judge you, and I know that everyone's journey is their own. I want to be your friend, Dillon. I'm sorry I didn't try harder to be that for you three years ago." He gave me a small smile. "I guess I was too distracted by your biceps and those sexy lips." His tone was light and teasing, and I appreciated the way he'd so easily relieved some of the tension that had built up from my confession.

And when our eyes connected, his were filled with compassion. Briefly, I wondered what he saw in mine because I was done hiding, and I prayed he was ready to see the real me.

Chapter 5

Chase

I'd been drawn to Dillon the first time we'd met at a mutual friend's party nearly three years ago. We'd talked the entire night and I'd spontaneously invited him to my friend Ethan's cookout a week later. We'd had a great time that night, too, and while I could tell he was inexperienced with men, we hadn't really talked openly about our histories. But sensing his nerves, I had kept things friendly and casual.

When he'd agreed to meet me for dinner a few nights later, I decided to test the waters. After dinner, we'd gone to a bar, and then I'd walked him back to his apartment not far from there. Only when I'd kissed him outside his front door did I realize he was far from ready to date a man.

At first, he'd responded to the kiss, and for a few short moments, it was one of the best kisses I'd ever had. But then he panicked and pulled away, mumbling an excuse about getting to bed early before practically slamming the door in my face. I'd been a little shocked and more than put off. I realized now, as I looked at his wide, dark eyes, I probably should have reached back out and at least tried to give him a chance to explain. But it was easier to just write him off as another jock too deep in the closet to ever be more than a fuck buddy on the side, and that was something I had no interest in. I wasn't about to hide who I was or be someone's dirty little secret, no matter how great the kiss was.

Hesitantly at first, Dillon shared his story. At times, I could almost feel his pain rolling off him in waves, pain that had him catching his breath and lowering his head. His anguish was a palpable thing pulsing between us. Some of the things he told me I understood in a way only a person with a similar journey could. The worries and concerns about what the people closest to you would think, wondering if they would treat you differently once they knew. Those things were real and valid. But while my coming out had been uncomfortable and my parents had spent years ignoring my sexuality, I had never encountered the deep-seated hatred Dillon had experienced. I knew my parents would not be supportive, but I also knew deep down they loved me and would never turn their backs on me. My high school best friends, Charlie and Everleigh, had stood by my side through it all, and even the guys on my football team had ultimately come around and shut down any homophobic comments, which had gone a long way toward the rest of our classmates accepting me.

Some of what Dillon told me about his father had me cringing in disbelief and frankly, it was much easier for me to understand why he'd denied his attraction to men for so long. Like me, he was an only child, but his dad loomed large over his childhood, and his heavy hand and draconian beliefs had informed the person Dillon grew up to be. He had spent many years living a lie so convincingly that he had nearly believed it himself.

Although Dillon maintained his composure while recounting his history, the moment he fell silent, I could see the toll his emotions had taken. He stared down at his hands, his broad shoulders hunched and his skin flushed. I finally did the thing I had wanted to do from the moment I had seen him at the bar. I put my arms around him and pulled him against me, burying my face in his neck.

He stiffened in surprise at the move, but I pressed my lips to his ear. "Relax. I've wanted to do this all night, and I think you need it too."

He immediately softened against me, and his arms crept around my waist as he returned my embrace. I could feel his heart beating against mine and as I tucked my face back against his neck, his pulse thundering rapidly under my mouth. I kissed him there. The sigh that came from his lips was everything in that moment, and my body heated as he slid a hand up to the back of my neck and pulled me in closer, encouraging me to continue.

I didn't want to take advantage of his vulnerability, but the feel of him so compliant in my arms was hard to resist. Nevertheless, my concern for his feelings outweighed my more carnal desires, so I gave him a squeeze and started to pull back.

"No," he pleaded, "just for another minute. This feels so fucking good."

I didn't release him but pulled back enough to see his face. He was still flushed, but the look in his eyes made my own pulse speed up. The pull of our mutual desire was an overwhelming force.

"Please," he whispered. " I promise I won't pull away this time. I need to know . . . to feel . . ." He leaned toward me, his intent clear, and I couldn't deny him because I needed to know too. I had to see if it was as good as I'd remembered.

I moved my hand from around his waist and put it on the back of his head, allowing myself to stroke his dark hair, so soft under my fingertips. He was inches away, his soulful eyes nearly black with desire as he watched and waited for me to close the distance between us.

"You sure?" I asked softly.

He nodded, and for a brief second, I saw a hint of a smile. His mouth started to move in answer, but I muffled his measured response as I crashed my lips to his.

I wasn't gentle, the pent-up hunger had me fisting the back of his shirt and sinking my fingers deep into his hair as I devoured his mouth with a groan.

He scooted closer, practically climbing in my lap, and his answering grunts and fevered hands stroking my back had my dick growing tight against my zipper. His mouth opened in invitation, and I slid my hot tongue between his lips. As my tongue touched his, he released a groan, and the sound had me envisioning all the dirty things I wanted to do to earn more of those sexy noises.

Our tongues tangled; we were lost in our kiss. Breaths quickened, and we panted into each other's mouths as we grew bolder, hands exploring over clothes, teeth nipping at tender lips, desire clouding everything but the need for more. More touching, more tasting, just *more*.

Needing to catch my breath before things went too far, I slid my mouth down to his neck, once again sucking at the spot where his pulse hammered. He tilted his head back, opening himself to me even more, and my body sang with need. It was as if he could read my mind as he slid his hard length against mine, giving me a little relief at the feel of him pressed against me.

I pulled back and put my hands on either side of his jaw, forcing him to look at me. He was so gone with lust, it took a minute for him to focus, and even when he did, he continued to grind circles against me. The friction from our erections rubbing together through our jeans made my eyes nearly roll back in my head.

I dropped my hands to his hips, holding him in place. God, he was so tempting with his kiss-swollen lips and dark chocolate eyes filled with a hunger that called out to every part of me.

"Dillon." I said it with a groan. "If you don't stop that, either things are gonna get out of hand, or I'm gonna come in my pants like a teenager."

His arms were on either side of my head, and he dropped his forehead onto my shoulder with a heavy sigh. I released my hold on his hip and stroked a hand up his back.

"Are you okay?" I asked him.

He looked up at me, his long eyelashes casting a shadow on his cheeks. His expression was filled with longing, and my heart squeezed in my chest. If I wasn't careful, I was gonna be gone for this guy.

"Yes, I've never felt more okay in my life."

I was surprised when he leaned in and pressed a kiss to my lips. I chuckled against his mouth even as my cock jumped in my pants at the simple gesture. He pulled back, giving me a genuine smile, and his whole face completely changed, like a light had been turned on inside him. Almost unconsciously, I reached my hand up and ran my fingers along his cheek.

His expression grew serious again as he stared at me. "I want more."

I could hear the quiver in his voice, and I didn't know if it was nerves or uncertainty. I looked him in the eye and knew my voice had a commanding tone when I spoke, but I needed to make sure this time.

"I think you're going to have to be specific, Dillon. What exactly do you mean by more?"

Chapter 6

Dillon

Chase's tone sent a shiver up my spine. I really fucking liked it. I liked him. Everything about him. He was better than I'd remembered. The way he'd listened when I'd told him about my dad, my girlfriends, even my unsatisfying (sort-of) hookups I'd attempted to temper my growing frustration with my personal life. Every gentle stroke of my knee, the encouraging sounds he made when I'd hesitated, and the warm understanding in his gaze all made me want him more. Now his commanding voice was asking me what I wanted.

And right now, sitting on his lap, feeling his muscular thighs under mine while his soft amber eyes glowed with interest, I wanted it all. I wanted every part of him. I wanted him to kiss me until I was so lost in the feel of his lips on mine, I couldn't think of anything else. I wanted to taste all of his secret places, bury my nose in his neck and breathe him in. I wanted to live in his world, his big, rough hand holding mine as we walked down the street secure in our relationship. Most of all, I wanted to know what it would feel like to be wrapped up in him, blanketed by his love. To know what it meant to be the main character in one of the rom-coms I'd always loved.

I desperately wanted my own happily ever after. And as I sat there looking at him, I could see all the promise shining from his open expression, his eyes warm, his lips set in a determined line, but just a tiny hint of a smile at the corners. He didn't say a word, just waited. It was as if though he was reading my thoughts, silently answering, reassuring, reaching for me. Something stirred in the deepest part of my soul, the part I'd kept buried, never wanting to feel the yearning and the disappointment of knowing what could be and unable to have it.

But this time, the yearning refused to stay buried, and I no longer had the strength to deny myself what I'd wanted for so long. What I'd craved since that day on my doorstep when I'd run away from this man. I'd never forgotten that kiss, and now he was here and holding me.

I wanted him more than I'd ever wanted anything else in my life.

As these thoughts tumbled through my head, Chase took my arms still slung across his shoulders and put my hands on his chest. I could feel the thump of his heart as he once again cupped my face with his hands. He ran a thumb gently across my bottom lip, and that tiny touch caused my skin to prickle and my hard-on to twitch.

"Tell me where you want this to go." His voice was husky, and I could feel the need behind his words. "Tonight and after?"

I understood the meaning in those words. He wanted to know if I was just scratching an itch, or if there would be more. I owed him the truth.

"I want everything I've been missing." I exhaled the breath I hadn't realized I'd been holding. "But I am scared. I don't know what will happen. With my parents, my friends." I felt a deep well of sadness at the idea of him walking away again. "But I'm more afraid of letting you leave. I want—no, I need to see where this goes."

His smile was brilliant, and the ache in my chest lessened at the sight of it directed at me so intently. He lifted me off his lap surprisingly easily given I wasn't a small guy.

"All right, then. Lead the way to the bedroom. I think it's time to get to know each other in a more relaxing way."

I sucked in a breath as he stood and reached for my hand, chuckling lightly at my panicked expression.

"Calm down, hockey stud. I have no interest in tonight being your first time with a man. We have plenty of time for that and I want to take things slow with you, Dillon."

Quicker than anticipated, I was completely naked and lying face down on my bed on top of a towel. Chase had managed to dig out a bottle of coconut oil from the recesses of my bathroom cabinet and, sensing my shyness, had thrown a small hand towel across my ass cheeks, giving me a modicum of modesty. Meanwhile, he was strutting around my bedroom in a pair of revealing blue boxer briefs, and despite my best efforts not to stare, the erection straining against the material continually drew my eyes. It wasn't a hard sell for him to convince me the best way to get to know each other was by giving each other massages, and he insisted I be the first recipient.

So that was how I ended up here, and I had no desire to complain, especially as he climbed on the bed and seated himself on the backs of my thighs, his knees on either side of me. I heard the pop of the bottle cap and felt warm liquid slide down between my shoulder blades (yeah, he insisted on heating the coconut oil in the microwave). Then his hands were on my back, firm palms running up to cup my shoulders as he leaned down and put his lips next to my ear.

"This is gonna be the best kind of torture. For both of us."

"Bring it on."

He responded by whipping the towel from my ass and sliding his hands down to grab my cheeks. I let out a low groan as he slid his hands slowly up my back again, his fingers expertly kneading away any lingering tension.

His low chuckle sent a shot of heat to my groin. "Sweet, sweet torture." His clever hands roamed my body, goosebumps rising in their wake.

"Just remember," I murmured, "it's my turn next, big boy."

He leaned down and placed a soft kiss on the side of my neck. "I'm looking forward to being at your mercy."

Chapter 7

Chase

"So what time is Dillon supposed to get here?" Everleigh asked impatiently, bouncing up and down in the chair next to me. "I can't believe you ran into him last weekend and you didn't even mention it to us before you left!"

"I already told you that I wasn't sure how things would play out and I didn't want to listen to your nagging if he shot me down or he was seeing someone else. And to answer your question, he was supposed to be here fifteen minutes ago."

Charlie, who was next to me on the outdoor couch, laid a comforting hand on my thigh. "He'll be here, Chase. He probably got hung up looking for a parking place. You know how busy it is on King Street, especially this time of year."

I wanted to believe her, but I couldn't deny the lump of nerves that had taken up residence in my gut when he hadn't shown up at 7:00 p.m. as we'd agreed. Charlie had reached out in our group chat to set up a pre-holiday get-together for grown-ups only. Her words, not mine. In addition to Luke and Charlie's little firecracker, Ethan and Everleigh also had a nine-month-old son, Jackson. They managed to get out more often, though, probably because Ever's parents were retired and constantly begging to have little Jackson for sleepovers with Gramma and Grampa. Charlie's parents owned a local bed and breakfast, so it was more of a challenge for them to babysit, and Charlie didn't trust very many people to watch Emmy.

Luckily, our mutual friend, Sebastian had said his mom, would have Emmy over to her house for a sleepover. Neither of her two kids had children yet, so she considered herself an honorary grandma to Emmy.

Once we had finalized the plans to meet here at the rooftop of Revival on King, the condo building that Luke, Ethan, and Sebastian owned, I had called Dillon and invited him to come out with us. I knew it was a bold move considering we had only just rekindled things between us, but he had already met most of my friends three years ago, and I really wanted him here. He'd seemed a little hesitant but agreed and said he would meet me here instead of at my house like I had originally suggested.

As I looked around the festive rooftop decorated with greenery and brightly colored holiday lights, I thought about last Friday night with Dillon. Things had turned out better than I could have hoped, especially after he had shared more details about his past and the reasons behind his wariness when it came to dating men.

I had thoroughly enjoyed teasing him with a sensual massage, and he had returned the favor, driving me crazy with his curious fingers and hot-as-fuck mouth. We had exchanged quite a few fevered kisses, and eventually, after we had worked each other up into a near frenzy, I had taken matters into my own hands, so to speak, and given us both some much-needed relief. The evening had been so erotic, I had come home and masturbated twice—his name on my lips, visions of his dark pupils blown wide with lust, the sound of him moaning my name as I made him come with my hand—before falling asleep.

I was afraid he would be awkward after all of that, but he mostly seemed happy and eager to spend more time together, exactly how I'd felt as I'd gotten in my car and drove home from his house that night. He assured me he was good and ready to take the first steps toward coming out of the closet. I'd hoped to see him again over that weekend, but he'd already had plans with his best friend on Saturday, and I had promised I'd help our friend Noah move into his girlfriend Samantha's house on Sunday. He'd emphasized once again that he didn't want to lose me, and he'd stayed in touch all week. Now as I sat here, my friends chatting happily on either side of me, surrounded by reminders of the upcoming Christmas holiday, I wondered if I'd once again be spending it alone.

My heart sank at the thought of another holiday with my friends, their significant others, and me, the forever odd wheel. After my evening with Dillon, I'd been floating on a cloud all week, hopeful for the first time since breaking up with Michael. Every conversation I had with Dillon, each text message, had solidified my feelings for him. We had capped off our week of flirting last night with a steamy Facetime call that had ended with us both masturbating and then falling asleep on the phone together. I'd never even done that with Michael.

As my spirits began to plummet, I closed my eyes and leaned my head back against the cushion, preparing myself for the inevitable disappointment of a call or text from Dillon with some lame excuse as to why he was bailing on me tonight. I felt a fingernail poking my shoulder, and an excited Charlie squeaked in my ear.

"He's here! he's here!"

My eyes flew open. His gaze caught mine, and it felt like so many words were exchanged in just that one look.

I've missed you. I'm so glad to see you. Damn, you look fucking hot!

Okay, that last one might have been me as I watched him walk toward me. His chestnut hair was tousled, and he had a light dusting of scruff on his square jaw. His jeans clung to him tantalizingly, bringing back the memory of his muscular thighs coated in oil as I rubbed him from head to toe. He wore a dark green sweater and a tan jacket, and suddenly I just wanted to take him home and unwrap him like the best Christmas present I've ever had.

"We'll be right back. Gonna grab a drink at the bar," Everleigh whispered as she and Charlie made a quick exit.

I stood as Dillon approached, invading my personal space, the tip of his shoes touching the tip of mine.

"I was beginning to think you'd changed your mind," I said, releasing the breath I'd been holding since he'd entered.

"Not a chance," he said with a small smile, and my heart swelled with all the promise I saw unwavering in his dark brown eyes as they held my own.

End

About Suzie Webster

Suzie Webster - Gypsy, Storyteller, Relentless Dreamer, Foodie, Happy Wife, Cool Mom of 3

Why did Suzie Webster start writing romance novels at age forty-nine? To Inspire women to realize that they are the owners of their life and that it is possible at any age to turn their story into a journey filled with laughter, steamy romance, and adventure just like their favorite book. Throughout her many careers from Northern Virginia to Charleston, Suzie has always loved mentoring and supporting other women who are trying to live the life they want and deserve. She has loved writing since childhood, and weaving stories is another way to share the message that love always wins. She is supported in her own journey by her very patient and tolerant husband Drew, who is always the inspiration for her sexy leading men and her three kids, Ryleigh, Percy, and Reese, who never fail to keep her on her toes and put her in her place. When she's not traveling (her favorite hobby), she can be found curled up with a good book and a tasty cocktail, preferably tequila.

Find Suzie Online:
Website: www.suziewebster.com
Facebook: https://www.facebook.com/suziewebsterauthor
Instagram: https://www.instagram.com/suziewebster_author/
Twitter: https://twitter.com/suzieQcanwrite
Amazon: https://www.amazon.com/Suzie-Webster/e/B07SGR7Y96?

Goodreads: https://www.goodreads.com/author/show/18874438.
Suzie_Webster

Edi-Snow!

By HM Thomas

Edi-Snow!

Contemporary

Joy Carter swore she wouldn't return to Edisto and the boy she left behind until hell froze over. Looks like the joke's on her. She just wants to hide out in her childhood home and forget her troubles, but Mother Nature has other plans. When a mix up in communication and a freak snowstorm leave Joy alone without electricity or transportation, there's only one man who can help her—Nick Parsons, the boy she left behind a decade ago. Only Nick's no longer a boy, and Joy's finding it hard to remember how she ever thought she could live without him.

Rated: PG-13

Chapter One

Snow drifted from the dark sky, landing with soft feather kisses on Joy's windshield. Under different circumstances, she'd take the time to admire the fluffy flakes. But these were not normal circumstances, and there shouldn't be snow. She'd returned home to South Carolina's Lowcountry, and although there were only two days until Christmas, there shouldn't be snow. It never snowed on Edisto Island.

Maybe she shouldn't have sworn to only return when hell froze over.

But apparently, karma had taken her words to heart. Not that the island was hell. For so many, it was paradise—Eden, if she were being biblical. The island hadn't driven her away a decade ago, and it wasn't drawing her back now. She'd left to build a life greater than what she'd ever be able to create on the sinking foundation of pluff mud. Unfortunately, as it turned out, concrete wasn't a great foundation either. And there'd been nothing but concrete surrounding her in Florida.

As she crossed the bridge connecting the mainland to the island, the snow fell harder. If she'd shared her plans to come home with her parents, they probably would've mentioned the snow. Not that it would keep her away since she had nowhere else to go.

Gripping the steering wheel until her knuckles turned white, she inched across the bridge. Yes, it was only snow, but she'd never driven in it, and she was on a bridge sixty-eight feet above the Intercoastal Waterway. Plunging into the chilly waters below was not how she planned to die. Not today anyway.

Six long miles later, her car sputtered to a stop in her parents' drive. Already, the snow was turning slick and icy. But she'd made it. Now, she could go in, warm up, and not leave until the storm ended. Knowing her mother, she'd have the fridge and cabinets stocked. She'd probably even have something cooking in the oven, preparing for Christmas. Joy's stomach growled at the thought. As she tried to open the car door, a gust of wind pushed it back against her. Now that the car had stopped, she could hear the wind whistling through the bare trees. Wind she understood. She'd lived through enough hurricanes and tropical storms on this island that, although wind made her cautious, it didn't scare her. But wind with snow? That was new.

Gathering her strength, she shoved the door open, stumbling out of the car and into the driveway. Picking over the snow in her low booties, she made her way up the icy steps to knock on the door. *Nothing.* Chafing her hands over her bare arms, she tried again. When still no one answered, she tried the knob. *Locked.* Shivering, she made her way around the porch, scanning the property for any sign of her parents or older brother. Although he didn't live here anymore, Jack was always around helping Dad with what little was left of the farm. But it seemed today was the exception. There was no sign of her family, though both her parents' cars sat in the driveway.

Pulling her cell from her pocket, she hit the speed dial for her mom. As she waited for an answer, she bobbed up and down, trying to stay warm. She couldn't remember the island ever being this cold, but she didn't worry. Her parents had both lived up north before settling on the island. They'd know what to do with a little snow and wind. Besides, in South Carolina, snow never lasted long. Tomorrow the sun would come out and melt the white stuff away. Then, when the sun went down, the ice would take over. Joy shook that thought away and instead conjured the image of the beach in the summer.

"Hello? Joy?" Her mother's voice came over the line, distant and a little distracted.

"Hey, Mom. Where are you?" She strained to identify any sounds in the background.

"Ummm. I don't know. Honey, where are we?"

"We're in Jacksonville, Mom."

At the sound of her older brother's voice and his answer, Joy's stomach dropped. Jacksonville? That was over two hundred miles in the opposite direction.

"We're in Jacksonville." Her mother's voice came back on the line. "I tried to call and see if you'd be in town. We were thinking of stopping by on our way back next week."

Joy's stomach tightened. "On your way back? Next week?" Her parents weren't here, and they wouldn't be back for a week?

"Yes, after the cruise. Remember? Jack and Stacy are taking us on a cruise for Christmas. You said you had to work."

Joy deflated. She'd had to work when they'd asked. Six months ago. When she'd still had a job. They hadn't mentioned it since.

"Yeah, yeah. I remember now."

"So, will you be in town? We get back January second." Some of the cheerfulness left her mother's voice. "We'd love to see you, honey."

Tears stung her eyes, but Joy pushed them back. She was cold enough without tears frozen on her face. "I'm . . . uh . . . I'm actually at your house." Her voice cracked. She'd come home wanting nothing more than her family and her old bed; instead, she found herself stranded on the porch, alone, in a snowstorm. Was this really her life right now?

"Oh my. You're at *our* house?" Her mother's voice rose, and the rest of her family's voices filtered through the phone. "Did I forget you were coming? I thought—"

"No, Mom. I didn't . . . I forgot about the cruise. It's my fault."

"Well, we could—"

"No, Mom." Her selfless mother would willingly sacrifice her own fun to save Joy from a lonely holiday. "You're not skipping this trip. I have a ton of work to do anyway." *Total lie.*

"Oh, okay, if you're sure. Do you have a lot of time off? You can stay at the house, make yourself at home. We'll only be gone a week." Her mother sounded worried.

"That sounds great, Mom. By the time you get back, I'll have caught up on work and can spend the rest of my time with you." If by "caught up on work" one meant "get her life together and find a new job."

"Perfect." A smile crept back into her mother's voice. "There's a key in the carport if you don't have yours."

Relief swept through Joy as she picked her way down the snow-covered steps toward the carport. Finally, she could get in, get warm and fill her belly. She wrapped her hand around the house key and turned back toward the house.

"Oh, Joy. You might want to run to the grocery store before they close. There isn't any food in the house."

Joy's cheerful mood deflated. She looked back at her pitiful excuse for a car. Looked like they were going back out in the storm.

Nick climbed into his pickup, cursing the snow as it fell in heavy, fat flakes. Snow! What the actual fuck? Sure, the weatherman had said it would snow. A blizzard he'd called it. A blizzard? In South Carolina? Since when did meteorologists actually get their predictions correct? How many times had they whipped residents (or more like tourists) into a frenzy over a hurricane only to have it rain? Too fucking many, that was how many. So why should he have believed them now? At thirty years old, he'd never seen a white Christmas, and damn it, he could've gone another thirty without one and been as happy as a strand-feeding dolphin. As a contractor, December was his favorite time of year to get work done. The temperatures dropped a few degrees below hell, the bugs stopped eating him alive, and no hurricanes lurked offshore. But now a damn blizzard had decided to steal that time away from him.

Slamming the door of his truck, he embraced the sour mood blanketing him. But he couldn't ignore the glaring truth. He didn't hate snow. In truth, it would probably melt quickly and let him get back to work. But did it have to come at Christmas? His plan had been to spend the holidays working on the new house he was building for a couple who were coming down after the New Year to check his progress. He'd planned to work through Christmas, so he'd have more to show them. No, that was a lie. Truth was, he wanted to work through Christmas, so he wouldn't have to think about how it was Christmas, and he was alone.

Not a fan of self-pity, he shook the thought away and backed out of the crushed shell drive of the new build. On the bright side, if the snow kept everyone at home, no one would come by his house expecting him to be cheerful and festive. He could sulk in his cabin with a six (or twelve) pack and Netflix. Not that there'd be any internet, but at least he had a generator and a wood-burning fireplace. He'd be better off than some of his neighbors.

As he drove down Palmetto Avenue, already covered in snow, he cataloged what was in the fridge at home. Maybe it wouldn't hurt to run into the Food Lion just to make sure he didn't run out of provisions.

Once inside the store, Nick immediately regretted his decision. What the hell had he been thinking coming in here? Like most people in the store, he didn't really need anything, but the idea of being stuck in his house made him antsy. Even more, the thought of being stuck at home and craving something he didn't have made him antsy. As he inched around the corner of an aisle, the sound of angry voices reached his ears.

"Well, you'll just have to find another one, girly." That creaky old voice belonged to Mrs. Abernathy. The woman was ninety if she was a day, but she insisted on doing everything herself. Today, apparently "everything" included fighting an underdressed blonde for a loaf of bread.

The stranger stood with her back to Nick, towering over Mrs. Abernathy's barely five-foot frame. "Please." The newcomer's voice was soft, almost desperate. "I just need a loaf of bread. You literally have four other loaves in your cart. I just need to make some sandwiches."

Mrs. Abernathy harrumphed and jerked the loaf from the younger woman's hands, ripping the plastic wrapping. Why the hell did everyone think they needed bread and milk in a snowstorm? Nick's gaze drifted to the older woman's cart—yep, two gallons. As for the blond woman, she had a half-gallon in her basket.

"Come on, Mrs.—"

"No. Look what you've done." The old curmudgeon cradled her loaf of bread, then placed it gingerly in the cart with the four other loaves.

"Hey, Mrs. Abernathy." Nick spoke up. The stranger's body tensed underneath her thin jacket. Yeah, she definitely hadn't come to the island prepared for a snowstorm. Not that anyone was prepared for what the weatherman had predicted.

Mrs. Abernathy turned her wrinkled face toward him and smiled. "Hello, Nicholas. It's so good to see *you*." She shot a glare at the woman, as if to make sure she realized her presence was not as welcome.

"Is everything okay here?" Nick stepped forward.

"Just fine." The old woman's smile was pure saccharine. "But I should run. I want to get my groceries home before the storm picks up." She shot another menacing look at the stranger, who only shook her head in response.

With her nose in the air, Mrs. Abernathy turned her shopping cart around and wobbled to the front of the store.

"Grinch," the stranger mumbled. "She always did hate me."

That voice. Nick's stomach tightened at the sound of it. But he must be mistaken because the girl he'd known with the voice of an angel had left long ago with no plans to ever return.

"You . . . uh . . . you know Mrs. Abernathy?"

The woman shifted, her head cocked to the side and her hip jutted out. The gesture screamed *duh.* He knew that move and the girl who'd perfected it. He swallowed, bracing himself as she turned.

Joy Carter.

For a moment, all the breath rushed from his lungs, and he couldn't figure out how to draw in more. Joy Carter had left this island almost a decade ago, stomping all over his heart as she did. Last he'd heard, she'd moved to Florida and was working so hard to climb the corporate ladder she couldn't make time to visit her parents.

"What are you doing here?" he blurted.

Her green eyes widened before turning to slits. "Trying to buy bread before this God-forsaken storm hits."

He shook his head. "No. What are you doing *here*? On the island?"

Her gaze darkened. Okay, so he could've found a nicer way to greet her. But in his defense, it was nicer than the goodbye she hadn't bothered to give him.

"This is my home, Nicholas. I'm here for the holidays."

"But Rachel and Will are on that cruise."

Her eyes grew big as saucers at that information about her parents. "*Rachel and Will?* Since when do you call my parents by their first names?"

He smirked. "Since I'm a grown-ass man no longer sneaking around with their daughter."

Her face went as white as the snow falling outside the store. When she swallowed, the muscles in her jaw tightened. Again, he could've been nicer, but . . .

"Well, I'm so glad they told everyone else about their plans." She turned away, squeezing between another shopper and a table of doughnuts.

As he stared after her, still trying to wrap his mind around the fact Joy Carter was *here* on *his* island, the realization hit him. Joy had come home to see her parents for the holidays, and they'd left her alone in a snowstorm. *Shit.*

"Joy," he called after her, but she didn't slow her pace. "Joy." He shoved through the aisle, not stopping until he almost ran into the back of her. "You didn't know?"

She shivered, probably from the burst of cold air let in by the automatic doors.

"No. It's my fault. I was trying to surprise them." Something in her voice didn't quite ring true, but if their past was anything to go by, Joy rarely spoke the truth.

"So, you really needed that bread?"

She turned to him, rolling those big green eyes that reminded him of fertile fields in the summer and Christmas firs in the winter. All things that, for him, no longer held pleasure. "Do you think I'd fight an old hag over a loaf of bread if I didn't need it?"

"That's not very nice," he chided, earning himself another eye roll.

"She's always hated me; you know that."

He suppressed the grin that threatened. He did know that, though he'd never understood why. Joy was all the Ps: polite, pretty, poised. *Perfect.* Maybe that was why Mrs. Abernathy didn't like her. Perfection was often an illusion. As Nick had found out firsthand.

"Here." He handed over the loaf of bread he'd found stranded in the produce aisle. He'd grabbed it in case, but Joy's sad eyes said she needed it more than him.

She stared at the proffered loaf without moving, so he shook it at her. "Take it. I have one at home, and it's just me."

Her gaze flashed to his. The impact was like a fist to the gut. So much for years weakening the connection between them. At least on his part.

Surely, Joy didn't feel the same zing when their gazes clashed. If she did, she wouldn't have been able to walk away all those years ago without so much as a phone call.

"Th—thank you." She took the bread from his hand, her fingers brushing against his as she did.

Warmth surged through him. Or maybe that was just the heat finally kicking on from the vent above him. Joy dropped the bread into her basket, then rubbed her hand on her designer jeans. Not that he knew if they were designer since he didn't have a fucking clue about things like that. He just assumed in the new life she'd chosen over him she'd wear only the best of everything.

"If you need anything while you're here—"

"I won't." She turned, entering the checkout line.

He nodded. *Okay.* He wasn't an idiot, and he wasn't a masochist. So, he'd just take his happy self to the next line and stay out of the ice queen's way.

Chapter Two

The stinging cold of the snow mixed with bits of ice barely registered as Joy focused on hurrying through the parking lot without slipping on the quickly freezing asphalt. Mother Nature must be having a freaking field day. Yet another hell-freezing-over moment: seeing Nick Parsons. She'd sworn to herself she'd never speak to him again, even if he came groveling. Of course, he'd never even tried to contact her after she'd left the island. Not that she'd expected him to, but a girl could dream, couldn't she?

As she tried to insert her key into the door lock, her hands shook. She'd blame it on the cold. The boy—strike that—*man* she'd run into in the grocery store surely hadn't affected her. Just because Nick had somehow become even more handsome in their decade apart didn't mean she'd noticed. And even if she had noticed, she hadn't cared. Ten years was a hell of a long time to carry a torch for a man who'd wanted nothing more than a couple of rolls in the back of his old pickup truck.

Damn, she missed that truck. No! She *did not* miss that truck. And she hadn't missed Nick. Not at all. Not much. Just a little. Sometimes. Every day.

Damn it.

Finally prying the door open, she placed her bags on the passenger seat and slid inside, slamming the door behind her. The inside of the car was cold, but at least the wind and snow couldn't reach her here. Her thoughts drifted to her car's pesky rear passenger door that didn't always seal properly. Hopefully, by the time the broken seal could cause a problem, she'd be back at her parents' house. Alone.

Inserting the key into the ignition, she gave it a quick twist. The engine sputtered, then died. Ugh! She tried again. This time, it didn't even bother to sputter. Just click, signaling that she'd turned the key to no avail. No! She tried again and again. Then one more time for good measure. All with the same result. Nothing.

She slammed her hand against the steering wheel. Really? How was this her life? She rested her head against the back of her seat and closed her eyes. Options. She just needed to sift through her options. She could call . . . well, no one. Her parents and brother were gone, and when she'd left ten years ago, she'd broken contact with everyone on the island. As if driving over that bridge to the mainland had erased her past. She could call a wrecker, but there wasn't a wrecker service or a mechanic on the island that would be open this late two days before Christmas. A cab? There weren't any cab companies, but maybe someone operated an Uber or Lyft. She'd just opened her eyes to check her phone for service when there was a hard rap on the window.

A slight squeal escaped her as she jumped. With the windows fogged from her heavy breathing in the frigid vehicle, she couldn't see who stood on the other side.

"Joy? You okay in there?"

Nick.

So maybe she did know someone on the island. Was she desperate enough to ask him for help though? The last time the two of them had been in his truck together—Her traitorous body heated at the thought. But what choice did she have? Taking a deep breath, she pushed open the car door.

As Nick stepped back, his dark eyes narrowed, studying her. "Everything okay?"

She stood from the car, rising to her full height, almost looking him in the eyes. "My. . . ugh . . . my car won't start. It's probably just the cold or the fact I drove it more today than I have pretty much ever."

Nick nodded slowly, his attention on her car. More snow piled onto the hood as they stood there. "Get your stuff and hop in my truck. I'll give you a ride to your parents'. Your car will be okay here for the night."

Joy glanced at the giant truck she somehow hadn't noticed until now. "I don't know."

"Oh." He smirked. "Was someone else going to pick you up?"

She let out an exaggerated huff. "You know they weren't."

His dark gaze narrowed again. "Do I? I can't say I really know much about you anymore."

As she leaned across the seat to grab her groceries, she could've sworn she heard him mumble, "Not that I ever really did."

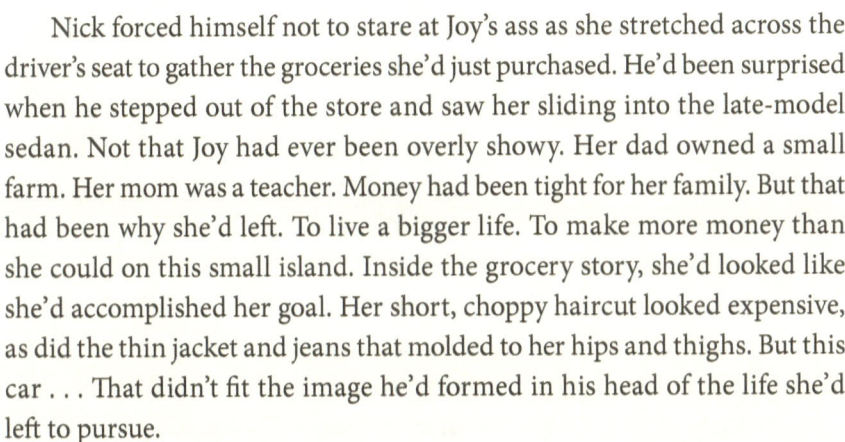

Nick forced himself not to stare at Joy's ass as she stretched across the driver's seat to gather the groceries she'd just purchased. He'd been surprised when he stepped out of the store and saw her sliding into the late-model sedan. Not that Joy had ever been overly showy. Her dad owned a small farm. Her mom was a teacher. Money had been tight for her family. But that had been why she'd left. To live a bigger life. To make more money than she could on this small island. Inside the grocery story, she'd looked like she'd accomplished her goal. Her short, choppy haircut looked expensive, as did the thin jacket and jeans that molded to her hips and thighs. But this car . . . That didn't fit the image he'd formed in his head of the life she'd left to pursue.

"Got everything?" he asked when she stood in front of him, holding her paper sacks.

She nodded. "But you really don't have to—"

"It's on the way." He turned and stomped through the snow to his truck. It was too damn cold to keep standing around talking. Yanking open the passenger door, he turned to her, then took the bags from her hands and placed them on the hump between their seats. When Joy stepped onto the running board, her foot slipped. Instinctively, he reached for her. His hands wrapped around her waist, and her back bumped against his chest. Heat washed over him like a flash fire in a dry forest. He hadn't felt that quick spark of lust in years. Ten years to be exact.

She cleared her throat, her gaze dropping to his hands still gripping her waist. Reluctantly, he slid them away, managing just a scrape of his calloused fingers across the smooth skin exposed by the rise of her shirt.

"You good?" he asked when he could again speak.

She nodded. This time, she gripped the handle before stepping gingerly onto the running board and pulling herself into the truck. Taking another deep breath, he closed the door and jogged to the driver's side.

They drove across the causeway in silence. What did he say to a woman he hadn't seen in a decade? A woman who'd been a girl the last time he'd seen her. Not that either of them had seen her that way at the time. Though the truth remained that they'd both been just dumb kids then. But now . . .

He slid a glance across the seat to where Joy sat with her hands in her lap, staring out the window. Now, Joy was all woman, and the scent of her soap or shampoo or lotion or whatever the hell girly thing she'd rubbed on her body was driving him wild.

"So," he offered as an icebreaker. "You don't usually visit. What brings you here this year?"

Her spine stiffened, and her hands turned to fists.

Sore subject. "You don't have to answer if you don't—"

"I missed my parents. I forgot about their trip." She shrugged as if the gesture would assure him there was nothing more to it.

Fine. He was just trying to make small talk. He didn't need to know her deep, dark secrets. He'd drop her off at her parents' house, then stick to his end of the island over the holidays. Before long, she'd be on her merry way back to sunny Florida. The less interaction they had, the better.

He pulled his truck into her driveway. Something he'd never done when she lived here. No, all the time they'd spent together had been on beaches and back roads. Or his dad's shitty trailer. Joy had never invited him to her house. Never allowed him to meet her in the driveway or, God forbid, her front door.

"Th—thank you for the ride. Really. You're a lifesaver." Her voice was quiet, and if he wasn't completely imagining it, even a bit humble.

As he nodded, some of the ice left behind at the way she'd kept their relationship a secret melted away. "If you need anything while you're here, give me a call."

She cocked her head, studying him with her green eyes. "I don't have your number."

A smirk lifted the side of his mouth. "Google me."

This time she rolled those evergreen eyes and slipped out of the truck, taking her bags with her. "Merry Christmas." She slammed the door behind her.

Nick watched her tiptoe through the accumulated snow in her ridiculous booties. She didn't look back as she pushed her way inside and closed the door behind her. He waited for the lights inside to come on. Any sign that she was safe and secure inside. Nothing. He peered through the snow. Maybe he'd just missed it. Or maybe she still liked the dark. A small flicker caught his eye, coming from where he knew her bedroom was located. Just because she hadn't invited him to the front door didn't mean she hadn't snuck him through that window once or twice. He waited another heartbeat, but something felt off. Pushing open the door, he dropped into the snow, then followed her footsteps to the front door.

"Joy." He knocked against the scarred wood. "Hey, Joy. Everything—?"

The door swung open. Joy stood wrapped in a thick blanket. The house behind her was in complete darkness.

His gaze drifted down to her feet and back up. "What are you doing?"

"What are *you* doing?" she countered. "You delivered me safely home. You can go now."

Fucking ice queen.

"Why are you wrapped in a blanket?"

She rolled her eyes. "Because it's cold."

He could see her breath. "Did you turn the heat up?"

Another blank look. "Of course." This time, her voice faltered.

"And?"

Her jaw tightened as she blinked back tears. "And there's no power, so there's no heat. I thought about starting a fire, but there's no firewood, so . . ." She motioned to the quilt wrapped around her. "At least I don't have to cook the loaf of bread."

"Come on." He nodded toward his truck. "Get your stuff. You can stay with me tonight."

She stood motionless. For a moment he worried she'd actually frozen, but then she blinked. "I can't . . . I . . . why would you . . . ? I'm fine."

"Uh-huh. Temperatures in the teens and dropping. No power. No heat. Sounds excellent. Come on." Without waiting for her response, he turned and stepped off the porch.

She followed him onto the porch, trailing the quilt through the snow. "Nick, you don't have to do this. You don't have to take care of me."

She was wrong about that. Ten years ago, when she'd left, he'd tried to convince himself of that same lie. Ten minutes back in her company proved he'd failed.

Chapter Three

Joy tensed as Nick pulled his truck onto the pitted dirt road. Not that she could see the road through the snow covering it, but she knew the road well. Nick had lived here ten years ago in a rundown trailer with his father. Her heart sank. She'd assumed Nick had moved on and made his life better than the one he'd hated.

"You ... uh ... you still live here?" It was the first thing she'd said since climbing into his truck with the suitcase she'd never unpacked and her few meager groceries.

He spared her a dark-eyed glance. Her stomach twisted. After a decade, just a look from him shouldn't affect her. But here they were.

"My dad owned the land outright. After he died, I didn't see a reason to move anywhere else."

She wanted to point out the fact he'd hated it here, that he'd wanted nothing more than to escape this land and his father, should've been enough. He could sell this land and make enough to rebuild somewhere else, somewhere without bad memories and falling shacks for houses. Only, when he made the turn down the snow-covered drive, there was no shack, no trailer. Instead, a small, but very modern house stood in the trailer's spot. She stared open-mouthed as Nick parked in the same spot where he used to park his rusted-out pickup.

"Surprised?" Without waiting for her answer, he slid out, slamming the door behind him.

She was still sitting in wide-eyed wonder when her door opened. Nick stood in the snow, staring up at her. He reached for her bags, taking as many as he could, and then turned for the house.

Sighing, she jumped down, careful not to slip on the running board, and took the rest of her bags. Lights were shining through the windows, each with a set of shutters that complemented the color of the cozy-looking home. She stomped through snow that now reached the tops of her boots. She'd never seen anything like this before. They'd be lucky to get out of the house tomorrow. *Christmas Eve.* Which meant she was stuck, alone with

Nick, for the foreseeable future. She wasn't sure how she felt about that. Although the swirling in her gut told her she just might be excited.

"No power issues?" she asked as she stepped inside. But that was all she could say because her breath caught as she looked around the small home. Nick had dressed the room in minimal decorations, making it feel larger than it actually was. A large couch took up most of the room, and just looking at the cushions made her suddenly tired.

"Maybe eventually." He deposited her groceries on the clean kitchen counter. "I have a generator and firewood, so we'll manage." He nodded to the stone fireplace where already dry wood was cradled in a metal basket and kindling sat on a grate. "You can put your suitcase in there." He nodded toward a room at the end of the hall.

Still taking in everything around her, Joy shuffled down the hall. She stopped short at the threshold of the room he'd shown her. The large bed and dark, masculine colors would've indicated to anyone that the room was Nick's bedroom. But for Joy, the strong, sexy scent she still recognized as Nick was her clue.

"Uh, Nick?"

"Yeah?" His footsteps came down the hall, the hardwoods creaking under his boots.

She turned to meet his gaze. "This is your room."

"Do you want extra credit for figuring that out?" He gave his head a little shake.

"I can't stay in your room."

His gaze drifted to the large, four-poster bed made up with a dark-blue quilt and two simple pillows. An inhale shook his body. Finally, his gaze returned to hers. "I'll be on the couch."

"I can sleep on the couch. You don't need to—"

"I'll take the couch, keep the fire going. You just . . . do whatever you need to do. If you want a shower, you might want to take it before the power goes."

Swallowing, she watched him retreat to the kitchen.

Yeah, a shower. Maybe a nice cold one.

What the hell were you thinking? That question repeated through Nick's brain as he heated soup on the stove and prepared to make grilled cheese. Joy was probably used to men treating her to much nicer meals. Not that he was treating her. This wasn't a date or a reconciliation. This was a stranded woman without power who needed shelter and warm food for the night. He could provide her with those necessities. He'd do the same for any stray.

He cringed at his own thoughts, but he needed those thoughts to keep him from thinking other, more inappropriate ones. Like how Joy was down the hall in *his* shower, in *his* bedroom. Naked. And wet.

What the hell were you thinking?

He couldn't answer that question. But one look into her green eyes, filled with tears she wouldn't let fall, and he couldn't have left her home alone in a snowstorm. Of course, as hot as she was, she could probably keep warm all on her own.

He kicked himself for that wayward thought. But it was the truth. Although Joy had been an attractive teen, he couldn't deny she'd only gotten better with age. *Damn it.*

The shower turned off. Nick glanced down the hall toward his bedroom door. Not that he could see anything. She'd closed the door. The bathroom door was likely closed as well, but a man could hope. It was Christmas, after all.

When his bedroom door opened, he tried to pretend he hadn't been staring at it, waiting for Joy to emerge. But then he caught a glimpse of her, all fresh-faced and comfortable—in leggings and an oversized sweatshirt with her hair in a messy bun—and he forgot about pretending. She still looked so much like the girl he'd fallen head over ass for years ago and hadn't quite gotten out of his system since.

Joy came to a stop behind him, chafing her hands over her arms as she watched the snow fall through the window beside him. "It's really coming down out there."

He concentrated on the grilled cheese in the pan and tried not to notice the heat from her body reaching out to him. "The weatherman says two feet." He shrugged. "But when are they ever right?"

"Looks like he's right so far," she mumbled. She moved until she could lean a hip against the counter next to the stove. "Thank you for letting me stay here." Her voice grew somber, serious. "I don't know what I would've done if you hadn't given me a ride . . . and if you hadn't stuck around."

She lifted her gaze to his. Her eyes had always held all her secrets. Her hair, her clothes—those things might have changed, but her eyes hadn't. In their depths, the girl he'd loved still hid.

Instead of being a smartass, he simply replied, "You're welcome." He flipped the sandwich, making sure it was golden on both sides, then slipped it onto a plate. "Bowls are in the drawer beside the dishwasher. Want to grab some?"

Swallowing, she nodded. He didn't watch her as she padded across the kitchen, but his body knew her every move.

"Your house is beautiful," she told him when she returned with the bowls.

He exchanged her plated sandwich for the empty bowls. "Thank you. I did my best. I tried to build something . . ." Different from the shithole he'd grown up in. Joy would get that more than most. Though her home hadn't been like his, she'd always wanted something bigger. Better. And that hadn't involved him.

"You built this?"

His pride prickled at the disbelief in her voice. "Yeah. I'm not just some island kid who—"

"I didn't mean that." She set her plate on the table and turned to look at him. "I knew you could do whatever you wanted. It's just . . . your home is . . ." She shook her head. "It's art, Nick. You did good."

Deciding to let her comments pass, he carried bowls of soup to the table, then returned for his own sandwich. Once they were both seated, they dug into their meal. A small moan purred in Joy's throat as she bit into the grilled cheese.

"Oh, my God."

"It's just grilled cheese," he mumbled. Hell, if she made such erotic sounds while eating comfort food, what sounds would she make if he—

Nope. Not going there.

"You always made the best. Do you remember . . . ?" Her gaze dropped to the table. She set her sandwich on the plate and wiped her hands on the napkin on her lap.

He remembered everything. Every stolen kiss. Every lingering touch. Every simple grilled cheese sandwich. He'd tucked all those memories away in a vault labeled *Stay the Fuck Out*. And now here she was in the flesh, breaking the lock he'd placed on that door.

Instead of reminiscing, he asked, "Why are you here? Rumor is you haven't been back since you left."

Her green gaze shot to his before she looked away again, shrugging. "I missed my family. It's Christmas."

She lied. Just like she'd lied when she said maybe they could keep in touch.

"You planning to stay until they get back or will you leave after the storm passes?"

A shadow seemed to pass over her face. "No. I'll . . . I'll be here."

"Everything okay?" He had to ask again. It might have been ten years, but he still knew her well enough to know when something was wrong.

She sighed. Her breasts caught his attention as they rose and fell. "I might be here for a while."

His stupid heart sped in his chest. "A while?"

She nodded. "I might be moving."

"Here?" Why the hell was his heart racing? Even if she came back, that didn't mean anything for him.

She shrugged once more. "I don't know if I can find work here, but maybe." Her green gaze met his, striking him like a punch to the gut.

Before he could open his mouth and offer her a job, he took a bite of his sandwich. Job or not, she wouldn't stay.

"Things in Florida . . . I'm ready for a change."

Wasn't she always? "And you think coming back here is a good change?"

Her face softened as she studied him. "Everything here wasn't bad."

Her quiet voice reached inside, squeezing his heart in an iron fist. No. Everything here wasn't bad. Some of it, like her, had been downright perfect.

Until it hadn't been.

He pushed away from the table, taking his empty dishes to the sink. "I think it's time for bed. I've been up since dawn and I . . ." He didn't have to explain things to her.

Her chair slid across the hardwood floor. "Since you cooked, why don't you let me—?"

"I've got it," he bit out more harshly than he'd meant. "You don't need to do anything. I'll just rinse these and put them in the dishwasher." He reached for the dishes, his fingers brushing against hers in the exchange. Warmth spread through his fingertips, reminding him of the warmth of her bare skin after a day in the sun.

She tensed and pulled away, fisting her hand against her stomach. "Thank you again. For everything."

This time, he couldn't even muster a weak *you're welcome*. Instead, he grunted and placed the dishes in the sink. With a last sigh, Joy turned and retreated down the hall.

One night. No matter what the weather was like in the morning, he'd get her back to her parents' house and out of his bed.

Even if that was exactly where he wanted her.

Chapter Four

When Joy woke up shivering, moonlight shone through Nick's plantation blinds. She rolled over to check the time, but on his bedside table, the clock was blank. *No power.* Well, that explained why she could see her breath in front of her face. Wrapping his quilt around her shoulders, she climbed from the bed. Her bare feet sank into the thick rug by the bed, but she dreaded stepping onto the hardwood. Quickly, so as not to touch them more than necessary, she made her way to the living room where Nick slept. She found him sprawled on the couch, one leg hanging off the side, an arm slung over his eyes—and his perfectly sculpted torso bare. A small fire in the grate kept the room warm. Trying not to wake him, she crossed the room and sank to the floor by the fire.

"What are you doing?"

So much for not waking him.

"The power went out," she explained. "No heat in the bedroom."

His dark eyes narrowed before he scrubbed his hands over his face and stood. "I'll go start the generator."

She jumped to her feet and grabbed his arm. He froze, his gaze going to her hand squeezed around his biceps like she had the right to touch him. Releasing her grip, she stepped away.

"It's warm in here. I can just stay in here till morning." When he looked at her as if she'd grown an extra head, she added, "If you don't mind."

His jaw tensed. He drew in a deep breath, then shook his head. "No. If you're okay on the couch, I can wait until it's light out."

Without waiting for an answer, he brushed past her and squatted in front of the fireplace. Although he'd stripped out of his shirt, he still wore his jeans. Against her better judgment, Joy admired the way the denim hugged his ass as he tended the fire. She also couldn't help but notice his muscles bunching and shifting in his back. Nick had always been fit, but the years had been good to him. If she kept ogling him like this, she wouldn't need that fire.

"What do you do now?" Maybe if they talked about their lives, she'd stop drooling over him.

"You mean besides rescuing women unprepared for snowstorms?"

A smile crooked her lips upward. "Yes, besides that."

He placed another log on the fire and, seemingly satisfied, rose. "I build and fix things. Houses mostly. With the weather around here, there's always a house to be repaired or built."

That made sense. He'd always been a fixer. "You built this house?" She dragged her gaze away from the well-built man in front of her to the well-built house surrounding her.

He nodded. "Like I said. My dad owned the land, so there was no reason not to stay here, but I had to get rid of that shitty trailer, you know?"

Yeah, she did. He'd hated that place and the life he'd had there.

"I would've thought you'd left here by now. You were so unhappy."

He gave a careless shrug. "It wasn't this place's fault." He met her gaze for the first time all night. "You can't outrun what you're unhappy with inside."

His words smacked with accusation. A reminder she'd left, that she'd tried to outrun her unhappiness. Only to end up right where she'd started.

"And sometimes, you have to go somewhere else to realize what you left behind."

He studied her out of eyes that had seen too much during his thirty years. "And is that what happened to you? Did you leave and realize what you'd left behind?"

No. She'd always known what she left. A small island that didn't offer her any opportunities and a boy who'd never give her his heart. But now she knew herself better. Now she could make wiser decisions. And now she needed her mom, just until she felt like herself again.

"This is . . . uh . . . a lot of heavy talking for the middle of the night." Truth be told, she didn't want to face those things. She didn't want to think about why she'd left and why it had taken her so long to come back.

Eyes narrowing, Nick nodded. "Yeah, we were never much good at heavy talking, were we?"

"You didn't seem to mind." He'd never been after her conversation skills.

He considered her for a moment before shaking his head. "Maybe it's best if we try to get some sleep." He took the blanket he'd pushed to the floor sometime in the night and settled himself at the end of the couch.

Swallowing, Joy nestled into the other end. She was tempted to pull the blanket over her head so he couldn't tell she was wide awake and would never fall asleep. But between the now toasty room and her thoughts of Nick, with the blanket covering her, she'd likely die of heatstroke.

If sexual frustration didn't get her first.

The first thing Nick noticed when he awoke was the fire was nothing more than embers. He should be freezing, but instead, he was warm, almost burning up. The next thing he noticed was the woman cuddled into his side, half on top of him. Her breath tickled the hairs on his bare chest, her soft skin plastered to him. Along with her soft curves.

Joy.

He hated to wake her, but he couldn't just lie here staring at her until she woke. If he did that, he'd end up wanting to touch her, and if he touched her, he'd want to kiss her, and if he kissed her—

He couldn't go down that road. He'd been there ten years ago, and she'd walked away.

Nick nudged her, hoping to wake her without frightening her. Of course, as far as he knew, she might be used to waking up in the arms of random men.

"Joy. Hey, hon, wake up."

"I don't wanna," she mumbled. "It's so warm." She snuggled closer, wiggling her body against his and moving her mouth closer to his neck.

He bit back a groan. "Joy, seriously. Rise and shine. I need to—"

She jerked awake, her green eyes widening. As she shifted, he rolled, teetering on the edge of the couch before falling and taking her with him. They landed on the floor, her under him. Him between her legs.

"Shit. Joy, I'm sorry. Are you okay?" He tilted to the side, trying to take his weight off her. Her legs slid farther apart, and he settled between them. Perfectly.

A sound somewhere between a moan and a whimper passed through her lips. Nick was rock hard in an instant. Joy's green gaze met his. Even as a girl, she'd never backed down from what she wanted. Head-on had always been her direction.

"Joy," he croaked.

She shifted, lifting her hips, pressing her warm center against his hard length.

"You don't know what you're doing," he warned her.

Those green eyes narrowed now. "That's not what you used to say."

And with that challenge, she rose and pressed her mouth firmly to his. Nick's eyes drifted closed as he focused on the warm, wet slide of her lips against his. He'd kissed plenty of women over the years, most of them only once or twice, but none of those kisses had compared to this. Joy clutched his back, her nails digging into his flesh. He rocked forward, rubbing against her. He felt, rather than heard, her answering groan. The years fell away, and he was twenty again, falling in love for the first and only time and wanting something he couldn't have.

A knock on the door brought him out of the rabbit hole of heartache Joy was dragging him into. He pulled his head away, looking at the door.

"Nick. You in there?"

Joy tensed beneath him. "Is that?"

He nodded. The local police chief and Joy's high school sweetheart.

Nick pushed off her, trying to get his body under control.

"Why's he here?" she scrambled up from the floor, running her hands over her hair before straightening her clothes.

He lifted one shoulder. "I should probably open the door so he can tell me."

Her eyes went wide. "You can't let him in here."

He stood, adjusting himself before his zipper left a permanent mark on his body. "He doesn't want in here. He's probably just—"

"Don't tell him I'm here."

Nick stopped on the way to the door. "Excuse me?"

Joy had disappeared down the hallway. "I don't want him, or anyone, to know I'm here."

Anger twisted in his gut. Surprise-fucking-surprise. He'd been good enough to save her from freezing in the damn parking lot or spending the night alone in her powerless home. Hell, a few more minutes, and he might've been good enough for a quickie on the floor. But as usual, when it came to facing the rest of the world, he'd never be good enough for Joy Carter. Well, fuck that.

He threw the door open.

"Hey, Nick." The chief stood with his hands shoved into the pockets of his uniform coat. A coat that hadn't been designed for the piles of snow on the ground behind him. "We found a car at the Food Lion registered to Joy Carter, but we can't find any trace of her. I checked her parents' house, called the resort, and the state park. No one's heard from her or has any record of her being on the island. You got any ideas?"

Clenching his jaw, Nick gave a curt nod. "Yeah. She's in my bedroom packing her shit."

Chapter Five

Staring out the window of her parents' house at the blanket of white covering the yard, Joy only saw red. She was going to kill Nick. As soon as the weather cleared and she could get back to his house, she was going to kill him. No. That would be too good for him. She'd castrate him. That would teach him. She'd clearly asked him not to let anyone know she was there. And what did he do? Five freaking seconds later, he told jackass Johnson she was in his bedroom. Oh, and he'd made it sound dirty too. Like she'd been there all night screwing his brains out. Well, someone must've screwed his brains out, because he was a dumbass. A dumbass who needed castrating.

Looking out the window, she decided the weather had cleared enough for her to make the trip to his house. Her mom's keys hung by the door. She'd just scoot over to Nick's, give him a piece of her mind, and be back before temperatures dropped again tonight.

Nick stood on his porch glaring at the snow that would eventually turn to brown mush and a whole lot of annoyance. When he'd come out to start his generator earlier, he'd heard the laughter and squeals of his neighbor's kids as they played. Everyone was having a great time enjoying the weather. Everyone but him. And probably Joy. When she'd left his house with Chief Johnson, she'd looked like she was headed to her last meal. Except for her eyes. Those had been shooting daggers right at him. Thank God looks couldn't actually kill. But if he wasn't mistaken, there'd been something else there too. Something almost like . . . regret. At least that was what the adult version of himself said he'd seen. Ten years ago, she'd had a similar look in her eye as she told him she was leaving. He hadn't read it the same way.

Sighing, he headed inside to grab his coat and keys. Power hadn't been restored to the island. If Deputy Dumbass hadn't been able to get Joy's generator going, or if he had and it went out, she'd be stuck in the house freezing her ass off because there wasn't a way in hell she'd call and ask for help now. Climbing into his truck, he idly wondered if he should've worn a cup as well. No doubt Joy would aim straight for his balls when she saw him.

He'd only made it a mile down his snow-covered dirt road when he spotted a car in the ditch. The vehicle didn't appear to be damaged, but it was definitely stuck. Exhaust still billowed out of the pipe, indicating the car was running and someone was probably inside. Pushing thoughts of Joy aside, he rolled to a slow stop by the car. Only as he did, he realized the small convertible stuck in the snow was Joy's mom's car. But her mother was on a cruise in the middle of the ocean. Throwing the truck into park, he jumped out and trudged through the snow to the car. He tapped on the fogged window. Slow as Christmas, the glass inched its way down to reveal Joy's scowling face. His heart slammed in his chest.

"What the hell are you doing out here?" He yanked her door open, checking her for injuries.

She smacked his hands away. "I was coming to see you."

This time, something like joy squeezed his heart. "Me? You were coming back?"

She yanked off her seatbelt and hauled herself out of the tiny car, rising to her full height and looking him in the eyes. "Yes. To tell you you're a dumbass."

Her words took a minute to sink in, but when they did, they had his hackles rising. "Dumbass? Me? That's interesting coming from the woman who drove a convertible in a snowstorm."

Glaring at him, she crossed her arms over her chest. "How else was I supposed to get here after you told Derrick to take me home?"

"You weren't supposed to get back here. You were supposed to go home with Derrick. Maybe now that you're both here, you can live that life you always wanted."

Her slitted gaze turned wide. "With him? I've never wanted to live a life with him. Why would I start now?"

Valid question. He, however, didn't have a valid answer. "You wanted him before you left. He was your boyfriend, the one you could tell your parents about, the one everyone wanted you with." While he'd been her dirty little secret.

"Everyone but me," she replied.

He nodded. She probably had a point. "You're right. If you want some-one, you can't just leave them."

Her jaw tightened, and her green eyes sparkled in the bright sunshine reflecting off the snow. "That's not true. Sometimes you leave people because they don't give you a reason to stay."

"And Derrick didn't give you a reason to stay?"

She glanced at her boots, kicking a clump of snow. "I'm not talking about Derrick. I never would've stayed for him."

"Then who? If the golden boy couldn't make you stay, then—?"

"You." She glared at him like he was both the most fascinating and frustrating thing she'd ever seen in her life. "I would've stayed for you, though I somehow kept expecting you to come with me."

"Me?" She'd never even hinted that she wanted him to come with her. He'd been a fling. He'd been fun. But she hadn't wanted him long-term. Had she?

"Yes. You." She shook her head, rubbing her hands up and down her arms to ward off the chill in the air despite the absence of falling snow. "I never wanted Derrick. He was a friend. A friend who wanted more and who our families thought would be perfect for me." She pulled her bottom lip between her teeth, chewing nervously. "He was never perfect for me. Never what I wanted."

His chest grew almost too tight to breathe. "And what did you want?" Or, more importantly, what did she want *now*?

"What I couldn't have." Her voice was almost a whisper as she turned back to the car still stuck in the snow. "Do you think you can help me get this out so I can get back home?"

Uh-uh. No way was he letting her get away now. Not after that cryptic reply. Wrapping his hand around her biceps, he spun her around to face him.

"You're not going back home."

"Of course, I am. Where else do I have to go?"

"With me." Where she should've always been. Where she should always stay. "I never told you I loved you," he blurted.

Joy's eyes grew wide as Christmas balls.

He swallowed, trying to find the right words to say what he felt for her. What he'd always felt for her. "I loved you . . . back then."

Her face fell. The hope shining there moments before vanished, leaving behind only confusion.

"I think I still love you now." Only he didn't think. He knew. The moment he'd seen her standing in the grocery store aisle fighting over a loaf of bread with mean old Mrs. Abernathy, all those old feelings had swamped him. He still loved Joy Carter every bit as much as he had ten years ago when she'd trampled his heart.

"I loved you too," she whispered. Tears sparkled in her eyes. "I didn't think I was supposed to, but I couldn't help it. I loved you. I've loved you every day since. Leaving didn't change that."

"Why didn't you tell me?"

She sucked her teeth. "Why didn't *you* tell *me*?"

"Would it have changed anything? Would you have still left?"

Her gaze fell away, the snow again becoming riveting. "Probably," she confessed. "But I wouldn't have left *you*. I would've visited until visiting wasn't enough and I had to come home sooner."

Warmth spread through his body, fueled by regret and happiness. It was a damn odd mixture, but eventually, the happiness won out.

He stepped closer, cupping her face in his gloved hands. "Come home with me now. Spend Christmas with me. Help me make up for all the ways I failed you before. Let me say all the words I should've said then."

A tear trickled down her red cheek. "Do you mean that? You . . . you love me? You want to start over?"

He brushed the tear from her cheek and pulled her close. "I've never wanted anything more. I love you, Joy." And instead of waiting for her response, he crushed his mouth to hers in a language they'd always understood.

End

About <u>HM Thomas</u>

HM Thomas grew up in SC creating bigger, more dramatic worlds than her own. After graduating from Clemson University and getting her own HEA, she began writing romance, oftentimes mixed with suspense. When not writing, HM enjoys camping and hiking with her husband, three children, and rescue dog.

Find HM Online:
Website:<u>www.hmthomaswrites.com</u>
Newsletter: <u>https://hmthomaswrites.eo.page/3v24z</u>
Facebook: <u>https://www.facebook.com/hmthomaswrites</u>
Instagram: <u>https://www.instagram.com/hmthomas_author/</u>
Twitter: <u>https://twitter.com/AuthorHMThomas</u>
Amazon: <u>https://www.amazon.com/HM-Thomas/e/B07ZS1Y9X7</u>
Goodreads: <u>https://www.goodreads.com/author/</u>
<u>show/19797388.H_M_Thomas</u>
BookBub: <u>https://www.bookbub.com/authors/hm-thomas</u>

Let Me Call You Sweetheart

By J. Lynn Rowan

Let Me Call You Sweetheart

Historical

Estelle Lealand has discovered the life – and love – she hoped for may be out of reach after breaking her engagement with one of Charleston's elites. But a chance encounter on a rainy December night reacquaints her with Wes McKenna and makes her wonder if happiness is still possible.

Wes McKenna has spent the past year in social isolation in order to control the shell shock that followed him home from World War I. Estelle is the first person to make him feel whole again and that there might be something in his future besides loneliness.

As they spend more time together, Estelle and Wes realize they may share more than common memories of life before the war. Could the unexpected feelings growing between them be true love?

Rated: PG

Chapter 1

December 23, 1919

Dust settled on Estelle Lealand's brand-new red velvet overcoat and matching hat as yet another car sputtered past her without stopping. The gravel edging the road bit through the soles of her heeled rhinestone-studded shoes, which had started the evening flashing with reflected candlelight as she danced the foxtrot and sipped champagne imported from France.

She coughed to clear her throat and wiped her stinging eyes, not caring if her makeup smeared. The tears were from the grit kicked up by the passing vehicles' tires, she told herself. Not the embarrassment and hurt pride of having to walk home from her best friend's Christmas party after telling her fiancé that she would not marry such an arrogant cad.

Someone probably would have given her a ride, but Estelle had stormed out without thinking. The gossip would be all over town by tomorrow morning and by dinnertime would be making the rounds in Beaufort, maybe even all the way up to Charleston. Her audacity at publicly shaming Bradley St. John. At throwing him over for an off-color remark while everyone else just tittered uncomfortably.

Estelle only mattered because her family saved the very lifeblood of their sleepy Lowcountry town. Her father used his government connections to bring much-needed wartime industrial jobs into the county. Her brother's gallant sacrifice in the trenches saved the lives of half the boys from the local battalion, allowing them to come home and marry their sweethearts and start new families.

Bradley had been one of those boys. Resplendent in a new captain's uniform, Estelle had met him on the dock in Charleston when she'd gone with her parents to retrieve her brother's casket from the troop transport ship in January. Still reeling with grief for her brother and dazzled by Bradley's epaulets, polished manners, and extravagant way of wooing, she'd fallen hard and fast. He proposed to her three months later, and Estelle's place in society seemed secured.

Unfortunately, Bradley's contempt for anyone below him in social status finally knocked the stars out of her eyes. She could walk away from Bradley for any number of reasons, but his snide, cutting comments about poor, shell-shocked Wes McKenna riled an anger in her that demanded an immediate break with Captain St. John.

Estelle came to the intersection with the main road, and hopes of hitching a ride the rest of the way home soared despite the late hour. But just as she picked her way over a wheel rut and turned toward town, the wind picked up, and three large raindrops splattered on her cheeks.

"Oh no."

Why hadn't she waited for someone to give her a ride or called home to see if her father could come get her?

The thickening clouds scuttled toward the moon and threatened to obliterate all light from the road, and she quickened her pace. Only a mile or so stretched between the intersection and Daisy Bell's grocery. Miss Bell would be long locked up and gone off to bed, but Estelle could hunker down on the covered porch until the worst of the rain passed.

She had no sooner decided on this plan of action when the sky opened up. The torrent of rain drenched her within seconds. She clutched the front of her overcoat with one hand and gripped her hat with the other, willing it to stay put until she could reach shelter of some sort. Trudging forward, trying to judge the edge of the road as best she could, she pressed on.

The downpour blurred her view of the road. She sloshed through gathering puddles, stepping once into a mucky pothole up to her ankle. Miserable inside and out, Estelle barely noticed the wavering light gathering from behind her.

A blast from a vehicle's horn snapped her to full attention.

She spun. Her heel caught the rough edge of the pavement. With a shriek and a windmill of her left arm, she tottered off into the muddy gravel. She struggled to stay upright. Pain radiated down her left foot and up through her ankle to the outside of her calf.

A pickup truck came to a stop in front of her. Estelle squinted through the rivulets of rainwater streaming into her eyes as the passenger door swung open.

"Get in!" The driver leaned across the seat, one hand outstretched to help her.

Estelle gave her eyes a futile swipe with the back of her hand. *Wes?*

Of all the people to show up on this road tonight, it had to be Wes McKenna.

Wes beckoned. "I'll drive you home."

"I can't." She gestured toward her ankle, which now throbbed with every heartbeat. "I think I sprained my ankle."

"Well, you can't stay here either way." He slid across the seat and hopped from the open passenger door. Before Estelle could protest, he scooped her up and deposited her inside the truck. After he closed the door, he dashed around to the driver's side to climb back in.

Estelle leaned back, grateful to be out of the rain, even if the water dripping from her clothes and body formed a puddle on the seat to rival the ones outside. She tried to elevate her foot, but there was nowhere for her to rest it. Wincing, she lowered it again.

"Why are you out in this weather?" he asked, putting the truck in motion.

"I hadn't planned on it." Her tone came out sharp. With a sigh, she turned her gaze out the window even though she couldn't see anything. "I was out at the Point, at Della's Christmas party."

"With Captain St. John, I assume."

Heat filled Estelle's cheeks. "Yes, I was."

"Why isn't he driving you home?"

Estelle clenched her teeth for a moment before answering. "I guess he won't be driving me anywhere anymore." Wes didn't respond, much to her relief. She waited another minute before speaking. "You haven't got a towel, have you?"

"There might be something under the seat."

Estelle leaned over to rummage beneath the seat. Her hand immediately came in contact with a shallow woven basket. Tugging it out just enough to reach in, she felt around until she closed her fingers on terry cloth.

The towel smelled clean, even if she couldn't visually confirm it. She dabbed at her face and squeezed the dripping ends of her hair, momentarily lamenting the carefully set curls that now clung to her neck. "Where were you going?"

"Home."

She turned to him, but Wes kept his eyes on the road. He drove slowly, hands firm on the steering wheel and brows lowered in concentration.

"I thought your uncle lived in the other direction. Toward Beaufort."

Wes flicked a glance in her direction. "I only stay out there for the busy season, and then just during the week."

"Oh." She chewed the inside of her lower lip. "Where's home, then?"

"Other side of town, almost to the lighthouse."

Why hadn't she known this? Estelle couldn't imagine Wes managing for himself, nor could she picture any houses on the low bluff near the lighthouse. She wanted to ask more, but then the first streetlights came into view, and Wes turned onto Main Street.

"Left on Garden Avenue," she told him.

"I know."

Estelle made a show of refolding the dampened towel on her lap. Of *course*, Wes knew where she lived. He and her brother had been thick as thieves as children.

The rain eased as Wes pulled up in front of her house. Estelle looked past him. The porch lights were still on. However, the inside lights were all off. Her parents weren't home from their party yet. She had to get herself inside.

Wes set the parking brake, hopped out, and circled the truck before Estelle could say anything. He opened the door. "I'll get you inside if you have your key." She should insist on limping up the walk herself. But Wes stood in the drizzle, waiting.

"All right."

She set the towel on the seat beside her and fished her key from her purse. Clutching it, she shifted toward the open door, preparing to slide out.

Wes moved before she could. Scooping her up, he carried her up the walk. He paused once they reached the shelter of the porch.

Estelle shivered. He had lifted and toted her as if she weighed nothing, and now he just stood there, with her in his arms. He felt solid, sturdy, and warm despite the dampness of his jacket. Her gaze shifted to the sharp line of his jaw, blurred by the shadow of a beard. Below his cap, his dark hair curled upward and glistened with rainwater.

"Your key?" He spoke quietly, with patience.

Their gazes met. Even with the illumination of the porch lights, his blue eyes lay in shadow. He stared, but not rudely. It made her want to nuzzle close under his chin, her cheek pressed to his chest.

She swallowed hard. "You can set me down."

"Not if your ankle is sprained."

"We can't do a thing about that on the porch, and I can't reach the lock if you don't put me down."

Wes hesitated, but then he lowered her until her feet touched the porch. Estelle shifted her weight to her uninjured leg, though even that foot ached and felt swollen inside her shoe. He steadied her as she fitted her key into the lock and opened the door. Once the way inside was clear, he scooped her up again and stepped through the doorway. Estelle indicated a lamp on the hall table, and Wes paused there so she could turn it on. Then he went into the front parlor and deposited her on the sofa.

"Will your mother be mad about the water?" he asked.

Estelle shook her head. She unbuttoned her overcoat and shrugged out of it, then unpinned her hat and tossed it on the other end of the sofa. "I'll explain everything in the morning."

Wes nodded, then gestured toward her feet. "Which ankle did you hurt?"

"The left."

"How badly?"

"It's agony, to be honest."

"I can imagine."

She almost made a comment about how he couldn't possibly imagine what it was like to hobble in heels with an injured ankle. But she bit her tongue, realizing how heartless she would seem if she hinted that Wes knew nothing about physical pain.

They stared at each other for a strangely long moment. Then Wes sat down on the floor in front of her and lifted both her feet into his lap. Gently, he unbuckled her shoes and took hold of her left ankle. She winced. Wes glanced up at her before he carefully began testing her ankle's mobility.

"I don't think it's sprained," he said. "But you'll want to keep it elevated and apply a cold compress."

Estelle nodded but couldn't find her voice. He closed both hands around her ankle and massaged the joint with soft, slow movements. No, more like caressed. Sparks leapt across her skin. Up her leg. Skittered through her veins. Her lungs seized. She had to remind herself to breathe.

Wes looked up at her, his expression tense. "Why didn't Bradley St. John drive you home?"

The question shocked her back to her senses. She eased her foot from his grip. "I don't want to talk about it right now, if it's all the same to you."

"He's a cad if he let you walk home from the Point on a night like this. Or at all, for that matter."

"I didn't exactly give him a choice."

Wes stood. "What does that mean?"

Estelle sighed and pushed off the sofa, waving away the hand he extended to help. She tested her ankle, finding it marginally better but still too weak and painful to bear weight. She sat down again. "It means, we are no longer engaged."

Wes gave her a curious look. "You had a fight?"

"It was more that I accused him of being arrogant and ignorant in front of everyone. Then I tossed a glass of champagne in his face, threw my engagement ring at him, and stormed out."

Silence filled the room. Estelle's face burned again. Why on Earth had she spoken so bluntly about what had happened at the party? Horror swelled within her. However, the look on Wes's face checked it. His lips were tight, but the corners twitched.

"Wes, are you *laughing* at me?"

"No." His voice sounded a bit strangled. "I'm laughing at how he must have looked during all of that."

Estelle balled her fists. "It's no laughing matter. I was right, but I should have done it in private. By the end of the week, everyone who's anyone from Beaufort all the way up to Charleston will know the story."

Wes's expression grew serious. "Do you regret ending your engagement?"

"No." She took a deep breath. "I shouldn't have accepted in the first place."

"Then what does it matter what people say? Bradley St. John is only important to himself and other people who think they're important as well. Though I do wonder what made you tell him off in public."

She gazed at Wes, remembering the nasty things Bradley had said about him at the party. He would hear the gossip soon enough. Sighing, she eased to her feet again. "I said I don't want to talk about *that*."

"That's fine." Wes stepped forward and took her by the arm. "You're cold. You've been standing here too long in dripping clothes."

He stood so close. Estelle had to tip her head back to look into his eyes. "So have you."

"I have experience with it."

Her breath hitched as his hands stilled on her shoulders. "If . . . if you can help me to the stairs, I can manage the rest of the way on my own. My parents should be home in a little while."

He took her hand and threaded it through the crook of his elbow. Together, they crossed the room and the front hallway until they reached the foot of the stairs.

"I'll check on you after Christmas, if that's all right." Wes held on to her. Her skin tingled from his touch.

"Of course. Please do. And you'll be careful driving home, won't you?"

"Don't worry about me."

She eased herself up onto the bottom tread and gripped the banister before turning to face Wes. He gave her a small smile.

"What is it?" she asked.

"Nothing much." His smile widened. "You're wet from head to toe, but you look lovely. I can only imagine how you looked before you got caught in that downpour."

"Oh." She smiled, too, glancing down at the beaded party dress the rain had ruined in short order. "I suppose I did look rather nice."

"Bradley St. John doesn't deserve you."

Her gaze swung to his. Surprised at the seriousness that had returned to his face, she reached out one tentative hand to cup his cheek. "You're a million times better than him, you know."

Wes laid his hand over hers for a moment, then stepped back, just out of reach. "Thanks for that, Estelle."

"It's true."

"I'm glad you think so. Most other people don't." He moved another step backward. "I'd better go. I don't think your father would take kindly to me being here alone with you at this time of night."

"He'd understand and be grateful. You're my knight in shining armor tonight."

"Maybe so. But all the same, I'll say good night."

With that, Wes turned and headed out the door.

She shivered against a chill, and it wasn't because she was wet. The warmth that radiated from his smile and his touch, Wes had taken with him. How was it possible she missed him already?

Chapter 2

The holidays kept Estelle somewhat isolated from local gossip. Her ankle—bruised but not sprained according to the doctor—made it impossible to do more than hobble about the house. Her parents were disappointed to hear about her broken engagement, but they offered understanding.

"If you weren't happy, he wasn't worth it," her mother had told her. "We would never force you to marry someone you didn't love, darling. Such a marriage wouldn't be true. But thank goodness for Wes McKenna. How lucky he happened to be out that night and willing to bring you home!"

A few days after Christmas, Wes appeared on the Lealands' doorstep. Her father greeted him and offered coffee while her mother fussed with Estelle's hair before helping her to the parlor.

"How have you been?" her father asked as everyone settled into their seats. "We don't see much of you these days."

Wes shrugged. "I keep busy. There's always work to do on my uncle's farm."

"A far cry from the factory, I'm sure," her father continued. "Takes a strong, dedicated man to work the land."

"I appreciate the compliment, sir."

Estelle caught her mother's attention. "Perhaps Wes could sit with me in the garden for a little while? The weather's been so mild, and I've been stuck inside for days."

"That's a lovely idea." Her mother helped her to stand and guided her through the house and out into the garden. Wes followed several paces behind, held up by her father's continued musings on farming versus factory work and too polite to try and break free. Fortunately, her mother understood and interceded, sending Wes out to the garden alone.

Wes paused on the back step. Estelle stood under the bare branches of a crepe myrtle tree, but even in the winter sun, she shined. A pretty young woman replaced the bedraggled girl from a few nights ago, and he saw the Estelle he'd known from before.

She beckoned for him to join her on the bench beneath the tree. She still favored her left foot as she moved.

"I had to think fast, or my father would keep you embroiled for ages." She smiled as he sat down beside her. "It's so good of you to come."

Wes set his hat on the bench between them, a reminder not to get too close even if they'd known each other all their lives. "I wanted to see how you were faring, if the ankle was any better."

"Not sprained, as you'd said. It's still achy, but the doctor said it should be all right by the end of the week." She glanced skyward, her blue eyes catching the sunlight. "You aren't working today?"

He shook his head. "I'll drive out to my uncle's later to see if there's anything he needs a hand with. But this week, my time is mostly my own."

"And what big plans do you have?"

"Nothing you'd find interesting."

"Let me be the judge of that." She gave him a smile. "Please?"

He'd forgotten what it felt like to sit beside a pretty girl and have a real conversation. Or to have a real conversation with just about anyone other than his aunt and uncle. He'd worked hard at keeping to himself over the past year. "I have some repairs to make on my house. A loose shutter, some clapboards that need to be scraped and sanded. That sort of thing."

She gazed intently at him. "You mentioned you live out on the lighthouse road."

Touched that she remembered, he nodded. "A little two-room bungalow, just big enough for me. Nothing to brag about, but it's mine."

"And you're out there all alone?"

"Sometimes on the weekends, I go up to the lighthouse and visit with the keeper. His eyesight is failing. Not enough to retire, but enough that he can't read like he used to, and he has an impressive collection of books."

"So you read to him?"

"Sometimes." He shrugged. "Sometimes we just sit and enjoy the view."

He lapsed into amiable silence beside her and took a moment to study her. The girlish roundness of her cheeks had disappeared since the war had started, and she had learned more polished manners and a sense of fashion. No wonder Bradley St. John had picked her out of a crowd. Wes wondered what she ever saw in the snobbish captain, though he was more curious about what made her break off their engagement. There seemed no polite way to ask.

"Didn't you work at Daddy's factory when you first came home?"

The sudden question startled him. "For about a week, I think."

"And then you went to work at your uncle's farm instead."

"It . . . The factory was too noisy. Too unpredictable."

Estelle made a soft sound of understanding. He hoped she didn't think less of him for not managing to keep his nerves under control for the sake of a well-paying job.

"I worked there during the war." Her voice carried a little note of pride. "Just as a secretary. Daddy wouldn't let me onto the factory floor. I told him I could handle it, but you know how he is."

A grin tugged at Wes's lips. He imagined Estelle in a factory worker's apron bustling between machines that cranked out war materiel, her honey-wheat hair tied back in a sensible bun under a cap. Somehow, the role seemed more suited to her than that of a secretary.

"I was still working there when Bradley started courting me." Her voice turned brittle as she continued. "He didn't like me working at all, never mind in a factory, even one owned by my father. Daddy didn't seem to mind when I told him I wanted to stop, though."

"You wanted to stop, or Captain St. John wanted you to stop?"

She shrugged. "It was all the same at the time, I guess. Most of the girls were leaving their jobs, anyway, what with the boys all coming back home. Do you think you'll keep on at your uncle's farm?"

Wes sat back and gazed up at the clouds. "It's hard work, but it's satisfying. I think my uncle would like to pass it on to me someday. If I only have myself to think about, I suppose I'd stay with it."

"Why wouldn't you stay with it if you have someone besides yourself to think about?"

He glanced at her. "Well, suppose I get married someday, and my wife doesn't want to live on a farm. Suppose she wants to live in town or move to a big city."

"I think you'd have to decide those things together. You can't make a life with someone when you want different things."

He shifted to face her. "Are you talking about me or yourself?"

Estelle fiddled with the frill on her sleeve cuff. "Maybe both."

The conversation lapsed, replaced by the chittering of winter birds. Wes checked the time. It was later than he expected. "I should be going. I'm glad to see you on the mend."

She tilted her head. "Were you worried?"

"A bit. About more than your ankle too."

Pink infused her cheeks. "That's sweet of you, Wes. Will you visit again?"

"If you like."

"Very much."

They gazed at each other for a few seconds. Then, shaking free of a feeling he couldn't quite name, Wes remembered himself and bid her good afternoon.

Why did she draw him in? He'd known her since they were children, and up until the night before Christmas Eve, he'd seen her as little more than his best friend's sister. What changed, and why? The questions unsettled and excited him. For the first time since coming home from the war, he had hope his life could be more than what he'd made it to be.

Chapter 3

Over the next two weeks, Estelle looked forward to Wes's daily visits. Sometimes he only stopped for a few minutes to say hello. But usually, he stayed upward of an hour. Their conversations revolved around childhood reminiscences or the doings of people in town. Wes talked more about the work he did on his uncle's farm and his little oceanside house on the lighthouse road.

He never talked about the war, except on one drizzly afternoon when they sat on the porch, and he'd expressed his regret that Estelle's brother had not made it home from Europe. Bound by a mutual loss, she'd held his hand in silence for a long time until Wes quietly declared he should be going before the rain worsened.

To her surprise, Estelle looked forward to his visits more each day. The excuse of her ankle allowed her to beg off from running errands in town with her mother. Wes came and went from her little bubble. She noticed little ways in which his presence found its way into her heart.

His smile when he saw her, his companionable laughter as they shared old stories, his ability to put her at ease. After a year of minding her demeanor with such care so as to not upset Bradley's expectations of her, Wes's presence brought joy.

And then, there were the little touches. A hand on her elbow to help her down the porch steps. The arm he lent for support on the short walks up and down the block once her ankle could handle the exercise. The linking of their fingers on the garden bench on a mild evening as they watched the stars wink into view.

"I'm glad Wes has been coming around," her mother told her one evening after she'd bid him good night. "You seem happier of late."

Estelle blushed but said nothing. Deep down, an old infatuation had dug its way out of her girlhood memory. Now, nourished by the daily attention Wes paid without fail, that infatuation blossomed into something else, something real. Bradley's callous treatment came into stark comparison, making it clear her engagement had been a sham.

About three weeks into the new year, neighbors started stopping by, remarking on Wes's appearance at the Lealand house, hinting about Bradley's absence. Della came bearing a Charleston newspaper opened to the society pages.

"You and Bradley are all anyone's talking about in Beaufort," Della told her. "And since your broken engagement is being speculated on in the society pages, I'd wager it's all over Charleston as well."

Estelle surveyed the gossip column with pursed lips. "Just a lot of busybodies with nothing else to do."

"Maybe." Della folded the paper and put it back into her pocketbook. "Honey, we all know you did the right thing. But Bradley won't stand for having his name in the press like this. I know he'd gotten quite nasty. However, that could be nothing compared to what he might say now."

Estelle hoped Della was wrong and tried to set the record straight among her neighbors. Enough of them had connections in Beaufort and Charleston that, with the right things said to the right people, it could all blow over, her broken engagement forgotten within a couple more weeks.

"Estelle, you have a visitor."

Her mother stood on the back porch, wiping her hands on a towel. Usually, her mother sounded cheerful when Wes arrived, but today she seemed nervous.

Estelle rose from the garden bed she'd been tending. Wes had traveled up to Columbia with his uncle yesterday and hadn't planned to be home until late. This was a nice surprise, but she wondered if something was wrong to make her mother anxious.

"Please, send him on through." She pulled off her gloves and removed the large gardening apron she wore to keep her clothes clean. The afternoon had been cool and her task leisurely, so she felt presentable enough for Wes. He'd seen her looking much worse, after all.

She drew in a sharp breath. Instead of Wes, Bradley strode through the back door. Dressed in one of his best tailored suits and his hair neatly slicked down, he held a large bouquet of red hothouse roses in one hand and his fedora in the other.

Estelle's welcoming smile fell away, a scowl replacing it. She crossed her arms. Bradley sauntered down the back steps, his grin self-assured.

"Good afternoon, Estelle. You're looking lovely, as always."

"What are you doing here?"

He stopped a few feet from her and offered the bouquet. An awkward moment passed. She begrudgingly took the flowers from him.

"I know you're upset with me, but I'm here to make amends."

"Amends? After more than a month and a half? I hardly think so." She plucked a dried petal from the bouquet and let it fall to the ground.

"You were quite angry. I thought you needed time to cool off."

"I think you're worried about the society pages."

His grin disappeared. He shoved his free hand into his pocket. "Aren't you?"

She shrugged. "I generally ignore the society pages."

"My mother is beside herself with the news."

"The news or the gossip?"

Bradley looked perplexed. "Why the gossip, of course. She couldn't believe the things they said in the society pages. I had to explain it all, how—"

Estelle held up one hand. "Wait. You didn't tell her our engagement was off? She didn't know until she read about it in the gossip rags?"

"Estelle, please. Don't be so crude." His face reddened. "I explained it all, how you'd had too much champagne and misunderstood something I said—"

"Excuse me?" If she'd been angry the night of the party, what could she possibly call the feeling that rose through her body with such violence now? "You told your mother I mistakenly called off the engagement because I was *drunk*?"

Bradley let out a nervous laugh. "You were tipsy. Emotional. Perhaps I went too far in my comments—"

"Too far? You degraded a man I've known my entire life. Someone who nearly died in France in service to our country, because of his shell shock!"

"Estelle."

She brandished the bouquet like a club. "Bradley St. John, if I wasn't clear enough before, let me be clear now. Our engagement is off. I do not want to see you again, *ever*. I suggest you leave now."

His eyes narrowed, his face turning an unattractive shade of puce. "And I suggest you think carefully before you send me packing. Marriage to me opens doors for you into the most esteemed and sought-after social circles in Charleston—all of South Carolina and Georgia, in fact! You were nothing, had nothing, until I marched off that transport ship in Charleston. And without me, you will again have nothing. I'm your ticket out of this backwater swamp!"

With a huff and a shriek, Estelle flew at him and brought the flowers down upon his head, repeating the blows until he stumbled backward down the garden path. He tripped over her box of gardening tools, nearly falling, before turning and jogging toward the side gate. Estelle followed, the limp, broken flowers extended like a sword. She chased him out to the sidewalk. There he straightened, squared his shoulders, rounded his car, and jammed his hat onto his head. He sent her one final condescending look before he got behind the wheel.

As he pulled away, Estelle pitched the ruined bouquet at the windshield, where it burst into a flurry of stems, petals, and leaves.

"Good riddance!" she shouted.

Frustration heaved through her body. Tears washed into her eyes. Rubbing them away with the back of her hand, she stormed into the garden and headed for the shed. Her brother's bicycle leaned against the wall inside the door. Wes had cleaned it and repaired the tires, thinking she might enjoy the exercise now that her ankle had healed.

Her mother came onto the back porch. "Estelle, what happened?"

Estelle walked the bicycle through the garden. "I'm going for a ride."

"It's late, almost dusk." Her mother followed her. "Darling?"

Estelle steadied the bicycle and prepared to mount it. "I need to clear my head, Mama. I'll be back later. Don't wait up for me."

With that, she gathered her skirt in one hand, flung her leg over the crossbar, and set the bicycle in motion. Her mother called after her once more, but Estelle pedaled away, toward the south end of town.

Wes had said he should be back tonight. She would go to him, even if it meant she had to ride all the way to the lighthouse and ask the keeper where Wes lived. He was the only person she wanted to see right now.

Chapter 4

By the time she reached the bare top of the rise leading to the lighthouse road, Estelle's breath came in labored huffs. She regretted the corset that pinched her ribs and wished she'd taken a moment to change into something more suited for cycling.

Wind buffeted her as she braked and set her toes on the ground. At first, the air refreshed her after her exertion. But it only took a minute for her skin to grow chilled. She added her lack of an overcoat to her list of regrets.

Estelle glanced inland, alarmed to see dark clouds obscuring the sun. *I'll have to make a dash for it and hope Wes's house isn't much farther.*

She pulled her hat down over her ears, put the bicycle into motion again, and headed down the other side of the hill. The road, already poorly lit due to the trees lining either side, fell into shadows. Clouds thickened to the west. Estelle alternated between furious pedaling and cautious coasting. She searched for any landmark that would indicate a nearby house.

At last, she saw a break in the trees on the ocean side of the road and recognized the end of a graveled drive. Heart leaping with hope, she slowed and coasted between the trees. The narrow driveway led to a squat little house flanked by moss-draped live oaks, scraggly palmettos, and a tidy yard. The house appeared well-tended for all its weather-worn appearance. An orange glow shone from the two front windows. Estelle gave a little cry of joy at the sight of Wes's pickup truck.

With renewed energy, she pedaled to the truck. After hopping off the bicycle and leaning it against the porch, she hurried up to the door and knocked.

Wes opened the door. Warm light spilled onto the porch. His eyes widened. "Estelle? What are you doing here?"

She smiled, spreading her hands. "I came to see you."

He glanced over her shoulder. A frown replaced his surprise, a line of worry forming between his brows. "*How* did you get here?"

"I rode my brother's bicycle." She realized his attention was focused on the storm. "May I come in? You've told me so much about your home, I'm just dying to see it for myself."

"Sure." With another glance at the sky, Wes ushered her into the house and shut the door. "You've picked a terrible evening for cycling."

"I guess I didn't pay attention to the weather when I set out. It's turning into a habit, I'm afraid." Estelle took off her hat and set it on a small table near the door. "I must look a fright."

Wes's expression lost some of its tension. "You look a bit windblown, but I'd hardly go further than that."

Estelle entered the main room of the one-story bungalow and took in her surroundings. A fire crackled cheerily in the hearth on one end of the room, and an old but comfortable-looking set of armchairs flanked a braided hearth rug. In the center of the room, a gaslit pendant light hung low over a table and mismatched chairs. A modest kitchen filled the remaining space. She imagined his bedroom lay beyond the closed door opposite the fireplace. A bank of windows spanned the entire back wall with a narrow door on one end. Most of the shutters were closed, as were three sets of heavy drapes meant to block drafts. Two large bookcases, completely filled, stood on the far side of the fireplace along with a small cabinet upon which sat a new-looking gramophone.

She turned to Wes, who still stood near the door. "You're quite cozy here. It must be lovely in the summertime."

"I'm comfortable enough." He cleared his throat and smoothed one hand down the front of his shirt. "I can't believe you came all this way just to see me."

A chill coursed through her, but she hid it with another shrug and a toss of her head. "My curiosity got the better of me."

"You're shivering." Her attempt to hide her shiver hadn't fooled Wes. He led her to one of the hearthside chairs. "Have a seat. I'll make some tea. After the storm's passed, I'll drive you home."

"I can ride home." She suddenly wondered if he minded her intrusion.

"You will not. That storm means business. Even a quick cloudburst will turn the roads to muck in minutes." He rattled about in the kitchen, exuding the echo of military efficiency as he lit the stove, filled the kettle, and set it on the burner. After setting out a tin of tea and two cups, he joined her at the fireplace and lowered himself into the other chair.

Estelle mentally fumbled for a topic of conversation, but the way Wes studied her made it impossible to think.

"Why did you really come all the way out here?" he asked.

"I told you, I wanted to see—"

"Nonsense." He leaned forward, resting his elbows on his knees and clasping his hands. "Something's got you upset."

"What makes you say that?" Her tone bordered on defensive despite her efforts to sound dismissive.

"It's hardly the time—or weather—for a three-mile ride out of town. And you aren't dressed for cycling. You rushed off in a hurry."

"You're the one talking nonsense now."

Wes gave her a look. "How long have I known you, Estelle?"

She dropped her gaze, relieved she didn't have to pretend with him. "About as long as I've been alive."

"I know when you're mad. So . . . ?"

The kettle whistled, and he rose to manage the tea. Estelle made a point of not looking into his eyes when he returned to hand her a cup.

"Does it have something to do with your erstwhile fiancé?"

She blew lightly on her tea. "Why would it?"

Wes set his cup on a chairside table, then sat down with a sigh. "The last time you rushed out into bad weather, you'd just thrown your engagement ring at him."

"Oh." The tea was still too hot, so she lowered it to her lap. "He came by this afternoon."

"What for?"

"To badger me into submission."

"What did he say?" Concern streaked across his face.

"It really doesn't matter. I told him off, sent him packing, and then set off on a leisurely jaunt into the stormy night to see you." She tried the tea again, finding the temperature tolerable.

"Estelle."

Wes frowned and rose from his chair. With a single stride, he crossed the hearth rug and sank to the floor, cross-legged at her feet. A vague memory surfaced, one from her childhood, when Wes had sat just this way to comfort her after an older neighborhood girl had teased her to tears over her scabby knees and unruly hair.

Eyes burning, she slowly spun the teacup in its saucer. Wes took the cup from her and set it on the floor, then wrapped his warm hands around hers. "This goes back to Della's Christmas party, doesn't it?"

"Oh, further than that, I'd say."

The memory of the night of the party drifted to the surface. Wes rescuing her from the rain. Carrying her into her house. Kneeling before her, testing her sore ankle.

Heat rushed to her cheeks. She snapped back to the present when he gave her hands a gentle squeeze.

"Can't you tell me?"

Worrying her lower lip between her teeth, she searched his face for any signs of insincerity. Finding none, she plunged ahead and shared all the increasingly nasty things Bradley had said over the past few months.

How she didn't need to thank his parents' cook because talking to the help was below her. The comments about her mother keeping house and how Estelle needed to rise above such a life once they married.

His embarrassment over her working at the local factory during the war even though he hadn't even known her then.

Worse were his terribly bigoted views, like how the families of the Black men who fell in Europe didn't need to have their names on local monuments to fallen heroes, that just being allowed to serve in the 10th Cavalry should have been enough for them.

She appreciated that Wes let her prattle on. Released from the propriety of her engagement, her indignation soared. She barely retained control of her tirade.

"And then at the party," she concluded, her voice quivering with tears, "he had the gall to say that any man who came home from the war with shell shock was a coward and an idiot and would have been better off dying in France, and—"

Wes leaned back, stunned.

She covered her mouth to ensure she said nothing else.

He dropped his chin to his chest, his gaze locked on the rug.

"Oh, Wes." She clasped her hands in her lap. "I'm so sorry."

He scrambled to his feet and retrieved both teacups. "It's all right."

"No, it isn't." She popped up and followed him. "Bradley is mean-spirited and arrogant. Nothing he said about you is true."

Wes set the teacups in the sink. "Estelle, you don't have to—"

"And I told him you're smart and brave and resourceful—"

He turned to her. "When did you tell him that?"

"Right before I threw my engagement ring at him and stormed out of the party."

A heavy silence hung over the room until he cleared his throat. "Well, I appreciate you standing up to him. What else did he say?"

"When?" She looked up at him.

"Today. Before you pedaled furiously into the storm to find me."

"It wasn't even sprinkling when I left." Tears further blurred her vision. She spun around to hide them. "I should go before it does start raining."

The words had no sooner passed her lips when the clouds opened up with a torrent of rain that hit the roof with a roar.

Chapter 5

Wes crossed his arms and studied the droop in Estelle's shoulders as the rain hit. "Well, you can't go anywhere now. Might as well tell me what he said."

She crossed to the windows at the back of the house and pushed one curtain aside with a trembling hand. She always was the sort of girl to let hurt hide behind anger, even as a child. But something told him this hurt went deeper.

The rain grew heavier. A tremor passed through him. Thunderstorms weren't especially common this time of year without heat and humidity to make them build up like in the summertime. He should have driven her home immediately, should insist on doing so now. The pickup could handle mud, and he could pull over to wait out a thunderstorm like he did when he was alone. Estelle might be fighting to keep her emotions in check, but he wouldn't be able to hold his own demons down if it thundered.

They both needed a distraction.

Wes's gaze settled on the gramophone. A memory surfaced—a lovely memory from before the war—Estelle at sixteen, carefree but looking a little lost on the edge of a dance floor. It was her first time attending the town's Independence Day social since her parents had decided she wasn't a little girl anymore. Her brother had escorted her, but Wes remembered how her smile had beamed across the torchlit space when she'd picked him out of the crowd.

Much had changed in the intervening years. But that smile, innocent and excited, forever seared into his memory, had kept him afloat in France and beyond.

He strode to the gramophone and rustled in the cabinet below. He only had a handful of records. Estelle might not care. He set one on the turntable and wound the crank before placing the needle. A staticky *hiss* filled the room for a few seconds before the strains of a ragtime song began.

"I suppose you've done more dancing than I have since the war." He turned to find Estelle staring at him.

She nodded.

Wes moved into the open space, extending his hand. "I'm out of practice, and we don't have much room. But would you like to dance?"

Another nod. She moved into his arms. The steps came back to him after a few turns. Though he had to switch the records every few minutes, they quickly settled into the familiar movements. After several dances, Estelle relaxed, smiling and laughing as they twirled in the small space.

Another song came to an end, and she gripped his shoulders to keep him from pulling away. Her posture and expression suddenly sagged, and alarm shot through him when a tear slipped down her cheek.

"He said I would be nothing without him."

Wes leaned toward her, silently urging her to continue.

"I was only important because I would be marrying him." Her fingers curled into the fabric of his shirt. "He said I was throwing away my only chance to get out of here—Wes, he called our town a backwater swamp!—and if I didn't marry him, I'd go back to being nothing!"

She seemed on the verge of tears again but somehow held it back. Wes took her hands and lowered them, holding them over his heart. "He's wrong, Estelle."

"Oh, I certainly let him have it," she continued. "I didn't have another ring to throw at him, but I whacked him with the bouquet of hothouse roses he thought would appease me."

He couldn't resist a chuckle at the mental image.

She echoed his laughter, though hers held a tinge of bitterness. "Maybe I am a nobody, Wes, and maybe I'll have nothing that people like Bradley think is important. A big house, fancy cars, jewelry, the esteem of other people who think all those things are important."

"Do you want all of that?"

"I'd certainly enjoy all those fine things. But, no, I don't want all of that." She shook her head to punctuate her certainty. "I want things Bradley could never give me. A home. A family." Pausing, she gazed into his eyes. "Love."

Wes hauled in a deep breath. "He doesn't deserve you, Estelle. He's the one with nothing. And you deserve someone who'll give you . . . everything."

Outside, lightning flashed, and his nerves sizzled with it. She didn't appear to notice. He pulled away to put on another record. He counted, gathering all his willpower to remain steady through the task, priming himself for the moment the thunder sounded. It came as a low rumble, and despite his mental preparation, his stomach still flipped. His diaphragm spasmed, forcing air from his lungs as if he'd been punched.

The storm would bring that thunder closer. He couldn't bear to have Estelle witness what thunder reduced him to. He *should* have brought her home immediately. They could have talked on the drive.

"Wes?"

"One more dance?" He tried to keep his voice light as he positioned the needle. The trip back to town would take a good half hour in the rain, but if he was lucky, he could at least get Estelle back home before the thunder got too close.

She peered curiously at him as he came back to her, but he took her in his arms before she could say anything.

I am dreaming Dear of you, day by day

Their gazes met as the lyrics started. "Golly," she murmured. "This was the song. The one playing when you asked me to dance."

"I remember." His reply came out quiet, choked.

"It was my first real party. I was so nervous, and then I saw you on the other side of the dance floor."

Wes couldn't muster any words. Another flash of lightning. He had to count, to focus. She pulled at his control as she eased closer until her head rested against his shoulder.

Keep the love light glowing in your eyes so true

The thunder followed, closer this time, a muted clap in the distance that rolled into a dull rumble. "Estelle."

"I was beside myself when you came over and asked me to dance. I was the luckiest girl in town. You were the first man I ever danced with, you know, besides my father or my brother."

Another flash, and this time the sharp crack came almost immediately, shaking the house on its foundations. He sucked in a hard breath. Closed his eyes. Prayed he wouldn't be pulled back into the muck. Into the terror.

"Wes?"

She had drawn away, and with great difficulty, he opened his eyes and looked at her. Worry etched a small line between her eyebrows.

"You don't like thunderstorms."

"No," he managed before another flash and crack simultaneously split the sky.

"Is it . . . the war?"

Closing his eyes again, Wes nodded. He could never explain it, never wanted to. How it felt to be caught on the barbed wire in the quagmire and the rain, bullets whizzing past while German artillery split the sky. Men dropping all around, screaming, dying. And the desperate prayers that the only thing that could be worse—the blinding, suffocating, deadly mustard gas—wouldn't come before help could arrive.

"It was thundering," he ground out. "I couldn't tell the difference between the thunder and the shelling."

Estelle laid her palms against his cheeks. "I'm sorry. I wish I could take the memories away."

You, alone, my heart can cheer, you just you

He released a shaky sigh. Her touch grounded him. His hands found her waist, settling just above the gentle flare of her hips. "You shouldn't be here. I never wanted you to see me like this."

"But I am here, Wes." She stepped closer, winding her arms around his neck and rising on tiptoe. "You're not in France. You're right here. With me. And I'm not leaving."

"People might talk."

"They're already talking. It doesn't matter. I trust you."

His arms went around her, hugging her tight. He breathed in the scent of her hair, ocean air mingled with some kind of flower. Her embrace was warm, comforting. Safe, in an unexpected way, and right, as if she'd always belonged there.

And he understood, clear as day, that she always had.

Outside, the thunder crashed again. But this time, instead of the echo of artillery in his ears, he heard the pounding of his own heart.

"Estelle." He rested his cheek against hers. "I would very much like to kiss you."

She released an endearing little gasp as she tipped her head back. Their gazes met, and a sweet blush infused her cheeks. "I would very much like you to kiss me."

With a nod to her consent, Wes pressed his lips to hers. The thunder, both real and imagined, drifted away.

Let me call you "Sweetheart", I'm in love with you!

Chapter 6

The early glow of morning twilight woke Estelle. For a moment, she stared out the window, blinking at the unfamiliar view. Then she sat up as her mind cleared. The sparse but tidy bedroom was Wes's, in his snug bungalow outside of town. And beyond the door, Wes had bedded down in front of the fireplace.

The events of last night rushed over her with the force of a tidal wave. The rational part of her mind reeled at the idea of spending the night not only at Wes's house, but also in his bed. He'd acted the perfect gentleman and respected her privacy and her person, bidding her good night at the bedroom door with a light kiss.

But oh! That first kiss! She never imagined a kiss could make her go hot and cold all at once, rooting her to the spot while her heart soared. Was that what all the poets meant in their songs and sonnets?

First things first. She went to the washstand, where Wes had put a jug of water the night before, and poured a little water into the basin. After washing her face and swishing the groggy taste of sleep from her mouth, she finger-combed and pinned her hair as best she could. After dressing in her limp outfit, she took a deep breath and stepped into the main room.

Wes was just setting a steaming plate of eggs and bacon on the table, and he gave her a sheepish smile when he saw her. "I thought you might like breakfast before I take you home."

"You're joining me?"

"There are a couple things I need to do outside." He retreated out the back door before she could say anything.

A bit deflated, Estelle sat down to eat. Her gaze wandered the room. The blankets Wes used last night were neatly folded and stacked on one of the hearthside chairs, and other than the coffee pot, the kitchen appeared squared away.

He's certainly efficient. Of course, Wes would be efficient. He was accustomed to living with a particular daily routine. Her appearance last night had thrown that routine into turmoil, but Wes had taken her into his home, made her feel at ease—and so much more.

Wes returned and paused by the door. "Why the smile? Are my eggs that good?"

Estelle dropped her gaze to her plate but couldn't banish her silly grin. "I'm just relieved."

"You might not be once I get you home."

Her parents would be beside themselves over her behavior. She stood and gathered her empty plate and utensils. "I suppose we should be going. Do you want coffee first?"

"I can live without it." He crossed to her as she started toward the kitchen. "You don't have to bother with that."

Giving him a teasing glance, she set her plate in the sink. "One thing I can do is clean up after myself. My mother taught me how to keep house."

"I'm sure she did."

He wrapped his arm around her waist before leaning down to kiss her. How natural it felt to be tucked against his side, how delightful the way his kiss left her a little breathless.

"What was that for?" she asked.

He strode to the front door and grabbed his cap and jacket off the peg. "I might never have the chance to kiss you again once your father finds out you were here all night."

His words dashed the warmth seeping through her. She sighed and followed him outside. He had already put her bicycle into the truck bed and now opened the passenger door so she could climb in.

The drive into town should have been pleasant, but Estelle internally squirmed with sudden worry. Wes said nothing the entire time, though just before they turned onto her street, he reached over to squeeze her hand. The gesture strengthened her resolve. She'd done nothing wrong, at least not in any way that mattered.

After parking, Wes retrieved the bicycle from the truck before helping her out. She took a deep breath and started toward the house. Wes walked the bicycle behind her. Maybe her parents didn't know she'd been out all night and she could slip up to her room unnoticed. But then the front door whipped open. Her father stepped outside with a glower.

"Inside," he commanded. "Both of you."

Estelle glanced over her shoulder. Wes's jaw hardened with tension, but he set the bicycle against the porch railing and followed her inside.

When she entered the parlor, her mother rose from the sofa and flew at her, enveloping her in a desperate embrace. "Where have you been? I went to check on you last night, and you weren't there . . ." She trailed off as Wes came into the room, hat in hand.

Estelle took her mother's hand and gave her father a pleading look. "I can explain."

"Please do!" her father barked.

She swallowed her nerves and sent Wes what she hoped was a reassuring look. "I was upset after Bradley left yesterday, so I rode out toward the lighthouse. I didn't realize how late it was or that a storm was coming in until I was too far to turn back. I didn't think I would make it back before it hit. So I stopped at Wes's house."

Her father made a low sound in his throat. "Why didn't you call?"

"I don't have a telephone line." Wes flinched when her father turned to face him.

"Then you should have brought her straight home."

"Yes, Mr. Lealand. But she was upset and cold from her ride. It would be rude of me to rush her back out again, with the storm about to get so wild." He exchanged a glance with Estelle. "It seemed foolish to venture out in the dark and the rain, so I let her stay."

She tensed, hoping Wes's explanation would be enough.

Her father grumbled under his breath, but her mother took a step toward Wes. "We do appreciate you sheltering Estelle during the storm. But you must realize the position you've placed her in."

"Mama," Estelle began. "You and Daddy know—"

Her father shot her a withering look. "Hush, girl."

Wes looked from one parent to the other. "Mr. and Mrs. Lealand, you've known me my whole life. I would never hurt Estelle. I'd do anything to protect her."

"Would you really?" Her father stepped toward Wes. "Her reputation could be in absolute shambles by noon."

A flurry of emotions raced across Wes's face. Estelle realized what he must be thinking, as well as what her father intended.

"Wait," she cried. "Mama, Daddy, please. There's nothing to worry about, I promise. You both *know* Wes."

Her father came to her, his expression softening. "And I also know the world, Estelle. So does Wes, and I expect him to do the right thing."

"Of course, I'd do the right thing," Wes said. "As long as Estelle agrees to it."

"She'll agree to it." Her father's tone brooked no argument.

Her eyes burned. The peace and joy she'd felt just an hour ago seemed suddenly out of reach. "I won't marry Wes just because we spent a stormy night together. Nothing happened!"

Silence descended on the room. Wes's shoulders drooped, his expression one of resignation. She realized her words, uttered on impulse and in frustration, had pierced him more deeply than any physical wound ever could.

Her mother murmured something about giving the two young people a few moments alone. Estelle waited until her parents had left the room before rushing toward Wes.

"I'm sorry, I didn't mean it the way—"

"No, I understand." His voice held no blame, no anger. Just sadness.

She grabbed his hands. "No, you don't."

"Estelle, you shared a lot about your hopes last night." He gently disengaged his hands from hers. "You deserve a man who can give you all you could ever want or need."

"Oh, Wes, you—"

He suddenly pulled her close, burying his face in her hair. "I don't ever want you to accept a life that won't make you happy. But the truth is that I love you. I have for years. I have nothing to give you, but if you were mine, you would be everything to me."

Stunned, she started to embrace him. But before she could respond in kind, he broke away and strode out of the house.

"Wait!" Estelle hurried after him. He had reached the truck before she made it halfway down the walk. He paused long enough for her to reach the gate. "You know how I get when someone backs me into a corner. You can't leave until I tell you the truth."

Lips tight, Wes came to her and stood with his hands in his pockets.

"It's not that I don't want to marry you—"

He took her by the shoulders. "You *do* want to marry me?"

"Someday. For now, I'd be proud just to be your sweetheart." She rested her hands on his chest. "I started falling in love with you the day you rescued me from the rain. And after all those weeks you spent visiting me, telling me about the things you wish for in life . . . I want the same."

"I don't have much to give you, Estelle. You've seen my home, know how I live. I don't know if I'll ever have much more."

"I don't need more. I just need you." She flung her arms around his neck. "If we love each other, we'll have everything we need."

Wes hugged her tight. "We'll talk your father into letting us wait a bit. But if you're sure, I'll do my best to make you happy."

"You already have." She tipped her head back to gaze into his eyes.

He smiled at her.

Then, right there on the front walk for everyone to see, he kissed her, long and sweet, full of all their promises for the future.

End

Author's Note: The song "Let Me Call You Sweetheart" was first published in sheet music form in 1910 by composer Leo Friedman and lyricist Beth Slater Whitson. The following year, the Peerless Quartet released one of many recordings, and the song remained popular through World War I and beyond. The lyrics used in this story are from the 1911 recording, which is part of the public domain and can be listened to via the Library of Congress (https://www.loc.gov/item/jukebox-646117/).

About J. Lynn Rowan

A writer since childhood, J. Lynn Rowan is currently published in romance, historical fiction, and academia. When not writing, she enjoys traveling, cooking and baking, and learning and teaching history. She lives near Charlotte, NC, with her own Romantic Hero of a husband and their children.

Find J. Lynn Online:
Website: http://jlynnrowanliterature.wordpress.com
Newsletter: http://eepurl.com/bt5Er9
Facebook: https://www.facebook.com/JLynnRowan
Twitter: https://twitter.com/JLynnRowanLit
Instagram: https://www.instagram.com/jlynnrowanlit/
Amazon: https://www.amazon.com/author/jlynnrowan
Goodreads: https://www.goodreads.com/jlynnrowanlit
BookBub: https://www.bookbub.com/authors/j-lynn-rowan

Maeve's Welcome Home

by Addie Bealer

Maeve's Welcome Home

Contemporary

Maeve Harper and Nate Weaver have been friends since childhood. Despite dating in college and becoming more serious afterwards, they let jobs and geography get in the way of a real romance. Now, thanks to a generous inheritance and perhaps the matchmaking skills of Maeve's late Uncle Harry, they are both back in Bees Ferry living next door to each other, about to become business rivals. Some strange setbacks befall them both, and old resentments keep cropping up, making it hard for the two to imagine a happily-ever-after. Between Maeve's determination and Nate's big secret, love should find a way.

Rated: PG

Chapter 1

"They're ready for you." A martian held up two green thumbs. At least Maeve thought they were thumbs. It was hard to tell, as the costume had several arms, several hands, and dozens of long pointy fingers. "Good luck."

Taking a deep, steadying breath, Maeve Harper stood and thanked the martian. Yes, after preparing for months, she did have this. Last year's decision to come back to South Carolina's Lowcountry from Raleigh had been necessarily fast, given her great-uncle's deteriorating health, but this plan of hers was well thought out. In the past few months since Harry's death, she'd organized every aspect of her life into neat, little boxes to make this moment perfect. Her work as a colorist for graphic novels and as a freelance illustrator was busy and fulfilling, and, as she'd discovered, didn't tie her to one place. As a bonus, she could keep those aspects of her professional life running and still manage a bed and breakfast. It was time to put down roots. She picked up her laptop and followed the martian through the double doors and up the aisle to the front of the meeting room.

Blocking every other thought from her mind, she concentrated on making eye contact with each town council member. She hoped she didn't burst out laughing; they were all dressed for the Halloween party that would follow the meeting. Luckily, she delivered her vision for Bees Ferry Township's very first B&B flawlessly. At the end of her speech, she was confident the decision would go her way.

"Ms. Harper, as you know, you were our last speaker this evening. We'll take a short break for council discussion. It's unusual to have two presentations for new business ventures on the same night," said Willa Nelson, the town council president. She was radiant as Padme Amidala. "And the same type of business, too."

Two presentations? Maeve's smile ratcheted down a notch from confident to cautiously optimistic. *Same type of business?* Her fingers turned white from their death grip on her laser pointer.

Willa turned to a fellow council member. "And on the same block, no less."

Same block! The world wobbled on its axis. That must mean—could *only* mean—

She turned toward the audience.

Nate Weaver.

There he was, sitting like he always did, one ridiculously muscular arm thrown over the back of the chair next to his, staring at her, mouth agape. Her best friend from childhood. Her occasional boyfriend during college. Her one serious lover in the past decade.

And currently, the bane of her existence. Maeve's heart flip-flopped, just like it did every time they saw each other, which was pretty often, considering they were neighbors.

Willa banged—well, thudded—her gavel on the plastic folding table.

"Twenty-minute break. Y'all go get some coffee and pie and mill around in the back for a while." Willa was also the owner and head pastry chef at Hive, the local bakery.

The assembled interplanetary visitors, ghosts, and sexy black cats headed for refreshments. The council, all dressed as members of the Galactic Senate from the *Star Wars* movie franchise, turned their chairs toward one another to conduct deliberations.

Maeve huffed, gathered her materials, and stalked to the back of the hall.

"What in the world are you doing, Maeve?" Rugged and virile as ever, Nate filled her vision and made her pulse quicken. Wearing khakis and a pumpkin-orange button-down, he was one of only two people not in costume.

She was the other. A sexy witch outfit had seemed inappropriate for a serious business venture proposal. "Me! Since when do you have time for anything but work?"

He folded his arms and rocked back on his heels. "You must have had to do some fancy dancing to come up with this plan at the spur of the moment. When did you find out I filed?"

"I've been working on this plan for months," she hissed at him. "I've ticked every box on my preparedness checklist, and I've been busy fixing all the problems that mysteriously crop up every time I turn around. I didn't even *know* you filed." Although she had wondered about all the tradespeople's trucks that had been at his place recently.

"Oh? Did your water get cut off when you were having new tile installed too?"

"No, and I've told you already I wasn't responsible for that. Would you care to revisit the fire that nearly burned down my toolshed?" Maeve poked him in the chest for emphasis.

Yep, it was still rock hard, and he didn't budge. Some things never changed.

"It barely scorched the grass, and I was the one who put it out, remember?" Nate said. "Don't go jumping to conclusions about that. Look, I gave a solid proposal, and I have a hell of a lot more to offer than wind chimes and watercolor classes."

Maeve caught herself before launching into a defense of her business model. She did wish she had heard his proposal. At least she'd know what she was up against. Instead, she'd sat in the hall during most of the meeting, running over her speech one more time and trying to quell her jitters. While the decision to open a bed and breakfast in the house she'd inherited from her great-uncle Harry had been rather impulsive, she'd subsequently put in hours of research and work to make it a professional venture. How was she supposed to know Nate had the same idea? It's not like they saw each other every day anymore, even though they were neighbors. That daily contact had become awkward when Harry died.

"What's really wrong, Nate? Afraid of the competition? Admit it, you don't want me to open my guesthouse."

"You're right on that score. I have a plan, Maeve, and you're about to ruin it. I've given this a lot of thought," he paused, putting his serious face on, "and I think Harry would love my idea."

Maeve cocked her head to one side. Uncle Harry had left a house to Nate as well. She guessed it had been his way of saying *thank you* to the two of them for taking care of him in his last days. It could also have been Harry's way of playing matchmaker one last time. He'd always wanted Maeve and Nate to get back together.

"Nate, why in the world would you want to run a bed and breakfast?" He hardly fit the mold of an affable host, despite being molded very nicely, thank you.

Nate uncrossed his arms and planted his hands on his hips. His voice softened. "Look, Maeve, trust me on this. There's a bigger picture here. I was planning on telling you. I wanted everything to be perfect first."

Their eyes locked. There it was again, that crackle of awareness between them every time they were together. The attraction was still there. Maeve felt herself softening toward him, like always. He sounded so sincere. She knew he'd loved Harry, and this did sound like a nice tribute. Wait a minute . . .

"Nice try, Weaver. I live in one of Harry's houses, too, remember? And I have just as much right as—"

"Children, children. Still getting along so well, I see." A man dressed as a riverboat gambler stopped before them. He twirled his cane and tipped his hat at them. At well over six feet and athletically built, Grayson Cooper drew admiring stares from people of all ages.

"Who the hell are you supposed to be, Grayson?" Nate's scowl said whoever it was, was ridiculous. He scowled even harder when Grayson bent to kiss Maeve's cheek.

"Why, a 'suhthen' gentleman, to be sure." He smiled before continuing in his exaggerated accent. "Would this little tiff be in relation to the highly amusing predicament in which you find yourselves this evening?"

"Your Southern accent is terrible, Grayson," Maeve told him. "We're discussing business, so if you'll excuse us . . .?"

Grayson Cooper's smile never reached his eyes. Ever since she had first met him, Maeve's inner voice had warned her to keep him at a distance. Being friendly with him she could manage, but dating him was another question, one which she always answered with a firm *no*. And with Nate Weaver right next door, why would she ever look at another man? The fates—or maybe Harry's ghost—must have brought them together again for a reason.

"Y'all wouldn't have this lil' ol' difficulty," said Grayson, "if you'd let me list your properties. I keep tellin' y'all I'd get top dollar for them."

Since neither Maeve nor Nate bothered to respond, Grayson shrugged and swaggered around his fancy cane.

"I'll ask you both again next week. I do love a good challenge," he called over his shoulder.

Willa's gavel struck the hollow plastic of the folding table again, calling the meeting back to order.

"Y'all come on back." Willa waved at Nate and Maeve. "Here's what we've decided: Mr. Weaver and Ms. Harper both gave excellent presentations. The council is impressed with the research behind them. If the Chamber of Commerce has its predictions for tourism numbers for next year right, it seems to us Bees Ferry Township could support a couple of guesthouses. We'll let both proposals go forward to the public question and comment phase and revisit them at next month's council meeting. Good luck, meeting adjourned, and be safe trick-or-treating."

Thud!

Chapter 2

After the meeting, Maeve unlocked her Jeep and slung her presentation materials into the back seat. Why was there a setback at every turn with this B&B idea? She didn't expect the road forward to be strewn with roses, but couldn't she catch just one break? She and Nate had called a truce before walking to their cars. That felt like a good start. And, they were going to go out to dinner to discuss things in more detail. That was definitely the kind of break she was looking for.

Nate living right next door was distracting on many levels, but not really an obstacle. Nate opening another guesthouse right next door, now *that* could be a problem.

Sighing, she wished for the carefree summers of their childhood. When they were little, life had been magical. For years, she and Nate had spent nearly every summer day together when her family traveled to the coast from Asheville. Maeve and her folks would stay in one of Harry's two houses on the sprawling property; her dad was Harry's nephew and loved the slower pace of life in Charleston in the summers. Nate would come over for visits with his grandfather, one of Harry's long-time buddies. After his grandad died, Nate continued riding his bike over on his own. They'd chase lizards, collect moss, or build forts. On rainy days, they made Black Cows with Harry's homemade vanilla ice cream and played Monopoly or checkers or cards.

Could it ever be that easy again? Planning actual dates with Nate seemed like a good place to start.

A few days after the council meeting, in a posh top-floor office of a historic building in downtown Charleston, Grayson Cooper waited in a Louis XVI chair. The Persian rug under his feet was plush and way out of his tax bracket. Though his instinct tended toward fidgeting, he distracted himself by imagining this was his office, his view of the city. He just had to believe in himself, like the Be Your Own Boss seminar had taught him. That, and deliver the goods. He could do that, right?

When the door opened, he twisted uncomfortably in his chair and looked over one shoulder. Unable to project "Confident Businessman About Town" from that position, he jumped to his feet, grinning.

Until now, Southern charm had kept him in the good graces of the powerful businesswoman who entered. Jennifer Lewis walked briskly, unsmiling. Hitching one hip up on the corner of the desk in front of him, she folded her arms. Grayson's gut spasmed uncomfortably.

"Sit. I thought you said it was a done deal."

He sat, hating himself for behaving like an obedient dog, and cleared his throat before answering.

"Jennifer, darlin', we are *this* close." He held up a finger and thumb an inch apart, hoping the perspiration forming on his forehead was invisible. "I promise."

"Your promises won't build this resort. The investors are getting impatient, and frankly, I don't blame them. Bring me signed contracts ASAP." Jennifer stood and moved behind her desk. "Or else you'll find a sad little black hole where your career used to be."

He sauntered out of the office, but Grayson's knees nearly buckled once in the hallway. Sure, he'd proposed the deal when he heard this company was looking for a chunk of land in his area, but if people didn't want to sell, how was that his fault? Hell, the old man hadn't wanted to sell either.

He'd tried making it difficult to keep the houses. He was doing everything he could.

Fine. He could be more creative. He'd get those contracts signed one way or another. He had to. The bills were piling up, his landlord was threatening eviction, and he expected a visit from the repo man any day.

Chapter 3

Nate congratulated himself on taking a day of leisure. Hell, he deserved it. His architectural design business had racked up two contracts last month, and he was bidding for a third job in the coming week.

Since the council meeting on Halloween night two weeks before, he'd taken Maeve out to dinner several times and carried drinks over to her back stoop on warmer evenings. They were getting back on familiar ground, and for that, he heaved a great sigh of relief. He'd told her more than he'd planned to about the guesthouse, but not so much that he'd spoil the surprise. Harry should have left both houses to Maeve. Nate intended to give the guesthouse to her once it was up and running.

He looked at the small velvet box on his kitchen counter, the one he'd purchased before the last time they broke up. Nope, it wasn't time yet.

Despite being a grown-ass man of thirty-one, he'd never gotten over his schoolboy crush on Maeve Harper, and honestly, he never wanted to. Nate frowned, recalling their last breakup. They'd both been entrenched in their professional lives, building their respective careers in cities more than five hours apart. Neither of them had had the guts to just pick up and move, so they'd called it quits.

Their foray into a platonic relationship began when he and Maeve had teamed up to take care of Harry during his illness. After his call, Maeve had come back to Bees Ferry and lived in Harry's vacant house while Nate stayed with Harry. They tag-teamed caring for the older man, juggling their careers, doctors' visits, and keeping Harry comfortable. They'd renewed their friendship along the way. All Nate wanted to do was nudge that friendship back toward romance status once more. He grew weary of the *off* nature of their on-again/off-again relationship.

Pouring a second cup of coffee, Nate glanced around the kitchen of the house he'd inherited from Harry Harper. The Harper and Weaver families had been connected since long before Nate was born. All the Weaver children had loved to play in this yard, feed Harry's chickens and ducks, and explore the property that sprawled for acres back to the marsh.

When Nate's mom had had her hands full with a brood of little kids and Nate had been itching to get into some real teenage trouble, Harry had provided an alternative, teaching Nate about woodworking and the basics of construction. Harry's tutelage had not only kept Nate out of bad company, but it had also given him direction in life. It was thanks to Harry that Nate's interest in construction projects like building greenhouses had grown into a love of architecture and design. Now, he was the proud owner of Weaver Architecture and the humble recipient of one of Harry's houses.

And . . . cautiously hopeful he and Maeve could put their last breakup behind them and start again.

He raised his cup in silent salute to Harry's memory and opened his back door to see how the newest additions to his garden were doing. His mellow mood evaporated.

Carnage!

The miniature gardenias and azaleas he had planted twenty-four hours earlier along one side of the property were all ripped from the ground, lying on their sides, mud everywhere. He plunked his mug down and trudged out to the yard.

A piece of paper wedged between two arches of his handmade wire fence read:

Sorry! My dog smelled the fresh soil and went on a digging spree.

There was no signature, no contact information, and no offer to help replant everything.

"Well, shit."

Who lets their dog pull up every single plant on the block? Nate figured he had two options. One, start walking all over Bees Ferry looking for a muddy dog, or two . . .

Fifteen minutes later, shovel in hand, he began replanting every single bush he had installed yesterday. All thirty-six of them.

After an hour of damage repair, he was sweaty in the warm November sunshine. His T-shirt came off and landed on the ground. Wiping the back of his hand across his brow, Nate wondered if spitting would make him feel better. He tried it out, the way a disgusted John Wayne would have done if the bad guys had just destroyed a peaceful town.

Yep, it helped.

Something about this whole mess was just *off*. Odd there weren't any paw prints in the mud.

As he was scooting soil around the last gardenia, Maeve jogged around the corner and stopped in front of him. His heart, already pounding from the exercise, kicked up its speed a few more beats per minute.

"What in the world are you doing?" she asked.

Just like every other time she was around him, a jolt of awareness hit him. The first time he felt it, they were little kids. She'd caught a turtle the day before Nate's tenth birthday and spent an entire afternoon at the library learning how to care for box turtles in captivity and writing out instructions. Then, she'd caught Nate's heart by giving him the turtle and the illustrated instruction book at his birthday party. He'd been hers ever since.

Even through those off years when they'd been in different cities or different states. Or different states of mind.

Now they lived in Harry's houses right next door to each other, almost like those summers when they were kids. It was torture to be so near to her and not be able to . . . what? Hold her for hours? Talk to her all night long? Kiss her senseless?

Fingers snapped in his face.

"Nate. Where'd you go?" Maeve gestured to the row of plantings. "Didn't you finish this yesterday?"

"Yeah, I did." Nate shook off his reverie. She was taking note of his gardening, was she? He hoped she liked it. "Somebody's hound upended all of them."

"Are you sure it wasn't the wind? All of my flags got blown down." She tucked a strand of hair behind one ear. Nate noticed her gaze drifting down to his chest and tried not to smile. "And some got stuck up in the trees. Can I borrow your tall ladder again?"

"Wind wouldn't have done this." He gestured to the newly restored line of plants. "Some jerk left a note. But the more I think about it, the less it adds up."

He grabbed his shirt from the grass and wiped his face with it before tucking it into his waistband, letting it hang at his side. Her eyes followed his every move.

Nate pointed to the ground and noticed her eyes stayed glued to his shoulders. "There aren't any paw prints."

Maeve shook her head as if to clear her thoughts and frowned. She flicked her hair back over her shoulders. Nate knew the gesture by heart. She would put her hands on her waist next and kick her hips to the left. She always did that when she puzzled over something.

"Can I see the note?" She held out her hand.

Nate handed her the piece of paper and watched her face while she read. He wondered if she would purse her lips in concentration. He contemplated kissing them when she did.

"Know any dogs in the area that would do this?" he asked.

"No, but let me grab your, um, gardening tools. We can get your ladder and head over to my place," she said, resolutely looking anywhere but at his bare chest. "I have something to show you."

Well, well, well. Nate enjoyed her enjoying him. If he had known working shirtless would capture her attention so thoroughly, he'd have been half-naked more often. Maybe she wasn't as immune to him as he feared.

He smiled and indicated she should lead the way. He was trying to take things slowly this time, not rush her. OK, so his plan wasn't exactly anyone's definition of taking things slowly, but once he'd made up his mind, he couldn't wait. He just had to keep it all a secret for a little longer.

When the shovels and hose were put away, Nate dragged his shirt back over his head and muscled the twelve-foot ladder out from behind a wall of other crap in the shed.

Maeve walked across his yard on stepping-stones that had been laid about a century before either of them was born. The path led to her yard via an ornate gate set in a fence that separated their properties.

Their yards abutted each other in the middle of what would be considered a city block if this part of Bees Ferry could be called a city. Nate followed Maeve to her yard where statues of various goddesses poured water into gurgling fountains, wrought iron benches lounged under jasmine-covered pergolas, bird feeders marched alongside pressed pavers, and raised garden beds sat shoulder to shoulder with un-raised garden beds. Plaques on shed walls and plants in pots vied for attention wherever one turned.

Other than the shrubs he'd just returned to the ground, his yard had grass.

"Look," she said, pointing toward the front of the yard. "It took hours crawling up and down that ladder last week to hang them and one night of wind to knock them down."

Nate opened the ladder near one of the trees. Maeve had said her buntings were prayer flags. They weren't so high up, but their blocky shapes got caught on leaves and twigs.

"I don't think there was enough wind last night to do this," he told her as he got the last strand out of the tree.

They walked around the yard picking up the fallen bunting. Nate helped Maeve collect it into a box for temporary safekeeping, then followed her into the house. She headed straight for the kitchen and dug around in the trash can for a moment.

"Here it is," she said, handing him a crumpled piece of paper. "Remember the two giant terra cotta strawberry pots I had outside of the front gate? Well, now I have one."

Nate unfurled the paper and read:

Sorry about the pot. It was blocking the sidewalk and my dog bumped into it.

"What a coincidence." Nate turned the paper over. No signature or contact information.

"I don't think this is a coincidence, Nate. That pot was heavy as all get out and it *wasn't* blocking the sidewalk."

He put the note in his back pocket along with the one he'd found in his yard that morning. He'd sort it out later.

Emboldened by the success of their recent dates, he reached out and wrapped one arm around her shoulders, kissing the top of her head. She relaxed against him, turning her cheek into his chest and wrapping one arm around his waist. Just like it used to be. Just like it should always be.

"Honestly, Nate, sometimes I wonder what the hell I'm doing. Next week is Thanksgiving, and the week after that we hear back from the council. Part of me is nervous I won't get approved because then what will I do?" She pulled away and faced him. "And part of me is terrified I will get approved because I'm not sure I can handle all these bizarre setbacks."

Nate took her hand. She was right. Two notes on two different days for damage that didn't look accidental was no coincidence. And coupled with the earlier grass fire by Maeve's shed and the curious incident of his water getting cut off on the one day he had tilers working, Nate decided he should start looking into the causes of all the accidents.

"Let's go sit out on the steps," he said.

He grabbed two Cokes from the fridge and pushed open the back screen door, twisting bottle caps off as he went. They settled in their usual places, a habit from childhood, Maeve on the top step, leaning against the doorframe, Nate two steps down, his elbows resting on his knees.

"You've done a beautiful job out here," Nate admitted. "I'd want to stay here if I were visiting the Charleston area."

"Thanks. The guest rooms are coming together too. But all these unexpected things come up, and they have to be dealt with immediately, so my time and attention and money are in more places than they should be. I knew my illustration commissions might be on hold while I got the B&B up and running, but I had no idea there would be this many hurdles."

Nate nodded in agreement, vowing to get to the bottom of things without piling more stress on Maeve.

"I hear you."

"Always something, right? It's not just the strawberry pot or the flags, you know," Maeve said after a swig of Coke. "Remember when Grayson stopped by to drop off some stuff from town? He said he saw someone looking in my front window, but they ran off when they saw his car."

"I do remember." Nate also recalled how annoyed he'd been that she'd waited hours to tell him about it. He'd helped her install motion-activated floodlights on all the corners of her house the next day. "And the fire. You do know that wasn't me, right?"

"Well, there *was* a Weaver Architecture matchbook on the ground right where the grass got scorched. I know you would never do it intentionally . . ."

"Those were swag from the last Chamber event. Everyone brought something, and anyone could have picked those up. But you couldn't resist jumping to conclusions again, right?" Nate twisted his head around to look at her and raised his eyebrows, daring her to prove him wrong. It had been their stumbling block since adolescence: fear to trust. The curse of overly independent kids and one of the reasons for their many breakups over the years.

"Well, it's no more ridiculous than you accusing me of having your water turned off."

Maeve's hands flew around as she talked. Nate loved that her whole body communicated what she was saying. It was like watching a spontaneous dance that didn't need music to be beautiful.

"I guess we're both looking for easy answers where there are none." He finished his soda, contemplating their recent mishaps. "Did anything unusual happen to you the week my water got cut off?"

Maeve dropped her chin onto her hands to think. Her lips pursed, as he knew they would.

"Around the same time I had all those deliveries go missing?" She scooted down to share his step, her right hip pressing into his left one, their shoulders jostling each other for room. His left arm moved up and around to cushion the small of her back against the hard cement.

Nate sighed as her cool skin connected with his still-warm body. Her scent filled the air around his face, citrusy and spicy. His consciousness redistributed space so that she occupied part of his interior. It had always been like this. They thought on the same wavelengths, the ideas clearer when their bodies touched. It felt good to get back into that familiar rhythm.

"Yep. Two suspicious events in one week. What happened with your packages?"

"They never turned up. I had to reorder all of the sheets for the guest beds and the linen napkins with the fleur-de-lis on them. My credit card company covered the loss, but it was the aggravation and the time, you know?"

"I know," he agreed. "Today felt like a rerun for me. This was going to be my one day to be lazy before the onslaught next week."

"Oh, yeah; they're breaking ground on Johns Island, right?"

Nate grinned. She'd been so happy for him when his architectural plan had been selected for the new community center and playground.

"Yeah, and if all goes to plan, that project ought to be well underway by the time I open the B&B in January."

Maeve grinned right along with him. "Do you know what you're calling the guesthouse?"

"I think so. If I get approved." He nudged her. "What about you? Change your mind about going into head-to-head competition with me?"

She snorted. "Not likely. Harper House will kick your ass." She looked at him expectantly. "Like the name?"

At that moment, she could have been asking if he'd like cold roadkill on a silver platter. If she served it, the answer was yes. Without allowing himself to think about it, he leaned in and kissed her.

With his mouth feverishly pressed to hers, his tongue probing her lips, Nate felt the depth of her reaction. She kissed him back with the same fervor he was feeling. The secret he was trying to keep from Maeve, the one involving that little white velvet box on his kitchen counter, was in jeopardy of being not-so-secret. *Timing, Weaver.* He did the only thing he could do to preserve his sanity. He broke off the kiss, thanked Maeve for the Coke, and headed for the relative neutrality of his own yard. It took him several deep breaths to bring himself under control.

Chapter 4

In celebration of the fact that Maeve's business application had been approved, as had Nate's, Willa, in her role as Hive Bakery owner, had served up fancy coffees on the house. She had also served up the opinion that Maeve should sort out her feelings for Nate.

Fine. When Maeve thought of Nate, two words sprang to mind: *hotter-than-hell hunk of beautiful man* and *impossible piece of stubborn granite.*

OK, it was more than two words, but what did Willa want her to say?

"Look, Maeve, all I'm trying to do is help you categorize your feelings. You organize every other aspect of your existence to within an inch of its life—"

"Can I help it if I like things to be in neat little boxes?"

"—so if you could decide once and for all if he is an enemy, a platonic friend, a temporary fling, or in the forever box, you could adjust your thinking about him and act accordingly. Your life would be so much simpler." Willa wrapped her hands around her mug of spiced-pumpkin-flavored coffee and sipped.

"Is there an 'it's complicated' category?" Maeve asked, wrinkling her nose.

"I've got to get back to work. Break's over." Willa said. "Think about what I've said."

How could she not? Nate was the first thing on her mind every morning and the last thing every night. He had always been there, in her brain and heart, even before she'd moved back to the Lowcountry, whether she wanted to admit it or not. Just because they'd stopped being a couple, she'd never really considered them *over.*

While she hadn't anticipated the radical turn her life would take in the past year, she was glad for the change. She'd been living in Raleigh, North Carolina, when Nate had called to tell her that her great-uncle Harry was seriously ill. It had been their first conversation since their last attempt at being a couple, which had ended badly. Still, packing her worldly belongings in her Jeep and driving down to Charleston had been a no-brainer.

For several months, they'd coexisted, falling into a platonic friendship. Putting their personal feelings—in her case that included regret, longing, aggravation, want, and lust—aside, Maeve and Nate had cared for Harry at his home. Friends and neighbors helped when they could, and Nate's mother had cooked for them every day. One day, Harry had declared he was moving into a skilled nursing home and asked her and Nate to look after the houses and land until he got better. He'd said it with a wink. Harry had passed away a week later, leaving half of his estate to Maeve, his only living relative. It included the house she currently lived in, so Maeve had decided to stay. Permanently.

The other half of Harry's estate went to Nate, the former wild child Harry had helped tame and come to love like the son he'd never had.

And now, here she was, living and working in Bees Ferry, in the house where she had spent all her summers, next to a man she had loved for as long as she could remember. A man she couldn't seem to live with or without. A man who exasperated her at every turn.

Last week, he'd paraded around his yard shirtless, then he'd kissed her *but good* and told her to be sure her doors were locked before dark. He'd gone home leaving her hot, bothered, and unable to stop thinking about his shoulders. And his chest. And the way his abdomen rippled with muscle and tapered so perfectly into those jeans that hugged in all the right places—

Holy hell.

Riding her bike home from downtown Bees Ferry, she gave serious thought to Willa's suggestion. She'd put Nate Weaver in a category if it killed her. He definitely wasn't her enemy. Business rival, maybe, but not enemy. And he was, of course, her friend. A very good friend and neighbor and all-around good guy who had her back even if there was competitive tension between them. And sexual tension. And intense attraction.

Could he be a temporary lover? The thought made her mouth water with anticipation, but she could picture the aftermath, and it wasn't pretty. Was there a possibility for something more long term? A true relationship including friendship *and* romance *and* sex? Dare she say commitment?

The one thing Maeve hadn't shared with Willa was her recent history with Nate. A couple of years ago, she'd been looking forward to a getaway from Raleigh. She and Nate had planned to meet at a favorite bar on Folly Beach for a long weekend. Maeve had arrived just in time to find a perky little local wearing short shorts and a bikini top wrapped around Nate like a beach towel. Instead of waiting for some flimsy explanation she'd convinced herself would be a lie, she congratulated Nate on finding such a stellar example of a woman. She slammed her drink down on the bar so hard that half of it plopped out of the glass and all over Nate. She'd left him standing outside the bar accusing her of jumping to conclusions. He hadn't even had the decency to call her later and explain.

What if she put him in that last box, the Forever Box, and "acted accordingly," as Willa recommended? It could be the ride of her life, or she could get her heart broken again. If she put everything on the line and was rebuffed, what then? Could she live and work next door to the man who made it clear he didn't want her for forever? Could they go back to *just friends* after that?

It would suck.

But would it be any worse than the position she was in now, wanting him and not having him? Maeve sighed and pedaled on. Could she juggle her day job, the illustration commissions, opening a guesthouse, *and* a romantic gambit all at the same time? In the back of her mind, she heard Harry's voice. He offered the same advice he'd given her when she was fresh out of college and worried about having too much on her plate.

"Give it a go," he'd said then. "You'll fly or you'll fall, but either way, you'll have an interesting view of the world."

OK, Harry. You were right the first time. You'd better be right this time.

When Maeve arrived home, she found a note from Nate stuck in her screen door. Would she join the Weaver clan for an early Christmas celebration? Yes. Yes, she would.

Chapter 5

"Mrs. Weaver, that was the best pre-Christmas dinner I've ever eaten," Maeve exclaimed, setting her napkin on the table.

"Thank you, sweetie. I'm so glad you came this year. We've missed you. Since we're fixing to go on that European vacation I've been promised for twenty years now, I figured we'd better get our holiday celebrating out of the way early." Mrs. Weaver picked up a stack of plates. "Besides, with everyone staying over and opening presents tomorrow morning, this can be kind of a run-through so Tater will know what to expect on actual Christmas morning when Santa has come to *his* house."

Tater was Nate's nephew, the only grandbaby so far in Nate's sprawling family. At just over a year old, Tater was waddling around the table from person to person, accepting little bites of whatever was left on everyone's plates.

"Mom, he won't remember this in two weeks, so don't go overboard." Nate's sister Estelle rolled her eyes at her mother's back. "He'll probably like the boxes and wrapping paper better anyway."

"You mind your own beeswax, Estelle Marie, and let me worry about what's overboard or not for my grandson," called Mrs. Weaver from the kitchen.

"I'll go help with the washing." Maeve grinned at the familial back-and-forth and took more plates from the table. All the siblings and their better halves joined in mock-chastising Estelle about her beeswax.

Talk in the kitchen ranged from the delicious dinner they had eaten to local news, the weird early cold snap, who was reading what, and, of course, tomorrow's menu of leftovers. Every sibling and their partner had an opinion on how to best prepare Turkey 2.0.

Maeve watched Nate look around at his family. She knew how much he loved them, and she knew the moment he'd had enough of them. Just like when they'd been kids and he'd need to escape to Harry's while his mom corralled all the younger ones, she could tell he was about to make a run for it.

She winked at him. He pulled her outside, one arm around her shoulders, which she figured was the only way to walk anywhere with Nate Weaver, and they headed for the swing by the little lake a few hundred yards from the house.

"This is such a beautiful place." Maeve sighed. It reminded her of the many holiday celebrations she had spent with the Weaver family after her parents had died. Accepting Nate's invitation to join them again had been easy, especially given the camaraderie they'd enjoyed over the past few weeks. It seemed like she and Nate had celebrated their respective business plans every other night in December so far. She still felt like he was holding something back, but oh it was good to see him and laugh with him almost every day again. After Harry's death, they had danced around each other's feelings, not sure if there was enough glue to hold them together without Harry as their bond.

"I've always loved it here," Nate agreed.

"Can you believe there are so many ways to reinvent leftover turkey?"

"Whatever they come up with, it will be great," Nate told her. "You should stay."

Maeve sat next to him on the swing, her hand on his thigh. His firm, sexy thigh.

Since deciding to "give it a go," she had yet to test the romantic waters with Nate. True to her promise to Willa, Maeve had put Nate in a category. She had decided on that blasted Forever Box, and come hell or high water, she was going to act accordingly. Their tacit agreement to keep things platonic, put in place when she'd first returned to Bees Ferry to help care for Harry, hadn't come with an expiration date, but Maeve decided that *friendship only* ended yesterday.

"What, stay here? At your parents' house?"

"Stay," his husky voice tempted. "Just for the night. Let's forget about work and the houses and what's around the corner. Besides, it's Christmas. We deserve the break."

"It's not Christmas. It's mid-December and—"

She didn't know what would have come after, and she didn't care. Nate looked at her with an intensity that stole her breath. He leaned his forehead on hers and closed his eyes.

"Shhhh," he whispered.

Maeve stopped talking, deciding instead to use her mouth for more pleasurable pursuits. She took his mouth with swift assurance, her hands on his face, letting his beard-roughened jaw scrape her palms and send pulses of awareness up her arms. His lips, warm and welcoming, opened for her searching tongue. He was deliciously hot on the inside.

She tilted her head and wrapped an arm around his neck, sending her fingers through his hair and deepening the kiss. He responded with all the fire and sizzle she craved. Platonic be damned; this felt right. Desperate need hit her square in the heart when he scooped her up and settled her on his lap.

"Hey you two!" a voice called into the still evening. "The annual Christmas Game-a-Thon is starting. Get in here, Nate, so I can kick your ass in Monopoly again."

Maeve pulled back first, panting and frustrated to end the kiss. Nate was breathing hard as well. And he *was* hard. Everywhere, if that bulge under her bottom was any indication.

"Say you'll stay," he commanded in a hoarse voice, his hands roaming across her back.

Maeve crawled off his lap, going against the desires of every fiber of her being.

"Fine," she told him, a wicked gleam in her eye. "But it's going to be a little payback for you, mister." She wanted him to squirm, just like she had done after that kiss on her back steps when absolutely *nothing* had happened afterward. "I already told your mom I'd be happy with the pullout in the den."

Much later that night, Nate lay wide awake. When Maeve had accepted his invitation to early Christmas, he'd gotten nervous. Not because she was coming home with him; she'd done that dozens of times before over the years. She fit right in with his boisterous family and had from the time they were kids. What made him antsy was the box in his pocket he'd been carrying around for the last few weeks.

Her kiss earlier had rocked him. She hadn't initiated any romantic contact between them since coming back to Bees Ferry. It was what made him hesitant about their relationship, since he didn't know how else to describe the *thing* that had always been between them. Friends, of course, but there had always been something more. There had been a time when they'd practically lived in each other's pockets.

After dinner, when he'd hauled her onto his lap on the swing, he thought she'd feel the hardness—of the box, of course—and ask about it. What would he have said? Could she possibly be surprised that he had serious feelings for her? She hadn't noticed the ring box, though, or at least hadn't mentioned it.

Christmas game night had been agonizing. He'd been teased about being preoccupied more than once by more than one sibling. They didn't know the half of it. What he was feeling was akin to pain. Anticipation was building inside of him that needed release. But could he propose in front of the whole family? Would Maeve want such an intimate exchange to be public?

It might be a good Christmas present. Then again, maybe it shouldn't be part of any other holiday celebration. In the end, he kept the ring in his pocket. And now here he was, stretched across the old twin bed in his old room, because sharing the den's pullout sofa with a woman whose hair smelled like cinnamon and vanilla cookies and whose round derriere would fit so cozily against his hip wasn't an option.

Maeve had been right; this was torture. He couldn't sleep. Hell, he couldn't even get comfortable. As much as he wanted to pull her into bed, his childhood bed in his parents' house held no appeal as the setting for great romance.

His one consolation: their on-again/off-again relationship certainly felt *on*, and it was damn well going to stay that way.

Nate leaned over the edge of the bed and grabbed his khakis from the floor. He shifted them around until he could get his hand in the left pocket. He pulled out the small box and flipped open the top. The center diamond sparkled at him even in here, where the only illumination came from the string lights his mother had put in every room of the house, including his old, unused bedroom.

"Hang in there, Weaver," he whispered to himself. "The right moment will present itself."

Chapter 6

Maeve heard the engine before she saw the car. It interrupted the quiet of a warm Christmas Eve morning as she was finishing up a few sketches for a deadline. There was no mistaking Grayson Cooper's souped-up convertible. He screeched to a stop in front of her house and got out. After using his sleeve to buff the smudges off the door when he closed it, he pushed his Ray-Bans on top of his highlighted blond curls.

Maeve stopped sketching as he approached her front stoop. The fashion-model smile and preppy wardrobe should attract attention all over Charleston, but Maeve never saw him with a date and wouldn't trust him with a friend. Her gut said Grayson was always on the prowl for the next best thing, never satisfied with what he had.

"Hey, Maeve. Not too cold for you out here?"

Grayson sauntered up her front walk. He reminded her of a game show host. That false cheerfulness set her teeth on edge.

She closed her sketchbook. "What brings you way out here, Grayson?"

"Mind if I join you?" Without waiting for an answer, he sat next to her on the step. "Congratulations on your B&B approval. I thought I'd talk you into having dinner with me to celebrate. Downtown, with a bottle or two of wine?"

Maeve scooted over to put more than a few inches between them. His proximity had all the little hairs on the back of her neck standing at attention, and not in a pleasant way.

"Aw, Grayson, I don't think it's a good idea."

After a moment, he took his sunglasses off his head and twirled them between his fingers.

"Well, I have to ask every now and then. Also, I, uh, wanted to talk to you about—"

An older pickup with "Weaver Architecture" emblazoned on the doors parked behind Grayson's sports car. Nate slammed the driver's door shut before stalking around the back end of the truck. He didn't have expensive sunglasses or a fashionable outfit or buttery leather loafers, but Maeve's pulse accelerated. He looked good enough to eat.

"Grayson Cooper, just the man I was looking for." Nate didn't look happy to have found his quarry.

"You were? Why?" Grayson jumped to his feet like a naughty child caught doing something wrong. He cleared his throat and stood up a bit straighter. "Actually, I wanted to talk to you too."

"Grayson invited me to dinner," Maeve said, "with wine."

"Did you, now?" Nate said, still frowning at Grayson.

"Yes, as a matter of fact, but you're invited too," Grayson said brightly, rubbing his palms together. "I'm afraid Maeve thought it was a date, but this is strictly business. All business, all the time. You know me."

"What business do you want to discuss with both of us over wine, Grayson? Would it be about these?" Nate pulled folded papers out of his back pocket.

Grayson took the papers from Nate. Glancing down, he paled. "Well, yes, but it's not how it looks, Nate."

"Why don't you tell Maeve how it looks. I haven't had time to share these with her yet."

Grayson shifted his weight from one foot to the other, tearing the papers in half and half again.

"These are nothing," he said. "It was a bit of a gamble, but, ah, do you think I could have something to drink?" He glanced desperately toward the porch.

Maeve had no idea what was going on, but Grayson looked like he was trying to swallow sand.

"Of course," she said, pointing a finger at each man in turn, "but nobody says a word 'til I get back."

As soon as she went inside, Nate reached over the gate with lightning speed and snatched up Grayson's starched shirtfront.

"Did you forget one of my sisters works in your office, dumbass?" he growled. "You'd better have a damn good explanation for why it looks like you were trying to forge our signatures on sales offers, Grayson, or I'm taking the originals and those notes you left us about your 'dog' destroying our yards over to the sheriff's office. His brand-new forensic handwriting expert can have a look at them side by side."

Nate shoved Grayson back on his heels as Maeve came out with three beers.

"Looks like we're all going to need these. Nate, I said no talking 'til I came back, so you're going to have to repeat it all."

"Originals?" Grayson stepped back out of Nate's reach.

"Yeah. You didn't think I was stupid enough to put the only existing copy in your hands, did you?"

"Copies of what?" Maeve asked.

"And do you want to tell her you busted her great uncle's antique planter, or shall I?"

Before today, Nate had had a sneaking suspicion the mishaps around his and Maeve's yards could all be laid at one door. He thought Grayson was jealous Maeve wouldn't go out with him; maybe the petty acts of vandalism were some kind of post-adolescent revenge. Immature but harmless. Then his youngest sister had called.

"Why are you selling your house?" she'd asked as soon as he answered his cell. When he denied it, she'd countered with, "I'm holding an offer acceptance letter in my hand; it looks like you were drunk when you signed it."

In a breach of office protocol, she'd saved the documents she'd found with Nate's name on them, and several similar ones in Maeve's name, all from the shred pile. Nate left his job site and drove like a maniac to get his hands on those papers.

"Look y'all, let me explain." Grayson wiped his hand across his forehead, swallowing several times. "There's a pile of money on the table for both of you. Way more than you'll ever get for these properties individually, and I can personally assure you—"

"Grayson," Maeve looked at him incredulously. "What part of *we're not selling* don't you understand? We've talked about this so many times in the past year. And what the hell did you have against my antique planter? I didn't even know you had a dog."

"He doesn't," Nate told her. "A dog would have behaved better. For some reason, our friend here thinks he can get away with forging our names on some sales agreement, and . . . Grayson, for the life of me I can't figure out your logic. The sales wouldn't have gone through."

Grayson sat heavily on the step again. Maeve watched him drain his beer, turning the empty bottle around in his hands meditatively, as if considering how much to say.

"I didn't need the sales to go through," he told them quietly. "My payday was coming with getting your signatures on those offer acceptance letters by tomorrow. They were going to give me a huge advance just to get you to sign the agreements. It was going to be enough to pay some bills and get me the hell out of here."

Maeve walked over to stand by Nate. "Who was paying you?"

"Jennifer Lewis. She's a piece of work. Knows how to turn on the charm until it's time to start turning the screws. She's the local liaison for a foreign resort developer. They specialize in putting exclusive retreats in backwaters because the land is cheaper."

"Well, I wouldn't call Bees Ferry a backwater," Maeve said, offended.

"That's not the point," Nate said. "So did you give them a signed offer, Grayson? Do we need a lawyer to get us out of this?"

"No. I couldn't go through with it. That's why the documents were in the box to be shredded. No one was supposed to know. I thought I'd give you two my best-ever sales pitch today, maybe convince you to sell." He looked away, wiping a shaking hand over his face.

"And the flags? And the fire? And the prowler," Maeve demanded. "Was that you?"

"Yeah, all me. There was no prowler, Maeve. I thought if you didn't feel safe here, well, all the better. Look. I'm sorry." He hung his head. "I'm not a bad guy, just a broke one."

Nate stalked a couple of feet in one direction and then turned and covered the same ground in the other before jabbing a finger at Grayson.

"For God's sake, Grayson," Nate said. "Get the hell off this property before I—"

Maeve put a staying hand on Nate's shoulder. "Just go, Grayson."

Grayson looked once at Maeve and avoided Nate's gaze. He got in his convertible and executed a U-turn in the middle of Monroe, tires crunching on the asphalt.

Chapter 7

Later that night over pizza, Maeve asked Nate, "How long have you suspected him?"

"Probably since we got those ridiculous notes about my plants and your strawberry pot. The more I thought about it, the more other things came under suspicion. The water company said my water was turned off as a precautionary measure after a call from a concerned neighbor. Grayson knew that would cost me money and time."

"When were you going to tell me about your suspicions? It's not like I'm hard to find." Maeve had been so busy for the rest of the afternoon, she hadn't had time to logically think through the day's events. She could only feel, and her predominant emotion was disappointment. She'd been left out of Nate's circle of trust. Again.

This isn't Folly Beach, she told herself. She felt betrayed anyway.

Nate looked at her, did a double take, and turned his whole body so he was facing her. He held her shoulders with both hands.

"I know that look, Maeve Harper," he warned. "Don't you dare go jumping to conclusions again."

"Were you keeping me in the dark on purpose?"

"No! I've been snowed under with work, just like you."

He gentled his hold and interlaced his fingers behind Maeve's neck. She kept her arms folded across her chest but forced herself to meet his gaze.

"Is that everything I should know?"

Nate averted his gaze. "I think so. For now."

Maeve didn't love the sound of that, but it occurred to her she could exercise a little trust. That was what you did for someone in your Forever Box, right?

"OK," she conceded. "But why would Grayson sabotage our yards?"

"His primary goal is money." Nate moved away from her to pace the length of the kitchen. "I think he's convinced it's everyone's motivation. That's why he gave us a pitch every time he saw us. When we didn't budge, he tried manipulating us into feeling frustrated and overwhelmed so we'd want to sell. In the end, he was desperate, but not desperate enough to commit a felony."

"Thank goodness for that, at least. What are you going to do now?"

"What do you want to do? This is as much your decision as mine, Maeve. We're a team, right?"

"I hope so." *Act accordingly*, she told herself. *If you want him for the long term, you have to trust him like you want to be trusted.*

Since the damage to their properties had been minimal, and although Grayson was surely a total jerk, they decided not to call the authorities.

After clearing away the pizza boxes Nate leaned against the kitchen counter, one long leg crossed over the other. "Maeve. I . . . I haven't been completely honest with you."

Maeve felt her stomach drop. *I knew it!* Her mouth went dry, and all the old doubts came rushing back. Willing herself not to be disappointed, she started making a mental list of all the things she'd have to do before she moved back to Raleigh. Hire a local cleaning service. Resign from local organizations. Figure out how to long-distance manage her brand-new business.

She almost laughed out loud. Grayson should've stuck around a little longer. He might've had at least one signed contract. She couldn't possibly stay here, not if Nate was keeping things from her.

"There's a reason I was so . . . shocked when you turned up at the council meeting with a proposal to open a guesthouse," he was saying.

"Was it because I was giving you some competition?" Maeve decided the best defense was a bitchy offense. "Or because you found out about *my* plans for Harper House before that and couldn't stand the fact that I might be able to do something without you?"

"Good God, woman, when are you going to quit jumping to ridiculous conclusions about my motives?"

"When you stop acting like you can string me along, then drop me like a hot potato," Maeve shouted. "Like when you invited me to Folly Beach, then spent the night prancing around with some other . . . person."

Nate ran both hands through his hair and sighed. "She was my best friend's little sister who had gotten engaged. I also hugged her fiancé. If you had stuck around for five more minutes, you'd have found all this out back then."

Maeve couldn't say a word. She felt like a fool. Nate was right: she did often jump to the wrong conclusions. She'd done so when they were kids. If something in their pretend world went wrong, she blamed Nate. She'd done the same when things had gone wrong with her guesthouse; it could have only been Nate, right?

"But what about every time we kiss? It feels like we're at the beginning of something, then you disappear or act like it didn't happen." Maeve hoped she didn't sound as pathetic as she felt.

Nate moved closer and gathered her in an embrace. "You didn't come back to Bees Ferry for me, remember?" he asked. "You came back for Harry. I've been trying to give you space, to give you time, to see that I'm a good reason to stay. We kiss because I can't help myself."

He demonstrated, kissing behind her ear and gently biting her earlobe. He trailed warm, wet nibbles down the side of her neck and licked the hollow above her collarbone. He worked his way around to the other side of her neck and up to her chin. His teeth grazed over her jawline before his mouth claimed hers in an all-consuming reckoning with the truth.

"And I walk away," he whispered, "because I want the decision for us to be together to be as much yours as mine."

Maeve open her eyes, which had drifted closed of their own volition. Her arms wound around Nate's shoulders. She clung for dear life. "But you're keeping another secret from me," she protested between kisses. "Why?"

"Crazy, right? I haven't had a cocktail splash in my face in so long, I was missing the sting of vodka and tonic in my eyes." The edges of those eyes crinkled as he smiled down at her. "I was keeping a secret because I wanted to surprise you. Even you should have been able to jump to that conclusion."

Nate stepped out of their embrace but kept Maeve's hand in his. He took something from his pocket.

"What, ah, what is that, Nate?" She didn't recognize the whispery, shaky voice as her own.

"Well, *this*," he said, opening a white velvet box and sliding a diamond ring over the third finger on her left hand, "is an engagement ring, if you'll have me. And this," he continued as he took a silver object out from under the velvet padding, "is the key to your new guesthouse."

"Is this what you haven't been completely honest about?" She stared at the glittering jewel on her finger, her heart pounding a staccato rhythm.

Nate's cheeks flushed and his throat worked to swallow. "Remember at the council meeting you asked me 'Why?' Why a guesthouse?"

"Yes. You said because Harry had welcomed you in his home."

"Well, it's that and the fact that it's still as much your house as mine. Harry should have left everything to you. I planned to give you the guesthouse as a gift, a profitable business venture since you already have a house to live in. As a reason to stay. I never told you what I'm calling it."

"What are you calling it?" Dazed, her heart pounded like a jackhammer. Surely Alice had been less disoriented when she fell down the rabbit hole.

"The sign arrived today. Want to see?"

At her nod, Nate linked his hand with hers, and together they crossed the backyards on ancient stepping-stones that led from their past straight to their shared future.

In Nate's front yard, the new sign hung from the gable over the steps. It declared the house to be *Maeve's Welcome Home.*

Maeve wrapped her arms around Nate. This man had bet his heart and his future on her. He had chosen her as his *forever* just as her own heart had recognized its true path.

"Oh Nate. I don't know what to say."

"Say 'yes.' And merry Christmas."

"Yes. And merry Christmas." She lifted her face for a kiss that went on and on.

Epilogue

Valentine's Day, Two Years Later

"Maeve, we're supposed to be getting rid of *everything* we don't use, remember? You never take your ring off, so why do you keep taking its box out of the 'to go' pile?"

"It's not a 'to go' item," she called from the porch.

Nate shook his head and muttered about organizational chores in general and his wife's organizational logic in particular. Fine, if she wanted to hang onto a small white velvet box that never got used, who was he to argue? It didn't take up much room anyway, and it would fit somewhere else in the house.

Maeve's Welcome Home had racked up a full slate of reservations for the summer again, and this year, they'd be using some rooms in their own place, Harper House, for overflow. That was fine for now, but when the baby came, he was putting his foot down. No more guests in their home. He didn't intend to share the two loves of his life with tourists.

Nate hauled what he hoped was the last box of stuff for the town's charity bazaar to the porch.

"I'm going to run this into town and stop at Hive to grab us both some lunch. Don't do too much while I'm gone, got it?"

"Nate, I'm pregnant, not incapacitated." Maeve kissed her husband, one hand resting on her baby bump. "Where did you put my ring box?"

"It's in the bottom of your armoire at the moment. I don't get why you hang on to that thing." He kissed her back, with gusto.

"Because, my love, that *thing* is my Forever Box, and I'm never letting go."

End

About Addie Bealer

Addie Bealer lives with her husband and a hound in Western North Carolina. She writes fiction and memoir, and has authored a collection of poetry, some of which has been published. When not writing, Addie enjoys romping through fields with her pup and travels for research, relaxation, or red wine.

Find Addie Online:
Website: https://addiebealer.com/
Twitter: https://twitter.com/addiebealer

No Regrets
A Marion's Corner Short Story

By Robin Hillyer Miles

No Regrets

A Marion's Corner Short Story

Contemporary

Cantley, a widow in her sixties, moved back to her small village to start anew. She's gone through a rough patch and is unsure how to let go of the past.

Alston, the single silver fox, is eager to meet people and explore the area. He's ready to settle down, but his time is spent working from home and caring for his elderly parents.

Will he be the distraction she needs? Will she give him the grand tour? Visit the Lowcountry in this seasoned romance to discover the answers.

Rated: PG

Chapter One

Thursday, October 31, 2019

Cantley Broughton tucked the recyclable shopping bags under her arm and entered the double doors of Marion's Corner's Piggly Wiggly. She grabbed a buggy, tossed the bags in the baby seat, and headed toward the candy section.

The town witch's adopted daughter stopped her at the bread aisle. "You've forgotten something. It's a blurry image. Do you want me to concentrate on it?"

"Hey, Kilby. I've been forgetful lately but remembered my bags and wallet." She pointed toward her bags and patted her back pocket. "I've got to hurry to get Halloween candy for tonight since—"

"Since the village ladies cautioned you against handing out only kazoos." The younger woman laughed.

Cantley laughed with her and shook her head. "Yes. Word travels fast."

Shoppers passed her with candy-laden buggies, and she quickened her steps. She ignored the deep voice urgently calling, "Miss! Miss!" that seemed to be directed at her.

A tingle ran across her knees, and the hair on her arms stood up. She scrunched her eyes shut and turned her head away but waved as she hurried past the next aisle. The haunted aisle. A few times, in this Pig, she'd caught a glimpse of a classmate's chatty ghost who still stocked groceries and called out to those he knew even though he'd died years ago. The locals said Marion's Corner was so lovely, welcoming, and friendly that no one wanted to leave, not even after death.

She opened her eyes as soon as she'd taken enough steps to get past the ghost aisle, and the hazy feeling left, but her heart pumped double time.

"Miss! Miss!"

Someone was definitely trying to get someone's attention.

She turned down the candy aisle and perused her sparse options. The middle rows, the ones in arm's reach that usually held copious varieties of mini-sized candy, were bare. She haphazardly tossed full-sized packages in her buggy, mentally calculating the number of children in Pinopolis. Movement farther up the aisle caught her eye. She hesitated, bracing herself, then looked. A silver fox sort of man around her age slow-jogged toward her. He grinned at her the entire time until he stopped in front of her buggy. She continued to grab candy as she stared.

Rarely did one find such good looks in Marion's Corner. She lost her ability to speak, so she wiggled her fingers at him. Golden-brown eyes held her gaze. His grin caused her to grin along with him. Thankfully, he was fully alive and unfamiliar. He smiled like he had a secret.

"Hi, I believe these are yours." He held up a set of keys, and the sun glinted off them from the windows at the front of the store.

Luckily her voice decided to work. "I don't think so."

"Are you certain?" He jingled his keys toward her like he was holding mistletoe.

No, not his set of keys, *her* keys. She recognized her Gamecock key fob. Cantley patted the front and back pockets of her jeans and then held her hand out to accept her keys.

"I *did* forget something. Kilby's never wrong."

"Kilby?"

"The town witch's adopted daughter; she has some magic abilities too."

"Yikes."

"Well, if you're going to be magic, Marion's Corner is the town to live in. Most of us don't pass judgment about it." She gave him the look she gave her children when they were unkind.

"Ah, sorry, I knew that. My first reaction needs some practice. I only recently moved here." He bowed his head slightly in apology. "Let's start over. I believe these are your keys as I saw you leave the car."

"Did I drop them in the parking lot?" She tucked the keys into her front pocket.

"No. Left them in your ignition. With your convertible top partially down and the driver's side door and the trunk wide open." He grinned again. "It's my lucky day. I'm not normally in the grocery store at this time of the day, but I'm officially off work for the next three weeks. My parents and I have a trip to Greece starting tomorrow."

"Gracious. I'd say it's my lucky day. Thank you." *Lucky in more ways than one. Menopause brain may have worked out in my favor this time.* "My mind was on grabbing the Halloween candy before it's gone. Sorry, you had to run after me and that I ignored you at first." She held out her hand. "I'm Cantley Broughton."

He shook her offered hand. "Cantley kinda rhymes with candy—how appropriate. It's nice to meet you. I'm Alston Pike."

Cantley thought she'd heard the last name before, probably at the Pinopolis post office where all the village gathered to share books and plants, read the bulletin board, and purchase ribbons commemorating different causes. The public side of the two-room building saw a lot of traffic.

"Nice to meet you, Alston. I grew up here. I realize I judged you, judging magic. Sorry about that."

"Oh, you weren't. I know I was, though. You've lived here all your life?"

"I grew up in Pinopolis but spent almost forty years in Columbia. After my husband died two years ago, I moved home." A flash of a happy time with her husband came to her, and she smiled. He'd always teased her about having conversations with strangers in stores.

"I'm sorry for your loss." His words sounded sincere, yet his face lit up a bit.

"Thank you." She smiled at him. "Welcome to the Corner."

"Thanks. My parents live in Pinopolis too." Alston nodded and then peered into her shopping cart. "Are you giving out full-sized candy? My great-nieces will clean you out."

"I'm giving out kazoos too. On Pinopolis Road." Cantley also perused her selections and tossed in more. "I don't need leftovers. Bring 'em on."

"My parents' house is near Wampee. We're taking Dad's people-mover to trick or treat. He went overboard with the thrill of owning a golf cart." He chose a bag of Atomic Fireballs and placed them under his arm.

"Do stop by. My house is between the post office and Land of Pines on the left if you're coming from Wampee. It's the yellow one, set back from the street, with the camellia and azalea bushes out front."

"I know your place. My mom wanted to find out who lives there so she can see the yard."

"Tell her to come over anytime. I'll give her a kazoo too."

"Please don't. She'll play it all the time—indoors, off-key, sitting as close to me as possible." He paused. "Why kazoos?"

"Kazoos have a Southern history. They were invented in the 1840s by Alabama Vest of Macon, Georgia. He introduced them at the Georgia State Fair in 1852. There's science and physics involved too. It's a cool little gizmo."

"I love learning origination stories. It helps me win at trivia." Alston grinned.

Cantley smiled in return. "Me too. After I retired as a pharmacist, I took history classes at the University of South Carolina for fun."

"Good use of your time. I'm a retired Navy vice admiral. I now work part-time for the telephone/cable company for a few hours most weekdays. I've been getting lost or losing my golf balls in the afternoons." He moved to her side of the buggy to make space for a customer looking at the candy.

"Admiral? Impressive." *That explains his perfect posture.*

"They kept promoting me. What was I to do?" Alston's eyes sparkled when he teased her.

They moved in unison to get out of the way when the customer gave them the side eye. They grabbed the buggy handle simultaneously, and their hands touched. Cantley's entire body buzzed, and not from a ghostly encounter. She'd felt this once, forty-something years prior as a college student, when she met her future husband, the college professor. That sense of knowing someone before you know them. That burn in her belly made her stand tall and thrust her chest a bit. That promise of one day they'd be in each other's arms. Heat spread up her body and warmed her cheeks.

"Hey. We seem to be impeding traffic. Want to grab a seat at the diner next door and continue our conversation? I would love to hear about the area from a true local." Alston wore a hopeful look. His face became even more handsome.

"Will your wife be joining us?" *Please don't be married.* Her heart thumped to the beat of the eighties song blasting from overhead speakers.

He jumped slightly and looked around. "I'm single. Well, divorced, to be accurate. I left her on the west coast back in the late 80s. I hope she's not here."

Me too, Cantley whispered to herself. *How is he still single?*

Her voice said yes before her brain could catch up. "I could grab a bite with you. Greece is on my bucket list. I'd love to hear more."

She began rationalizing with herself. He was new to town. She should show the famous southern hospitality, right? Taking care of a sick husband, the subsequent widowhood, and menopause had taken away her libido and desire to be nice. Her children kept hounding her to get out of the house more, find new friends, meet up with old classmates, and visit old haunts. After taking a friend's recommendation to try bioidentical hormone therapy, she'd just started feeling like herself again. She'd have been more likely to say no, but he looked like a model from one of those underwear ads she kept seeing on social media. The doctor had said she'd start getting horny as her body adjusted to the hormones. They seemed to be kicking in.

"Sure. Let me buy your jawbreakers and lunch as thanks for not stealing my car." She snatched the bag from him, turned her buggy around, and headed to the register before he could protest and see her blushing.

"Atomic Fireballs, I'm taking them on the trip. Should help me stay awake on the flight so my body'll be acclimated to the right time zone. But I'm taking care of lunch." He'd caught up with her again. "And helping take your bags to the car."

She placed the divider behind the groceries on the conveyor belt while he gathered candy bags in his hands.

"I don't think there're this many kids in Pinopolis."

"Then every child shall get two bars." He'd distracted her to the point that she had too much candy, but she wasn't going to let him know.

He helped bag the groceries and carried them to her car before they headed to the diner. Their strides matched despite his extra foot of height.

"I swear this restaurant has the same menu selections they had in my childhood." She looked up from her printed sheet.

"Says here on the menu it's been in business for seventy-five years. Must mean it's good food and service." He looked at her over his reading glasses, and her heart skipped a beat. "What do you suggest?"

She moved her gaze from his eyes to her menu. *It would not do to kiss a stranger in the town's mom-and-pop restaurant when half the diners stared at you, and the rest had phones in their hands.*

The menu came back into focus. "You can't go wrong with the meat and three option. Their cup of soup and sandwich combo usually hits the spot for me. I'm going with the veggie chili and grilled cheese."

"Sounds good. Though the blue-plate special might be calling my name."

They placed their order, took sips of water, and started speaking. She hushed so he could go first.

"No awkward pause. Nice," Aston said. "You go first."

"Are you excited about your trip?" *Of course, he's going to say yes—it's Greece!* Cantley placed a napkin under her water and mentally kicked herself.

"Definitely. As I said, I'm taking my parents on this trip. It'll be some work for me as I'm in charge, but it will be fun. We travel together often." He paused. "Thank you for dining with me. I've been hoping to meet local people besides workmates, but it hasn't happened since I work remotely and rarely."

"You're welcome. You said you moved here to be closer to your parents?"

He kept looking her in the eyes while they spoke. No one had looked her in the eye except for her grandbaby in a long time. A shiver ran down her spine.

"Yes, I did. I moved around and out of the country so much that I only saw them every couple of years. And they're in their eighties. You know the drill."

"I bet they're stoked you're here for them. I would love to have the opportunity to spend time with my parents. I had a tough few years. The nurse we hired after my husband broke his hip attempted to get him to sign stuff over to her. He finally came to his senses right before he died. And then my parents died."

"Wow. That's rough. Did you have to get a lawyer to fight the nurse?"

"We had everything in my name since he was twenty years older. The lawyer had it locked up tight."

"Good for you." He nodded.

"I don't know why I'm telling you all my horrible secrets. I guess I needed to talk."

"You've had quite a few stressors. Deaths of parents and spouse, lawsuits, and moving. The Navy drilled mental health awareness into us the last few years I was in service. I can offer sympathy and steps to take, but I'm certain you've done all that."

"Oh, I've received help. It was rotten, but I've got happy memories. What's the saying: the past is a tiny circle, the future is a tiny circle, but the present is a huge bubble, and we need to pay attention before it bursts into the past circle, and a new bubble appears?"

"Sounds like a perfect philosophy."

"Thanks, I saw it in a meme on social media somewhere." She leaned back to allow the server to set down their plates. "My daughter, her husband, and my grandson live nearby, so it helps. My son is busy gallivanting and living his best life between taking pharmacy school courses. Tell me about your parents. How long have they lived in Pinopolis?"

"Just a few years; they wanted to be by the water. Dad tasks me with chores. Mom feeds me. I haven't had to cook since I moved close by. Need to get to Jimmy's Gym more often because Mom likes to use real butter." He patted his flat belly. "Which reminds me, I was at The Pig to get butter and quart-sized plastic baggies for her. I got distracted."

"Uh-huh." She tried not to focus on his body as the "what's under the clothing" images in her head made her squirm a bit in her seat. "Do you have brothers or sisters? I was a single child. I always wanted a sibling. Wait, you have nieces, so you have one or the other."

"I have an older sister. My nieces are her granddaughters. Their parents have a work function tonight they can't miss. This will be my first Pinopolis golf cart Halloween and my first with small kids. I'm looking forward to the experience."

"If this weather holds out, the kids will be sweating in their costumes. My grandson is going as a lion. His parents are taking him to a trunk or treat but brought him over for a trial run last night." She showed him the photo she'd taken on her phone.

"Cute. The girls are going as Wonder Woman and a cat. At least, that's what they were doing yesterday. They've changed their minds a few times."

"I look forward to oohing and aahing over their final selection."

After lunch, they chatted beside her car. Alston promised to stop by her house later to trick or treat.

That early evening, Cantley set up an umbrella with a table and a chair near her driveway. This eliminated trick-or-treaters traversing her dirt road with its looming camellia and azalea bushes, and crape myrtles dripping with Spanish moss impeding the path. She knew the kids in the village thought it spooky, as she'd overheard them talk about it. She placed an oil lantern on the table and lit it before returning to her house to pour a large portion of wine into a Tervis cup with a lid and a Gamecock design. She pulled the candy bowl and the box of kazoos out in a wagon she'd bought for her grandson.

Word had gotten out about her treats, and traffic held steady until it was almost too dark to navigate the long stretch of Pinopolis Road. Disappointment settled in her stomach. She'd worn a denim button-down with white jeans and sneakers, donned silver jewelry, and done her hair. Not a single Wonder Woman or cat had appeared at her table. She finished the last sip of her wine.

Golf cart lights came whizzing up the road. The driver zipped past her station, then did a U-turn and stopped in front of her. Alston had mom-armed the two little girls sitting next to him to keep them inside the cart while he spun it around. They were bent over laughing.

"Grand Alston, that was fun. It's more fun riding with you when Mimi and Gigi aren't here." The cat girl next to him patted his shoulder.

"Don't tell them."

"We won't." Wonder Woman jumped out of the cart and headed toward Cantley. "Hey, Miss Candy, I hear you have kazoos and big bars of candy.

My name is Scarlett, and I love both of those things. This is Charlotte." She pointed at her little sister.

"Sorry, we're late." Alston helped the younger girl from the cart. "My sister made them have supper before they could trick-or-treat. And then I didn't realize how many houses would have treats out. We had to unload, which took a while because they," he paused and nodded toward the girls, "started dividing out the spoils."

"I'm glad you made it." She handed the girls their choice of candy and then dumped the remainder of her supply, adding extra kazoos "for Mimi and Gigi" to the overflowing jack-o-lantern buckets.

"I was hoping to spend more time with you, but I have to get the girls in as they have school tomorrow."

"I don't understand having school on or after a holiday." Scarlett spoke with authority.

"I agree with you," Alston commiserated. "But y'all need to finish categorizing your candy and go to bed eventually. You can't stay up all night. Mimi is taking you to school tomorrow since we're going on our trip, and she won't see you for a few weeks." Alston helped the smaller girl back to the cart. "Are you staying out a bit? Can I stop by after I drop them off? I wanted to—I don't know—I wanted to spend a few minutes with you. How did the adults react when you gave out the kazoos?"

"As expected." Cantley helped load Scarlett into the cart with her candy and kazoos. "I'm sorry you missed it. The kids loved the double treat, but some adults wore the face of a third-grade parent whose child brought home the recorder."

"I remember getting a recorder one year. I believe Mom made me practice outside as the acoustics were better." He grinned at the memory.

"I'm doing a burn bowl for Samhain later. Stop by, and you can join me."

"Can I have a beer while I'm burning the bowl?" The children's laughter caught his attention.

"Grand Alston, you don't burn the bowl. You write stuff on paper and burn it, so you'll forget it." Scarlett had her hands on her hips while she spoke.

"How the heck do you—you know what, never mind. I got stuff to forget."

"And you can have a beer or two too." Cantley winked at him as she folded her jack-o'-lantern tablecloth.

An hour later, they sat on her screened-in back porch overlooking the lake cove.

"This is mighty peaceful." He took a swig of beer.

"Thank you. I wanted to ask, why do the girls call you Grand Alston? Aren't you the great uncle?"

"Scarlett is a piece of work. She said that since my sister is her grandmother, it makes more sense that I'm her granduncle. No one could argue with her logic. Granduncle Alston was too wordy for Charlotte. Now I'm Grand Alston."

"Smart girl. Okay, have you written down what you wish to release that no longer serves you?" She waved a folded sheet of paper at him.

"Yep. When do we set this sucker on fire?"

"Now, if you'd like. The fire is ready. Want to walk down?" She rose and took the cushion from her chair. "Bring your cushion. I have everything set up down by the lake."

They walked the hundred yards to the lakeside, where she'd dumped a heap of sand and placed an iron cauldron on a stand in the sand. Small flames leaped from the black cauldron the size of a car's tire.

"Are you a witch too?" Alston whispered.

Chapter Two

Cantley's peal of laughter rang out across the smooth water. "No. You don't have to be a witch to incorporate rituals into your life. I've been doing this for a couple of years. It helps clear my brain. But I am going to ask you to meditate and breathe with me, okay?"

"Can do. I went to a few yoga classes at the base gym." He set his cushion down at the flickering flames. "Where'd you get the cauldron?"

"My mother. It's a family heirloom. She kept plants in it. I do, too, when I'm not using it for pagan rituals." She motioned for him to sit.

She led him in setting intentions and grounding themselves. The night enclosed them. An owl hooted in the distance. Leaves rustled. The cypress trees on one side of her property gave off their smoky, balsamic scent, joining the smell from the fire. He sat as still as she until she stood and held her paper to the flames. He waited until she dropped the remains in the fire and turned to face the lake. He took his turn and joined her.

She wiped a tear from her eyes, took a deep breath, and stared over the water. "Another beer, water, or some tea?"

"Do you mind if I head home after I put out the fire?"

"Nope. Completely understand."

She walked him to his car after he'd ensured the fire was out.

"Can I text you when I'm in Greece? I'd like to keep in touch." Alston stood with the door open.

"Yes, please."

They exchanged numbers.

"Thank you." He pocketed his phone.

"You are most welcome. Safe travels."

"That's the plan, and I'm a planner. This trip has been fine-tuned to the nth degree. If everyone stays healthy, it should be fantastic."

"Share photos."

"Will do." He got into his car. Closed the door. Opened it. Got out. "I will have one regret on this trip, and it's if I don't ask you if I may kiss you."

She nodded. He walked toward her.

"No regrets." She opened her arms and wrapped them around his neck. The warm, soft kiss turned firm and urgent. They broke apart. He pulled her in for an embrace. She rested her head on his chest, listening to his pounding heart.

"That should hold you until your return." She bussed his cheek and patted his shoulder, resisting the urge to drag him into her house to her bed.

"Not quite, but I'll make do." His long look gave her shivers.

Friday, November 22, 2019

Alston updated Cantley with frequent texts and photos of his time in Greece. In the meantime, she took care of things she'd been putting off and worked out at Jimmy's Gym. Her attitude had improved immensely, per her daughter.

Just landed his latest text read. He told her he would drop off his parents and run errands for them.

Anything I can do to help? she texted back, holding on to a small hope she would see him in person today.

No, but thanks. Need to unpack their meds and pick up a package at the post office before they close. I wanted to see you. I'm exhausted.

Still on for our date tomorrow night? We have a seven o'clock reservation at 82 Queen. She replied.

It's highlighted on my calendar. Can't wait to see you when I'm not thinking about my pillows or my underarms. We've been in airports for twenty-four-plus hours.

Cantley puttered around her empty house and then decided she might be able to "casually" catch Alston at the post office. She walked down Pinopolis Road, bouncing a tennis ball off the pavement. No car was parked out front of the post office. She peeked in the foyer but didn't see anyone. Then she wondered why she did that at all. He was exhausted. He surely would not have walked up to get the package. She waved at the postal worker and left.

Deep in her thoughts, she continued bouncing the ball from hand to hand and headed toward the tip of the Peninsula. A car approached. She caught her ball and automatically moved toward the grass, ensuring the driver saw her.

"Hey," Alston said through the rolled-down passenger window. He pulled over and stepped out of the car. "I had hoped I'd get to see you."

"Me too." She walked to him. "I know you had a wonderful trip, but I'm glad you're back"

"My parents teased me about being on my phone more than usual. They noticed that I seemed happier than usual." He gave her a quick hug and pulled away, looking into her eyes. "Does it seem weird that I missed you when we just met?"

If he didn't hear her heart thump louder in reply, the look on her face must give her away. "Not weird. No regrets, remember?"

"May I kiss you?" He waited half a second for her to nod yes before pulling her deeper into his arms and giving her the kiss of a lifetime. He grabbed her hair and twisted his hand into it. "You have lovely blond hair. I think I will dream about it."

His lips met hers again. He tasted like cinnamon.

He patted his heart when they released one another. "Now I can sleep."

"Glad to help." She wasn't certain her legs would get her back home. Her entire body wanted to take him in the backseat of his Mercedes.

"I will pick you up at . . . wait, did we decide? No? See you at eighteen hundred hours? Will that give us time?"

"Yes, tomorrow, six o'clock." She stepped back to the grass.

He waved his arm out the driver's side window and over the roof as he drove away. She tottered on her feet before heading back home.

Saturday, November 23, 2019

The next night, they walked into the alley leading to the host stand at 82 Queen. The host led them to a patio table on a small half-circle-raised area. The ride downtown had been filled with conversations about Greece and traveling. Now they sat in silence, looking at the menus.

"Is this where you've taken all your first dates?" Cantley adjusted her menu to read it better.

He'd put on readers. "You are my first, first date here. In the past, I'd take my dates to the club on base because face it, I was a boring Navy admiral who didn't know better. I had a lot of first dates that never had seconds, except for Donna."

"Your ex?"

"No." He sighed. "I'm ashamed of both stories, actually. My ex got pregnant when I was on deployment and tried to make me believe the baby was mine. The math didn't work. Like at all. I got a quickie divorce, and she married the father."

"Wow."

"Yep. And I would have loved to have been a daddy. Anyhoo, I don't think I'm ready to tell you about Donna yet."

"You brought her up, but I won't pry. We'll wait until the right time." The sip of wine she took next didn't taste as good as the others, and she was sure her conflicted emotions reflected on her face.

"Hey, look." He leaned over to take the hand she'd rested on the table. "I'll tell you now and get it over with." He visibly took a breath. "Donna had visions of being an admiral's wife. We'd gone out a few times. I liked her but not like that. She kept coming over unannounced, claiming me at parties and booking tee times with my group if there was an opening. I swear she took a house key as I'd find her inside at times when I knew I'd locked the door."

"A stalker?"

"Definitely." He let go of her hand and rubbed his face. "Sadly, I was lonely and enjoyed the attention at first, but when I would go out with other women, she'd scare them away, or she'd tell them we were dating when we weren't."

"Poor thing. She sounds like she was lonely too. Where is she now?"

"In Tennessee. I partially moved to start fresh and to make a clean break with her. I tried not to hurt her feelings, but I'd done that for years."

He paused. "She and my mom became friends somehow. She calls Mom on the regular, and they talk. I've been ignoring Mom's questions about her. Mom can be a bit overbearing in some ways, but she means well."

"Oh dear. That's sad. Has Donna contacted you since you left?"

"She texts, and I text back single-word replies a few days later, or she'll start calling." He showed her the text history on his phone.

She noted the incoming texts were long and frequent, and the outgoing were few and short. *Not a liar, thank goodness.*

"I'm blocking her now." He pressed a few buttons on his phone. "Do you tell people you're blocking them or just do it?"

"I have no idea."

"Well, it's done without a forewarning, but she's had many. I don't want her bothering me when I'm with you." He gave her a hopeful look again. "Whew, I feel relieved. I should have done that sooner."

"Perhaps." Under the small wrought iron table, she rubbed his knee that had invaded her space.

Their server interrupted the moment to take their orders.

The after-dinner walk took them down King Street. The normally bustling city sidewalks were silent the week before Thanksgiving. They walked through Charleston Place, ended up on Meeting, cut through the City Market's open shed area, and continued to the Cooper River.

They turned to face one another. He lifted a hair that had blown into her face. She took a step forward, and they embraced. All the feelings—the tingles, the heartbeats, the warmth low in her belly—happened instantly.

A family walked past them, the children giggling. One made a kissing sound.

"I would love to continue this somewhere not so public." Alston took her hand and they returned to his car.

Cantley fastened her seatbelt. "Okay, let's change the subject. Do you pull for Carolina or Clemson since you have no dog in the hunt?"

"I pull for the Naval Academy first and Carolina second; my mother graduated from there. I like to increase my chances of inheritance when possible." He laughed. "I'm kidding about the inheritance part, you know."

"As long as you don't pull for Clemson, I don't care." She lightly squeezed him in the shoulder.

By the time they reached her house, it was after ten. He'd yawned the last few miles. "Can I see you in and then find my pillow?"

"You don't have to get out of the car." She started to open her door.

He reached over to stop her. "I am opening your car door, escorting you to your front door—"

Cantley interrupted his words by grabbing his face to kiss him. The warmth of his mouth and the eagerness of his reaction tempted her to climb over the console to gyrate on his lap.

Chapter Three

They laughed at the fogged-up windows after they pulled apart and exited the car. The porchlight led them to her door. The vibrations from the kiss drifted to her hand. She had difficulty getting her key in the lock.

"Here, let me help." He took the key, sliding it in easily.

She caught herself mid-sigh and took back her key. "Thank you for a lovely evening."

"I hope to spend even more time showing you off in the future. After I get over this jetlag." He yawned.

She turned him around and pushed him toward the porch steps. "Text me when you get home, so I don't worry. Are you certain you won't sleep here? I have extra bedrooms."

"I have a cat. You've probably noticed her black hair. I try to wear black to disguise it. Anyway, she's pissed at me for being away so long. I'm trying to make up with her."

"What's her name?"

"Guess."

"Hmmm, black cat, how about, Midnight?"

"Bingo. I didn't use much imagination in naming her. I need to head home to cuddle if she'll allow it. I'm glad you accepted my invitation tonight."

"Me too."

She waited on the porch until she saw tail lights turning left.

As she got ready for bed, a twinge of envy ached in her chest as she envisioned his arms around a purring black kitty instead of her body.

Her phone pinged with a text notification.

"Sweet dreams. I meant to ask if you'd like to go do something tomorrow. Visit Mepkin Abbey or Cypress Gardens? I have a list of places I want to see around here. I could pick you up at thirteen hundred hours if you don't mind a late lunch."

"Yes. See you tomorrow. Get some rest."

Sunday, November 24, 2019

Alston greeted her with a kiss at the door before escorting her to his car.

"It's going to get up to sixty-six degrees today." He put his Mercedes in gear and did a three-point turn. "I meant to tell you; my parents expect me at their house every Sunday at six o'clock for supper. Or did I tell you?"

"You did not. My kids call me every Sunday night about that time." Cantley adjusted her seatbelt over her garnet long-sleeved T-shirt topped with a Carolina zip-front sweatshirt. "Where are we going?"

"Mepkin Abbey. Check the backseat. I brought a cooler and a picnic basket. My tour guide neighbor makes these delicious charcuterie-filled boxes. I asked her to fix up the entire food and beverage detail for our outing today."

"Perfect. Trina makes beautiful cheese boards." She peered in the backseat.

"Ah, you know Trina, of course. She gave me notes for the day. Have you ever been to the Abbey?" He pulled a sheet of paper out of his pocket.

"I haven't been to Mepkin since the monks started growing mushrooms instead of eggs."

"Well, good, you can help me find my way. I'm used to Southern directions, but I found myself nodding my head at Trina when she rattled off how to get there." They both laughed.

"Keep drivin', and I'll tell you where to turn."

Cantley filled the scenic drive with local stories and gossip. When they arrived at the Abbey, Alston stopped in the gift shop so they could use the facilities and gave a generous donation before leaving it.

"When I was little, there was nothing here but a pole with a bell. You'd park your car, ring the bell, and the one monk who was allowed to speak would talk to you." Cantley gestured in the direction of the bell's former location.

Alston held her door open for her. "Now, that would have been an experience."

They took the road to the public gardens and unloaded the picnic supplies. They chose a sunny spot on the riverbank near a live oak dripping in

Spanish moss and the ubiquitous resurrection fern. Trina had included a thick blanket and all the accouterments for a perfect picnic.

"Want me to read Trina's notes while we dine?" Alston waved a sheet of paper.

Cantley nodded but groaned a bit. "I love pickled okra but hate pickles. Am I weird?"

"Maybe, but I'll try not to judge. She made individual salads, too, and included these tiny bamboo forks. They are like toothpicks."

Cantley tossed him a bottle of hand sanitizer. "Eat with your hands. It's a judgment-free zone."

He weighed down Trina's paper with an apple. "Okay, here goes. Cusabo people called this area Makkean. Henry Laurens purchased it from the person who took it from the Cusabo. He or someone before him called it Mepkin. It's most likely a derivation of the Cusabo's word. Laurens owned about three hundred enslaved people. She wanted to ensure we note the hardships these people suffered in the mosquito-laden heat, their work, and their freedom denied."

"Human history was not kind to a vast group of humans."

"It was not." They chewed their last bite, swallowed, and sat looking over the Cooper for a moment.

Alston continued reading. "Wait. Here's an interesting maybe-fact: Henry Laurens was one of the first South Carolinians to be cremated, and the monks have a columbarium now."

"Full circle, interesting." Cantley brightened as she remembered a tidbit of her own. "Have you seen *Hamilton*, the Broadway show?"

"Yes."

"Alexander Hamilton's friend, John Laurens, the one who wanted to arm the enslaved, let them fight against the British, and receive their freedom?"

Alston nodded.

"He's buried over there." She pointed to her left.

"No way."

"Folks around here say if the monks didn't own this land, it should be a national landmark because John's father, Henry Laurens, was our real first president. This is our Mount Vernon. Though the house is gone, it was over there." She pointed in the other direction.

"Trina says Henry was the president of the Continental Congress when the Constitution was signed. He was captured by the British and held in the Tower of London."

Cantley refilled their wine glasses.

"Henry Luce and Clare Boothe Luce bought Mepkin Plantation in the 1930s and hired the famous landscape designer, Loutrel Briggs, to create the gardens. They're buried here, too, this other Henry and Clare, and Clare's mother and daughter," Alston read.

"Clare wrote *The Women*, another Broadway play," Cantley remembered.

"I've seen it; had no idea who wrote it, though. She was an ambassador and the first female congresswoman from Connecticut."

"They were a power couple since he founded *Time* magazine. If memory serves, they split this land after her daughter died in a car crash, sold part to a lumber company, and gave the rest to the Trappist monks."

"Why do I need this write-up when you know everything she wrote?" He folded the paper and tossed it into the basket like a frisbee.

Cantley shrugged. "Trina knows way more."

"I'm glad you enjoy being a tourist in your hometown. Want to pack up and explore?" Alston wiped his mouth with a napkin and gathered his debris.

"Yes, sir, please."

They took their time walking the grounds, holding hands as the day wound down.

They took a break from walking, and Alston leaned on a railing. "This is nice, but they're closing up. My mother expects me at her house in a bit."

"It has been lovely. Thank you for inviting me." She turned her face toward his. They stood close. It felt right to tilt her face for the kiss, which turned into another, giving her a tingle all the way to her toes.

Monday, November 25, 2019

"The worst part of being off work is making up the days instead of exploring the area with you." Alston had called her the evening before; it was now Monday lunchtime.

"I'm enjoying this sixty-degree day and getting some stuff done in my yard."

"I am taking Wednesday off. Dad and my brother-in-law got a tee time." He paused. "Are your kids coming for Thanksgiving?"

Cantley sighed. Her son had arranged to go to his roommate's home in Pennsylvania. "My son's skiing, and my daughter's with her in-laws in Summerville."

"Come to our house. There will be plenty of food. Mom says she has a surprise for me, which means fried peach pies for dessert. If I'm lucky."

Wednesday, November 27, 2019

Cantley boiled water, then grabbed dish soap and a scrubbing brush. She'd set up the umbrella near the end of her road again and took down the six bluebird houses she'd hung around her property. This task had been on her list since August, but she felt like doing it today. She washed the bird-houses and left them to air dry on the table. Next up, she pressure-washed the stepping stones leading to her dock and back porch.

Exhausted, she took a shower and made a cup of herbal tea. She dropped the towel she wore and climbed into her bed for an afternoon nap. As she stirred from her sleep, she revisited the dream about Alston she'd been enjoying. She opened her bedside table and perused her toy collection. She had her favorites but thought she needed to spread the joy to the others, as they might feel neglected. Lately, she'd been using them a lot. She sent a mental thank you to her doctor and whoever invented hormone replacement therapy.

A flash of lightning caught her attention and sent a memory of her umbrella sitting near the road. The wind blew rain at her window. She dropped her vibrator. Throwing on one of her late husband's oversized Carolina T-shirts that came below her knees that she'd been using as nightshirts. Not bothering with pants, she ran down the steps to her front porch, peering at her driveway. Sheets of rain pelted the earth. She ran toward the street.

"I really need to get this paved," she thought as she slipped on the wet dirt. "Crap."

The umbrella was gone. The wind hit her back, so she figured the umbrella's flight would head toward the end of the peninsula. She took off after it.

A dark car passed her, and a wave of water splashed her legs.

Chapter Four

The driver slowed to a stop and opened his door. He got out in the pouring rain and shielded his eyes from the torrential downpour. "Cantley?" Alston called out. "Why are you running in the rain? Without shoes?"

She caught up with him and sputtered, "Umbrella." She pointed in the direction of the tumbling umbrella.

"Get in my car. We'll catch it. Dad's in the front seat. Jump in the back."

"I'm soaked."

"Me too. Get in the damn car."

"Yes, sir." In she got, and off they went in pursuit of the errant umbrella.

The umbrella stopped its roll into a ditch. They cautiously approached it. But as soon as they were close, it took off again.

"If you can touch it, you can catch it," Alston's dad hollered from his lowered window.

"Dad! We don't need your coaching." Alston dove for the object, and it flipped over, knocking him in the shoulder.

"Are you okay?" Cantley yelled over the storm's roar.

"I think your umbrella is possessed."

She triumphantly caught the umbrella as it slid toward the ditch that ran by the side of the road. "Got it!"

"Score." Yelled the older man who'd stepped out of the car and now made a touchdown motion with his arms.

Cantley and Alston brushed rain and tears of laughter from their eyes. She fought to close the umbrella until Alston came to her aid.

"Let's take this apart and put it in my trunk," he suggested, obviously trying not to stare at her chest.

Cantley glanced down to see what held his attention. Her nipples stood out from her wet shirt, emphasizing her curves.

"Best wet T-shirt contest ever," he muttered.

"Excuse me?" She teased.

He shook his head and took the umbrella from her. "Get in the car."

The ride to his parents' house took seconds. He helped his dad in while she tried to clean his seats with the towel he'd tossed her from the trunk. The house looked familiar, but the darkness and the rain obscured her view. She could swear her old house was across the street, but she'd taken out her contacts before her shower, and everything was a blur.

Alston returned to the car. "Let's take you home." They both got inside, and he looked over his shoulder as he backed out.

Cantley kept pressing the towel on the wet marks she'd made. "I've ruined your leather seats."

"It's leather. Cows stand in the rain a lot."

"Eww."

"You mean moooo." He slapped the armrest.

"Oh, my word. Okay. Get me home. I'm wet."

"Then I'm halfway there."

"Ha ha—oh shit! All I'm wearing is a T-shirt. I am used to wearing them like they're dresses around the house. Your dad saw me."

"You look beautiful."

They'd arrived at her home, and he'd stopped in his regular spot. He helped her out of the car when the hailstorm began. They ducked their heads.

"Drive under the carport. There's room. My car's in the garage. Go." She pointed the way.

He did as he was told.

She stood under an outside shower hose washing dirt off her legs and feet.

"Are you trying to turn me on?"

"Maybe. Why? Are you turned on?" She flipped the hose to aim it at his chest.

"Very."

"Me too."

He grabbed the hose from her hand and streamed the water over them both. She laughed and wrapped her arms around his neck.

"There's a nice king-size bed upstairs." And then, the memory hit her. "Wait—"

"Sweetie, I don't think I can." His lips captured hers.

She whispered in his ear. "I think I need to tell you something."

"Hurry."

"I was, uh, taking a nap. And naps make me, uh, horny. I—crap, you're going to see anyway." She tugged his arm and led him into her house and bedroom. He looked over her bed at the toys strewn all along the cover.

"Which is your favorite?"

"See, I was trying not to play favorites, and you—"

He kissed her again.

"Ah, you just want me for my body," he whispered in her ear, sending shivers down her spine.

"It's a nice body."

He pressed her into the bed. "So, I'm better than a toy?"

"Perhaps."

He proved himself right.

Thursday, November 28, 2019—Thanksgiving Day

"I've never enjoyed a holiday more." Alston kissed the top of her head.

"It's been nice. What time are you supposed to be at your parents' house?"

"In a couple of hours. I have a few things I'm supposed to bring, like . . ."

"Butter?"

"Yes. Butter and eggs, as those are things my mother runs out of most, though my brother-in-law is doing most of the cooking."

"I can make a quick macaroni pie casserole."

"Don't go to any trouble."

"It's an easy family recipe. Should I go to the gym first to work off the calories?"

"Let's have one more work out here, and it'll suffice."

After he left, Cantley boiled the noodles, grated the cheeses, and brought out the saltine crackers, pepper, milk, and butter for her recipe.

When Alston arrived again a few hours later, she met him on the porch, casserole in hand.

They pulled into his parents' driveway, and she began laughing. "I know this house. It looked familiar last night. I grew up across the street. One of my best friends lived here. We had a treehouse near the water. It can't still be there."

"Remnants are standing. Dad wants me to fix it up for the girls. Let's go check it out before we go in." Alston opened her car door. They giggled like school children on their way to the water leaving all the items they brought in the car.

Once they reached what was left of the treehouse, they dove for one another, and he pressed her against a pine tree.

"You need to work on my treehouse." She pulled him closer.

"Then we can fool around inside it." He pulled up her sweater to kiss her breasts. She did not protest.

Cantley entered the back bathroom and shut the exterior door to fix her hair before catching up with Alston. Knowing the house had its perks. She ran her fingers through her hair to remove some bark and pine needles. She flipped her head upside down to brush out more into the tiny trash can. The pocket door that led into the house slid open, and a tiny face leaned down to see her. Cantley straightened up and smiled.

"Scarlett, isn't it? We met on Halloween. I'm Miss Cantley."

"I remember you, Miss Candy. Whatcha doin'?"

"Fixing my hair before I meet the rest of your family." The glimpse she caught of herself in the mirror didn't look promising. Being upside down had brought all the blood to her head.

The child's face brightened, and she crawled onto the closed toilet seat. She stood on tiptoes and reached into a basket, holding a comb in her small hand. "Turn around; I comb Mama's hair and I'm gentle."

Cantley did as requested and felt a tug on her scalp but didn't yelp as she'd have liked.

"Where's Grand Alston?"

"Getting the macaroni pie out of the car for me."

"Is it sweet?"

"What? The pie? Oh. No. You'd probably call it macaroni and cheese."

Another pull of hair and a grunt came from the girl. "That's my favorite."

"I'm glad that I made it then. Almost done?" Tears formed in Cantley's eyes.

"Yep. Miss Candy?" She handed the comb to the woman. "Can you have two dates for Thanksgiving?"

"Thanksgiving changes dates, but it's always the fourth Thursday." The child had done a surprisingly good job, even if the comb was filled with blond hair. Cantley cleaned the comb and deposited the debris in the trash can. She handed back the comb for Scarlett to place it where it belonged.

"I think Grand Alston's in trouble." Scarlett patted Cantley's shoulder and hopped down from the toilet lid.

"Why is that?" A sense of dread came over her. Her stomach flip-flopped.

"You're prettier. I like your sweater." Scarlett touched the stitched rosette on Cantley's top.

"Thank you. Prettier means you are comparing me to someone. Why is Grand Alston in trouble?"

"It's not my secret to tell, but take a deep breath. Everything's going to be okay. I'll hold your hand." Scarlett led her out of the bathroom and down the hallway to the sunroom.

The sunroom hadn't opened to the breakfast area when she'd last visited her friend at this house. The elderly man from the night before sat in a recliner watching a rerun of Macy's Thanksgiving Day Parade. Cantley pressed her free right hand on her cigarette pants to wipe off a sheen of sweat. Her heart thumping against her ribcage was a deafening sound in her ears.

"GG Pete? This is Miss Candy. She gave us big bars of candy and kazoos at Halloween." Scarlett tightened her grip on Cantley's hand.

The older man lowered the foot of the recliner, looking over his shoulder toward the kitchen and back at Cantley. The confused look on his face spoke volumes.

He peered at Scarlett. "Can you go find Grand Alston for us, please?"

Scarlett pulled on Cantley's hand and forced her to lean down. "I told you he was in trouble."

"Scarlett? Did you hear me?"

"Yes, sir. But I promised Miss Candy I'd stay with her."

The man stood and approached them. "I see. Well, I agree. Keep holding her hand. I'm Pete Pike." He held out his hand. "You can call me Pete. Now let's go see where that son of mine might be. Though I think it's GiGi who's really in trouble, Miss Candy."

"It's actually Cantley."

"Cantley. Got it. Vivian!" he hollered as he entered the breakfast area.

"I'm right here. You don't have to shout." A woman about Pete's age wiped her hands on a kitchen towel as she rounded the wall. "Oh." She stopped and bumped her hip on the counter. "Hello."

A knock at the French doors in the breakfast area called their attention away from one another.

"Grand Alston!" Scarlett waved at him, pointing at Cantley and then toward the kitchen, eventually making the sliced-throat gesture before she noticed her great-grandparents and Cantley staring at her. "I found him." She wiggled her fingers in his direction.

Chapter Five

Cantley released Scarlett's hand, straightened her back, and walked to the French doors. She opened them and took her casserole dish from his hands. He had a bag of items he'd brought in the other.

"Thank you. Why is everyone staring at me? What's going on with Scarlett?" Alston kissed Cantley's cheek, which caused the adults in the room to gasp and the child to giggle.

"Scarlett?" GiGi had her hands on her hips.

"Yes, ma'am?"

"Take the bags to your mother."

"But I have to hold Miss Candy's hand."

"Scarlett, I'm not asking." Gigi pointed.

"Yes, ma'am."

Alston handed the girl the bag and gave her a quizzical look. "Am I in trouble?"

"It's complicated." The girl took the bag and skipped her way into the adjoining kitchen.

Cantley placed the macaroni dish on the breakfast table and extended her hand to the older woman. "I'm Cantley Broughton. I own the yellow house with the flowering bushes out front. My best friend lived here when I was growing up. I lived across the street." She gestured in the general direction of her childhood home.

"I'm Vivian. Welcome back."

They shook hands.

"I seem to have been invited without the hosts' knowledge. I think I might be the third wheel. Or have I interpreted the situation incorrectly?" Cantley spoke to the older woman.

Pete answered instead. "I like this one. She can read a room." He nodded at his son.

"Mother, I told you I'd have a date. Who'd you invite?" Alston crossed his arms over his chest.

241

"I assumed it was Donna, of course." Vivian looked over her shoulder toward the kitchen and back at him, making a shush gesture.

Three women entered the breakfast area almost simultaneously. They all stopped laughing when they saw the group before them.

The older-looking one spoke. "Um, we have carried out all the trash and loaded up the garage fridge. Who do we have here, little brother?" She stepped forward.

"This is Cantley. My date." Alston inched closer to Cantley and placed his arm around her waist.

A gasp arose from one of the other two women. "Alston, you're dating someone behind my back. Is this why you moved? For her?"

"Donna. We've talked about this. We have never been in a relationship."

Cantley stepped away from Alston. "I gotta go. Y'all enjoy the macaroni pie and rolls." She stepped toward the French doors.

Alston placed his hand around her wrist. "Please don't leave."

"It's fine. The weather is perfect for a walk. It was nice to meet you." She waved to the older couple and left.

Donna walked to Alston and took his arm. "I've been looking forward to spending this weekend with you and your family."

"And had anyone," he paused and directed this statement to his mother, "bothered to ask me, I would have nixed this plan. I thought blocking you on my phone would have been the final bell."

"You blocked me?" Donna's face turned red. "Was it because of her?"

"Donna. Don't start. This has nothing to do with Cantley. I need you to understand."

"But I don't . . ." Tears streamed from Donna's eyes. "We can make a go of this. I can move here. We can date. Start slow."

"No. A thousand times no." Alston looked at his family. "I told y'all there was a stalker. Well, she's here now. Will y'all kindly help Donna figure out her next move? I will pay for her flight home, no matter the cost. I need to check on my date."

"Go, son. I got this." Pete took Donna by the arm and led her to the couch, giving his wife the stink eye the entire time.

"Thank you. And here I thought my surprise was fried peach pie." Alston sighed and walked out.

"Fuck!" He took off at a jog toward his car.

He caught up with Cantley near the post office. "Please get in the car. I need to talk to you."

She shook her head no.

"Please, we can salvage this day. Let's talk," he begged from his window.

He sped up and parked at the post office. Getting out, he waited for her with his arms open.

She walked past him. "So that's Donna."

He jogged to keep up with her. "I had no idea she'd be there. She must have cajoled Mom into inviting her."

"I'm embarrassed, I'm mad, and I'm sad." She plopped onto the post office's short steps.

He sat beside her. "Are you hungry too? We can try the Waffle House. They're always open."

"No, thank you." She leaned on his shoulder.

"No, I didn't know. I'm not playing a game here. I'm sorry that happened. My mom meant well, I suppose." He wrapped his arm around her.

He took her home and returned to his parents to straighten things out. He texted her updates as the day wore on.

Friday, November 29, 2019

A knock came early the next morning at Cantley's door. Alston's mom stood on her porch with her casserole dish and a covered plate. They exchanged greetings. Cantley invited her to sit in a rocking chair after offering to get her a drink.

"I'm here to apologize. I ruined Thanksgiving for everyone."

"Apology accepted, though you aren't to blame for all of it."

Vivian bowed her head. "I didn't know Donna was a stalker. She seemed so nice on the phone."

Cantley nodded. "I hope she gets some help."

"Yes." Vivian nodded too. "Oh, my word, the children were so confused. Scarlett sent you this." She handed her a full-sized candy bar from her purse. "She said when she's sad, she eats chocolate, which makes it better. We probably need to work on her coping skills."

Cantley took the candy. "I think she has a lot to teach us."

They had a long conversation, and Cantley gave the older woman a tour of her yard. After the visit, she walked down to the post office and found a line out the door. A neighbor waved at her.

"What's the holdup?" Cantley stood on her toes to see into the post office.

"I'd say a good-looking man is checking his mail, and word got out, but he can't remember the code to open the box."

"Oh dear. I think I know who that is." She caught a glimpse of the back of Alston's head as she peeked in the window. "Let me go help him."

Everyone stepped aside to let her through.

She tapped Alston on his shoulder. "Why are you trying to open my mailbox?"

"I'm opening my parents' . . . no, I'm not. No wonder I couldn't crack the code." He moved up a box. "I'm discombobulated today."

"I bet." She patted his shoulder and returned to the back of the line.

He walked out with rolled-up magazines under his arm. "Can we talk?"

All the people in the line waited for her to answer. The neighbor she'd been speaking with nudged her.

"Give me a sec to grab my mail." She nudged her neighbor back to get her to move up.

She grabbed her mail, and they headed to her house. Once there, she settled herself on a porch rocker.

"Let me apologize for a horrible Thanksgiving. I made my mom cry. I haven't made her cry since I was a teenager."

"Oh, I bet you've worried her more than she lets on."

"Point taken. She said didn't know the stalker was Donna. I'm a grown-ass man. I am ashamed this happened."

"Oh, honey, I don't think it was your fault. That had to feel awful." Cantley had been rocking her chair but stopped at his last sentence.

"It won't happen again. I'm not planning on breaking up with my current love."

"Love?"

"Truthfully? Yes. Wow. I can't believe I'm saying this. I've fallen hard for you." Alston scooched his chair closer to hers.

"I'm going to need more time." Her heartbeat and the rock of the chair competed for sound space in her ears.

"I should have nipped it in the bud quicker. The older you are, the more the lessons and heartache, right?"

"Indeed. Speaking of, where's Donna?"

"She flew back to Memphis this morning. The ticket price was astronomical."

"Bless her heart. It's weird to feel sorry for her and be glad she's gone too."

"Exactly."

"Want to do something this evening?" She stood and held out her hand.

"I do. Do you like cats? Midnight needs attention. Dinner and a movie at my house?" He stood and brought her in close.

"I love cats. Wanna watch the Palmetto Bowl tomorrow?" She ran her finger along his chest.

"My parents asked me to invite you to their house for the game and a second try at their version of Southern hospitality." He lifted her chin and kissed her.

She pulled away to speak. "Oh, by the way, your mother stopped by to apologize, and your dad didn't mention seeing me basically naked, so I'm happy." They moved to the bedroom.

Later that evening, Midnight accepted Cantley. By the end of the night, the three of them were snuggled in Alston's bed.

Saturday, November 30, 2019

Alston picked Cantley up two hours before the noon kickoff. Clemson won, but Carolina scored a field goal. The celebration for not getting skunked included fried peach pies, kazoos, full-sized candy bars, the cat separating the new couple on the love seat, and no regrets.

End

About Robin Hillyer Miles

Robin is a native South Carolinian, born in the Upstate and raised in the Lowcountry. She lives happily in a small town on the outskirts of Charleston with her husband, son, and dog. This is her second published short story. She writes contemporary romance with a hint of magic realism.

Follow Robin online:
Facebook at https://www.facebook.com/ RobinHillyerMilesAuthorTourGuideYoga
Follow her on Instagram at https://www.instagram.com/rhillyer_miles/
Follow her Amazon author page at https://www.amazon.com/~/e/ B07YN9P3T6

Second Chances

By Victoria Houseman

Second Chances

Suspense

Dr. Tessa Stone's world fell apart when her fiancé, Detective Graham Fincher, accused her of murdering a terminally ill patient. Throwing herself into her work at the hospital, Tessa's determined to forget about Graham.

When Tessa's best friend is almost murdered, she vows to focus only on Ethan's healing and helping the police find Ethan's would-be murderer.

When Graham is assigned to Ethan's case, Tessa doesn't know if she can keep her heart protected.

The moment she sees Graham again, looks into his beautiful eyes, she wonders if she was wrong about him. Could she love him again?

Rated: R

Prologue

Valentine's Day is a made-up holiday. The cringeworthy cards, way too much chocolate, over-priced special dinners for two. I knew it, and I just didn't care. I loved Valentine's Day, especially with my love. It's said love at first sight doesn't exist, but it does. It happened to me. The figurative bolt of lightning between the eyes, my heart beating rapidly when Graham was near, the weak knees. It's all true.

We spent our first Valentine's Day together at my home. We cooked a simple meal, watched a movie, made love, and then got engaged. When he'd asked me, I couldn't say yes fast enough.

The day after Valentine's Day, it all fell apart.

Graham accused me of murder.

Chapter One

I stayed up during the night holding the hand of my best friend. He'd been shot. The nicest, most giving man in the world and some maniac sent a bullet tearing through him. His brain activity looked good, so my fear of having to turn off the life support machine was a low rumble in the back of my mind. If I could keep him stable for at least forty-eight hours, there was hope he'd make it.

I talked to him about our friendship, beginning when we met when we were nine years old. I covered a quarter of a century of memories until I couldn't talk anymore. I took long, slow sips from the water bottle a nurse had left for me, feeling only slight relief as it soothed my parched throat.

"Ethan, I vow I will find out who did this to you." My voice barely above a whisper. I looked out the window. The lifting darkness brought dawn over the ocean with colors of orange and yellow streaking the sky.

After ER staff worked on him, and surgeons did their thing to repair the damage from the bullet, it was past midnight. He was brought to the ICU where I was the chief physician. Fortunately, I wasn't the doc on-call tonight. They put him into an induced coma and intubated Ethan to give his body and his brain a chance to heal. The machines helping him breath, tapped out a steady rhythm. I found their dependability soothing. The quiet repetitiveness.

"Tessa."

The deep, familiar voice caused me to tense, my back ramrod straight, putting my stomach in knots. This was not a conversation I wanted to have, especially not with Graham Fincher. Detective Graham Fincher of the Charleston PD.

"Tessa…" He kept his deep voice low, soft. Memories of our time together came flooding back.

"Graham." I refused to turn around and look into his beautiful face that held so much betrayal. "You need a statement from me?" Now, more than ever, I needed to stay angry at him to keep my heart safe. This was about finding out who shot Ethan, and not how Graham had shredded my soul last year.

One of the nurses entered to check on Ethan.

"I'll be in my office. Let me know, immediately, if anything changes." I didn't mean to sound like a bitch, but stress, exhaustion, and now Graham was a terrible combination.

"Yes, Dr. Hughes." Janey and I had worked together for years on the ICU, but I could tell by her wide-eyed expression she was shocked at my tone when speaking to her. Letting out a heavy sigh, I tried to give her a smile, but my face felt frozen and the most I could muster was a nod of my head.

Getting up, I almost knocked into Graham's chest, not realizing how close he stood. My heartbeat rapidly, and my palms started to sweat. Damn him for still having an emotional hold on me.

Thrusting my hands in the pockets of my lab coat, I walked to the door. "Follow me to my office." Trying to hold my voice steady while my insides were roiling around took major strength.

Graham walked a few paces behind me, not talking. He knew me well enough to know not to speak when my stress level exceeded any measurement on a scale. There would be no wrapping myself in his strong arms, while crying against his chest. Not this time. This meeting would be only about Ethan.

Closing my office door behind me, I motioned for him to take a chair across from my desk as I sat down behind it. For the first time since he'd arrived, I couldn't avoid looking at him.

"I'll help you and the department any way I can in finding who did this to Ethan." Putting on my best professional face, I looked across my desk.

Graham gazed at me, into me, my heart and soul, and my breath left my body. His eyes were the first thing I'd noticed when we'd met. An ancient amber that held the wisdom of centuries.

Say something before you go across this desk and throw yourself on him, your body melting into his.

"Tessa, I'm so very sorry about Ethan. I need you to tell me everything you can, even if you think it's not important." He ran strong fingers through wavy dark hair. Fingers that were at times gentle as they touched every part of my body and fingers that could whip my body into a frenzy. I missed his hands on my body.

"I have no idea, I really don't. The whole thing is baffling." Focusing on who could've shot Ethan took my mind off Graham and...us. What we had, what could've been.

We discussed Lawrence Chambers, Ethan's ex-boyfriend. Lawrence worked at a high-end jewelry store. His designs are gorgeous, but as a boyfriend, he sucked.

"They only dated for six months, but you know Ethan. He loves with his entire heart." I sighed at my friend's terrible choice in men. "He thinks every guy he meets is 'the one'".

"But Ethan was living with you now?"

"He caught Lawrence with someone else...in bed. It broke his heart, but he packed up and came to my house that day. One thing about Ethan, he doesn't try to keep something going that has no hope."

"Is Chambers an angry person? Violent?" Graham took notes on a tablet.

"He's definitely a player, but a murderer? No."

After forty-five minutes of telling him every single detail of Ethan's life for the past few months, I wanted to wrap this up. Fortunately, other docs on the unit were helping me with my patients, but I wanted to get back to my friend and away from Graham.

I walked to the door and opened it.

Graham followed me and when he stopped, he stood way too close for comfort.

"Tessa," he whispered. His hand moved as though wanting to touch me, but he dropped it back to his side. "Please talk to me." I fought allowing the pain in his voice to shatter my carefully constructed shield around my heart.

"About?" Bitchiness came out, and I didn't care. "You have a job to do – find out who shot Ethan and why. My job is to keep him alive."

He opened his mouth, then slowly closed it again.

"Unless, of course, you think I did it just like you thought I murdered my patient last year." The arrow hit its intended target. His eyes shuttered as he backed away, ever so slightly.

"Tess. I never thought…" He sighed, running his hands through his thick, black hair. "I'll keep you apprised of anything I find out. Please let me know if Ethan's condition changes."

I nodded. I began to shut my office door as he was exiting, but he suddenly grabbed it.

"Tessa. Just so you know. I asked for Ethan's case."

Before I could say anything, Graham was halfway down the corridor.

I sat at my desk, trying to sort out the last hour with him. I hadn't seen him since the day I threw him out of my life. I thought I'd spent the last year healing my heart, mending my soul. He asked to be assigned to Ethan's case. Why? To run into me.

I left my office to go check on Ethan. I didn't want to think of the implications that Graham wanted to get back together.

Chapter Two

Before checking on Ethan, I called my younger sister, Delia. While as different as two sisters could be, we had an unbreakable bond.

She owned an art gallery in the heart of downtown Charleston. Thanks to her head for business and marketing, her gallery had become one of the most prominent in the South. Delia loved fine clothes, perfect makeup, and high heels that if I wore, I would break my neck. I wore scrubs at the hospital and sweats with oversized T-shirts at home. My make-up consisted of a swipe of lip gloss with a tint of color. We never judged one another. We had a glass of wine a couple of times a month and talked about life. Delia and Ethan loved to dress me up for dates. The dates usually sucked, but I looked great.

She answered on the first ring. "Tess?"

"Ethan's stable. But I'm not. Graham is the detective on the case." I refused to cry.

"I know, Tess. He's already called me. He wants to meet with me to talk about Ethan. See if there is anything I can think of that would help solve who did this."

"I'm going to check on Ethan, and then I'm going home to take a hot shower and rest for a bit."

"I'll meet you there."

Ethan made it through the first twenty-four hours without any crisis. Healthy color flooded Ethan's cheeks and his vital signs were stable. I kissed his forehead and whispered, "All right, E-man, don't let me down. I love you big time."

The drive home at dusk under a February sky always soothed me, gorgeous colors of peaches and blues streaking the sky while the sun slowly disappeared for the night. I drove with the window slightly down to breathe the crisp air deeply into my lungs.

Lights shone in my house letting me know Delia was inside. The wine glasses would be full, and appetizers would be artfully arranged on a plate. Eighteen months apart in age, we were further apart in everything else. Delia's blonde, silky hair fascinated people, while my dark curls couldn't be tamed. Lithe and petite, people always said Delia looked like a porcelain doll. Our family applauded me for my scholastic intelligence. We were both gifted with our mother's to-die-for blue eyes. No matter our differences, Delia and I would do anything for one another.

Walking into the kitchen through the garage, I was greeted by one hundred pounds of pure black Great Dane. At nine months old, Sampson stood taller than me with his paws on my shoulders. He knocked me into the closed door, and I winced.

"Sampson, down." He immediately went to his belly at Delia's command. Ethan's wonderful dog training showed.

I looked at her, my eyes wide.

"What can I say?" She grinned. "I have a way with dogs." Her smile faded. "If he's going to stay here, Tess, you're going to have to learn how to get him to listen to you. Especially a dog his size."

From the moment Ethan agreed to foster and train Sampson, they were inseparable. Sampson was a foster-fail at its finest.

"I let him run around the backyard once I let him out of his crate. He ate a good dinner and now it's time for you to eat." Delia pointed to the food and drink on my coffee table. "A combination of tomatoes, mozzarella, basil, and extra virgin olive oil. Pita chips. Nothing heavy, but you need something in you."

"You sure as hell didn't find this fine food in my fridge."

"I came prepared." Dee grabbed two small plates of food and nodded to the two glasses of wine. I picked them up and followed my sister out to my patio, Sampson right behind me.

We stretched out on wooden lounge chairs and ate our food in silence. Delia's cooking was legendary, but tonight's meal went down my throat like lead. I ate a few more bites, then put the plate on the side table and grabbed my wine.

"Thank you, Dee, delicious as always."

Dee looked at how little I'd eaten but didn't say anything. Instead, she picked up her wine glass and leaned toward me.

"To Ethan."

"To Ethan." We clinked glasses.

Sampson laid on the deck beside my chair. At the sound of the glasses, he put his giant head in my lap, gazing up at me with soulful brown eyes. I stroked his head while he pressed his cheek into my palm.

"You know I'm doing everything I can, puppy, don't you?" He let out a soft sound, almost like a moan. "We'll find who did this."

After washing the dinner dishes, I took the bottle of wine and our glasses to my sofa. With so little food in me, the alcohol wasted no time in giving me a slight buzz. I laid my head back on a cushion, feeling the wine course through every part of my body, down to my toes.

The doorbell rang, pulling me from my barely five-minute rest.

Delia walked to the door while Sampson stayed glued to my side

"Damn it," She muttered, "Lawrence, what are you doing here?"

I looked to the front door.

Ethan's ex, Lawrence Chambers, stood there, his normally perfectly pressed clothes disheveled, his eyes red-rimmed. He sobbed deep sounds that made his body shake.

Delia and I looked at one another, then looked at Lawrence. His crying seemed so disingenuous after the way he'd treated Ethan.

"Come in, Lawrence," I said.

Delia looked at me, her blue eyes opened wide. "What the hell?" she mouthed.

I shook my head, shrugged my shoulders. "Lawrence, would you like a glass of wine?"

"No, Tessa, I won't be staying long." His crying stopped. Pulling a monogrammed handkerchief from the pocket of his expensive shirt, he dabbed at his eyes.

"At least sit down while you're here."

He sat next to me on the couch. Delia sat in a wingback chair across from us, her eyes never leaving Lawrence. I rolled my eyes at my sister but gave her a small smile. At any second, I expected her to do the two-finger sign for "I'm watching you" to Lawrence.

Minutes passed, but Lawrence stayed silent. He sat like stone on the sofa, staring straight ahead.

I cleared my throat. "Lawrence, why are you here?"

"I really did love him." He sniffled. "I loved him more than I've ever loved anyone."

"If treating people like shit is how you show your love, I would hate to see how you treat your enemies," Delia said.

"Delia." I looked at her.

Delia raised her hands. "What? It's true."

"She's right, Tess. I'm not good at relationships."

Playing his therapist wasn't in my wheelhouse. "Look, Lawrence, it's really late."

"When he moved out, he accidentally took something of mine. I, um, I really need it back." He looked nervously around my living room.

"Excuse me?" Was he joking? "Lawrence, Ethan is in the hospital, hooked up to all kinds of machines, fighting for his life, and all you can think about is going through his belongings to find something of yours you say he took?" Suddenly I felt very sober and incredibly pissed off.

"I…I never loved anyone the way I loved Ethan." He repeated.

"Lawrence, I want you to leave. I have no idea what's wrong with you, but you're being creepy." I stood and walked to my door.

Sampson never took his eyes off Lawrence. Sampson stood when Lawrence stood. Though nowhere near the expert in dog behavior like Ethan, I sensed Sampson didn't like Lawrence. Ethan always told me dogs know who's good and who's evil.

Lawrence walked to the door with Sampson as his escort. Halfway out the door, Lawrence abruptly stopped and turned around. He looked down at the puppy sitting by my side.

"What is that ugly collar on Sampson? Ethan would never put him in such a common collar." He waved his hands in the air when he said 'common' as though it were a dirty word.

What the hell was he talking about? "I bought it for Sampson. It's a perfectly fine collar."

He pointed toward the sturdy collar on Sampson's neck. "Where's the one I made for him?"

I took a steadying breath. "Lawrence, Ethan could die, and this is what you're worried about? A dog collar?"

I slammed the door in Lawrence's face as he was about to say something. Never in my life had I'd done that, but damn, it had felt good.

Before I could sit back down, my doorbell rang. I pulled the door open with force.

"Lawrence, I told you--" I stopped. Graham stood in my doorway, wearing the blue jeans he knew drove me wild because of the sexy way they fit his beautiful ass and long legs. They looked like they were tailored for only him. His slightly wrinkled denim button-down shirt all but sent my need for him into hyperdrive.

"Graham..." Any other words stuck in my throat.

"Lawrence Sommers was just here? What did he want?" Graham became the suspicious detective.

"Tess, let the man in the house." Delia came up behind me.

I stood aside, allowing Graham to enter.

"I asked Graham to come over." She said, avoiding my gaze.

"Delia, it's almost ten at night." I made my voice as incredulous as I could. "You could've met Graham at his office in the morning."

"Tess, I have a lot going on at the gallery this week. This is the only time I have to speak with Graham about Ethan." She shrugged her shoulders. She motioned Graham to a chair in the living room.

Delia needed to understand that I had no intention of reuniting with Graham. Inviting him to my house so he could interview her was a weak excuse to get us in the same room.

Curling up in a chair, I half-listened to Delia and Graham's conversation. Adrenaline from Lawrence's bizarre visit left my body, and pure exhaustion set in. I laid my head against the back of the chair and closed my eyes.

Strong arms lifted me in the air, held me close. I nestled my forehead in the crook of his neck and curled into his arms. The safest place in the world – in his arms. For the first time in a long time, I could breathe.

"It's been an awful day for you, my love," Graham breathed into my hair. "You need sleep."

He gently laid me down on my bed, my head resting on my pillows. Drawing blankets over me, I felt him stretch out beside me, pulling me length-wise against him.

A feathery touch of lips grazed my temple, so soft, it might've been angel wings.

"If I could take back what happened last year, Tessa, I would. I knew you didn't kill your patient. I handled it like such an ass." He sighed, a sad sound. "I will love you until the day I die and beyond. If you never come back to me, if it means I die a broken, old man, I will carry you in my heart and soul, always."

I moved closer into his warm embrace, never wanting to leave. "I love you, too." I murmured, as. I sank deeper into his arms and drifted into sleep.

Sunshine flowed through my open blinds, landing brightly on my closed eyelids. I pulled the quilts over my head, but then everything rushed back. Especially my bizarre dream about Graham. Sitting up in bed, I noticed the bedding rumpled next to me, warm to the touch. Dreams didn't leave the sheets crumpled and warm.

"It's about time you woke up." Delia came in with a tray of food and steaming hot tea.

I sat up stone-like, staring at her.

"Here, take this." She handed me the mug of tea. "Yes, Graham stayed all night."

"What…" Now I knew it wasn't a dream. I'd slept all night in his arms, and it was the best sleep I'd had in over a year. I felt loved.

"You passed out on the chair while he and I were talking about Ethan. He carried you to bed and put you under the covers."

Too many thoughts and questions crowded my brain. I sipped my tea, not sure what to analyze first.

"Tessa, in all transparency, he tried to leave, but I wouldn't let him." She handed me the plate of a bagel with cream cheese and jam. "Eat."

"Delia. It's been over for a year between me and Graham." My argument sounded weak, even to me.

"Bullshit. Tessa, no matter how 'over him' you try to appear, Ethan and I know you want to get back together." She made a flourish of taking a bite of her bagel.

"He accused me of killing my patient. I thought he was my soulmate, the father of my future children, my ride or die, my person." My voice cracked. I took a large gulp of my tea in hopes it would stop me from crying.

"He never accused you of purposefully killing your patient. He questioned you, as is his job. He wanted to find out if there was maybe something you knew to help his case, but you immediately assumed the worst."

"What are you saying?"

"Tessa, bottom line. You jumped to conclusions, accused him of not trusting you, of not believing you, and you dumped him. You succeeded in slashing his heart and your heart to shreds."

I shook my head. "You're wrong."

"And you, my big sister, are totally stubborn. You'll never find anyone like Graham. The two of you were…magical." Delia looked wistful. For the first time I wondered if my successful, businesswoman sister was lonely.

"I need to shower and get to the hospital to check in on Ethan." My entire body felt grimy and I could barely work my fingers through my messy curls.

"You're changing the subject."

"Yes, I am." That's my safety mechanism when I didn't want to talk about something.

A hot shower with soap that softened my skin felt like a piece of Heaven on Earth. I stood under the showerhead while the water flowed over me. Water soothed me, calmed me, healed me.

It took all my willpower to turn off the water and wrap myself in an extra thick, warm towel. The towel Graham had wrapped around me after we'd showered together for the first time. We'd washed one another slowly, kissing, no words, just our bodies moving together under the hot spray. He'd carried me to my bed, laid me down, and we made love. Throwing the towel on the ground, I grabbed another one.

I dressed, went into the kitchen, and grabbed my car keys. Samson whined and put a huge paw on my thigh. "I'm sorry, baby, I didn't mean to ignore you. I'm going to see Ethan." I stroked his head. "Want me to give him a huge, slobbery kiss from you?" A deep woof told me all I needed to know.

"I'll be here when you get back. What do you want for dinner?" Delia shouted out to me as I walked to the garage.

"How about you gone? Seriously, Delia, please stay out of my love life."

"Okay, grilled steak it is." I didn't see the smile on Delia's face, but I knew it was there.

I whirled around. "Delia, Graham and I are over, kaput, finis. Please, I'm begging you, leave it alone." Too bad I couldn't make it sound convincing.

The most beautiful site greeted me in Ethan's room. His vital signs were better than I could've hoped for, especially his oxygenation and negative inspiratory pressure, the sign of his own ability to breathe on his own.

I squeezed his hand, kissed his forehead. "Keep coming back to me, Ethan. I need my bestie. I have so much to tell you. Sampson sends big, slobbery kisses."

Where's my grilled steak?" I called out to Delia when I got home. "I was looking forward to the wonderful smells of steak a la Delia on the grill."

"I'm in Ethan's bedroom."

Walking in, I saw Delia sitting on the bed, going through a box of Ethan's belongings. Boxes were strewn on the floor. Sampson sprawled beside her but wiggled his tail at warp speed when he saw me.

Sitting on the floor amidst the contents of Ethan's belongings, I gave Sampson a huge hug. "That's from daddy Ethan." His massive tail wagged so hard, it felt like fan blades on high. "Dee, what the hell are you doing?"

"Something Lawrence said bothered me. He wanted to search Ethan's things. He appeared nervous and agitated. What's he looking for?"

"I have no idea." I thought for a minute, then grabbed an unopened box. "We have no clue what we're looking for, but you're right. Lawrence's behavior was totally out of sync for him."

For the next hour, we searched the boxes Ethan hadn't yet unpacked when he moved in, hoping we would know 'it' when we found it.

Sitting back, exhausted, I pushed the last box aside. "This is futile, Dee. Ethan's clothes, some decorative items, nothing unusual in any of these boxes."

"The clothes hamper." Delia pointed to it in a corner of the closet.

I turned the hamper upside down, strewing its contents on the floor. Sampson let out a loud woof and came over to us. He stuck his nose in the clothes while pushing everything around with his paws. Dogs liked the scents of their person and Ethan's scent was all over the clothes in the hamper.

Sampson stopped, and looked at us, one large paw on a black draw string bag buried between the clothes.

When I opened the bag, a dog collar with gaudy rhinestones fell out. Totally not Ethan's style. A note lay deeper in the bag.

"Tessa, if you find this, you'll know what to do. I love you big. E."

I handed the note to Dee. "What the hell does this mean? Did he know he'd be shot?" Questions slammed into one another into my brain.

"Tessa." Delia turned the collar with stones around under the lamplight on the nightstand. I don't have my loop with me, but I'm pretty sure these aren't rhinestones. Those stones are real diamonds." She dropped the collar onto the bed as if it had burned her hand.

We both sat staring at the collar for a long, long time.

Chapter Three

'I don't understand." I turned the collar all around, staring at the stones, having no idea how to tell a piece of glass from a real diamond.

"Tess, remember all those shopping trips I took with mama? While you and daddy looked at dissected things under a microscope?" She took the collar in her hands. "She taught me about jewelry and art and everything designer. If these are real, they are near flawless and worth an obscene amount of money."

A chill went down my spine. What in the hell would Ethan be doing with these expensive stones? Definitely not his style. "Delia, do you think this is what Lawrence wanted? Do you think he shot Ethan for this collar?" Nothing made sense.

She sighed, running her hands through hair as straight as mine was curly. "We have to call Graham."

Graham turned the collar over in his gloved hands before putting it in an evidence bag. "Quite the expensive dog collar, don't you think, Sampson?" Sampson gave the bag a sniff and walked away. "I don't blame him. I wouldn't wear it."

Delia chuckled, but I made myself busy in the kitchen. I refused to acknowledge last night happened. "Who wants coffee?"

"Tessa." Graham stood behind me, so close we almost touched. Electricity crackled in small space between our bodies.

"You still take your coffee the same way?" My shaking hands dropped the bag of coffee in the sink.

"Tessa." The softness in his voice tore through me. He placed his hands on my shoulders, turning me to face him.

"Graham." The words stuck in my throat.

He cupped my face in his hands. "I love you, Tessa. That will never change. The day we met you unlocked my heart and claimed it for your own. Last night, you told me you still loved me."

"I remember." I thought I'd dreamt it, but I knew it was true.

"Tessa?" Delia interrupted, her voice soft. "The hospital called your cell phone. I answered it for you." She handed it to me.

"This is Dr. Hughes." I listened intently to the nurse on the other end, frowning. "I'll be right there." I ran for my keys. "It's Ethan."

Delia and Graham followed me out the door.

I reached his room just as the doctor on call removed the endotracheal from his throat. Ethan sputtered and coughed during the process. I wanted to cry because it meant he could breathe on his own. Delia and Graham stood behind me, their hands on my shoulders.

"Damn, you scared us, E-man." Delia's voice quivered. "We thought you'd taken a turn for the worse."

Ethan gave a weak smile.

The nurse gave him a cup of water with a straw.

"Just a few sips, E. No gulping." I said. I fluffed his pillows behind his head, straightening his covers until he put his hand in mine.

"Stop fussing." Ethan rasped.

"It's good to see you healing, Ethan." Graham said. "I'm so sorry to have to do this, but I need to ask you some questions about who shot you."

"Are you kidding me?" Everyone in the room looked up when I snapped. I glared at Graham. The doctor and the nurse quietly left the room.

"Tessa, it's fine." Ethan voice sounded like a frog. "I want to talk to Graham."

"When you've regained your strength."

"Tessa." Graham's voice was stern.

"Yes, Graham, I know. It's your job." My voice was raised and terse.

Ethan gave my hand a slight squeeze, letting me know he wanted to talk. Turning to look at Graham, I saw pain in his eyes, and etched in his features. I did love him, so very much. Would I punish him forever for doing his job?

"I'm sorry, Graham. I shouldn't have yelled." The two hardest words in the English language. He reached for me, but I backed away. "I'll leave the two of you to talk."

Chapter Four

Sampson's growl woke me before the breaking glass. The time on my phone told me it was after midnight. I reached beneath my bed and grabbed the baseball bat I kept there just in case…. This was definitely a just-in-case moment.

Sampson pawed furiously at the door. He wanted to find the source of the broken glass. I didn't want him charging at anyone. What if they had a gun and shot him? I could never live with myself. I tried a verbal command.

"Sampson, don't leave my side, do you hear me?" Of course, he heard me, but did he understand? I saw dog training in our future if I made it through the night. Actually, human training as I was the one who needed to know what to do with a dog.

I crept down the hallway to the living room while Sampson growled.

"Shh, quiet." He lowered his growl to a deep throaty vibration.

My living room nightlight showed the room was just as I'd left it before I went to bed. Nothing amiss. A thud had me turn back in the direction of the bedrooms.

Noises got louder the closer I got to Ethan's room. "I have a gun and I'm an expert in using it," I yelled, giving my best badass impression, but probably coming across as bad movie cliché. "The police are on their way." No, they weren't because I hadn't thought to call them while searching my house.

I forcefully threw open Ethan's door so it would crash against the wall and turned on the overhead light. A figure dressed in all black, stopped rifling through the drawers. There was something about the height, the way he stood over the drawers, his eyes visible through the black head covering.

"Lawrence, is that you?" I raised the baseball bat high over my head steps. "Damn it, Lawrence, get the hell out of my house."

The ninja jumped out the broken window and fled into the predawn light.

"You did what exactly?" Graham couldn't hide the fury in his voice. It matched his pacing in my living room. "Playing heroine is not in your job description." Damn, but he looked sexy when upset.

"I had a baseball bat, and Sampson." I pointed to Sampson and the bat, which was now lying on the kitchen floor. "It had to be Lawrence. I even called him by name."

Graham stopped and glowered at me. "Well, did he confirm your suspicion?"

"No, he turned and went back out the broken window."

"You can put plywood over the open window after we check for prints and DNA, but as of now, it's a crime scene. No one without permission is allowed to enter it." He pulled me into his arms. "And, for God's sake, Tessa, please do not put yourself into harm's way again."

I pulled back and looked up at him.

"Are you going to arrest Lawrence Chambers for shooting Ethan?" Anger kept my fear at bay. What if it wasn't Lawrence who broke into my house? Adrenaline rushed through me at the realization I went after an intruder in my home.

"With what evidence, Tessa? I want to find Ethan's shooter as badly as you do, but we need proof." He paced back and forth. "Ethan has no idea who shot him."

It hit me. "The diamonds in the dog collar. He wanted the diamonds in the dog collar."

"My gut tells me you are correct. I'm going to interview the owners of the jewelry store tomorrow where Chambers works. What more can you tell me about Richard and Barbara Clarence besides the fact that they are transplanted snobs from New York City?"

I thought for a moment. "Ethan took me to the opening night at their jewelry store. Very glitzy. High end jewelry. They'd hired Lawrence before they even moved here to do their custom work. Say anything you want about him, but he creates beautiful designs. His craftsmanship is perfect."

"What about the guests? Did you know anyone?"

"Charleston has changed so much. The restaurants, the shops. The television reality shows, Dear Lord. So much history seems to be slipping away, which wasn't a totally bad thing considering all the pain in Charleston's history."

The Clarences, while older, are targeting this crowd. Young with money to burn. I sighed thinking about the changes to my beautiful city. At thirty-five years old, I felt out of place in the young crowd at their opening night party.

The adrenaline was slowly leaving my body, exhaustion taking its place.

Yawning, I stretched my arms high over my head.

"Pack a bag, Tessa. I'll drop you off at Delia's."

"Sampson and I are staying in our home."

"Damn, but you are as stubborn as ever." He half-smiled. "I'll stay on the couch."

Our eyes locked. We both knew his sleeping on the couch wasn't an option.

I took Graham's hand and led him to my bedroom.

We stood in the dark, holding one another.

"Graham, I…" He pressed a finger to my lips.

"You call the shots, Tessa. Being here with you, holding you in my arms, is enough."

I slipped off my robe and got under my quilts. Graham unbuttoned his shirt and shrugged out of it then unzipped his faded jeans and shoved them to the floor. As if no time had passed, as if my heart hadn't been shattered into thousands of pieces, I felt my body respond to the sight of his. The events of the past few hours faded away. Graham was here with me and that's all that mattered.

He slid beneath the covers and wrapped me in his arms.

I cupped his beautiful face in my hands and brought it close to mine.

"Tessa."

"Shh. No words." My mouth sought his. We kissed, soft, tender, our tongues seeking, slowly dancing. I moved onto my back, guiding Graham on top of me.

"Tessa." He groaned.

"It's what I want."

He shoved my nightgown up with one hand while pulling my panties down with the other. I reached for him and guided him to me. I couldn't get him inside me fast enough.

"Don't go slow and, please, Graham, don't be gentle."

I found the sensitive spot on his neck, and I bite it. He lost his mind, pounding into me while I locked my ankles high on his back. He grabbed my wrists, pulling then above my head, pinning my upper body to the bed. I raised my hips, meeting him thrust for thrust.

We were one.

Chapter Five

"I can't arrest Chambers without sufficient proof. I can't even arrest him for breaking into Tessa's home." Graham's voice came from the living room. I'd slept past eight in the morning. A definite luxury.

Sleeping in one another's arms. Graham was up early, working hard on Ethan's case. It all felt so normal. But, opening my heart up to Graham again terrified me. If he hurt me again, this time my heart would stop beating.

"Okay, thanks for the update. I'll be in soon." He ended the call, turned to me and smiled. The smile lit up his face, made him look boyish and mischievous.

"Hi."

"Hi, back." He reached out an arm, grabbed me around the waist, pulling me onto his lap.

"Want coffee? I don't have much in the way of food, but I do have coffee." I slid off his lap and went into the kitchen.

"Tess, you okay?"

"It's just been a lot, you know? Ethan being shot, almost dying. That dog collar with the diamonds. Someone breaking into my home." I didn't mention last night, and neither did Graham. He knew when I needed space to process.

I heard his sigh, and my heart broke a bit. I wanted so badly to trust him again. To feel in my soul that he'd never believed I killed my patient.

Memories of last night's lovemaking flowed through my head, washed through my body. Confusion followed.

I placed the two steaming mugs of coffee on the kitchen table.

"Come and get it." Wow, I didn't do chipper very well.

"How did Chambers react when Ethan broke up with him?" We were back to Ethan's case. A nice, safe topic.

"How do you react when the person who loves you catches you in bed with someone else? Lawrence's ego was bruised, but more from being caught than anything."

"So, Lawrence wanted to be able to say he ended the relationship?"

"Graham, I have no idea, but like I told you, I didn't think Lawrence was a would-be killer."

Taking a few more sips of coffee, he said, "I'm going to talk to the jewelry store owners."

"Please keep me posted."

"It's an active investigation, Tess, but I'll tell you what I can."

I rolled my eyes at him, but this would have to do. "I've taken a couple of days off to be with Ethan. I'm going to the hospital soon." I saw the look of concern in his eyes. "You don't have to wait for me to leave. I'm fine."

"Please promise me something. No more heroics. OK?"

I stared, not answering. If I promised, it would be a lie.

"I'll keep an eye on her, Graham." Delia heard the last of our conversation as she entered from the garage.

They both looked at me. "Let me know when the two of you want to stop treating me like a child." I tried to sound angry but ending up smiling. I knew they cared about me.

After he left, Delia turned to me. "I didn't hear you promise."

"Were you expecting one? You know, dear sister, I don't like to lie."

"Tessa, please, let Graham do his job."

"I'm not stopping him. I'm just going to help him out a bit. Behind the scenes."

Delia sighed. "That's what I'm afraid of."

Chapter Six

Dee came with me to the hospital to see Ethan. We entered the Medical Stepdown Unit for patients recently discharged from the ICU, then found his room.

We'd barely walked in his room when Ethan croaked out, "Sampson? How's my boy?"

"He's fine. Fed, walked, and getting more love than he knows what to do with." I smiled while putting a cup of water to his lips.

"Hey, handsome." Dee kissed him on his cheek.

He gave a big smile. "My two favorite sisters in the entire world."

"It's so good to see you." Delia's eyes got teary.

"Alive, you mean. Go ahead, Dee, you can say it. I'm happy to be alive, too."

"E, Graham said you have no idea who did this to you? Is this true?"

"Just jump right in, Tessa, now that we all know I'm going to survive."

"Geez, Tess, let the man rest." Dee said.

I poured more water in his cup. "I'm sorry, Ethan, you know I'd never do anything to hurt your recovery, but none of this makes sense."

Ethan looked away. The blank expression on his face told me all I needed to know.

"What are you hiding from me?" I kept my tone soft. "Ethan, since we were nine years old, we've never judged one another for anything."

"I'm so ashamed, T." A tear pooled at the corner of his eye. "Why do I have a habit of picking the wrong men? Thinking 'he's the one' the minute he says 'hello'?"

"Did Lawrence shoot you?" Delia stepped up, squeezed his hand.

"No, he was with me."

"Ethan, did this have anything to do with the diamond dog collar?" He looked at me with wide eyes. "Yes, we found it and your cryptic note."

I told him about the 'ninja' who'd broken into his room and how we'd found the pouch with the diamonds in the dog collar.

Ethan tightly shut his eyes, but tears escaped and traveled slowly down his face. "I just want to go back to work as a dog trainer. I love my four-legged clients. And they love me, unconditionally."

We sat in silence, not rushing Ethan. He told us that even if Lawrence hadn't cheated on him, the break-up was inevitable. Lawrence gambled – and lost – an obscene amount of money. He borrowed money to keep gambling.

"These are some very bad people. To pay them back, when customers came to the jewelry store to have him design a piece of jewelry with stones they owned, he took the best diamonds and switched them with moissanite. Most of these customers had no idea how to tell a well-cut moissanite from a near flawless diamond. They just wanted to flash and sparkle around Charleston."

"He hid the real stones in the dog collar." Delia commented. "Very creative, when you think about it."

"Yes. I found it by accident and confronted him. He'd refused to do the right thing and return the stones or go to the police about the loan sharks. I took the stones and hid them before he could fence them for cash. It all happened so fast. Then I was shot and… well, here I am."

My cell phone started to vibrate. "My house alarm is going off." I pulled up the live video and saw two people breaking in through my front door. My screeching alarm didn't seem to deter them. "I have to get home."

"Sampson." Ethan sounded frantic. "Please don't let anything happen to Sampson."

I frantically pulled into my garage. "Tessa, don't go inside." Graham's voice boomed behind me. He must've been alerted about my alarm sounding off from the police station.

"I have to check Sampson." Ethan had been through enough and if anything happened to Sampson, I wouldn't be able to live with myself.

Graham pulled his gun from its holster, keeping it pointed it at the ground while inching toward my kitchen door. "I'll check Sampson. You get back in your car, drive away. I don't want you near here."

Sirens sounded nearby. Graham's backup was close.

Sampson howled in pain. The pitiful sound tore through my soul. With every ounce of strength that I had, I shoved Graham out of the way, and ran into my house.

Chapter Seven

"Give us the diamonds and we let the nice doggy go." Richard Clarence, the owner of the jewelry store, stood in my living room. The leash attached to Sampson's collar was wound so tightly around Richard's wrist that it had Sampson's head held at an odd angle, causing him to whimper. *We?* A huge hulk of a man came up behind me, putting a gun to my temple.

"Let him go, you son of a bitch." Nothing mattered but Sampson. "I'm guessing that you were the person who loaned Lawrence the money?"

"Oh, Doctor Hughes," he tsked. "I would never do anything so beneath me. Lawrence was a really bad boy. Stealing from me and my wife."

"Please call off your baboon." He nodded to his henchman, who lowered his gun. "Lawrence didn't steal from you; he stole from your customers. Those diamonds weren't yours."

Sampson began pulling hard at the hold Richard had on the leash. He pawed the floor relentlessly.

"I don't have the diamonds."

"I have them." Graham came up behind me. "Let her and the dog go, and you can have the diamonds."

"Who are you?"

"The guy who has what you want. The diamonds."

Richard released Sampson and the puppy came straight to me. Sampson sat next to me, glued to my side. I stopped talking. I had no idea what Graham was planning.

"Take Sampson, get in your car, and get the hell out of here." Graham spoke low, but I heard panic in his voice. "Now."

"Oh, no, the doctor isn't going anywhere until I get the diamonds." Richard said.

We both looked at him.

Richard eyes glistened with anger. He motioned to his silent wall of a person. "Take her into one of the bedrooms with the dog. If she tries anything, shoot them both.

Graham and I stood motionless.

"No matter what happens, I love you, Tessa." This time, he spoke low enough so only I could hear.

We went into my bedroom and shut the door. I looked at my unmade bed, remembering making love with Graham. If we both made it out of here alive, I would spend the rest of my life making it up to Graham that I ever doubted him. I would apologize to him daily for thinking he would ever think I could murder a patient.

Sampson became agitated, pulling on his leash, pawing the floor. He sensed something and he definitely didn't like Richard or his goon.

Gun shots came from inside my living room. Sampson pulled out of my hands and ran to the door, jumping, pawing, barking to get out of the bedroom. Mr. No Brain Cells raised his gun, aiming directly at Sampson.

With him focused on Sampson, it gave me the seconds I needed to grab the baseball bat from under my bed. I smacked the man as hard as I could across the shoulders and back. I kept thwacking him harder and harder, until he fell to the ground, unconscious.

I knew this baseball bat would be put to good use.

I opened the bedroom door and before I could stop him, Sampson ran out, his leash trailing behind him.

I scanned the room and froze. Graham was in a heap on the ground near the fireplace, blood everywhere. I started toward him until the sound of a gun being cocked stopped me.

"You didn't tell me pretty boy is a cop." Richard's body twitched. He'd been shot. Blood gushed from his side.

"You both need medical aid." I grabbed Sampson's leash and told him to sit beside me. Thankfully, he listened.

He waved the gun at my wingback chair. "Sit."

"I want to check on the Detective, unless you want to face a charge of murder."

The kitchen door creaked. I flinched. Much to my dismay, Richard saw it. *Please, Delia, don't come in this house.*

"Whoever you are, come on in and join the fun." Richard winced. He wouldn't be able to stand much longer. "We got a Detective who I hope bleeds everywhere, and I have a gun on the doc and the cute doggie. Get in the house now, or they all die."

He aimed the gun at Sampson. The next few seconds happened in slow motion. Sampson pulled out of my grip and lunged at Richard. Shots fired and they both slumped to the ground.

Someone screamed, a blood curdling sound. I realized it was me.

Chapter Eight

Everything happened in a blur. Officers swarmed the house while I stared from Graham to Sampson. One of the officers started yelling orders. "Ambulance", "Officer down".

"Miss, you can't be in here. It's a crime scene." An officer tried to block Delia's entrance.

"That's my sister and this is her house. Try to stop me." She shoved past him and came to me. Grabbing my arms, she shook me, hard.

"Tessa. TESSA". Dee screamed in my face. "Whatever is happening to you, get the hell over it."

I snapped out of my trance.

"Please, please do something about Sampson." I ran over to Graham, knelt by his side. "I'm a doctor." The officers working on him moved aside so I could get to him, too. The bullet went into his shoulder. "Help me roll him just a bit."

The officers gently lifted him. There was no exit wound. EMTs came in with a gurney and started an IV while I gave them statistics about his health history.

I needed to perform a quick trauma assessment. I was concerned about there being no exit wound, and with a shoulder wound, I expected him to have some level of consciousness. I knew he had a high threshold for pain. As they were strapping him onto the gurney, I examined Graham for other bullet wounds.

Then I saw it.

Blood on the corner of the fireplace glistened bright red in the sunlight steaming through a window. My stomach tensed. How could I have missed this.

"His head." The EMTs saw it at the same time I did. A deep wound ran from his temple to the middle of his forehead. The EMT at the top of the gurney started wrapped Graham's head with gauze, as tightly as he could to stem the bleeding. The bullet wound wouldn't kill him, but this head wound might. Icy tendrils wrapping me in fear.

I escorted the gurney to the waiting ambulance, squeezing Graham's hand, praying he would squeeze mine back, but his hand was limp and cool.

As they loaded him into the back of the ambulance, I leaned forward and whispered in his ear. "Don't you dare die on me, Graham Fincher." I kissed his forehead. "It's almost Valentine's Day and you know how much I love it." Defenses down, the full strength of my love for this man washed over me and through me like a Tsunami. "I love you now and always."

Jumping out of the ambulance, I slammed the doors shut and they were off, sirens screeching in the air.

Officers brought Sampson out in a blanket carry. He had been shot in his right rear leg. His breath made his chest rise and fall in a steady rhythm. My knees buckled and I could barely stand. Ethan and Sampson were going to be okay. Getting to the hospital to be with Graham became my priority.

"He's one brave dog, Dr. Hughes." One of the officers said. Dee came right behind Sampson.

"I'll go with him to the vet, Tessa. I really think he's going to be okay. He's a bit dazed right now." She hugged me, hard. "Get to the hospital, Tessa. Be with Graham."

Before I reached my car, EMTs brought Richard out on a gurney and took him to another ambulance. I stopped them and went over to look at him.

"He's lost a lot of blood, Dr. Hughes. In all probability, he won't survive."

"I pray he does," I said.

The EMTs looked at one another in surprise and then at me.

"It's simple. I want him to live so I can see him rot in jail for the rest of his miserable life." I waved them on to get him in the ambulance.

My phone alerted me to a text. In all the commotion they'd already gotten Graham to the ER. I couldn't get there fast enough.

Chapter Nine

Swiping open the ER doors with my identification card, I looked around frantically for Graham.

"Detective Fincher. Where is he?" Please, please don't let him be dead.

A nurse came to me, put an arm around my shoulders. "He's in CT, Dr. Hughes."

"Please text me as soon as anyone knows anything. I'm going to my office." I walked out of the emergency room before anyone could answer. I had to let the ER docs do their job.

A physical therapist helped Ethan stand with the aid of a walker.

Ethan's eyes brightened when I walked in the door. "Sorry, can't, my doctor is here. I have to get back in bed."

"Oh, no, sir, you're going to take that walk. You need to gain your strength. Keep your lungs strong so you don't get pneumonia." The physical therapist meant business.

I held the door open as the physical therapist held the back of Ethan's gown while they walked out the door.

"I'll get you for this," he said with a smile while planting a quick kiss on my cheek. My Ethan was getting back to normal. I closed my eyes, willing Graham to come back to me, too.

Pacing Ethan's room, I kept looking at my watch to see how much time had passed. I needed news about Graham and Sampson. News they were going to be okay.

The male physical therapist helped Ethan back into bed after their walk. He left the room, but not before telling Ethan he would see him tomorrow.

"What is it, Tessa?" Ethan asked as he settled into the bed. "The look of fright on your face tells me something is terribly wrong."

I opened my mouth to catch him up when Delia walked into the room. "Sampson misses his human daddy and wants to know when you'll be home?"

Delia winked at me as one more weight left my chest.

An ICU doctor poked his head in the door. "Dr. Hughes, I need to speak to you." The lack of expression on his face turned into a big smile. I took a huge breath and went out into the hall.

Chapter Ten

Graham spent the night in the ICU as a precaution due to his head injury. Where the bullet had entered was not life threatening. I refused to leave his side. In the middle of the night, I pulled the blanket higher on his chest to keep him warm. Suddenly a strong arm lifted me into the bed beside him.

"What are you doing?" I whispered. "Your other arm is in a sling, and you don't need to be lifting me."

"I want you next to me every night for the rest of our lives. Starting now."

"We can start when you're discharged." I tried to get off the bed, but he pulled me closer.

"Doctor's orders."

He smiled. "Then you must stay right here beside me, all night. You are my best medicine, my love."

I couldn't argue with him.

Graham was moved to a regular room the following day. Officers, detectives, the Chief of Police, all paraded in and out of his room. I finally told the nurse's station no more visitors for the next couple of hours so he could rest.

Hours later, a detective asked to speak with Graham and fill him in on the Clarences. The police discovered they had a long criminal history, with a lot of assumed identities. They traveled the country, opening jewelry stores with some of the money they'd stolen from customers in other cities. They fenced high-end jewelry for cash and moved on, getting richer in each city. Before coming to Charleston, they'd made it onto the FBI's most wanted list.

"We caught the wife trying to leave the country."

What they hadn't counted on was Lawrence stealing from customers, too. It put a glitch in their well-oiled plans. The henchman Tessa had knocked unconscious was the one who shot Ethan. The Clarences put out the hit, but it was meant for Lawrence. Ethan got in the way. Collateral damage.

Lawrence turned himself in for stealing the diamonds, which would work well in his favor, but he would still do jail time.

Ethan and Graham were released from the hospital on the same day. Going to my house was no longer an option. Once all the blood was cleaned, it was going on the market. I wouldn't live there again. Too much bad energy.

My parents had a great house on the Isle of Palms. Plenty of bedrooms for everyone. I took an extended leave of absence from work so I could keep an eye on Graham and Ethan's healing process under one roof. Even Sampson got a new, plush doggie bed and lots of soft toys. Delia agreed to move in to help me out around the house and cook some of her gourmet meals.

My favorite part of the house was the covered porch off the kitchen overlooking the Atlantic. Growing up, no matter the weather, I could sit there for hours, looking out at the endless ocean, it calmed me.

Graham wanted us to share a bedroom. "On one condition."

"What?" he asked, looking worried.

"You forgive me. If I hadn't gone rushing in the house to check on Sampson, you wouldn't have come in behind me and gotten shot."

"Tessa, it's not your fault. This is my job." Graham reached out to me. "You wouldn't be you if you hadn't rushed in to save Sampson. And you wouldn't be the woman I gave my heart and soul to the minute we met."

Wrapping my arms around his waist, I laid my head on his chest. My head hit just the right place to feel his heart beating, a beautiful rhythm.

Epilogue

Nothing in the world matched Valentine's Day on the beach in Charleston. Waves crashed on the sand while gentle breezes floated in the air. Graham wrapped a blanket around the both of us while we drank wine and watched the sunset. We looked into one another's eyes, filled with so much love.

He stood up, the blanket dropping to the sand. I took his hand as he led me back into the house and into our bedroom.

Our lovemaking had never been so pure, so transcendent. No one else lived in this space but us. Afterward, we held one another without a need for words. Our souls were joined forever. He kissed the ring he'd placed on my finger, and I kissed his lips.

When we woke the next day, I knew it was the beginning of our forever.

END

About Victoria Houseman

When a wrist injury at my counseling job left me with a 50% loss of use of my dominant hand, I had to learn computer skills. I took this as a sign to fulfill my dream of becoming a writer. I left counseling, started writing, and I've never looked back.

Find Victoria Online:
Website: https://victoriahouseman.com/
Facebook: https://www.facebook.com/victoria.houseman21
Instagram: https://www.instagram.com/victoriabauthor/
Amazon: https://www.amazon.com/Victoria-Houseman/e/B0B57SCZC6

The One That I Want

By Elaine Reed

The One That I Want

Contemporary

Dana Dahl only moved to Charleston to make her mother happy. Despite pining for her hometown in North Dakota, she lets her mother book her on a food tour. The savory delights Charleston has to offer remind Dana of home in unexpected ways, until Camille Lewis sits besides her. The glamorous local shows Dana all Charleston has to offer and serves up possibilities for a new life.

Rated: PG-13

Chapter 1

Dana kept her gaze on her plate, carefully separating the shrimp from the grits. She'd taken a mouthful with both, as the guide on the tasting tour had recommended, and hated the grits. They reminded her of eating at her grandmother's house and how Gran would never soak the beans, or the corn, or any other dried foodstuff long enough.

Dana closed her eyes for a moment to rein in the emotional tide that swamped her. She hated Gran's cooking, but now that she couldn't have it, it was on the long list of things Dana most wanted. Everything on the list happened to be back near Lake Sakakawea in North Dakota, while she was exiled in Charleston, South Carolina, not even allowed to visit for Thanksgiving. Of all the things that had happened over the last six months, being kicked out of her life—that was how it felt—had been the worst.

She glanced around the table before lowering her gaze again and grimacing. Thankfully, this dish came with a nice glass of wine. Dana swallowed as much of the grits as she could before drinking. There was no point in sullying a good, crisp white. When her mouth was clear, she took a deep drink of the wine.

"You look like you could use a refill." A woman with flowing model-esque hair plopped down next to Dana, gently stilled her hand holding the glass, and filled it to the rim. "Hurry, take a sip before it drips on ya." The woman gave Dana a bright smile.

"Thank you," she said, her voice low. Dana hadn't noticed if the woman was one of the guides on the tasting tour, but she figured someone this affable, and with a bottle of wine to boot, probably had authority over the group. Dana took a healthy drink and thanked her again.

"It's my pleasure. From where I was sittin', the wine seemed to be the only part of this dish you're partial to. I figured you'd need more."

Dana fidgeted before taking another sip and setting her glass on the table. "You could see that?"

"You're pretty stoic, but your whole face changed when you tasted those grits." The woman topped off her own glass. "I'm observant. It's part of my job. I doubt most others saw. You're safe."

Dana forced a smile. Indeed, she was safe in Charleston, and it was nice to have someone on her side. "I knew you were a guide. Which dish are you in charge of?"

"Oh no. I'm not a guide. Well, not on this tour. I work at some of the historical sites. My tours rarely include wine." The woman tinkled a laugh. "Say, maybe if you add more butter." She plucked a small ramekin of what Dana presumed was an arty hand-churned butter from the center of the table.

Dana held up her hand. "No, no. Thank you. The flavor was fine. It was the texture."

The woman set down the butter. "I bet you don't like oatmeal or cream of wheat, either, huh?"

Dana closed her eyes for a moment, appreciating the effort to understand her. "It's not sensory. The texture of the grits reminds me of my grandmother's cooking. She grew up poor and keeps a healthy store of dried beans, among other things. She never soaks the beans, or really anything, long enough."

The woman nodded, then dug a paper with the tour logo out of her purse and unfolded it. "I think this is the only serving of grits, which is unique since we're in the South. But let's be sure. Then we can strategize."

Dana narrowed her eyes. "Are you sure you aren't running this tour?"

The woman giggled again. "Positive. No more grits, see?" She handed the menu to Dana. "Make sure everything else seems okay. If not, we'll make a plan."

Dana took the paper while keeping her gaze on the woman. She'd found an ally out of thin air and wanted to make sure this woman was real.

"Go on, look."

Dana glanced at the menu, then back at the woman. She wore a bubble-gum pink cardigan set, with dark green slacks. She should've looked like a watermelon slice, but somehow, it worked. A small cross-body purse scraped the edge of the bench where they sat. It couldn't have held much. A slim wallet, phone, keys. Lipstick? Not nearly all the things Dana needed to appear as comfortable and put together as this woman did. "What's your name?"

"Oh! Silly me. I forgot I'm not a guide right now and haven't announced my name." The woman held her hand out. "I'm Camille Lewis. And you are?"

Dana wiped her hands on a napkin before grasping Camille's. "Dana Dahl."

"It's very nice to meet you. What brings you to this tasting tour tonight?" Camille tinkled another laugh. "I'm sorry, I've only had one glass of wine and already I'm alliterating."

Dana didn't know how Camille had managed it, but between her flowy hair, her not-a-watermelon outfit, and that delicate little laugh, she'd fallen under Camille's spell.

"It's a gift from my mother. She wanted to help me get to know Charleston better." Dana inched toward Camille. "What brings you here?"

"Are you on vacation? Enjoying our city?"

"I moved here over the summer."

"Oh, I hope you got to spend a good deal of time at the beach or on the water."

Dana shrugged. "Some."

"Anything we need to work around as the tour progresses?" Camille gestured toward the paper in Dana's hand.

Dana looked at it and smiled. "I'll read this menu, but don't think I haven't realized that you haven't told me why you're here."

Camille scooped some of Dana's grits onto a small plate, then replaced them with more shrimp. She picked up the plate of grits and made a show of adding salt and pepper. "Mm-hmm, what else am I gonna have to eat for you?"

Camille strolled along the sidewalk beside Dana, her impulse to thread their arms together so strong, she held her hands behind her back. Something about Dana put Camille at ease. So often she had to be "on" when she was with other people, and not just because she gave tours. People expected a certain something from her. Dana seemed like the type of person who'd be perfectly happy sitting quietly, not expecting to be doted on or entertained. It was refreshing.

That was what her brother had been trying to accomplish when he gifted her this tasting event, but she hadn't relaxed until Dana called her out for evading questions. Dana had noticed *her*. Not all the factoids she peppered into conversations, or the doting.

"Do you ever give walking tours in the city?" Dana asked.

"Not yet. I'd like to, but I made commitments to several historical homes, and the scheduling doesn't fit with the companies that tour the city."

"That's a shame." Dana bumped her with her elbow, causing Camille to shiver.

She desperately wanted to show Dana some affection. Nothing too familiar, but enough to feel like they were a unit.

"Have you considered starting your own tour company?" Dana stopped walking and faced Camille with an inquisitive expression. "I'd buy a ticket."

Camille pressed a hand to her cheek, hoping to fight back the growing burn. "You don't need to. I'll take you on a tour whenever you want."

Dana glanced away and smiled, then returned her gaze to Camille. "I'd like that."

They resumed their walk, having fallen to the back of the group. Camille knew they were close to their next stop, so she wasn't concerned. She liked the sense of privacy. She snapped out of her semiswoony state when Dana grabbed her arm.

"Look, it's you!" Dana pointed toward a shop window where a mannequin wore a winter version of Camille's outfit.

Camille giggled. "I do love the bright colors so many Charlestonians wear. They give me energy."

Dana smiled. "I can see that. Plus, they flatter you."

"Thank you." Camille lifted her chin and winked. "I do occasionally wear black." She nodded toward Dana's outfit: a black button down top tucked into high-waisted black cigarette pants. It was very chic, and Camille had several variations of it in bright, bold colors. The black was perfect on Dana.

Dana huffed a laugh. "I was trying to channel Audrey Hepburn from *Funny Face*. I watched it with my mom last night." Dana sighed and pushed at the bobby pin near her temple. "I'm more Rizzo from *Grease* than Jo Stockton, though."

Camille straightened her posture and gestured for Dana to continue their walk. "Rizzo was the best character in *Grease*. She was strong and sexy as hell. She was so great that Sandy turned herself into Rizzo. Rizzo's the best. She didn't change herself. She embraced herself. We should all be Rizzos." Camille glanced at Dana to catch her staring with wide eyes. "Oh, I'm sorry. I can get a little carried away."

"No. That was fantastic! I've always thought Rizzo got a bum deal. Everyone was judgy, and she should've gotten more screen time."

Camille clapped her hands together and pressed them against her smile. "You really live here now?"

"Yes."

Camille gave into her impulse and threaded her arm through Dana's as they walked the last few feet to rejoin their group. "We're gonna be great friends."

Chapter 2

Dana sat in awe at their last table of the evening. "It's over already?" While the food had been tasty, it hadn't made the impression Camille had. Dana wanted more time with her.

"This is it." Camille patted her mouth with a napkin before laying it beside her plate, the coconut cake reduced to a few small bites. "Not a bad way to end the tasting."

"Mm." Dana furrowed her brow. If she were back home, she'd know how to get more time with Camille. But here, everything was different. Even *she* was a little different. She should've thought about this before now. What was she without a game plan? Most likely a woman who would continue to spend her free time alone.

Dana followed Camille as she said her final farewells to their tablemates, tipped the tour guides, and made her way outside.

A sandy-colored midsize sedan pulled up to the curb, door locks clicking as it idled.

"That's my brother," Camille said. "He was worried I'd get tipsy." She sighed. "I wish we didn't have to end the night so early. I'd love to show you more of the city."

"I'd like that too." Dana grabbed Camille's hand and gave it a light squeeze, hoping Camille would continue to walk with her. Usually, she wouldn't want to risk being on foot at night, but Camille's presence soothed her and pushed those concerns to the back of Dana's mind.

The car window slid open. "Come on, Camille. Kelly's gonna go into labor."

Camille rolled her eyes and turned her head toward the car. "Eventually."

"Someone's in labor?"

"His wife's about three months along. She has a while yet."

Dana smiled. "Phew."

Camille grabbed Dana's other hand, leaned forward, and popped a kiss next to Dana's lips.

Dana froze for a moment, stunned. She blinked. Someday she'd get used to the cordiality in Charleston. "Love that Southern Hospitality."

Camille shook her head. "No, that was because I like you."

Dana didn't have time for Camille's declaration to set in before Camille's brother honked his horn.

Camille sighed and let go of one hand. She took a few steps before letting go of the other. "I have lunch at Brown Dog Deli on Broad Street most Thursdays around twelve-thirty."

"I'll be there," Dana said as Camille slid into the car.

Chapter 3

Dana had to make an effort not to stomp her way through Marion Square. She was brooding, and she didn't know how to stop. Well, she knew what would settle her. She was clueless about how to get it, though. Her therapist would tell her to redirect her thoughts, but since she couldn't plan away her mood, Dana wanted to brood. She resigned herself to shopping the Charleston Farmers Market on the last Saturday before Thanksgiving.

A display of colored glass items caught her eye. The tent held mostly jewelry, but there were some wind chimes and one small lamp with a web of pink glass sewn to the shade. Dana shifted her gaze between the lampshade and a wind chime.

"We have the wind chime in pink as well," the proprietor said.

"Actually, I like the chime as it is. It would be striking as a light fixture."

"Yes, but I'd have to learn how to do that. Otherwise, there'd be a small, naked bulb dangling in the center."

Dana made a face as though she'd taken a big bite of grits. "You can't do that."

The proprietor shrugged. "If you join our mailing list, you'll know when I've figured it out." The older woman handed Dana a clipboard with a handwritten form asking for a name and email.

Dana stared at the page, allowing herself a moment to think. Every night, her mother reminded her Charleston was home now. She might as well act like it. She cleared her throat and handed the clipboard back without her information, forcing her lips into a smile. "I make light fixtures." She brushed her finger along the bottom of one of the chimes. "I can convert this one so you have a model to learn from."

The proprietor took the chime from its hook and laid it on tissue paper.

Dana held up a hand. "Oh, I'm sorry. I didn't mean to offend."

"No, no, no!" The woman smiled. "I'm wrapping it for you." She handed Dana a business card with a Queen Street address. "You turn it into a light and bring it to my shop. If it looks nice, we'll work something out where you can convert more, or I'll pay you to teach me."

"What?"

"You heard me." She taped the tissue paper closed and slipped the chime into a gift box, then into a paper bag. "I watch the sunlight stream through them and think how nice it'd be to see the glass lit up at night. If you can make that happen, we should make a deal."

Dana reached into her messenger bag and rifled for her wallet. She pulled out her debit card. "Can you run this, or do you need cash?"

"Sweetie, put that away. If you break it, we'll talk. Otherwise, I trust you."

Dana froze. "I'm a stranger."

"Who shares my vision. I'm Joyce, by the way. If you can make this a pretty light before Christmas shopping season ends, we might both have a jolly December." Joyce slid the handles of the carrier bag over Dana's hand and dropped them on her wrist.

"Thank you."

"See you soon." The woman bent and looked at Dana's card. "Miss Dahl. See you soon."

For the first time in weeks, Dana gave a genuine smile.

"You gonna stand there all day, or you gonna go make that into a light?"

Dana's heart took off in a gallop.

She turned until she found Camille and put a hand on her hip, even as Camille's presence put breath back in her lungs.

"Three weeks! I've been at Brown Dog Deli every Thursday for three weeks. Where have you been?"

"I'm so sorry." The doe eyes Camille threw her way almost distracted Dana from the rust-colored dress that made her look cuddly, which was paired with white canvas low-top sneakers. "They shifted my schedule and I've been up on Meeting Street. My lunches have only been thirty minutes. That's not enough time to walk to Broad Street and back and eat."

"You should've told me."

Camille's eyes went wide. "I couldn't. I don't have your number."

Dana rummaged through her messenger bag again and came up with a business card. She thrust it at Camille. "Now you do. All my numbers. My email. Everything."

Camille's cheeks turned a pink so pretty that Dana almost lost her balance.

"Thank you." Camille pried the case off her phone and slid the card in, then put it back together. "So I don't lose it."

Dana nodded, the adrenaline slowing and taking her ability to speak with it.

"Since I made you eat alone for *three* Thursdays in a row, can I buy you lunch now? There's a cute little place right across the street."

"You don't want to eat from a booth or food truck here?"

"I want to sit and talk with you over a meal."

Dana blinked a few times and pushed at the hair clip over her ear. Was this a date? Did she care? She'd somehow manifested Camille. She wasn't going to walk away. "Okay."

Camille gave Dana a smile so bright it lifted her broody mood. "If we're still hungry after lunch, we can get dessert out here. I know the best ones."

Dana tilted her head. "I bet you do. Lead the way."

As though no time had passed from their last meeting, Camille threaded her arm through Dana's and led them to a café across the street.

Camille considered herself lucky that Dana had not only agreed to have lunch with her, but when they finished eating, she'd asked her to go through the rest of the farmers market with her. Camille talked as much as she could so she wouldn't give in to her impulse to fully lean against Dana. She managed not to slip into tour guide mode either; having someone interested in what she had to say without an agenda was a novelty.

"I can't believe I had a bowl of fresh fruit for lunch. In November." Dana pushed back the barrette near her temple, then smoothed her hair over her ear. "The only fresh produce in North Dakota this time of year is carrots and onions." She twisted her mouth, then nodded. "And cabbage."

Camille grinned. "That's a great start to a soup."

Dana looked into the distance. "I do make tasty soups."

"Will you make some for me? I love soup." And spending time with you, she silently added.

"Sure. Usually, I've made a bunch of soups by now." Dana pulled them toward a produce stand with leeks and potatoes. "I'm falling behind."

"Too busy?"

"No." Dana stopped and frowned. "It hasn't been cold enough. I guess I'm still adjusting."

Camille took in Dana's outfit of sleek black leggings and a spaghetti strap tank in ocean blue. Most locals would've at least had a jacket with them. "Getting used to a new place takes time. Especially when it's so different. What brought you here?"

Dana stiffened and looked away. "Work." She selected several white and sweet potatoes and paid for them.

Camille gave Dana room to finish her transaction and move to the next stand before she took the carrier bag and hooked their elbows together. "Did you have to move or else lose your job?"

Dana tensed again and closed her eyes for a moment. "I had a great job, but my mother insisted that I needed a change. When my company opened this branch, instead of helping write job descriptions, I volunteered to come here. It's still a great job, and moving got Mom off my back, but maybe it wasn't the right decision."

"Why?" Camille fidgeted with her purse strap, fighting the urge to spout all the facts and feelings she had to convince Dana that Charleston was the best place to be. She'd learned long ago that people had to come to their choices on their own.

Dana stopped at a stand with honey and selected several jars, along with a few honey dippers and rests. She paid and asked for special wrappings, all the while taking peeks at Camille. Once the seller handed over Dana's purchases, Dana turned to Camille and smiled. "Sorry. I didn't mean to stop you short. I thought this would be a good gift for my Thanksgiving host."

Camille nodded.

"But you deserve an answer. It's just hard to formulate. My job isn't why I left Lake Sakakawea. It's what got me here. The reason I left is why I speculate about my decision. And I'm not quite ready to talk about it."

"Okay." Camille pressed her lips together, considering her next question. Dana looked more at ease than she had at the tasting, but a North Dakota ball cap dangled from the strap of her messenger bag. Did she like anything about Charleston? Could Camille help Dana find some contentment in her new city? She adjusted the bags she held to keep herself in check. "Does Charleston feel more like home now than when we first met?"

Dana winked. "Mm, you're definitely helping."

Camille smiled and looked away. While she liked Dana's answer, she recognized it as a dodge. "Have you made many friends so far?"

"A few from work, and you." Dana gave Camille a warm smile that filled her with guilt.

"And I abandoned you right out of the gate. I am *so* sorry." Camille squeezed Dana's arm.

"It wasn't on purpose. And you found me again."

Camille tapped her fingers against her lips. "I need to make it up to you." She took a breath and dropped her hand. "Let me take you out."

Dana lifted her eyebrows. "Take me out?"

"Yes." Camille firmed her resolve. She wasn't often this straightforward, but she'd missed Dana for those three weeks, and seeing how adrift she was in Charleston, all Camille wanted to do was make her feel better. Plus, if she got Dana to see Charleston the way she did, maybe she wouldn't have to worry about Dana moving back to North Dakota. "I'd like to take you on a date. A unique one. Something you haven't done yet."

Dana shuddered. "Please don't say parasailing."

Camille laughed. "I wasn't going to, but that's good to know. We'll have to unpack that later."

"There's nothing to unpack. It's really windy here, and how do you land without drowning?"

Camille patted her arm. "There's a winch! You don't even get wet."

Dana shook her head. "Not sure I believe you."

"Okay, no parasailing, but you've given me an idea. Do you get seasick?"

Chapter 4

Dana took a big bite of her sandwich wrap and tried to keep her gaze off Camille while they spoke. "I finished the light fixture."

There was plenty of scenery at Liberty Square. It sat right on the water and had a lot of natural shade along with flowers and plants. Dana sat with her back to the inlet, so she kept her focus on nearby flowers instead. Aside from finding Camille again, making the light had been the most exciting thing in her life. She wasn't sure she was ready to admit that to Camille, but she wanted to keep her up to date on the project. "Do you want to meet for lunch again tomorrow when I return it to the shop?"

"Absolutely. I can't wait to see it." Camille reached over and squeezed her knee.

The contact was a prize. Dana had never considered herself a touchy person, but ever since that first night when Camille had linked their arms together, all Dana wanted was more reasons for this woman to touch her.

"It's only been a few days. How did you get it done so fast?" Camille asked.

"Sunday was quiet. Plus, I wanted to keep it simple so I can teach the lady how to do it herself and still make decent money selling them." And if she were being honest, Dana liked the idea of working on commission. She loved her job, but watching classic movies while on Zoom with her mom and grandma was getting old. She needed more to do and still wasn't comfortable going out in the evenings on her own.

"Can I see it early? Do you have a picture?"

Dana wrinkled her nose. "A picture wouldn't do it justice."

Camille shook her head. "You have to play hard to get, don't you?"

"Says the woman who disappeared for three weeks."

Camille held up her hands as a breeze came off the water and blew her hair behind her like a shampoo commercial. "You got me."

Dana grinned. "I hope so." She cleared her throat. "Eating out here is nice. I wish I'd noticed this space before. It's beautiful and close to work."

"Well, there is a museum right here." Camille gestured to the building across the green from the aquarium.

"I don't understand how you're not running one of them. You know everything about everything."

"Not really." Camille took a bite of salad, swallowed, then said, "But I'd like to have my own tour company."

"What's stopping you?"

Camille shrugged as she stabbed at her lettuce. "Money and competition."

"There are a ton of museums here."

"And I can take you through all of them." Camille set her salad down and dug into her purse, pulling out her phone.

"Is that what we're doing on Friday?"

"Nope." Camille's giant grin sent a shiver down her spine that settled low in her belly. "But you should wear pants. And maybe a light sweater."

"Huh." Dana hadn't expected the request for pants.

"Oh shoot. Can we go to the shop tomorrow after work instead of at lunch?"

Dana blinked a few times, reminding herself to breathe before she answered. "How late do you work?"

"Oh, we all close at five. So, five-fifteen? That okay?"

Dana willed herself to relax. The sun would start to set by five-thirty, but she wouldn't be alone. She'd be with Camille. It was worth it. Her therapist would be proud of her for taking this step.

"Okay. Tomorrow. Queen Street. Five-fifteen. *Don't* disappear."

Camille put a hand over her heart. "On my honor, I will be there."

Dana considered texting Camille with the exact location of where she'd parked in the Queen Street garage but talked herself out of it at least a dozen times. She didn't want to seem weird or needy. Except she was. Parking garages creeped her out to the point of nightmares. That she'd been able to find a spot on the first floor near a light and an exit, and all the things safety experts advise, was a miracle. In the end, she compromised with herself. She texted Camille with which garage she'd parked in—the shop was between two—and forced herself to calm down. She gathered the small box with the light and her supplies, secured her car, and hightailed it to the store.

She paused as the door closed when entering the shop, taken by the displays of jewelry, glass sculptures, and other art. The music of the door chimes broke her from her reverie.

"Gosh, it's beautiful in here." Camille's hushed voice washed over Dana.

She turned to the other woman and smiled. "So are you. Like a breath of fresh air."

Camille kissed her cheek. "You took the words right out of my mouth."

"Mm." Dana couldn't describe what had come over her. Maybe she was relieved to be out of the parking garage or excited to deliver the lamp. Maybe she didn't realize how lonely she'd been until she'd met Camille. Even when in North Dakota. She'd loved her life there, but when she moved, the only people she'd left behind were a handful of friends, and her mother, and grandmother.

"Can I help you all?" a slender man with dark hair near the cash register asked. "It's okay to come in and browse."

Camille giggled. "We needed a minute to appreciate how lovely all this is."

"Thank you," the man said. "My mother works very hard."

"Is Joyce here?" Dana gestured with the box she held. "I have a light to show her."

"I'll get her. Please peruse the art." He disappeared into a backroom.

Camille stepped forward into the space, wonderment personified. "He says that like he has a difficult time making sales, but look at this place! They must sell out constantly!"

Dana followed, alternating her glances between the glasswork and Camille. She enjoyed Camille's reaction as much as she did the glassworks.

"There you are, Miss Dahl!" Joyce, the woman from the farmer's market, swept into the room, smiling brightly. "I didn't expect to see you so soon."

Dana returned the smile, her nerves finally making her stomach flip. It had been ages since she'd shown anyone her lights. "You said you wanted to sell them during the holiday season. Black Friday is the day after tomorrow. I figured it was the perfect time."

"You're so considerate. I thought it would take longer."

"I've been working with lights for a while. I have a few tricks."

Joyce took out a metal stand and set it on a nearby table. "Then let's see."

Dana set her box on the edge of the table and took out the glass wind chimes she'd turned into a small light. "I have this wired two ways. I can adjust it to the one you prefer." She hung the fixture from the stand and touched a switch tucked in near the hook. One half lit up.

"Oh!" Camille gasped. "That's stunning. What did you do on the other half?"

"It's a little different." Dana clicked another button and the rest of the glass pieces lit up. "On this side, I outlined the glass, and on this one—" Dana pointed to a specific piece "I put the lights against the glass so they almost—"

"They glow," Joyce said. "That is amazing. How did you do that?"

Dana rolled her shoulders back, trying not to seem too proud. "The outlines are tiny rope lights. Very easy to do. These other ones, my mom calls them chandelier lights because each light is on its own wire. I can put them anywhere on the glass." She moved one of them from the top to the bottom of the piece of glass.

"You can make a whole new pattern like that," Camille said. "And the way you placed them, it brings out the best parts."

Dana's cheeks warmed. She'd considered the placement of each light for precisely this reason. The glass chimes Joyce had made were gorgeous, but for the lights to be worth it, they needed to be in the best possible places. "I brought supplies to adjust this to whichever design you prefer, Joyce."

The older woman pressed her hand to her cheek. "I see the beauty in both. Matthew!"

The man who'd greeted Dana and Camille earlier joined them. "How can I help?"

"Look at both sides of this. Which do you like better?"

He studied the light, lips pursed. Eventually, he scratched his beard. "We can sell them both."

Joyce sighed. "Yes. But which do you prefer?"

Matthew pointed to the side where the glass glowed. "Some people will want the other side for brighter light, even though these aren't meant to illuminate spaces."

"Do you have another one I can work with?" Dana asked. "It won't take me long to apply one style to this and then start another one. I have everything with me." She patted the small box in front of her.

"Really?" Joyce asked.

Dana nodded.

"Follow me."

Dana handed Camille the light she'd made and collected her box, then they followed Joyce to a workshop in the back of the store with several completed glassworks and many more in progress.

"Take your pick." Joyce held out her arm, inviting Dana into the space.

Dana set her box on an empty worktable and turned to Camille. "I'll take that. You choose the next one."

Camille clapped her hands and moved through the space, inspecting each work. Dana removed the glowing lights and showed Joyce how she'd outlined the glass with the tiny rope lights and finished the original fixture as Camille returned with another.

Joyce handed Camille the finished light. "Please take this to Matthew and ask him to display it with the lights on."

Camille nodded and took the fixture to the front of the store.

Dana spent the next twenty minutes working with Joyce. She showed her how she attached the power switch and the lights while Joyce selected the areas on each piece of glass where the light would look the best. When they were done, the light was truly stunning.

"This is what we're going to do," Joyce said. "We'll display these and take special orders this weekend. Are you comfortable with people picking which pieces they want lit?"

Stunned by the woman's quick decision, Dana nodded, taking a moment to find her voice. "Yeah. Yes. I'm comfortable with that."

"I sell these starting at fifty dollars each, but your lights add tremendous value. We're going to start at eighty. You'll get a thirty percent commission on each sale."

"Thirty percent?"

"If you can turn them around the same week, forty percent. I'll have my hands full making new ones, and people get excited when they can have what they want right away. You can work here, or I'll have Matthew deliver the pieces to you."

Dana's head spun. She pushed at the bobby pin near her temple. "Really?"

"Yes. Let's bring this one to the front." Joyce took the light and swept out of the room.

"Are you sure I can't buy it?" a woman was asking Matthew as they returned to the storefront.

"I'm sorry, it's for display only," he said.

"But we can custom make one for you." Joyce took out another stand and set it next to the first light, hanging the second fixture on it. "Choose whatever you like, and we'll add lights."

The woman's eyes went round, then she smiled. "I'll be right back." She slipped around them and headed toward the part of the store with the blue and green glass.

Joyce turned to Dana. "I have drawings for ornaments and chandeliers. Would you consider working together on those?"

Dana almost passed out on the spot. "I—what?" People back home had always complimented her work, but no one had ever offered to buy it. That was why she was a project manager at a construction firm. She knew how to build and light stuff, but not how to be profitable at it.

Camille tinkled a laugh. "I think you shocked her." She picked up one of Dana's hands and patted it. "You're lighting up people's lives, roughrider."

Once again, Camille snapped Dana out of her stupor. "Roughrider?"

Camille's cheeks turned a pretty pink. "I did a little research on North Dakota, and we're in the South. Everyone gets nicknames here."

Dana pulled Camille toward her and kissed her cheek, then turned to Joyce. "Yes. Let's do it. I have a full-time job, but I can work on these in the evenings. My job doesn't have overtime, and when it rains, work is slow. I can fill orders."

"Perfect." Joyce clapped her hands together.

The woman who'd been admiring the lights returned with a wind chime double the size of the ones Dana had turned into fixtures. "This one, please." She pushed the chimes toward Matthew.

"There is an added fee for the lights," he said as he took the piece.

"That's fine," the woman said.

"That will bring this to one hundred sixty. I can ring you up," Joyce said.

The woman and Joyce moved toward the register.

"Should I box this for you?" Matthew asked Dana.

"Can you show me how?" Dana asked. "I'll have to repack it, and I want to make sure I do it right."

Once Matthew had the glasswork wrapped and packed in a box, Camille helped Dana gather her things and take them to her car.

"We have to celebrate," Camille said as Dana closed the trunk. "Husk is right down the street. Let me treat you to dinner."

Dana looked around, noting the brightness of the lights in the garage and how dark it had gotten while they'd been with Joyce. Her impulse was to say no and get home to safety. But her mother, her therapist, and even her grandmother, reminded her regularly that she shouldn't live in fear, even though *their* fear had sent her to Charleston.

"Hey." Camille touched Dana's arm. "Where'd you go? Are you okay?"

"A little overwhelmed, but I'm okay." Dana nodded. "Let's go to dinner."

Chapter 5

Tucked in the bar at Husk, they'd gotten through the appetizers, and Dana was halfway through one of Husk's signature cocktails, when she said she needed to tell Camille something.

"You're a fairy, aren't you?" Camille joked. "That's how you make those lights work."

Dana gave a small smile and shook her head. "Life would be much more interesting then. I'd be able to fly, I could nap in flowers, it'd be lovely."

"You want to nap in flowers?" Camille's mind spun, thinking of places to take Dana where they could lie in a lush field in bloom.

"No, but the drawings of fairies in flowers are very cute."

Camille nodded her agreement.

Dana cleared her throat and fidgeted with the bobby pin near her temple. "I need to tell you why I moved away from Lake Sakakawea."

Camille wanted to reach for Dana, but wasn't sure if Dana wanted her to. So she sat prepared, waiting for whatever Dana had to say. "I'm ready when you are."

Dana took a sip of her drink and set the glass on the table. "About a year ago, a man attacked me in a parking lot."

Camille sucked in a breath. Her hands crept forward, but she fisted them. Dana's hands were in her lap, and her eyes were down. Camille waited for Dana's next move.

Dana looked toward the ceiling. "Wow. It took a shit ton of therapy for me to be able to say that calmly." She nodded, then looked at Camille. Her whole expression changed, and she waved close to her chest. "He didn't hurt me. Not really. I pushed him off, but he rallied." Dana gave a hint of a wry smile. "I was a school bus driver in college and carried a taser. I'd had it so long I didn't think it worked anymore, but it did."

"Put him on his ass?"

Dana nodded. "The way he fell, I'd stomped on his hand as I ran away. I don't know how I could've done the damage he claimed, but that doesn't matter. He went to jail. A judge cleared me of all charges because security footage showed the whole thing."

"Did he hurt you?"

"Not physically." Dana finished her drink and rested her hand on the table. "But I spent months wondering why me. And when the judge closed my case, his friends taunted me."

"Oh no." Camille reached across the table and wove her fingers through Dana's. "Did *they* hurt you?"

Dana squeezed Camille's hand. "Not physically. I applied for restraining orders, but none of them had actually touched me or gotten within arm's length. It was difficult to get one."

"Meanwhile, you're facing them and recovering from the initial assault, and it gets dark real early in the winter in North Dakota," Camille said.

"You got it." Dana leaned back in her seat but kept her hand in Camille's. "The positive that came from all this was that I knew I could take care of myself. I didn't freeze. I used the taser correctly. I'm capable, and that felt damn good."

"But?"

Dana nodded again. "My mother and grandmother were concerned that his friends outnumbered me. I laid low for a few months until the time change, when it didn't get dark so early anymore. That didn't help the thugs forget. Then I got mad. I have the right to live there. They shouldn't be allowed to push me out of my home. I was determined to get back to my life. But one day I got to Mom's early, and I heard her and Gram worrying over me." Dana pulled away from Camille and pushed her hands into her hair, squeezing her forehead. "I moved in with her for a while so she'd see I was safe. When my company had positions open in Charleston, I applied."

They spent the rest of the dinner talking about how Dana's company had supported her in the days after the attack and when she'd decided to move. At her request, her new coworkers made sure she never had to walk to her car alone, plus they invited her to everything. Dana accepted invitations often enough not to seem ungrateful, but she took time to work through things on her own.

Camille had never admired a person more. When they finished eating, Camille walked Dana to her car, then Dana drove Camille up a few floors to where she'd parked. They texted each other when they arrived at their homes, and then Camille set to work on plans for their date.

She'd stayed true to her word about taking Dana somewhere unique that she would enjoy, but with this new information, Camille made adjustments. The first was searching her closet to find all her black clothes. She didn't have anything quite as chic and cute as what Dana had worn the night they'd met, but she had a dress she liked, plus boots and a long sweater coat. She'd be warm and in Dana's seemingly favorite color.

Next, she hired a car.

Camille's brother would drive her anywhere, anytime, but she didn't want him dumping cold water on her first big date with Dana. Then she arranged for a hot dinner to be waiting for them when they arrived at the date. All she had to do was get herself to calm down and treat Dana the way she always had.

Dana's story had inspired a deep desire in Camille to make sure Dana felt safe with her. She liked her as much—if not more—than before and she didn't want Dana to think she was doing a tour guide thing. She wanted Dana. In Charleston. In her life. And she wanted that shadow of sadness and suspicion Dana carried in her eyes to fade away.

Camille shushed the little voice in her head that said the sooner Dana found her feet, the sooner she'd leave. Tour guides were accustomed to sending people on their way after a short while. Camille was determined to break that pattern with Dana.

By the time she knocked on Dana's door, she'd managed to get herself mostly under control. She was still excited about their date, but she wasn't afraid she would treat Dana with kidgloves.

Camille held out her arms and smiled when Dana answered her door. "I wear black!"

Dana laughed. "You look stunning." She pointed to her forehead. "I have bangs!"

Camille brushed her finger along the edge. "I like them."

Dana wrinkled her nose and took a step back, gesturing for Camille to follow. "I thought I'd look like Jessica Biel. I was wrong."

"They're pretty on you," Camille said.

Dana blew the bangs off her forehead. "They're growing out. I need to find a hairdresser." She stopped at a small table a few feet from the door with a mirror hanging above it.

"I can help with that."

Dana combed her bangs to the side and snapped a jeweled barrette in place, then faced Camille. "Ready."

"You're stunning." Camille held out her arm. "Let's go."

Dana had surprised Camille with a jar of honey from the farmers market, along with a dipper and small porcelain rest.

Camille blushed when she saw the southern lady fern painted on the rest and gave her tinkly laugh, kissing Dana's cheek and declaring it perfect.

Camille had a bigger surprise for Dana, though: a sunset cruise, complete with a full dinner. The other passengers on the boat had to buy appetizers from the snack bar, but Camille had sweet-talked her way into bringing a feast onto the boat for the two of them.

"Do you know everyone in town?" Dana asked.

Camille giggled. "Seems that way, doesn't it?"

Dana looked back at the water. A dolphin leaped, not far from the catamaran. "This is so much better than parasailing."

"I bet you could see more parasailing."

"Nope. I'm good." Dana sipped some wine.

"Not afraid of sharks?"

Dana tugged a lock of Camille's hair and wrapped it around her finger. "No. North Dakota was full of sharks. Nothing to be afraid of."

"Aren't y'all landlocked? I thought sharks live in salt water, not fresh water."

Dana pulled Camille against her, back-to-front, as they approached a lighthouse. "The Dakotas used to be home to huge glaciers and then a seaway that connected the Canadian Arctic to the Caribbean. Plenty of sharks in those waters. And they left us incredibly fertile plains."

"You lived by a lake, right?"

"Yes."

"And now you live by the beach."

Dana adjusted her hold on Camille so they could move to see the details of the Ravenel Bridge the captain had pointed out. "Yes. In a corporate apartment."

"You're a water girl."

Dana heard the smile in Camille's voice.

"I guess I am."

"We can go fossil huntin'. We've got some great beaches for it and expert tours."

Dana let go of Camille and nudged her until the women faced each other. "This is amazing. I never would've thought of taking a sunset cruise. And I will hunt for fossils with you anytime and anywhere."

"I sense a *but* on the way." Camille straightened her posture.

"You don't have to plan big activities for me." Dana kissed Camille's cheek. "I want to spend time with you. I don't need to be entertained. We can sit around and hem weights into your dresses. I'll love it because you're there."

Camille gave Dana a stern look. "No one sews weights into dresses anymore."

Dana lifted her eyebrows.

Camille crossed her arms. "They have double-sided tape. No sewing. And how did you know I put weights in my dresses?"

Dana shrugged. "It's windy here."

Camille hugged her.

Dana held her close, a little more loneliness floated away. It was still bullshit she had to leave her home when those assholes got their nuts in a twist, but this. If she was being honest with herself, she'd been living half a life before she met Camille. Even before the attack.

When the cruise ended, Dana held Camille's hand as they walked to the waiting town car.

"I had an idea for what we could do next, but it's after dark. I don't want to push you."

Dana went to adjust her barrette, then stopped. Instead, she pulled her bangs out of the clip and blew at them before smiling. "You're not pushing. I'm having fun."

"Good." Camille gave her a quick kiss on the lips and gestured for Dana to get in the car.

Dana scooted across the backseat and told herself not to overthink her next question as Camille got in behind her. "I'd love to see what else you had planned, but if you don't want to do that anymore, we can go back to my place. I can show you the bajillion wind chimes Matthew delivered this morning for lighting."

"Oh yes! That." Camille gave the driver instructions and then sat back, peppering Dana with questions until they reached the apartment.

Dana dropped her keys on the hallway table when they entered and directed Camille to a bedroom near the door. She flicked on the lights, and the wall lit up.

Camille entered the room as if in a trance and walked straight to the painting Dana had made when she first moved to Charleston.

"This is amazing," she said in a hushed tone. "It's Lake Sakakawea?"

"And the night sky and all my favorite little spots." Dana leaned in the doorway, studying Camille as Camille got close to the art and slowly made her way across the wall.

When Dana had first moved, she'd been so homesick that she constantly doodled her North Dakota life. Eventually, she'd measured the room and bought enough plywood to cover one wall. She'd added edging at the back to make space for her lights and transferred her doodles to the wood, then drilled small holes for the lights to create constellations, glimmer on the lake, and every other lit thing she could conceive. Finally, she'd painted it.

At first, she'd thought for sure she'd ruin it. She only had experience painting actual walls, not art, but somehow, after two months, it looked beautiful. After another two months, she'd stopped spending every spare moment sitting in front of it wishing she was in one of the places she'd painted. Now, she appreciated it as a new type of art she could make and left it on when she worked on the glass pieces for Joyce.

When Camille turned to Dana, there were tears in her eyes. "I don't know what to say. This is amazing."

"You said it." Dana gave her a gentle kiss near her temple. "Don't cry. Let's put on a movie or something."

Camille nodded and followed Dana to the back of the apartment. The far wall was a giant set of sliding glass doors that looked out on the ocean. "*This* is a corporate apartment?"

Dana shrugged. "My company really wants me to stay in Charleston."

"They're not the only ones."

Dana woke the next morning with Camille in her arms. They were tangled in bed in the big bedroom with the ocean view—the one Dana hadn't slept in much because it was so different from what she'd been used to. This had been the first time she'd fallen asleep in here without getting up in the middle of the night to move to the front bedroom.

Camille was why.

"Waking up to a view of the ocean is always amazing, but waking up next to you is even better," Camille said.

Dana hummed and pulled Camille tighter to her. They were naked, and Dana took advantage of this, running her fingers everywhere she could reach while still holding Camille. She wasn't willing to end any part of their contact. Camille peppered Dana's cheek, neck, shoulders, and chest with kisses.

"Tell me you don't have some important Southern thing you need to do today. Tell me we can stay right here," Dana said.

"I don't. You better not have some special midwestern thing to do either."

Dana chuckled. "The only thing I have to do is spend the day with you."

"Perfect," Camille said before kissing Dana.

Chapter 6

The next month flew by. Camille spent the time between holiday parties and tours preparing her own walking tour with one of the more prominent companies in the city. Dana started a new project at her construction firm and took on a variety of art projects at the shop on Queen Street. The pair hadn't officially moved in together, but they rarely spent a night apart.

Once Camille had secured her new tour contract, Dana had been her test audience, giving her opinion on the length of the tour, the most interesting stops, and whether the information Camille shared at each one was compelling. Dana had seemed the most captivated by the Old Charleston Jail. Camille hoped it was because of the building's history and all the ways it'd been used over the years, not because it reminded Dana of the person who'd gone to jail for assaulting her. He'd earned his place there, but Camille didn't like the idea of Dana dwelling on it.

She shimmied her key into the lock of Dana's apartment, she needed to get her change of clothes, and Dana, and get to the tour office well before her tour time. The tour had been pre-sold, with every ticket reserved for the next two weeks. Camille was jittery with nerves and excitement. She pushed the door open and smiled as Dana came toward her with her garment bag.

She looked beautiful with her new layered bob haircut. It was short in the back and had a whisper of her former bangs brushed over her ear where she used to wear a bobby pin or barrette. Her purple sweater was just bright enough to qualify as a "Charleston color," as Dana put it.

"Do you also want makeup?" Dana asked.

"I have some in the car." Camille gave Dana a quick kiss, then backed out of the apartment. "You promise to ask questions if the group seems bored?"

"They won't be bored."

"They might. This tour is different."

"Camille." Dana put a hand on her shoulder when they reached the car. "You're great. No one is gonna be bored. You're the best tour guide I've ever met, and after all the tours we've attended, I'm an expert in what's the best. You're it, hon."

Camille gasped. "You called me *hon*."

Dana smiled.

"I knew I'd get you to say something at least a little Southern." Camille hugged her, crushing the garment bag between them. She cherished these little moments when Dana actually seemed like *hers*, not on loan from another life.

"Get in the car before we're late." Dana opened the door for Camille, then put the garment bag in the back before getting in herself.

Camille took the long way so she could drive her route before checking in for the tour.

Dana frowned at the construction signs as they passed the Old City Jail. "I'm surprised you kept the jail in your tour."

"It gives me the opportunity to tell everyone how stupid the death penalty is since murder's illegal. Though when this jail was in use, life in prison probably would've been worse."

"It was pretty squalid."

Camille nodded. "And violent."

"Lavinia Fisher was in this jail," Dana said.

"Yeah." Camille gave a sad sigh. "She was framed. Lavinia never should've been there. She'd been forced from her home by a lynch mob, accused of crimes she didn't commit, and hanged for a crime they never bothered to charge her with."

"They took everything from her," Dana said in a hushed voice.

"She thought her friends would stand up for her, help her get her life back. She spent about a year in the jail, and when she was brought out to be hanged, none of them said a word. I have no proof of it, but I imagine that pushed her anger to a whole new level."

Dana paled, then shook her head. "It would've for me."

Camille pulled into the tour company's staff parking area. "My brother said he'd be here early. You'll have someone to chat with while I welcome everyone."

Dana took the garment bag from the backseat. "I can welcome them with you."

Camille beamed, appreciating Dana's unwavering support. "I'd like that."

The rest of the night passed in a blur. Camille smiled non-stop, welcoming her customers and telling stories as she walked them around Charleston. She was triumphant by the end and used it as an excuse to light sparklers on the beach when they got home. Watching Dana through the cheerful lights, Camille was overcome with happiness. When they burned out all the sparklers, Camille pulled Dana into a tight hug.

"I love you," she whispered into Dana's ear.

Dana pulled back, shock on her face. "You do?"

"How could I not?"

Dana closed her eyes. "I've been waiting for you to get tired of me."

Camille huffed a laugh. Funny, she'd felt the same way. "I could never."

Dana hugged Camille again. "I love you too."

Chapter 7

Camille shouldered her way into the apartment, loaded down with groceries. Dana had made a list of foods her mother liked, plus things she wanted her to taste during her Valentine's visit. She'd made Camille laugh out loud in the store when she'd sent a follow-up text that said, "No grits!"

Excited that Dana finally had things she loved about Charleston and wanted to share, Camille had gone a little overboard. Even as she struggled to balance the bags, she regretted nothing.

Once she lined the sacks up on the kitchen counter, she hustled to the bathroom. As she washed her hands, she noticed the counter looked sparse. None of the usual toiletries were out. She peered into the shower and discovered the same thing. The products were all gone.

Clothes were missing from the closet too. She retreated to the living room in a daze, looking for her phone to call Dana. A box with her hair products and makeup sat on the coffee table. Camille's stomach sank. She'd long suspected she'd always be temporary in other people's lives—the way tour guides were to visitors—but it had never been laid out so starkly for her.

Camille rushed back to the kitchen and grabbed her purse, digging through it for her phone. She needed it and her keys, then she'd grab that box and go. Dana not wanting to face her made this worse, but Camille didn't want to cry in front of her. It was shitty, but it had that one benefit.

"Camille!" Dana's voice carried through the apartment from the door. "I saw your car! Where are you?"

Camille sniffled, then fixed her expression and stepped into the hallway, box in hand. "The groceries are on the counter. I'll get out of your hair." She started down the hallway, hoping Dana would move clear of the door before she started to cry.

Dana shut the door. "What are you talking about?"

Camille gestured with the box. "You packed my bathroom stuff. My clothes aren't in the closet. I can take a hint."

"Oh, my god, no." Dana paled and moved toward Camille. "My clothes aren't there either."

320

Camille backed away. "It's fine. I'll come back for them when you're not here."

"No!" Dana held her arms out, filling most of the narrow hallway and blocking the door.

Camille nodded. "As soon as I saw that mural, I knew. It's just a matter of time before you go back to North Dakota. It's okay. Your heart is there. I understand."

"Camille, I moved my clothes too." Dana moved toward Camille, her eyes wide and glassy. "And that box has *our* bathroom stuff."

Camille scrunched her forehead and looked in the box. It did seem awfully large for only her things.

Dana cleared her throat. "Mom called from her layover. My grandmother decided to come, too, and they got her a last-minute ticket. Since they'll be here for a few weeks, I figured you and I would move to the front bedroom and let them have the ocean view."

Camille didn't move or speak, letting the explanation sink in.

Dana ducked into the front room and turned on the lights. "Look."

Camille followed and watched as Dana opened the closet, revealing their clothes.

Dana took the box and set it on the counter in the ensuite, then came back to Camille and held her face. "Why would you think I'd drop you without a word? I love you. I can't wait for you to meet my family, and I don't want a day to pass when I'm not with you."

Camille blinked fast. "Ever since my new tour, you've been distant. You've only been excited about your mother's visit. I thought—"

"You said something I needed to process," Dana interrupted.

"About?"

"Lavinia Fisher. How everything had been taken from her, and she'd been accused of crimes she didn't commit."

Camille took a step back. "Huh?"

"I was mad about moving. I felt like I'd been forced from my home, like that guy and his dumbass friends had taken away everything I loved and then tried to get me in trouble to boot. But people stood up for me. My mom, my boss and coworkers, you. I can be mad that I had to leave my home and still appreciate the life I have here. The *better* life I have here. You helped me realize it was okay. I'm okay." She laid her hand gently on Camille's chest. "My heart is *here*."

Camille didn't care if Dana saw her cry anymore. "You're not leaving?"

"No. And you better not leave me."

Camille laughed through tears as she hugged Dana. "Absolutely not. There're at least a dozen more historical places I need to show you."

"And we haven't taped weights into your dresses yet."

"See? So much to do." Camille wiped tears from her face.

"I love you." Dana kissed Camille, then held her close.

Camille sniffled and squeezed Dana. "Welcome home."

END

About Elaine Reed

Elaine lives in South Carolina's low country. When she isn't writing, she can be found exploring Charleston, taking in live music and searching for shark teeth on the beach with her family. She has three full length novels and several novellas published. She is a contributor to the Love in the Lowcountry anthology series.

Find Elaine Online:
Website: https://www.elaine-writes.com/
Newsletter: https://www.elaine-writes.com/newsletter/
Facebook: https://www.facebook.com/elainereedwrites
Twitter: https://twitter.com/_elainewrites
Instagram: https://www.instagram.com/_elainewrites/
Amazon: https://www.amazon.com/Elaine-Reed/e/B07YNCV6LP
Goodreads: https://www.goodreads.com/author/show/16599589.
Elaine_Reed

The Watchman's Remedy

By Victoria R. Benson

The Watchman's Remedy

Time Travel

Cora has one task to complete at work: search the dungeon. Heading toward that final chore, her perceptions of Charleston's infamous Old Exchange Building are instantly questioned when she finds herself facing an imprisoned pirate. Pranks and ghost stories run rampant in her imagination. However, Cora's reality is no longer life in 2022, but in 1718. Though concerned by his friend's confusion, Jonathan Harris quickly secures the genuine affections of this modern day woman. Cora embraces that her role as Watchman has shifted from caring for a building to saving this man from a Christmas Eve death sentence.

Rated: PG

Chapter 1

"Is the Great Hall clear?" Cora asked.

"It is. I checked the Isaac Hayne Room as well. The second floor is officially closed."

"Good. The main floor is ready too. That just leaves the dungeon, and I'll take care of it."

"Want company? I hate that place at night," Andi replied with a visible shiver.

Cora smiled and said, "No. It doesn't bother me. You can leave. I'll just do a quick walk-through, turn off the lights, and lock up."

"I can wait for you. I don't mind."

"You don't have to. It will only take a few minutes. Tomorrow is Christmas Eve. We have another big day ahead of us with two formal events to host. Go home and get rested. I'm fine. Besides, I *am* the official night watchman."

The young ladies laughed.

Convinced, Andi left Cora to finalize the closure of the Old Exchange and Provost Dungeon for the night. Cora followed her co-worker to a backdoor of the building and kept eyes on her until she was in her car and driving away. They exchanged quick waves, and the lone building manager returned to the now dimly lit, eerily silent foyer.

"You don't believe in ghosts. You don't believe in ghosts." Cora chanted to herself as she pushed her arms through the holes of her black, woolen cape.

Once bundled, she stopped at the greeters' stand to retrieve a flashlight from the lower shelf. "Just in case," she muttered as she slid the switch up, checking to ensure it was in proper working order. An expression of relief was followed by a deep inhale. "To the dungeon!" Cora called out while pointing her flashlight upward and in the direction of the stairwell like a saber.

The walls, ceilings, and fixtures had been watching people come and go for hundreds of years. Cora was one more occupant in a long history of guests. The heels of her lace-up boots tapped the marble floor, sending reverberations throughout the observant archways. A mob cap held snugly to her head, and the floor-length, yellow brocade, colonial gown she wore had long since become a normal part of her wardrobe. It was as if the building itself had chosen the staff's attire.

With feigned confidence, Cora descended the stairs. Her full attention was on standing straight. She was determined to convince herself she was not the least bit creeped out by the countless stories she had heard of the spirits that lingered about in the dungeon when their audience had dwindled. Step after step, Cora thought only of her shift's final duties. Logic was her mindset.

Despite her efforts to be nonchalant, Cora nervously rattled her keys in one hand and continued to grip the flashlight in the other. Her pace quickened . . . until the toe of her boot caught in the front hem of her dress. A disturbed squeal pierced the air, and down she went.

Barely cognizant of what had actually happened, Cora opened her eyes. Her cheek pressed against the dampened dirt floor while the rest of her body was sprawled above her on the steps. At first, she realized she wasn't even able to *try* to stand. She lay in a reverse incline from what nature intended and assessed her pain by slowly moving a few muscles at a time. Some shallow exhales were joined by moans of complaint.

"How could you be so careless, Cora?" she whispered to herself.

As moments passed and Cora became certain that nothing was broken, she lifted her head to check her hands for injury. Looking at her soiled palms, frustration swelled when she noticed they were both empty. "My keys," she whined, and she immediately lowered her throbbing head back to the surface beneath her.

"Miss? Miss? Are yeh well?"

Cora gasped. She raised up onto her elbows, hoping her imagination was her only company.

"Since I see yer able to move, I hope yeh don' mind me asking, yeh didn't spill my tea, did ya?"

The question immediately irritated her. Certain she was not imagining things, Cora searched for the voice's owner without getting up. The expanse of her workplace's lowest floor was not what she beheld. Instead of arched ceilings constructed of bricks, wooden flooring, wall hangings, dioramas, and artifacts, Cora's setting was a very small room. It was partitioned by floor-to-ceiling bars and barely lit by the glow from one lantern atop a table placed just out of reach from the strange man sitting on the other side of the bars.

The ache in her back from her curved position on the floor signaled it was time to move. Cora pulled her legs toward her core. They slowly slithered down the wooden planks like two snakes. When finally seated in a position that made her feel like her body parts would work in unison again, Cora analyzed her surroundings once more.

Thankfully, the unsolicited chatter had subsided. This gave Cora time to refocus. Nothing made sense. "Did I take the wrong stairwell? Is this a room I've never been in?"

"Speak up; I can't hear ya."

Cora turned her attention to the stranger. "Who *are* you?"

His reply was a snort accompanied by a soft chortle.

"Do you work here? Are you new?"

The chuckle grew louder.

"Stop laughing! I could have broken my neck!"

"'Tis not an outright laugh you hear, miss. 'Tis merely the melody of me being mildly amused. Yer neck has come through that ordeal unscathed. What would've been worse is you coulda knocked out some of those teeth I've grown to enjoy grinning at me during each of my evenin' meals. Yeh should be more careful."

"I don't grin. At anyone. Ever. And I don't even know you," Cora chided.

"Yeh grin at me, Miss Cora."

"How do you know my name?"

"Yeh told me yer name."

Dumbfounded, Cora gaped and stared. The man who sat at a distance before her didn't appear to be very old. Perhaps he was in his twenties. He could be one of the guides who decided to get drunk and sneak back into the building. Maybe he'd accidentally locked himself in this unoccupied room. He was in costume, although his clothing was dingy and shaggy, and brown curls framed his scruffy face.

"Seriously, who are you?"

More snickering and a strongly accented response was received. "I'm a man who's thinkin' yeh hit yer head in that nasty spill yeh just took on those stairs. I hope this doesn't mean we won't be friends anymore. You forgettin' who I am an' all."

Cora realized that despite her refusal to accept the rumors that plague her workplace, they might hold some truth. "Oh no, no, no. You're not a ghost, are you?"

"Lord, I hope not. I'm hangin' onto every bit o' life I have left. I am still breathin'. At least until your father leads me to the gallows."

"Father? Gallows?"

"Have you also forgotten that Captain Laurent of the Court of Guard of Charles Towne sired yeh? And if he gets his way, I'll be meeting my Maker tomorrow at sundown."

"Ah! I've stumbled upon an overzealous actor. This is a reenactment. I'm being punked." She then addressed Jonathan, "My father is Michael Dupont, and hangings were abolished as an acceptable method of public execution in the 1930s. So, tell me, in your setting, what year is it?"

The man stood from his seated lean against the wall and stepped inquisitively to the bars. He first looked at Cora with a pinched brow and tilted head. He then looked around. With raised arms he asked, "1930s? What year is it? We are in the same place, miss. We're here at the Court of Guard. It's December 23 in the year of our Lord 1718."

Having watched a pirate trial in the Great Hall, Cora was officially convinced this man was truly part of an elaborate prank on her. She placed her fists on her hips and smiled. "All right, is Andi here somewhere? Did my boss put you up to this? Are my coworkers messing with me?"

"Miss Cora, I'm thinkin' while yer sittin' there, yeh should take care and gather yer thoughts. Yer words are makin' no sense. The only mess I see is the one you made when you dropped my supper in yer fall. I know no Andi, yer boss is Captain Laurent, and a lady of your standin' does not work. I believe you've been . . . uh, touched." He tapped his temple with his index finger.

"I'm fine! What's your name? Oh, and, nice accent. It's very authentic. But you can drop the act now. I know why you're here. I've figured everything out. Very amusing."

"I'm not a performer, Miss Cora. My name is Jonathan Harris. I am twenty-six years old. I'm awaiting my trial tomorrow morning for piracy. The South Carolina Navy took me from a ship on the first day of October. There's not one soul left of the crew except me. Everyone else has found death or freedom from their accusations."

"I know the story. After all, I am a docent for the building." Cora reviewed lists of infamous pirates in her mind, eyeing Jonathan all the while. "I don't recall your name though."

"You've made that clear, Miss Laurent. Listen, while yer ponderin' or recollectin', will you scrape what you can of my supper from the ground and bring it to me? I'm only fed once a day. Yer homemade biscuits with slices of ham and warm tea have been on my mind since I 'woke this morn."

Cora looked to her right and sure enough, there was an overturned plate and a tipped teapot a small distance from her. She studied the china from where she sat, then scanned the area again for her keys and flashlight. After a quick glance at her dress and boots, she crawled to the plate, turned it over, and marveled at the two biscuits and two slices of ham. Immediately, she righted the teapot, noting it still had some tea in it.

"So you'll be bringin' that to me now, yes?" Jonathan inquired.

"I'm dreaming. That's it. I'm in a strange dreamlike state of consciousness," Cora rationalized to herself. "Just go with it."

To her current companion she said, "Uh, yes. I'm bringing your supper, Jonathan. I think I'm feeling a bit better."

"Glad to hear it."

The food was replaced onto the plate. Cora moved to a kneeling stance and picked up the teapot. "Do you have a cup?"

"Aye. Yeh know I do."

"No, I don't," she spoke under her breath, shaking her head. Then audibly she replied, "I'm just asking. No need for sassing."

Her defensive remark was met with a pleased yet inquisitive reply. "Yer sounding quite audacious this evening, now aren't ya?"

331

Jonathan watched her approach. His intense observation of her every move was not without notice.

"Your stare gives me the sense that your thoughts should be kept silent," Cora accused him.

"Yer perception is incorrect. I'm not ogling. I'm searching for signs of swooning."

"Swooning? As in attraction or distress?"

"No need to be so uppity about yerself. Perhaps I just don' want ya to drop my supper again. I see that the dirt has had the pleasure of drinking most of my tea."

Once within reach of her new acquaintance, Cora said, "I'm sure I can get you more tea."

"Not 'til the mornin', if they allow you to visit."

Cora handed what could be this young man's last meal to him through the bars. He took the plate and held it level while she set the food on it. His other hand pushed a cracked porcelain cup toward her, and she poured what bit of warm libation that remained in the teapot into it.

"You'll stay a while?" he asked.

Having decided to accept her strange situation, she replied politely, "As long as you wish."

"Those are words of liberty, Miss Cora. Those aren't yer words."

"If I'm not free, why am I allowed to come here?"

"No one else wants to feed me. They see bringin' me food as servants' work. They'd rather me starve. I'm thankful that you'll have none of that. Yeh've convinced yer father that yer doin' the Lord's work. No one argues."

"So, I'm nice?"

Jonathan held a biscuit and had just taken a bite of it, so he covered his mouth with the back of his hand. Apparently anxious to answer her question and still be polite, he swallowed hard and said, "Yer very nice."

Cora raised her eyebrows. "Well, I hope the new me isn't disappointing."

"Yer not disappointing to me! You have my solemn promise on that."

A comfortable silence rested between them while Cora watched Jonathan eat and sip. He seemed to be a gentleman. His manners were polished, and even in his unbathed, unkempt state, he was ruggedly handsome. Cora was glad he was the cohort in whatever one could call her circumstance.

"Jonathan, have I been coming here since you first arrived?"

"Very near the beginning. Once you learned they weren't going to feed those who weren't executed, you began gathering what you could for us."

The research she'd done stated one of the pirates had been hanged on December 10, so for the sake of clarification and reassurance she asked, "Have you been alone for very long?"

"Though I've tried not to keep track o' the days, I'm aware that it's been a fortnight since my ship's captain passed."

An ominous rumble of thunder groaned above them.

"'Tis a sign," he softly declared.

"'Tis weather," she corrected.

"Miss Cora, the most likely truth is that tomorrow, the eve of our Savior's celebrated birth, will be my final day on this earth."

"Why tomorrow?" she asked.

"My reckoning is that the well-to-dos want to awaken on their holy day with souls free from the stains of their pride and obstinance. With this cellar empty, they will perceive themselves as holy as the Christ-child himself."

Cora knew most pirates were not as blameless as they claimed to be. Many clutched onto self-images of being the good guys of seafarers even though they might not have known they shouldered a Robin Hood complex. Jonathan's innocence would have to reveal itself. She planned to hear all he had to say on his own behalf, though her intuition told her to doubt nothing he said.

Cora removed the lantern from what she saw was a milking stool and sat. Jonathan lowered to the floor in sync with her and continued savoring his small meal.

"Jonathan, how old am I?"

"Yeh worry me. You're eight and ten years, Cora."

She huffed a nearly inaudible puff of air from her nose thinking about being eighteen again. Cora of the twenty-first century was twenty-four.

His presence was beginning to cause her heart to beat faster. "Have we ever been on the same side of these bars?"

"Aye. Once. I had a fever, an' yer father allowed you to swab my head with a cloth until I recovered. I wanted to stay sick until I heard the angels singing."

"I'm glad you recovered; otherwise, I would have never gotten to meet you."

"Yeh just aren't makin' any sense."

"Perhaps not, but from my perspective, you, and *this*," she paused and motioned to their surroundings, "are new, and I am in control of it all."

"Control? Nay. Yeh need to awaken, Miss Cora. Ye are helpless, and I am hopeless." Though his words were saturated with despair, his eyes gleamed with peace and love.

She blinked away a tear, and pressure in her throat momentarily kept her from responding. Cora wanted to unlock the door, face him without obstruction, and tell him there was always hope. He had nothing to fear. "I am *not* helpless, and as long as you have breath, you are not hopeless," she said with conviction. "Look at me, Jonathan."

He did, and the corner of his mouth could not suppress a smile.

"I may look like the same girl who visits you every day, but I'm not her. Not anymore."

"I believe you, love."

"You should."

The cap on her head was becoming an irritant, so Cora pulled it off and rolled the laced edge between her fingertips. She watched Jonathan and he watched her.

When his mouth was clear, he asked, "A docent you say? What is a docent?"

Still disbelieving all that was occurring, Cora responded, "I teach people about the Romantic period in the history of Charles Towne when the pirates descended. I tell stories of how they pillaged and plundered, of their trials, and even how the architecture of many buildings was designed during the era when pirates roamed the streets of the city."

Jonathan drifted into a thought-filled trance. Unblinking eyes watched a scene visible only to him. "Romantic, eh? Yeh should know, the screaming is real. The blood is real. The tears of grown men desperate to survive is real. The awareness of a life wasted is real. There is no *romance* in pirating.

It's a brutal, shameful, hungry, hard existence. Why men choose it, I'll never understand. I didn't choose that life. A strong and violent man chose it for me. My heart wanted to escape, but my mind didn't know where to go. It's funny how finally being caught and placed in this cage has given me my first memories of freedom . . . and my first feelings of love. I always dreamed of having a wife and children and land bejeweled with a glorious home and fertile fields. For many years, I've imagined myself as a dignified and respected man."

"I don't really know you, but you certainly seem to be a very dignified man, at least compared to a lot of other men your age I've met. You will have all you dream of, Jonathan. We'll figure this out. Together."

"No, Cora. If yeh help me, yer father will not be able to save yeh from the assemblage of the nobles and lawmakers. Yeh'll be sentenced for yer interference."

"Listen! I didn't fall down those stairs and wake up here for no reason. This is my dream, too, and I am not going to let it end without doing everything within my power to resolve your predicament. I'm going to enjoy every minute of this. I have studied records for so many hours they surely amount to years of my life by now. We're getting you out of here!"

"Yeh certainly are different since you came to terms with your insanity. I thought yeh were always going to be a polite, obedient, and somewhat frail, if yeh don mind me sayin', daughter of a watchman."

"No. I'm a watchman, and we are going to save your life."

"Corabelle?" a deep voice called out, breaking their connection.

"Who's that?" she asked Jonathan.

The question sounded strange coming from her. However, based on the way she had been acting since her fall, Jonathan didn't seem surprised by her ignorant state. Taken aback, his brow pinched, and he replied, "That'll be yer father, Miss Cora."

"My name is Corabelle?"

"Aye. Corabelle Laurent."

"Corabelle, you've been down there long enough. Come now. It's time for you to go home."

"What's my father's name?"

With each inquiry, Jonathan grew more and more concerned. "Miss, yer father is Romain Laurent, Captain of the Guard. He is the commander of the watchmen." He then raised his voice. "Sir?"

"Shh!" Cora hissed.

"Sir? Captain Laurent, your daughter has taken quite a spill."

"Then she'll need to clean it up!" her father growled.

"Why would you tell him that?" Cora asked indignantly, but she also couldn't help giggling at Romain Laurent's reply.

"You're going to need a reason for not knowing anybody. Why not start with the truth? Better to admit that you've bumped your head than end up on trial as a witness for the devil or traitor or sympathizer. I heard tales from the old mates on board the ship of women young and old being accused of the strangest acts. Men believed them cursed. O' course from where I sit, I see now how easy it is for the ignorant to be convinced."

"You were on a pirate ship, Jonathan. The claims against you are not fabricated in feeble minds. Your situation is nothing like the ones you've heard from other colonies. The men on those ships *are* guilty of theft, murder, abduction, and worse."

"Not I, Cora. And before you got your sense knocked out of yeh, yeh trusted me."

"I'm not saying I don't trust you, but tell me, did you fire cannons or muskets at the Navy?"

"O' course! When someone points a gun to yer head and says 'LOAD!' yeh load! 'Tis my age that keeps me from being seen as innocent. My purpose, since I was placed on the ship at the age of nine, has been to stay alive. I'm proud of the fact that I got quite a will to do so." Jonathan smiled with pride at his innate determination.

Cora grasped the bars that separated them. She calmed at the knowledge of his persistent faith in his dreams. She offered an endearing smile in return. Each word, story, and glance from Jonathan was securing her affections. With a flirtatious raised eyebrow she accused him, "You're still a pirate."

"I never claimed to be good; I'm just sayin' I ain't bad."

Humored, Cora released a deep breath. "I just can't remember the name, Jonathan Harris."

"Corabelle! Don't force me to carry you out of that hole myself!" her "father" persisted.

Her attention turned to the top of the stairs until Jonathan asked, "How many times are yeh going to tell me you don't remember me?"

Cora's eyes widened and she shrugged. "I guess until I do."

Jonathan ran his finger down hers. "Remember me, miss. Yer my last hope. Yer the only one who can remedy the course of my life."

Cora understood why any woman would find such a man to be alluring. Without ignoring his heartfelt sentiment and pre-established attachment, she turned and projected her voice toward the stairs. "I'm coming, Father." She then asked Jonathan, "I do call him 'Father' right?"

His joyous laughter fully aroused the butterflies in her belly. "Yes! Yes, you call him 'Father!' I don' mind repeating it; I believe yer touched." Jonathan again tapped his temple. "Be careful out there."

She pointed. "I think in *here* is where I should be careful."

He winked.

As she walked back up the stairs, she heard his sultry whisper. "I like the new Cora."

Chapter 2

At the top of a very steep set of stairs was a distinguished gentleman. His attire was functional yet elegant. The style was not ornate and had no traits of being militaristic. He wore a dark blue wool coat adorned with pewter buttons. Beneath the open jacket was a deep red waistcoat topped with a wing-tip collar and a white linen cravat tied into a bow. The man wore tan knickers, white stockings, and black moderately heeled shoes embellished with a buckle.

"Come, daughter!" He waved his inviting hand impatiently. "Why are you dawdling? Rain will soon be falling, and it is nearly dark."

Cora gathered her skirt and undergarments in her hands and lifted them. She immediately noticed that each step barely had enough depth to secure the front half of her foot. "No wonder I toppled down these," she muttered.

When she was within reach of her "father," he took her elbow and lifted her out of the cellar. With her feet planted and her balance sure, Cora raised her eyes. She was definitely not standing in the Old Exchange Building. The room she was in was dull, utilitarian, and brown. It had one table and one chair. Each wall had a small shelf that held an oil lamp, and the wall opposite the entry had a rack with hooks for coats and slots for muskets. The history buff inside of her wanted to walk and observe every inch. However, the man who loomed over her with an impatient glare was never going to allow that.

"Off to home with you, Corabelle."

"Alone?"

"You've nothing to fear. The watchmen are posted."

"I'm not afraid of the dark. I, uh, I . . ." She wasn't sure how to say she didn't know where "home" was. Cora stepped to the door, leaned as if she were afraid something was going to rush in, and looked out at the scene beyond the porch.

Even in the shaded gloom of the pre-storm dusk, Cora beheld the antithesis of the Watch House. She awed at the colorful masonry, wood, clay, and stone buildings that lined East Bay Street to the north and south.

"You what, daughter?"

"I, um, would like for you to walk with me, please."

"The house you fear is quiet. There will be no taunting tonight."

Having been listening intently to every word, Jonathan called from below, "Miss Laurent?"

Cora rushed to the opening in the floor. "Yes?"

"You stroll past that house of ill-repute to the dock twice each day donning your yellow finery."

She gasped and whispered to herself, "I live in a yellow house on Queen Street—I mean, Dock Street—two away from the tavern. Of course, the old French Quarter."

"How do you know?" she asked Jonathan.

"'Tis what I've heard."

"Thank you, Jonathan."

Captain Laurent interrupted their awkward exchange. "Corabelle, come. I'll escort you home to your mother and younger sisters. It will afford me an opportunity to verify all bastions are manned."

Her father extended his arm, and Cora exited one world and entered another. A dull flash lit the sky, and another dismal rumble of thunder drummed above them. The gentleman allowed his eldest daughter to set their pace. She marveled at the sound of the waves lapping the sea wall. The aroma of the marsh was familiar, though purer. It lacked the petroleum fumes from the boats and ships that populated the harbor in her modern era.

"High tide," she commented.

"Mm-hmm," her father replied.

"The burning fish odor? Is that oil in the lamps?" Cora remembered the fuel for the lanterns would be whale blubber.

"You are correct again."

Along the bay, they strode until she was led left. More of the same architecture lined both sides of this street as well. It was all even more colorful than in the twenty-first century. Past homes and probably businesses, Cora gathered every detail into her senses until her father said, "Inside," and pointed her toward a three-story home.

"So this is where we live?"

Captain Laurent pulled from her hold and shifted, creating space between them. Cora received a look from a man who was almost fed up. However, his irritated expression didn't deter her next question. "Do we have a cook, a laundress, a housekeeper?"

"Yes. You! You! And you! Now why are you so bewildered this night?"

"I am only asking because I'd like to be reminded of how we live."

Romain Laurent clearly was beginning to take offense. "This is all very odd, Corabelle! Why you are seemingly ignorant this evening is beyond me. You know we left France and only arrived in the Colonies by the grace of King George. This new land is our refuge, but we came with nothing. We all work." He moved his finger in a circular motion. "Therefore, you work. You, your mother, and your sisters are all accountable for maintaining our household. Someday, we will purchase land outside of the city; but for now, we appreciate the opportunity to live with modesty. A show of gratitude from you would be appreciated."

Cora wanted to fit in with the era, so she tailored her response to one of an apologetic daughter. "Please, please don't be angry. I am grateful. I guess I have to confess, I fell down the stairs at the Court, and I haven't been feeling quite like myself since. My senses will return soon. No need to worry."

"Is that what the prisoner meant when he said you'd taken a nasty spill?"

"Yes. You misinterpreted what he said."

"You seem well enough now."

"Yes, Father. I am regaining my wits."

"Go eat and rest. I'll be home in a while."

A tapping sound began, then quickly increased in frequency. Cora scurried into the house, avoiding the raindrops. Three women sat properly in silken upholstered chairs near a fire. Cora greeted them collectively with a nod and smile while she observed the well-furnished small room. Then, to avoid conversation, she excused herself and went directly upstairs. On the second floor, she tiptoed about until she was certain she had found the daughters' bedroom, and she sat on one of the beds to gather her wits.

Every single person, building, smell, and sound was all very real. Cora had never felt so alive, so immersed in a dream before. She couldn't decide if she was going to wake up or if she should return to the Court of Guard to be with Jonathan. Only one thing was certain: she was not in a reenactment.

Chapter 3

The rains fell in such volume that no one could see beyond the width of one house. Concerned that ill-intended persons would find the deluge to be an ideal covering, Captain Laurent called the entire guard unit to patrol the streets for the night.

This was a blessing and a misfortune for Cora. She would be hidden beneath the sheets of rain, but she would also have more of a challenge evading the numerous watchmen as she made her way back to their headquarters.

The first thing Cora did while planning her escape from their quaint little home was listen to the three ladies on the first floor chat about chores and schedules. She learned her "sisters" names were Alyce and Emilee, and they had already served supper and cleaned the dishes.

Cora's chores had been completed before she'd set off for the jail because she was responsible for the morning meal. Next, she heard their father would be returning, which he had already mentioned. Finally, she learned a most important piece of information: their family would be hosting a Christmas Eve gathering for neighbors and visiting politicians.

Having eaten and finished with eavesdropping, Cora had decided she would go back to Jonathan. "But how am I going to get out of here?" She searched for something in sight that might give her reason to leave the house again. "Wait, I don't need permission. I'm in charge here."

Cora stood, opened the armoire, withdrew a cape, and headed out of the room and down the stairs.

"I'll return home later!" she called casually as she grasped the brass knob of the door.

"You'll go nowhere," her "mother" replied. "A young lady does not wander the streets at night. You've no escort and no assignment. Sit in here or retire to your room."

A memory from her studies flashed into her thoughts; in the early 1700s, there was a barn and a plot of land for farming at the northwest corner of the fortified city. "I'll be back, Mother. I forgot something at the barn."

"No! You have not!"

"I am responsible for collecting eggs. Our stock needs replenishing. The rain may only continue to fall, and the ground will be far more unstable and soft. By tomorrow, walking out there could be like trudging through the marshes. Let me go now."

"Not a consideration."

Boldly, she asked, "And if I leave, without permission, what will happen?"

"Your father will lose his position due to having a daughter with questionable morals. You are in until the sun rises."

Her lips tucked in the side of her cheek exhibiting her momentary defeat. "Very well, I'll wait."

Cora ascended the stairs and returned to her room. The thought of stuffing a makeshift body beneath one of the blankets occurred to her, but she wasn't sure which bed she slept in. Therefore, she stepped to the window and noticed the second level wasn't very high. She decided she could hold the sill and drop to the muddy ground without injury. Cora pulled the hood of her cape over her head, lifted the wooden frame, and proceeded to swing one leg at a time through it. She twisted, lowered until her body dangled, and with one small push away from the house, she released.

Sure enough, the surface below had turned to mush.

"Uck!" she groaned.

The cold rain was the definition of misery. Cora crossed her body with both arms and splashed from the alley behind her house to the front corner. She looked left, then right. The immediate vicinity was vacant of all humanity. Since no one was in sight, Cora ran east on Queen Street toward the bay.

At the crossroads of what she knew to be Queen and Church, to ensure she would not find herself face to face with Romain Laurent, Cora went south. The black cape that covered her grew heavier, and though the weight became cumbersome to the ease of movement, her truest discomfort was having her feet slosh in her boots.

Like a mysterious invader, Cora advanced toward Broad Street. Under the best of conditions, the visibility would have been subdued, but in the pouring rain, she could only raise her head every few yards to verify her immediate path was clear of any other people.

Soon, Cora found she was traversing an intersection. Knowing the vicinity, she paused and marveled, "Wow! It really is pink! Appropriate for a rumored brothel, I suppose." Unable to withdraw her attention from a remarkable structure that had stood the test of time for those moments, she didn't mind the rain that dropped aggressively upon her cheeks and into her squinting eyes. Cora would not be deterred from committing the moment to memory.

With a mission being her driving force, Cora proceeded. When she arrived at Broad Street, she stopped and attempted to hide by pressing her back against the wall of the building on the corner.

Evidently the recent invasions had instilled an extreme sense of caution among the men because guards saturated the main thoroughfare of the town. Studying the numbers, it was indisputable the entire perimeter of the city and the docks would also be heavily manned. The watchmen were intent on protecting property under the obscured conditions.

Though her progression had begun as a run, it slowed to a walk, and was now a trudge as puddles deepened around her ankles. Charleston was not immune to flooding during a storm that delivered an average accumulation of rain, therefore Cora was not anxious to see what was going to result from this downpour.

Drenched, the water running down her face and dripping in steady streams from her hair, Cora panicked. "The prison, the cellar, I wonder if it'll fill or if they've sealed it somehow!"

Despite the distance to the Half-Moon Battery still being a bit too far and knowing she wouldn't make it there undetected, Cora proceeded. She stayed low and alert and moved along the fronts of the buildings until she was close to the Guard House. When the only distance that remained was crossing East Bay, Cora emerged from a crouched stance and appeared like a ghost in the street.

Entering the building undetected was going to be an impossibility. Therefore, she called out in distress, "Hello!"

An immediate response followed, and a man was seen and heard splashing toward her. "Miss! What are you doing out here?"

Under the pretense of disorientation, Cora explained, "I was going to our barn and somehow went the wrong direction! Where am I?"

"Corabelle?"

"Yes!"

"You're at the waterfront. Your father is inspecting the perimeter. He'll not be back anytime soon. I'll walk you home."

"No! I'm so cold. Will you please let me warm up in the Watch House? If I've wandered this far, I'd rather just get inside as quickly as possible!"

The gentleman didn't want a woman in the chamber at night, but he also didn't want to leave his post for the length of time it would take to get her back home.

"Very well! Come with me." He offered her his elbow. "Though we are only steps away, I don't want to lose you in this weather."

Together they rushed toward the shelter. Thumping up the steps and into the building, Cora and her escort sighed. "Thank you . . ." She waited for him to supply his name.

"Maxwell," the guard replied.

"Oh yes, Maxwell?"

"Flemming! Maxwell Flemming! You've known me for over a year, Miss Laurent."

"I'm sorry, Mr. Flemming. I'm feeling out of sorts, my vision is blurred from the rain, and getting lost in the cold has me stymied."

"'Tis understandable. Not a concern. Do you need anything?"

"No. You can return to your post. Now that I have my wits back, I'll go home once I've warmed up."

"I may be able to get you there in a while, miss."

"Thank you."

Cora removed the heavy-laden cloak and hung it on a hook behind the desk.

Her escort bid her a quick adieu. "You'll find me just outside if you need me."

Cora nodded and thanked him again.

Her curiosity became all-consuming. There was a blueprint on file in the Old Exchange's records room of the original building, the building in which she stood. Cora had only been able to imagine the scene for so many years. Before visiting Jonathan, she decided to give herself a tour of the interior.

Below, Jonathan had heard the pounding of boots over his head, but with the cellar door closed, he couldn't discern the voices of the occupants nor their exchange.

Cora took an inventory of all she beheld. There were ink jars, quills, boots, and uniforms, and she even noticed a key hanging nearby. She took the key from its hook, but her obsession was the history that surrounded her. She marveled at knowing Charleston's first police force distributed uniforms to its officers.

In the attic, she found the armory. Weapons and barrels of gunpowder were stored at the top level. Modern-day speculation was the ammunition had been stored in the cellar.

"The cellar! The attic is the storage because the cellar does flood!"

Her footsteps pounded down the wooden stairs and across the floor of the entry to the trapdoor. She lifted it, descended halfway into the cellar, and bent to see Jonathan.

"It'll flood in here, won't it?" she asked with urgency.

"Aye. I won't be needing that trial tomorrow morning, after all."

"I'm not going to let you die, Jonathan!"

"So that's you I've heard tapping around up there?"

"Yes! Look what I found?"

Cora held out the key to the lock of his cell.

"I'll not be leavin' here, miss. They'll kill us both."

The water was seeping in and rising. It was at Jonathan's ankles. "I need a few more minutes," Cora said as she jumped upward and disappeared. When she returned, her arms and hands were full.

"Be careful. 'Tis not the time to take another tumble," he advised.

Cora laughed and cautiously eased her way down each step. Once on solid ground, she propped all she carried atop a box against a wall and rushed with the key to the bars. She inserted the molded iron bit into its complementary hole, turning it, a grinding clink forced a grin to appear.

"See, I told yeh I've seen ya grin," Jonathan reminded her.

"We did it! You can leave with me!"

Jonathan held up his arm to show the thick links that kept him attached to his prison.

"Is there a separate key?" she asked.

"I'm afraid so," was his melancholy reply.

"Ugh! I'll be back."

Cora gathered the massive layers of fabric that weighed her down and high-stepped through the water back to the ladder. Up she went to the desk, rummaging through it once again, and then she slammed the drawer shut.

As she began another descent, a thump was heard. Cora turned and watched the latch of the front door lift. Hearing the same sound, Jonathan pulled the gate so it looked closed, and he froze. Cora rushed back to the desk, sat in the chair, and waited.

Maxwell Flemming peeked inside. "Are you ready to return home?"

Terrified he'd notice the trapdoor propped open, Cora stepped to him. "I'm enjoying the sounds of the storm. I'm also not anxious to go back out into this downpour."

His eyes narrowed and his head tilted. "You look guilty, Miss Laurent."

She thought for only a quick second and replied, "I've been writing . . . at the desk. I'm not allowed to do that at home. Please don't tell my father. If you can give me a few more minutes, I'll be done."

He cocked a suspicious eyebrow. To secure her excuse Cora asked, "You won't tell, will you? My father will be so disappointed."

"I'll not tell, but stay out of the cellar. This rain will be continuing all night, so the prison cell will fill."

"Shouldn't you move, Mr. Harris?"

"No. It'll save the time and trouble of a trial. Just stay out of there."

"You don't need to worry. He doesn't even know I am here."

Maxwell pulled the door closed. Cora fumed and stomped back down to Jonathan. Slogging to him, she growled, "Oh, you are leaving!"

Another key was withdrawn from her pocket, and she released his wrists from the shackles. Cora grabbed him and pulled him out from behind the bars.

Rubbing his wrists Jonathan said, "I don't know yer plan, but I am anxious to hear it."

"My plan is to send you out into the world so you can make a fresh start."

Despite how entertaining she had been, Jonathan turned solemn. His informal dialect faded, "Corabelle Laurent, you aren't thinking through these decisions. Everything you are doing is dangerous. You may not remember, but you have my heart. I cannot let you do this."

"I don't need to remember anything. I only need to know you're alive."

"The book learning you mentioned haunts you, doesn't it?"

Finally, her obsession made sense. Cora didn't know of Jonathan because the only names she could recall were those of the captain who was killed and the three pirates who were acquitted. "Please. I beg you. Let me do this."

"First tell me, in the world you've created in your mind, does Corabelle Laurent exist?"

"No, she doesn't," she confessed.

"Then perhaps 'tis fate that we are here."

"Yes. I believe this is fate," she replied.

"Tell me, what are my orders?"

Cora smiled. "Jonathan, you have to remove all of your clothes. We have to make it appear that you've drowned."

His look of shock told her that was not what he expected to hear. "I'll not be shimming down to my bare flesh with you watchin'!"

"Don't argue, just hurry! I can get you out of here, but you have to leave your clothes behind. I've found some boards. I'll put them inside your clothes so they'll look like you're floating. It will buy us at least a day or possibly two so you can get out of Charleston."

"Oh no! I'll not be allowing you to see me frigid and meek. 'Tis not the impression I want to leave on an innocent lass."

Fully understanding his innuendo, Cora bent until she could curtail her boisterous laughter. Once she was upright, she took a deep breath and responded, "Don't worry about being frigid and meek! Worry about being alive! And take off those filthy clothes." Continued giggles could not be suppressed.

"I'll take death over misinterpretation of my manhood, Miss Cora."

They were running out of time. Cora knew Maxwell would undoubtedly return to check on her soon. Though his modesty was still very amusing, she pleaded, "Jonathan, I am actually begging you to remove everything. I'll make a dummy, attach it to the chains, and lock it in the cell. No one is going to want to remove a lifeless body from this place. Please!"

He pondered her idea for a brief moment and conceded, "Ugh! I'll do it. But turn yer back."

Being coy, Cora replied, "I'd rather not."

Jonathan placed his hands on his hips. The water had reached their kneecaps. Biting the inside of his lip, he calmed and stared into her eyes. She offered a raised eyebrow that was accompanied by an amorous smile.

He began to disrobe. As he unbuttoned his linen shirt, he said, "Keep yer eyes up, missy."

"I'll try," she replied flirtatiously.

Clearly Jonathan decided he was going to enjoy instead of dread the moment. His movements were sultry, and he never lost eye contact with the young woman he had grown to love.

When all had been slipped from his body, Cora cheated. She stepped back, observed the smooth, lean yet muscular physique before her, and she rushed toward him. He wrapped his arms around her, and they savored their first kiss.

Neither wanted to part, but the level of the pooled water was creeping higher. As it eased its way to their thighs, it was time to prepare the makeshift mannequin and get Jonathan somewhere safe.

They released one another.

"I do like the new Cora," he complimented.

She chuckled, turned away from him, grabbed a roll of cloth, and with an extended arm said, "Here, put these on while I tie your old clothes to the wall over there."

Jonathan looked at what she handed him and chided, "Yeh've stood here gawking at me, kissing me, touching my nakedness, and all along yeh had a shirt and breeches sitting right there?"

"I wasn't *gawking*, I was drinking you in with my eyes."

"Oh my, the crude words you put together. Yeh sound like a woman who spends her time at a brothel."

"How dare you insult me!" Cora gaped with feigned offense.

"*That* was a compliment."

Cora giggled.

Seductive and confident, Jonathan asked, "What kind of ruddy demon are yeh, Corabelle Laurent?"

It was time to move this plan for his liberation along. A quick kiss was planted on his lips, and she said, "I'm the kind of demon who doesn't know what tomorrow will bring. There was no way I was going to miss an opportunity to collect all of this," she paused, waving her finger up and down while pointing at him, "and store it away safely in my memory."

"Yer naughty. I'd very much like to keep yeh."

"I'd like that too. But for now, let's get out of here."

Cora waded through the water into the cell with Jonathan's clothes and three boards. While he dressed, she slid the boards into the arm and leg holes and tied the garments together. She then managed to attach the cuff of the chain to the wrist of the shirt and floated the clothed planks so they would appear to be a body face down on top of the water.

She gathered her skirts and draped them over one arm, then pulled awkwardly on the cell door with her free hand. Once it was closed and locked, she joined Jonathan waiting near the steps and told him, "I'll go up first and check the street. You're dressed like a watchman, so as long as you don't have to talk to anyone, you should be able to escape."

"And where shall I go without you?"

His soft tone made her throat tighten. Standing a few steps above him, Cora looked back and downward into his innocent, yet wanting eyes. She turned, sat on a stair, and pulled him to her for another deeply affectionate kiss. Jonathan's hungry hands filled themselves with all they could in that moment, and his body pressed against her craving freedom and connection.

Cora whispered, "You'll go anywhere but here. Go far away from Charleston so I'll know you're alive."

"I'm not sure I want to be alive without you."

"Don't be noble, Jonathan. Be free. Live that dream of having a farm and a family."

"Listen to her, lad!" a stranger's voice coaxed. "Come with me."

They both looked up in shock. A neatly coiffed man stood over them.

"Who are you?" Jonathan asked.

"Rumors got out that one more lived. We brethren weren't going to let you die. I've got a boat anchored out in the harbor and a ship quite a bit farther out. We're going . . . now!" He looked at Cora. "Thank you for making my job a lot easier, miss."

Cora climbed up the steps with Jonathan clambering behind her. With no time to plan, Cora rushed to her cloak and swung it around her shoulders, pulling the hood up she said, "Please go, Jonathan!"

He pressed one last kiss to her lips. When he released her, she waved goodbye and ran from the building.

From the corner of her eye, Cora saw the two men watching her get the attention of a nearby officer. She lead him north on Bay Street. One final glimpse over her shoulder had Cora hoping to see them escape to freedom.

The stranger and the handsome young pirate stepped from the porch, kept their backs to the wall, and disappeared around the south corner of the Charles Towne Court of Guard. No footprints would be seen, no evidence of an unknown comrade's presence would be found, and no record of a rogue young pirate's escape would make the history books. Jonathan Harris vanished from the world on December twenty-third, seventeen-eighteen.

Cora sheltered her head from the unrelenting rain. *I'll tell your story. I'll remind the world that you existed.*

Chapter 4

I'm still here.

Bright light aroused Cora from a deep slumber, lying in her warm bed the night watchman studied her setting. "I'm still in Captain Laurent's house?"

The memory of the previous night momentarily consumed her thoughts. After some time of staring at the ceiling, wondering what had happened to her pirate, listening to the continuous rainfall, and dreaming of Jonathan, she had finally fallen asleep.

The patriarch's voice called, "Corabelle, rise. We've much to do, but no task can be completed until we've been fed."

The sunshine was irresistible, so the window was her first stop once she was on her feet. The alley behind their home was certainly still flooded, but the skies were clear. Cora rushed to dress and join her family in the parlor.

"Did the dungeon fill?" she asked her father.

"Aye. When that much rain falls, it always does."

"What about Mr. Harris?"

With eerie nonchalance, Romain replied, "He is either sitting in judgment with the Almighty, or if he is tall enough, he may still be alive."

"And when will we know?"

"The rains have flooded the roads into Charles Towne; all are impassable. The trial of Jonathan Harris will be postponed until after the Holy Days."

Continuing her pretense, Cora asked, "Will I be allowed—?"

"No! You'll no longer be caring for that man. You shall feed your family, then help your mother and sisters prepare for the soiree we are hosting this evening."

"Yes, Father." Obedient and secretly ecstatic, Corabelle Laurent followed her father's commands.

The entire morning and afternoon, she was the ideal daughter and the very model of pleasantness. When the first hint of dusk blanketed the sky, Cora selected an impressive silk gown embroidered with roses to wear, and she awaited a return to reality.

Guests arrived, and the Laurent family greeted them with utmost joy and respect. The hosts' three daughters circulated about the room offering refreshments and treats. Smiles adorned their lovely faces.

Lingering in each other's vicinity, Alyce spoke into Cora's ear. "Corabelle, Father appears to be making arrangements on your behalf." Alyce nudged her head in the direction of Captain Laurent.

The moment her father had her attention, Cora received a motion to join him. She set the silver tray she carried upon a table and nervously walked to the gentlemen.

"Corabelle, this is Mr. Joshua Harper. He has arrived from Virginia. He was to visit relatives in the area, but the storm sent his boat off course a bit. His misfortune is to our benefit."

Her focus and full attention turned from Romain Laurent to the guest. Cora offered her hand for greeting, curtsied with lowered eyes, and then raised them with a gasp.

"I'm in need of a bed for the night, and your father has been kind enough to make arrangements for me. As he said, my name is Joshua Harper, and it is my exclusive pleasure to be introduced to you, Miss Corabelle Laurent."

Jonathan stood with a more elegant presentation than any other man in the room. His clothing was exquisite; his manners refined; his hair cleaned, cut, and styled; and his face was free of whiskers and absolutely flawless.

She stared.

"I'll leave you two to get better acquainted." Captain Laurent bowed and backed away from their company.

When she was sure no one was listening, Cora scolded in a hushed tone, "How dare you come here!"

Jonathan smiled. "Exhibit only pleasantries, love."

Their gaze created a magnetism, a desire, that would not be denied for much longer.

"I'll make an excuse for my departure. Go to the barn," she ordered.

Jonathan sipped the wine he held and casually exited the room. Cora left through a side door that led to the carriage house and kitchen. She hurried to the barn down the street.

The heavy door was slightly ajar. Cora gave it a slight pull, entering through it, then closed and latched it behind her. She ran to him. "You *are* why I am still here, Jonathan."

"Careful, love, you must call me Joshua now."

Without giving her a chance to speak again, he kissed her. She accepted his gesture and moved them into a more intimate position.

From their recline in the dark, Joshua said, "My life isn't worth living if I can't have this every day."

With her head resting on his shoulder she asked, "How did you get back here?"

"The shortened version is: the man who came to rescue me from the noose asked me who the lassie was beneath me in the cellar, and I told him you were a girl,"

"Girl?" she interrupted.

"Pardon me, you are the one and only *woman* who was able to get me out of my knickers, and I was sure you would've had your way with me if we'd been anywhere else in this world."

Cora smirked because he was absolutely right. "Obviously."

Another salacious kiss was placed and he continued, "Sir Robert gave me quite a regal set of raiment, rowed me up the river, planned a tale for the folks of this town, and set me off to come back to you. Oh, I have this for you as well."

Joshua pulled a necklace from his pocket. Hanging from the chain was a small golden owl with diamonds for its eyes. He held it up, and its delicacy awed Cora. Before he latched it around her neck, he turned it over. "Look, Corabelle, I've engraved it for you."

On the back was an etching that read, *Love, JH*. Cora turned and lifted her hair in acceptance of the gift. The clasp was hooked and his lips again enjoyed all that finally belonged to him.

Nestled in the private comfort of his arms with his body next to hers, Cora asked, "Why an owl, Jonathan?"

"No, Corabelle. My name is Joshua."

"Why an owl, Joshua?"

"My love, eagles watch over the day, but owls watch over the night. The owl is revered as a virtuous and wise protector."

"A night watchman," she lovingly agreed.

Chapter 5

"Cora. Cora."

Disoriented, Cora heard a deep exhale. She heard it again, and then once more before she realized it was coming from her own body.

"Jonathan?"

"No."

"Joshua?"

"No, Cora. My name is Nate."

There was no glow from any lights detected. The room had to be nearly dark. Cora squinted, barely allowing her eyes to open. "Who are you?" she asked before even attempting to identify her surroundings.

"I'm Nate, a paramedic. I brought you here to the hospital yesterday."

"Hospital? What day is it?"

"It's Christmas . . . Christmas night, actually. Your family has been here all day, but they left a little while ago. I'll call them and tell them you're awake. They are going to want to come back to see you."

With a raspy voice, Cora slowly said, "Wait. No. Tell me what happened."

"You fell down some stairs at work. No one found you until yesterday morning when the manager opened the building. He called for an ambulance, and we arrived. You could have died. You have quite a head injury."

"It was so real," Cora muttered as tears rolled from her eyes into her hair. Nate leaned over her and wiped the streams as they fell.

"Shh . . ." he soothed as they continued to flow. "You will probably be very emotional for some time, but you're going to be all right."

Distraught that all she had experienced was over, she asked, "He's just gone?"

"Cora, who are you talking about? Your dad or brother?"

Her chest heaved a few times, and she placed her hand on her forehead. "I'm so confused," she sputtered.

"Do you mind if I turn on the light over your bed? I'll keep it dim. I'd like to help you sit up so you can sip some water. That might help you wake up a bit."

Cora gave her permission with a nod.

Nate pushed the button on her bedside remote, and one fluorescent bar illuminated. He then pressed another button to raise the head of her bed. "Is that okay with you?" he asked gently.

Again, she nodded.

The tray table was placed on the other side of the bed from where he stood. The caring paramedic reached across to get Cora's tumbler of water.

Her eyes fully opened. "What is that?"

"My watch?"

Her throat was dry, and she was now trying to speak through the sobs, but she said, "Yes! Your watch! That's mine!"

"Um, no, Cora," he replied delicately. "This watch is mine. My mother gave it to me on my eighteenth birthday. It's been in our family for generations."

She looked at him. "No. It's mine. That owl inset in the watch face is mine. It's engraved. 'Love, JH' is on the back."

"How do you know that?!"

"I know it because it is mine," she insisted once more.

Nate recalled what his mother had said the day she gave it to him. "*You are to take care of the watch; it belongs to you. But the owl in the center belongs to the woman who will watch over your heart.*" The men in his family had always given the owl to their wives, and when the oldest son became a man, the owl and watch were passed on to them.

He smiled and replied to her, "We'll talk more about it belonging to you later . . . a lot more."

The man who cared for her was feeling familiar. She said, "Your eyes, they remind me of someone. And your voice, I feel like I know it."

"I've been here talking to you, reading to you, and waiting for you. When the man at the Customs House told me your name was Cora, I felt very attached."

"Why?"

"I have ancestors named Joshua and Corabelle Harper. Cora is a very unusual name. I had to hear the story of how you got it."

Cora's heart rate increased. "What's your full name?"

"It's Jonathan Nathaniel Harper."

"JH," she whispered.

"Are you feeling better?" he asked with kindness and hope.

"Yes. I think I am." Then, after a moment's pause, Cora asked, "What book were you reading to me?"

"Well, your parents said you are quite the history buff and pirate tales are some of your favorites, so I was reading you the accounts of a pirate and his crew who attacked Charles Towne three hundred years ago."

"Was there a man named Jonathan Harris in those records?"

"No. I've never heard of him."

Disappointed, she muttered, "He was real."

"I believe you."

"What were you going to read next?"

"I was going to read about those who protected our Holy City, the night watchmen."

Cora rested her head back on the pillow. "Don't bother. I know that story too. I'd rather write the next tale."

"I can't wait to read it," he said.

Nate smiled and placed his hand over hers. Cora looked at him, somehow he reminded her of the man in her dreams. Cora turned her hand over and lifted her fingers so they fit perfectly between his. A comforting squeeze from him eased her pain.

He then asked, "So are you able to answer the question I have waited thirty-six hours to hear?"

Her brow pinched with curiosity.

"Your name?"

"Oh yeah. My answer is rather boring." Cora shrugged. "I'm named after my great-grandmother. It's possible her parents had a more interesting reason to name her Cora, but mine did not."

"Is it possible that JH and Corabelle wanted us to find each other? Could this just be fate?" Nate asked with a hopeful smile.

"His name was . . . he was Joshua Harper. And yes, I believe this is fate."

END

About Victoria R. Benson

A native South Carolinian and graduate of USC, Columbia, Victoria has taught 4th-6th grades and high school Math for eighteen years. Though always an educator, when a long lost passion for writing revived, Victoria heeded the inspiration and authored her first romance novel. See her works at blackdressbooks.com.

Find Victoria Online:
Website: https://blackdressbooks.com/
Facebook: https://www.facebook.com/blackdressbooks
Instagram: https://www.instagram.com/victoriarbenson/
Twitter: https://twitter.com/blackdressbooks
Amazon: https://www.amazon.com/Victoria-R-Benson/e/B081GB6HS7/ref=aufs_dp_fta_dsk
Goodreads: https://www.goodreads.com/author/show/20432723.Victoria_R_Benson
BookBub: https://www.bookbub.com/authors/victoria-r-benson

When It's Meant to Be

By Danielle Gadow

When It's Meant to Be

Contemporary

George Caldwell seems to have it all, but double work leaves no room for a personal life he didn't realize he was missing until Thanksgiving Day. An injury, after the morning 5K Turkey Run, brings Amber to his side. She ignites his attention with first, her beauty, and then, her advice to ensure his recovery.

Late afternoon dinner with friends brings Katlyn, a long-ago, one-night fling, back into his life. The connection they made at a college bar provoked an undeniable interest in each other. The early morning hours ended when Katlyn left before realizing they never exchanged the most pertinent information, their phone numbers, or last names.

Rated: PG

Chapter 1

George Caldwell spotted his fraternity brothers, hollering, "Another beautiful day!" as he completed his slow-paced jog and stopped in front of them. "Thanksgiving is my favorite time of year, and I wouldn't miss Charleston's Annual Turkey Day Run, for anything."

"You're the last one here," Victor noted. "Just like you'll be the last one to cross the finish line." He patted George on the shoulder as he walked by and laughed. "Just like last year!"

"Being the fastest isn't everything." George threw a cocky smile back at Victor while fist bumping Dennis a hello.

Dennis and Victor were George's closest friends, and the 5K run had become a tradition during their college days as fraternity brothers at the University of South Carolina. The day trip from the big campus in Columbia to Charleston never deterred anyone. Traveling to Charleston for the run, then back to Columbia for dinner at Ms. Daisy's house was as much a part of the holiday tradition as turkey and mashed potatoes. Now that they lived in the Charleston area, their Thanksgiving Day activities started and ended there, with an afternoon drive to Ms. Daisy's for the meal in between.

Blue skies and forty degrees made it a downtown Charleston race. The three proceeded, one behind the other with a walking-lunge rhythm toward the Meeting and Calhoun Streets starting point. Although they weren't die-hard competitors for any category wins, they were focused on their friendly three-man competition. Dennis participated for fun and the T-shirt, Victor wanted the bragging rights, and George enjoyed the camaraderie and adding to his weekly mile count.

"Any bets?" Dennis asked. "I've got ten dollars that says I don't win." They all erupted with laughter.

"I've got twenty that says you don't win too." Victor slapped Dennis on his shoulder as they continued to stretch and walk to get to the starting point.

George, the notorious big spender, chimed in, "I've got a fifty that says I beat you both."

"Bet's on!" Victor accepted the challenge, extending his hand in the air for high-fives from everyone. They slapped palms to seal the deal.

An air horn caught their attention, then a blaring voice announced, "One minute to start. Take your places, and if you aren't in the race for the official competition, please move back and let the competitors in front."

Everyone who was participating in the run got ready for the start at the line.

"On your mark. Get set," the announcer yelled loudly into the mic. Then, he pulled the trigger of the cap gun.

Bang!

The run began. Nine thousand or so bodies began the trek toward the Battery. This self-paced historic run passed Citadel Square Baptist Church, the historic Market, Gibbes Museum of Art, The Mills House Hotel, and the Four Corners of Law, which consisted of Charleston City Hall, US Post Office and Courthouse, County Courthouse, and St. Michael's Episcopal Church. Of course, they saw beautiful historic homes all along the way too.

George, Dennis, and Victor ran together at a steady pace, taking turns leading their group along the route on Murray Blvd. that led them by White Point Garden and Fort Sumter House onto South Battery. Then Victor sped up.

"Every man for himself!" he yelled over his shoulder, and off he went.

The turn onto King Street, named after King Charles II, shifted the surroundings from historic homes to a shopping district as they crossed Broad Street. They were almost in the home stretch.

The historic Frances Marion Hotel marked the finish line and led runners back into Marion Square.

Victor crossed the finish line then turned and waited, watching for George and Dennis. Within seconds, George crossed the line, then Dennis.

Victor laughed. "Whew, what took you so long?"

Dennis waved him off. "You got me, I don't even have an excuse."

The men continued toward the open area for drinks and snacks. Victor walked slightly ahead toward a refreshment booth.

"The crowds," George complained while making a quick turn to avoid a run-in with a child darting in his direction, but his foot slipped on the wet grass, making him twist his ankle, and then his knee, as he went down.

Dennis stopped short of tripping over George. "Are you OK?"

George sat for a second, trying to decipher exactly what just happened. He massaged his knee with his right hand while stretching to grip his ankle with his left. "I'm sure I am," he said through clenched teeth. "It was my fault."

"Ah, no it wasn't," Dennis said. "I saw the whole thing, and I assure you that kid wasn't paying any attention. Where are his parents anyway?"

"Help me up." George extended his arm for Dennis to pull him up on his uninjured right leg.

"What happened?" Victor asked, walking up with a banana in one hand and a drink in the other. He consolidated his items in one hand and helped George on his left side, opposite Dennis.

"Grrrrrr," George growled quietly, hoping he wasn't drawing attention to himself. His jaws flexed as he gritted his teeth together. He adjusted carefully, using both Dennis and Victor for stabilization, and was able to hop forward on his right leg. He cringed when anyone swiftly walked by their left side, fearing someone might accidentally cause the slightest bump.

"Sit down for a minute," demanded Dennis.

"I'll be all right," he insisted but took Dennis' advice and didn't complain as they lowered him to a firm sitting position. "Give me a second; it will be OK." But the pain radiating up his leg and beyond his knee, told him otherwise. *Damn, this could be serious.*

Before he could dwell on that, a woman's soft-spoken voice flooded his ears, drawing his attention as she leaned over in front of him.

"Can I do anything to help?"

Chapter 2

George's eyes roamed the young woman's face and body—and where else could they land if not straight on her chest, which was inches from his face and pressing against the sweat-dampened shirt that clung to her?

"What happened? she asked.

His eyes quickly steadied on her face while he tried to come up with a better excuse than *being tripped by a kid*. She had beautiful dark-brown hair that was perfectly straight and captured by a purple ribbon, the ends just touching the top of her shoulders. The race badge number 0624 pinned to the bottom of her Adidas pink-and-purple flower-patterned shirt validated her as a competitor in today's race.

"My name is Amber," she said, looking around at everyone, and drawing her attention away from George.

Dennis stood straighter, proceeding with his usual protector mode to look as if he were George's personal bodyguard.

"I'm hoping I can help you." She smiled while looking directly at George. "What happened?

After trying to give a verbal explanation and assurance he was all right, he shook his shoulders, twisted his torso, and wiggled his fingers as if those body parts had anything to do with the injury.

"There's nothing wrong a cold shower won't cure," George said, in an attempt to get back her attention.

Amber shook her head and looked around at his friends. "You're talking to yourself because no one believes you."

She explained she was a Doctor of Physical Therapy and highly recommended he see a physician.

"Do you mind?" she asked. When George shook his head, she lightly touched his ankle and helped straighten his leg. "Does this hurt?" She continued to slowly massage up toward his knee.

"Whoa," George shrieked after a moment. "That's the spot." He lightly placed his hand on top of hers, hoping she wouldn't continue to apply pressure. His jaw clenched with the pain he didn't mean to reveal.

Amber looked directly at George's face and cringed when she saw his pained expression and recognized his undeniable discomfort.

His jaw tensed.

"I'm so sorry." She moved her hands back down to George's ankle, lightly touching it. "How is this?"

"Not as bad as my knee," George replied.

The concern of this unknown, beautiful woman mesmerized him. He stared at her, thinking he'd take the pain as long as she didn't leave his side. He noticed a slight flutter in his chest as if his heart was trying to tell him something but disregarded the feeling as quickly as it appeared. He didn't have time for this nonsense.

He spotted his friends looking pointedly at each other.

"And nothing is wrong, he told her," Victor repeated George's earlier explanation dryly.

"I've seen that expression before," Dennis said in a low voice. "He better get his head out of the gutter." He laughed.

George purposely ignored his friends, preferring to focus on Amber. There was no point in denying she'd pushed the accident from George's mind. His attention was on this woman, not the pain.

Amber spoke to his friends. "Maybe you could help him get up again. Secure each arm, letting him use your shoulders for leverage."

He appreciated her direction as his friends lifted him to his feet with much more care than last time.

Amber shook her finger at the three of them. "Get him to a doctor's appointment to be sure there is no tear or break."

All three men looked at each other as if a doctor's appointment was foreign to them. "Any suggestions?" George asked.

"Actually, I do know a great specialist." She replied, looking at George. "I intern for him. This means I can go into the system and create an appointment for Monday. I'll be working that day, so I can help explain the situation and add you to my patient list."

"Will do." George measured his words as she made him nervous. He spoke to people all the time. A communications introvert he was not until Amber had him captivated.

They exchanged phone numbers, and Amber said she would text him the appointment time as soon as she had one.

Dennis left to find the white Chevy Traverse George had parked in a nearby parking garage. Apparently, it'd taken him several stops to explain why he needed to drive closer to Marion Square to pick up an injured runner, but eventually, he and Victor were able to get George in the front passenger seat and head to George's home in Summerville where they all would shower and change clothes before driving to the Thanksgiving celebration at Ms. Daisy's in Columbia.

Ms. Daisy had hosted Thanksgiving dinner since the three men had all become friends at the fraternity. Back then, Ms. Daisy was the house mother of sorts. Now she lived alone and continued to prepare a Thanksgiving feast every year for the fraternity members who were also alone during the holiday. The late afternoon meal gave them plenty of time to drive to Columbia after the race.

While Dennis was driving, George's phone pinged with a text message. Amber confirmed his Monday appointment. His heart beat faster, and his hand shook while holding the phone as he turned to show the text to the guys.

"Wow, she's quick," George said.

"What does it say?" Dennis asked, not taking his eyes off the road.

"Must be good; look at George's expression," Victor commented.

George read the text to them. "Your appointment is Monday, 11:00 a.m., downtown Summerville office. I'll be there too. Sorry, we must meet again under these circumstances." She'd included a sad face emoji too. "Who would think I'd be happy about a doctor's appointment?"

"It's not the doctor," Dennis assured. "It's the girl!"

"No, it's not, and her name's Amber," George said with a smirk.

"OK, I'm still right. It's Amber you're excited about and don't even try to deny it." Dennis turned to glare at Victor in the back seat. "Give me some help here. You saw how he acted when she tried to help after the accident."

"Yeah, I can't deny it, George. You were in la-la land with her presence. She's cute and all, but when's the last time you were ever struck silent by a woman?"

"Ah, shut up. You guys don't know what you are talking about," George defended himself. "She was just nice, sincere, and saw someone she thought needed help."

"Uh-huh, that's all it was." Dennis shook his head, and the three remained quiet most of the way to Columbia.

George took advantage of the silence, thinking about how she had all the qualities he looked for in a woman. Her genuine concern, professionalism, and quick smirks she'd shot off during the limited conversation told him she had a great personality. Her physical beauty was just icing. Yep, everything that interested him in a woman.

George lightly pounded his chest with his clenched hand as his heart fluttered again.

At Ms. Daisy's house, the reminiscing over the good-old fraternity days began. Usually, the same stories were repeated every year, including how Ms. Daisy helped keep them out of trouble.

Everyone grabbed a sturdy disposable, Thanksgiving-decorated plate with orange plastic utensils and bright napkins printed with a cartoon turkey. Ms. Daisy served buffet style. The walk around the counters where the food was displayed gave each the opportunity to choose to their liking. The guests jockeyed for seating as tables and chairs were scattered both indoors and out.

The doorbell rang, and Ms. Daisy jumped with excitement and scurried to answer the door. All the guests were engaged in their own conversations and eating their delicious Thanksgiving favorites. No one seemed to notice the new guest hugging and joyfully speaking with Ms. Daisy until Ms. Daisy spoke up.

"Everyone," she announced. Her guests gave their full attention. "I'd like to introduce to you KatieLynn Spaulding. I call her my granddaughter artist."

"I was extremely close with her family back in Wyoming. Her mother passed when she was young, and I was there to ensure the masculine homestead didn't take away her love for art and ballet, but mostly art." Everyone laughed as they knew of Ms. Daisy's love for all things art.

"Thank you, Ms. Daisy," KatieLynn replied. She gave Mrs. Davis another hug. and began a personal conversation, while the guests resumed their chats.

Dennis got George's attention with a soft punch on his upper shoulder. "Are you OK? You look a little pale."

WHEN IT'S MEANT TO BE

Chapter 3

George shook his head to tweak his thoughts while bracing himself as he adjusted his injured leg.

"George," Dennis said again. "Everything OK?"

"I'm fine," he said, "I was just thinking about the university's spring semester coming up." He was taking over as the interim chair for Visual Art and Design at the University of South Carolina Beaufort for a brief period, a favor for both a dear friend while she was on maternity leave and the university.

Ms. Daisy reminded everyone there were desserts sitting out on tables in the covered patio area. Almost immediately, guests headed that way, including Dennis and Victor.

George shifted in his seat and stood without putting any pressure on his injured leg. He hoped to speak with KatieLynn Spaulding.

He gingerly moved toward the patio where he'd last seen KatieLynn speaking with some guests. He braced himself on the dessert table until he spotted her talking with Victor. No surprise, Victor could make conversation with anyone, especially a pretty woman.

"Hey, George, let me introduce you to Kate," Victor looked at Kate and motioned with his hand to follow him toward George.

George used a crutch he'd brought from home to hobble a little closer before settling his right foot firmly, leaning slightly against the wall, and extending his hand to shake hers. "It's very nice to see you again, Katlyn." He smiled as he continued his reach to shake her hand, then changed his mind and reached further to offer a hug while giving his friend the get lost signal.

The infamous signal had been used many times between fraternity brothers. Victor did what he knew to do. "It was nice to meet you, Kate. I hope to speak with you again later."

"It was nice meeting you too," she replied.

George waited to ensure Victor had left and no one else was going to interrupt before speaking again. "So, long time no see." He gave her a cocky smile. "What have you been up to? Tell me, what is it: KatieLynn, Katlyn, or Kate?" He hesitated, realizing he may have sounded a little irritated.

She smiled, taking a step back from George. "My name all depends on where you rank in my life."

George continued to lean against the wall, taking more pressure off his leg. He was in deep thought, trying to remember the details of the twelve-hour relationship between him and Katlyn, or whatever name she was going by these days. *Relationship* was probably too strong of an identifier. There really had been no romantic relationship. Friendship was even questionable. *Immediate attraction* and a *great time* could describe those twelve-plus hours adequately. George recognized Katlyn as cute now as she was then with her shoulder-length, dark-blond hair. He couldn't help himself and continued to stare.

Katlyn had been a graduate student when she bumped into George at a college bar many years ago. She was at the university working on her master's degree in education.

It had been a girls' night out when Katlyn and her friend picked their favorite Five Points college bar. The bar was crowded, typical for a weekend, but it wasn't shoulder-to-shoulder crowded. Katlyn had been trying to get the bartender's attention to order a drink when she felt a solid hip bump against her right side. She turned to see George looking directly at her as he rested his elbows on the bar in front of her. He smiled and asked, "Where have you been all my life, good-looking?"

What a line, Katlyn had thought to herself, but he was so handsome, she couldn't take her eyes off of him.

George banged his fist on the counter to get the bartender's attention while never losing eye contact with Kate. "I'm buying. What'll you have?"

That had been all she needed to hear. How could she turn down a free drink?

"Surprise me," she had told him.

The two had been inseparable the rest of the night. After losing contact with her friend, they'd walked to his apartment where they'd continued the conversation and drinking, and then explored each other from head to toe.

Katlyn's phone had rung in the predawn hours; it had been the friend she had started the previous evening with.

"Where the hell are you?" she'd yelled when Katlyn had answered.

George had given Katlyn the address to tell her friend so she could pick her up, and they'd gone outside to wait. Her friend had pulled up to the front of the apartment building within minutes, and things had gotten awkward. It had been as if neither George nor Katlyn had known what to do or say to each other. Suddenly, after hours and hours of nonstop talking, laughing, kissing, and fondling, they started acting like strangers. Sure, technically, they were, but *total* strangers?

Katlyn had turned to George and said the first thing she could think of. "Thanks for the drinks; I had a great time." Then she had gotten into her friend's car.

George might have replied, "Me too," or "Let's do it again," but Katlyn couldn't remember exactly now. She regretted they hadn't exchanged phone numbers.

Yet more than five years later, here they were now at Ms. Daisy's Thanksgiving dinner.

Chapter 4

"It truly is good to see you again," George said. "I'm shocked."

"You're not the only one," she replied.

He shifted his weight to his good leg. That movement threw him off balance, and he instinctively placed his bad leg on the floor. Pain shot through him, making him grunt.

"Oh, oh, oh," Katlyn hollered and instantly reached for him as if she could help stop a fall.

"It's OK; I'm good," George responded as he caught his balance again. His face whitened. "I'm going to wish that didn't happen."

Katlyn grabbed a folding chair and set it down beside George. "Have a seat. How did you hurt your leg?"

"Good idea and thank you." George eased into the chair. "Just an accident dodging a kid about to run me over this morning." He gave a few details of the accident and how another runner came to his rescue, and that he had a doctor's appointment on Monday.

Katlyn gave her brief history of the last five years in return, which included finishing her master's degree and working as an elementary school art teacher while being a jewelry designer on the side.

"The stories I could tell you," she said. "And here I am today, recently hired to teach college students. Beginning in January." She smiled.

"Kate Spaulding," George said her name slowly while looking her up and down. With her beautiful blue-green eyes, he remembered having what he described as specks of glitter that made her entire face glow. The memory of that one evening and everything that went with those eyes began to flood back to him.

"You are the Kate Spaulding filling in for Dr. Frihart during her maternity leave next semester, right?"

"Yep," she said, tilting her head with a questioning look. "How did you know that?"

"Long story short," he said, "I just signed your paperwork. Does Dr. George Caldwell sound familiar?"

Katlyn sat with that revelation for a moment before she interjected with delight, "It absolutely does now! I never knew your last name."

George filled her in on his temporary position as interim chair of the Visual Art & Design Department at UofSC Beaufort while Carolyn had been in and out with pregnancy issues—mostly out—and was to go on official maternity leave after Christmas. She'd been adamant about her replacement while she was gone, and that had been Kate Spaulding, a previous summer-school student of hers at the Savannah College of Art and Design.

"So, I guess you're my boss now?"

George laughed. "Exactly."

"Let's go," Dennis announced from George's front porch. He was driving George to the doctor's appointment Amber had set up for him, so George didn't even think about driving himself.

"Can you stay here and wait," George asked Dennis as he hobbled with two crutches toward the front desk to check in for his appointment. Dennis nodded.

"I'm here to see Dr. Patrick," George said when it was his turn to check in. "Amber set up the appointment for me. I'm George Caldwell." He blushed, feeling somewhat ridiculous.

"Yes, Mr. Caldwell, it will be a few minutes. Meanwhile, I'll let them know you have arrived."

Within seconds, Amber walked out to the lobby, wearing typical medical scrubs, only hers were garnet. "Hey, George. How are you doing? Hope you have been resting and taking care of yourself."

"As best I can," George replied. "I see you are Gamecock loyal." He nodded toward her scrubs attire, referring to the color.

"Wouldn't wear anything else," she said as she waved her hand toward the door. "Follow me."

Amber guided George into a large room filled with various workout equipment and padded tables. "Are you able to sit here?" She tapped the padded table and chuckled, knowing full good and well he would be able to sit down on the table. "Let me know if you need any help."

After George sat and got comfortable, Amber instructed, "Bring both legs up, flat on the table. Lie back and relax."

A gentleman dressed in black slacks and a white lab coat walked in. No doubt, the doctor. He raised himself up, leaning on his elbows.

"Hello, Mr. Caldwell. I'm Dr. Patrick," he explained. "Amber tells me she met you at the Turkey Day Run." George tried to sit up more, but Dr. Patrick shook his head. "Please lie back Mr. Caldwell. I'm going to look at your ankle, and then your knee."

Dr. Patrick began to prod and poke, asking about the pain and how George felt today as compared to last Thursday when the accident happened.

"The pain isn't too bad," George told him. "Although, I've been extra careful using the crutches and all. The crutches are more annoying than the pain."

"I have no doubt you feel that way," Dr. Patrick said as he chuckled. "I don't necessarily think you have done any major damage; however, I would like to be sure with an MRI, which we can conduct here if you are agreeable."

"That would be fine. When will this be scheduled?"

Dr. Patrick looked at Amber for an answer.

"There's a patient in the MRI room now," said Amber. "It will be another thirty minutes or so before that scan is completed, then we should be able to send in Mr. Caldwell next."

"Perfect, if that is OK with you," Dr. Patrick said, speaking to George. "Another thirty minutes, maybe forty-five, then you're next. Your ankle and knee should only take about fifteen minutes each."

George thanked Dr. Patrick as he left. Amber stayed and asked if there was anything she could get him while he waited. "Would you like something to drink? The building has a small cafeteria. I'd be happy to get you something while you wait."

George smiled, enjoying the attention, then remembered he needed to let Dennis know what was happening. "Could Dennis come back here while I wait? I need to let him know what's going on since he drove me here."

"You know," said Amber, "I'd be happy to drive you home after the MRI, so your friend doesn't have to wait. My shift will be over by the time your MRI is completed."

Before George could come up with an excuse or even open his mouth to respond, Amber had walked toward the door. She turned and said, "Really, I don't mind. I'll tell him so he can leave, and I'll drive you home." She walked out quickly without turning around for an answer.

George smiled to himself. Wondering what this was all about. There was nothing more appealing than an extraordinarily nice, confident, professional woman who showed him any attention at all, regardless of the circumstance. His professional life kept him busy with two jobs. The temporary academic position and his entrepreneurial startup of *Sporting Design* didn't leave much room for anything personal. It was obvious, that they had one thing in common, running, and he would bet money there was much more. Something about Amber made him not want to be so busy anymore. She was flirting with him, ever so subtly, but he recognized flirting, and he wanted to explore what else they had in common. He needed, he wanted, someone like Amber to share his personal life with. The instant appearance of butterflies in his stomach, made him feel giddy and he welcomed the feeling and hoped it would continue.

The MRI was as quick as described. Dr. Patrick told George he should have the results within twenty-four hours, and he would call to discuss a physical therapy plan. Although he assured George, from what he could see, he felt this mishap would resolve itself with a little rest.

Amber helped George to her Volvo, walking closely beside him with her hand around his bicep as he continued to use the crutches to ease the weight on his left leg. It wasn't as if she or George thought she could do anything to stop a fall, but it was the thought that counted. She opened the front passenger door for George and grabbed both crutches so he could adjust himself to sit down. She went to the other side and put the crutches in the back seat before getting in and pressing the ignition button.

George's stomach fluttered and his mind raced in romantic directions. Was he imagining things? Was she as attracted to him as he was to her?

Chapter 5

It was a relief when Dr. Patrick called the next day to say the results looked good, with no tears or anything to be concerned about. The ankle was a sprain, and George twisted his knee when he tried to keep from colliding with the kid. With it all happening at the same time, it was like a double whammy, for someone like George who was in fit condition.

"Two minor sprains, so between rest, elevation, and pampering," Dr. Patrick told George, "And you should be back to normal, but let's see you in the office again in two weeks, just to be sure." George agreed and the call was transferred to the front desk to schedule the appointment.

Following the doctor's orders, George spent the next two weeks at home, both shopping online for Christmas gifts and scheduling meetings with his business partners, Dennis, and Victor.

Two weeks later, George drove himself to the doctor's appointment and walked in without any assistance from the crutches. He gave his name to the receptionist and found a seat.

"George Caldwell," was announced by a female voice he quickly recognized before looking up from the *Sports Illustrated* magazine he had selected to pass the waiting time. He saw Amber with what he assumed was his chart in her hands. She had a mischievous smile on her face, and he responded quickly with his own.

"It's so good to see you again, Miss Amber." He said while walking toward her and realizing he didn't know her last name.

"You, too, Mr. Caldwell," she professionally responded. "Follow me, right this way." She directed him into a private patient room where they would wait for Dr. Patrick.

"I guess you know the MRI results," George questioned.

"I do, and you look great and seem to be walking well," she said. "I hope you're having no more pain."

His chest seemed to twitch or was that his heart? The sensation caught him off guard as he smiled. "Let me thank you and take you to dinner," he said. "Somewhere in Charleston? How about Hyman's Seafood?"

Her voice was soft and sincere, as she looked down holding the patient chart close to her chest. "Thank you, but you don't need to do that."

"I want to do this for you. It's just a thank you."

Again, Amber thanked him but deflected. "Hyman's wouldn't be my choice, but I appreciate the offer."

George was shocked when she denied the offer. "Really?" He burst out. "Hyman's is one of the best restaurants on Meeting Street. Not many people would turn that down?"

She smiled but didn't say any more.

If only she could read the disappointment on his face. Had he truly misread, what he had previously hoped was some sort of connection that had formed between them even if in such a short time. "Another place, then? Your choice." He wasn't about to let his instincts about Amber be wrong. At least not this quickly.

"I work there, nights and weekends," she said smiling even bigger.

He laughed. "No way! Why didn't you just say that? How long have you worked there?"

"It's been a couple of years now since I started PT school. A girl's got to have spending money, you know."

"How could I ever have missed you?" George replied. "I eat there quite often. I take clients there all the time, and don't think I've ever seen you."

"You've got to open your eyes," Amber sarcastically said. "I've seen you. In fact, I knew who you were when I saw you on the ground at the Turkey Day Run. Why do you think I stopped and offered to help?"

George was totally confused but focused on Amber's face. Maybe she did look familiar?

"And Dan, my boss at Hyman's, happens to be a fraternity brother and one of your best friends." She stared back with a satisfied smile. "Am I correct?"

George cupped his hands over his mouth, trying to hide the smile and hold back the laugh. "You got me, that's for sure," he admitted. "I can't believe Dan never told me. He's in big trouble now."

"Why would he even say anything about me?" Amber held back a laugh.

"Well, hell, let's make it easy," George suggested as he imitated what Dan should have said to him. "'Hey, George, I've got the best server of all time working for me. She's super smart, good-looking, and *single*.'" George raised his voice for emphasis. "Yep, that would have done it for me. That's all he would have had to say." He paused, looking more intently at Amber, "You are single, aren't you?"

Amber seemed to glow as she took two steps closer to George. Lifting herself onto her toes, she reached around his neck and paused while looking into his dark-blue eyes. This first move was all George needed. He leaned down to kiss her lips ever so lightly. When she returned the kiss, as if giving him permission to proceed, he slowed the kiss to an end and backed away. He hoped that didn't cause her concern, but his heart was pounding in his chest, and he knew he needed to stop, or things might get out of control. Thank goodness, there was a knock at the door.

Instantly, the two backed farther away from each other, wiping their lips with their hands, hoping to clear away any tell-tale sign of even an innocent kiss.

"Come in," George said once they felt presentable.

Dr. Patrick opened the door and entered. He paused, looking back and forth between Amber and George. "It's good to see you again, George. Have a seat on the exam table."

George leaned against the table and pulled himself upward to sit, his legs dangling over the edge. He was almost sweating, vacillating between *Oh shit, we just got caught!* and *Damn, I hope she doesn't get in trouble.* He tried his best to stay focused as Dr. Patrick reviewed both his ankle and knee, asking if there was any pain when he touched the areas.

"Not at all," George replied. "You've confirmed the diagnosis and remedy perfectly."

"You have Amber to thank for that. Her recognition of a potential problem and setting up the appointment was the first step. Even though she is still an intern, I left this case to her completely. She is going to be an excellent PT when she finishes her degree. The diagnosis including a couple of weeks of rest was all her."

Done with the follow-up appointment, Dr. Patrick stood and headed for the door. As he was about to leave the room, he paused, his hand on the doorknob. "Amber, I'll leave Mr. Caldwell's chart in your hands to finish up."

Even though George and Amber were trying their best to convince themselves nothing inappropriate happened between them before Dr. Patrick walked in—or nothing that could be proven—the embarrassed looks on both their faces were priceless, leaving Dr. Patrick with one more direction for Amber. "Remember, Amber, I don't charge follow-up appointments, so whatever recovery plan you decide is up to you." He gave what appeared to George to be a devious smile before he finally left them alone.

Amber proceeded with Dr. Patrick's directions, explaining to George she felt he did need

further *personal* PT appointments, and it would be in his best interest if he agreed to house calls.

There was no argument about house calls. Physical therapy appointments were scheduled for the next day.

Amber's first professional house call was held in George's living room and started with typical PT questions about how his ankle and knee were feeling.

"What's your pain level?" she asked. "Between one and ten, with ten being the most painful."

"Two, maybe three."

"Let's stretch some," she directed him as she stretched out her own left leg to show him some moves.

He followed her direction, copying every move she made, stretching and bending both injured locations, proving he had no issues with the injury.

Amber confirmed, "You're doing great."

"You're the professional," George assured Amber. "Maybe my case requires more personal PT specific to all the activities I am normally involved with." He smiled at her cleverly, waiting for her to pick up his hint.

"I hear you. Swimming is always a PT favorite." She was looking at his backyard pool, which was visible through the sliding glass door. "I'll have to add a swimsuit to my PT accessory bag, just in case."

"And it's heated, perfect for this time of year," he said. "Then maybe you can let me help you plan additional PT activities to make sure this injury doesn't hinder my golf game, starting here at the twelfth hole, water skiing with my boat on Lake Moultrie, or kayaking on the Ashley River."

"That's quite a list," she agreed. "I will be more than happy to make sure all those activities are worked into your personal PT schedule—regardless of how long it may take or how many times we may have to repeat an activity." She smiled. "Now that we have a plan for the types of PT activities to schedule, let's spend today doing . . ." George assumed she purposely paused to make sure he was paying attention. "Yoga!"

They both laughed.

"Are you familiar with yoga?" she asked.

"I've never done yoga if that's what you are asking," he said.

"Then I'll have to give you a close, personal demonstration."

"Close and personal? Sounds like I'll need that," he assured her.

"Since both were wearing shorts, we're already dressed for this activity, and it will be fun."

Amber pulled two yoga mats out of her activity bag, unrolling them both and tossing each on the floor. "Have a seat on the mat."

She sat too. "Yoga is done with slow movements and deep breathing. It can improve flexibility and strength while stretching your muscles and even relieve stress and anxiety."

George sat with his legs crossed, not so comfortably, and stared at Amber in her short shorts, before realizing her athletic shirt completed a matching set. A fashion statement he had seen before. "Relieve stress and anxiety," he repeated. "That's not working here." He reached for her hand. "Maybe you need to get closer, help make sure I'm doing this right."

"You're so goofy," she said but moved closer anyway, sitting on his mat with him. "Feel better now?"

"I'm about to," he assured as he leaned toward her, playfully knocking her over and then hovering over her upper body, straddling his legs on each side of her hips. He sank down, careful not to crush her with his weight, and began kissing her with full intention. Their mouths opened and tongues played. He moved his kisses down her neck, over her shoulders, and up to her mouth again.

"Now that's the kind of yoga I like," he said as he continued kissing and nibbling all over.

"Who's overseeing the session here?" She pulled up to reverse positions with him, straddling his waist and imitating his moves. "What was that you were saying about stress and anxiety?"

The personal PT appointments, as they were called, continued every chance they could get together, only pausing during Christmas break when Amber went home to see her parents in Rome, Georgia, and George visited his parents and Ms. Daisy in Columbia.

Chapter 6

The first week in January, a ping sounded the text alert on George's phone. It was Katlyn.

I'm headed your way. Hope to be in Beaufort around 5 pm.

George thought for a moment. It was Friday and he wasn't in Beaufort. He only stayed at his apartment in Beaufort Monday through Wednesday, leaving on Thursday afternoons so he could be home in Summerville Thursday evening through Sunday.

Not wanting to text while he knew Katlyn was driving, he called her.

"Hey, George," she answered.

"Hey, Katlyn, how about a change of plans?"

"I'm up for anything," she responded. "What's up?"

He explained his living arrangements between Summerville and Beaufort, then suggested she get on I-26 and head toward Summerville and stay with him. They could both drive to Beaufort on Sunday, which was time enough to get her settled into her apartment before office hours started on Monday and classes the following week. He continued with reassurance he had already pulled her class schedules, list of students, and syllabi Dr. Frihart had put together for each class. He could give everything to her when she arrived.

"It sounds like a plan," she said.

George gave her his address. "Call me if you have any issues."

"Will do," she said before hanging up.

Now she was wondering why her stomachs seemed to flip. It has been a long time since she had seen George—not counting the Thanksgiving dinner at Ms. Daisy's—and since she wasn't seeing anyone herself, maybe this would be a rekindling of a relationship that never happened.

"Maybe."

She smiled at the thought and continued to think of her short-term encounter with George. She remembered how captivated she'd been by the unexpected attention she received from a very handsome, older gentleman, no less. She considered herself an introvert; therefore, interacting with unfamiliar people was unlike her. Yet, this connection had been different from any other she'd ever experienced. She'd dated and even had a few lengthy relationships in the past five years. Why, she questioned herself, was she even thinking about a possible rekindling with George?

As expected, the GPS didn't fail. She slowed her Jeep to a crawl as she turned into the driveway and noticed George on the front porch waiting. The house looked like a historical treasure—two stories with an attic above. Hand-carved balusters accented the entire wrap-around porch. Tall, thin French doors opened from inside spaces from more than one side. It was covered with a copper-tin roof and cedarwood siding. Every window was encased with elaborate detail in various shades of pastel accents framed by hurricane shutters painted Charleston green.

She parked by a three-tier water fountain serving as a driveway accent and took her time getting out of the Jeep while she gazed around. "Wow!" She looked at George before saying again, "Wow!"

Of course, she was talking about the house, but after George hopped down the porch stairs and landed directly in front of her, it was all she could do to hold back another "wow" as she looked up at him. He wore khaki pants, a dark blue polo shirt with an embroidered logo *Sporting Design* on the left chest, and leather topsider shoes.

"I'm glad you made it." He paused briefly. "I should tell you there are options." He went on to explain his home had historic colors with every bedroom being different. "Take your pick: a purple room, baby blue, slightly pink, or—not my favorite—ordinary white. Each has a bathroom, too; how can that go wrong?"

She looked at George with a playful smile, remembering her younger self from years past when pink was her staple color. "Pink. I can never get enough pink."

George smiled back and he glanced through the rear driver's side window. "Do you have any luggage I can help carry inside?" He walked to the back and peeked through the rear window. "Looks like you do."

Katlyn unlocked the back door for George.

"Pink is definitely your color," he confirmed as he pulled out two pink paisley suitcases. "I'll show you to your room, then let me take you to dinner."

In less than thirty minutes, they were both in the living room. "Ready?" asked George. "I thought I would take you to Halls Chophouse here in Summerville. It's one of the best steakhouses around and hasn't failed me yet.

"Sounds great," Katlyn assured him. "It's a date."

George walked her to his SUV in the driveway and opened the passenger door. Yes, that was a standard date move, but it was also his gentlemanly character. This wasn't a *date*, and he was sure her comment was just an offhand remark.

They pulled into the restaurant parking lot and walked inside. "The place looks busier than I expected."

"Good evening, Mr. Caldwell," said the hostess. "Would you like a drink at the bar? It will be just a few minutes before I can seat you."

"That would be perfect," he walked Katlyn toward the bar with his hand on her lower back. "Do you still drink Old Fashioneds?" It was the only drink he could remember from way back when.

"I haven't had one since you bought me a drink or two," she admitted. "I don't know why because I remember liking it. I'd love one."

When the bartender approached, George placed their order.

"Great choice," said the guy standing next to him.

George turned and realized it was Dr. Patrick.

"Great minds *drink* alike," said George. "It's nice to see you somewhere other than your office." He smiled.

When the bartender set down the two drinks, George handed Katlyn hers and lifted his with a simple "Cheers" and a nod to everyone. He put the drink back down in front of him.

"Cheers to you too," said Dr. Patrick. "Let me introduce you to Ali, my wife."

George shook Ali's hand. "It's nice to meet you."

"You as well." She shook George's hand with a strong grip signifying self-confidence. Her petite five-foot three-inch frame might have sent a different impression as she stood aside her husband towering over her, adorning a build of pure muscle.

Suddenly, George realized he hadn't introduced Katlyn. "My apologies, this is Katlyn Spaulding, I mean *Kate* Spaulding. I met Kate back when she went by Katlyn; sometimes I forget." He looked directly at Katlyn and mouthed "I'm sorry."Katlyn smiled at George signifying no worries, then shook hands with the couple. "I'm subbing for some art courses at UofSC Beaufort." She was feeling nostalgic, remembering the past with George. She leaned against George while squeezing his bicep as if to confirm their relationship. "George was gracious enough to offer that I stay with him until we drive to Beaufort and I get settled in my apartment."

George pulled his arm back, and she released her hand. Then she impulsively reached around to his back, massaging in obvious circular motions, and looked into George's eyes while she scooted even closer to him and gave him a side hug.

She smiled as she straightened and brought her hands back to her side. *Now, this was a date,* she thought to herself. The moves she just made on George could surely be recognized as her interest in him. Was she trying to recapture a relationship from the past she knew, deep down, wasn't a true relationship? Or could it be a relationship? She wouldn't know if she didn't try.

"Excellent," said Dr. Patrick. "I hope things go well for you." He then looked at George. "How is Amber?" The expression he sent George's way, made George feel, without a doubt, *You are going to have questions to answer.*

"She's been wonderful," George answered slightly louder than necessary as if that might erase any suspicion. He clenched his jaw, hoping not to bring attention to his frustration while also trying to inch away from Katlyn. "She's been spending time with her parents over the holidays."

"Yes, I'm aware," said Dr. Patrick. "She's well-thought of and we'll miss her in the office when she rotates out."

George smiled. "No doubt." He hoped there was no emotion on his face that might imply anything to validate what Dr. Patrick knew, or didn't know, about his relationship with Amber.

"Dr. Patrick, your table is ready," the hostess called out. She spotted George and said, "Your table is next," before guiding the couple to the other room.

George picked up his drink and gulped the entire thing in one swallow. He sat the glass down, looking at the bartender. "Another please."

They decided to forgo dessert when George mentioned an upset stomach. He just wanted to go home after his panic upon Dr. Patrick seeing him with Katlyn at dinner. *It's not like I've done anything wrong*, he kept telling himself, but he hadn't told Amber about Katlyn's unexpected visit.

He sat in the living room with Katlyn, discussing her schedule of classes as he passed the class rosters, schedules, and syllabi across the coffee table.

Ping.

George looked at his phone. It was Amber. No surprise as they had been texting regularly since she'd been away. While he would normally be elated, now he began to sweat. The coincidences of Amber's text, seeing Dr. Patrick, and Katlyn being in his living room were too much.

"I need to reply to this text," he said, as he walked to open the sliding glass door and step onto the patio.

The text included an adorable puppy gif. **Miss You! Dr. P texted. Said it's busy and he could schedule me in the office next week.**

George was searching through "miss you more" gifs to pick from while wondering what else Dr. Patrick might have said to Amber and why did he text her. Then he began rationalizing with himself: *I haven't done anything wrong; Katlyn's a friend, a coworker—subordinate to be exact. I'm helping her out, being nice. So, what am I worried about?*

He found a perfect gif listing every day of the week and ending with "I miss you more" and touched send. Then texted, **Is it OK to call?**

Yes!

He immediately tapped her number stored at the top of his favorites list.

"That was quick," Amber answered with a happy voice.

"Wasn't quick enough," he admitted. "So, you're coming back early? That's awesome!"

"Yep," she said, "my final rotation is specifically with pediatric patients. He asked if I'd like to start early. I'm getting paid, so how could I say no?"

"Pediatrics?" George teased. "I guess that's why I'll have to continue with private PT sessions since I don't fall into the pediatric category."

"Exactly, you're a *big boy*." She exaggerated *big boy*, and continued, "I've decided to drive back tomorrow. I'm packed and should be on the road by eight in the morning. I can schedule you for a private PT session around two-thirty," she offered in a flirting voice.

The earlier excitement in her voice turned solemn when she spoke next after he'd paused for a beat too long. "If you would like?"

"I want you to stay here with me," he said, finding his voice after Katlyn has popped into his head and he knew there might be a problem.

"I hoped you would say that."

Amber felt the fine hairs on the back of her neck rise to attention as she considered George's pause over the phone. "What's up," she said softly.

"Nothing," he replied almost as soft, "I just miss you and wish you were with me right now." He paced the patio, holding the phone out with the conversation on speaker.

"Well, OK," she replied, her voice stronger, sounding more confident.

Still pacing the patio and around the pool, George made another turn and walked directly into Katlyn. "Whoa!"

"I just wanted to tell you I was going to call it a night. Take a shower and head to bed. I'll see you in the morning," Katlyn confirmed with a smile.

"Oh yeah, great." He countered back, and Katlyn left. Then he heard another voice.

"Excuse me, George." It was Amber's voice. "What was that? Who was that?"

Damn speakerphone.

"That was a woman's voice," she sounded very certain.

George immediately tapped the speaker button and lifted the phone to his ear. "I'm so sorry, it's nothing, Amber, really nothing to worry about."

"I beg to differ," she said more firmly. "I think I heard enough. Taking a shower? Going to bed. Did I need to hear more?"

"Wait, listen—"

"And it was a woman's voice!" her voice sounding louder. "That I am sure of."

"Amber, let me explain," he tried to remain somewhat calm while he stared at Katlyn, wishing she would walk away.

"Oh, please do explain. I can't wait to hear this."

Chapter 7

"Kate is the substitute art professor while Dr. Frihart is on leave. We know some of the same people and ironically had met one another years ago. I needed to go over a few things with Kate before school starts. She arrived today, and I invited her to stay in one of the many guestrooms, but not mine. She was at Ms. Daisy's house on Thanksgiving. I told you about her. It's a weird coincidence." George took a deep breath and sighed, giving Amber a moment to interject. She didn't say a word.

He took another deep breath. "I'm sure I told you some of this, some-time during one of my private PT sessions." The memory made him smile to himself. "We've talked about so much; I've never held anything back intentionally."

"Maybe so," Amber admitted softly.

That was progress and all he cared about at this point.

"You know me," he said to Amber. "I invited Katlyn without thinking, without realizing how the offer to stay at my house might appear otherwise and upset you. This meant nothing to me." He paused, hoping Amber was listening closely. She was quiet.

George continued. "I told Katlyn to drop by my Summerville house and stay with me over the weekend since I had all the paperwork she needed for her classes, and we could review everything before returning to Beaufort on Sunday."

Still no sound from Amber.

"Please, Amber," he begged again. "Think this through; don't give up what we have going for us now because of someone I *barely* knew years ago. *Years ago*," he repeated for clarity. "It was a one-evening fling, and even that is giving it too much of an unrealized definition."

Still no sound, no comment coming from the other end of the phone. Until finally, "This has been a lot, more than I expected. I've got to go. I've got to think.

"Amber, please."

"I'll see you tomorrow," she said. "I promise." She hung up without hesitation.

It was a long night for George. He repeated over and over in his head what had happened, and what he could have done differently. But nothing could be changed now. He worried about what to say when Amber showed up this afternoon. He had no idea what to expect when she arrived.

Wide awake now, George walked to the kitchen to make some coffee and was surprised to see Katlyn was already there.

"Do you want me to leave before Amber gets here?" Katlyn asked as she poured herself a cup of coffee she had already started. She didn't want to leave. She wanted to meet Amber. She wanted to know who this woman was. Maybe it was the thought of competition, but she knew George would never be more than a friend and coworker.

"No, Katlyn, absolutely not," George was sincere. "If you leave, that could only make things worse, as if I did have something to hide. Please stay," he confirmed. "But give us some space when she arrives."

"Maybe you should start by calling me Kate now." She poured another cup of coffee. "Katlyn was then, Kate is now. Grown-up now. If you keep calling me Katlyn, it's like there's some special relationship; and as you said, twelve hours doesn't make it special. It's just an encounter."

George walked toward her and accepted the cup of coffee she handed to him. "Thank you, Kate, for understanding." He pulls the cup to his mouth to take a sip, then hesitates and blows over the rim of the cup to cool the coffee. There was nothing that could ease his own thoughts of how he had unintentionally hurt Amber.

"I'm going outside," George said to Kate. "I'm going to sit on the front porch and wait. It's all I can think about, so I'll just wait."

"It's going to be fine." Kate patted his upper shoulder. "I'll be inside."

If he'd timed it right, Amber should arrive soon. His nerves were rattled, and his hands were shaking causing a slight spill of his coffee on his pressed khaki pants. Hoping for text messages, he kept checking his phone, only to be disappointed each time there was none.

The morning was gone and the afternoon had begun when Amber's car turned into the driveway. He jumped to his feet, walked to the top of the steps, and watched her park alongside Kate's Jeep. Before she could cut off the ignition, George scrambled down the stairs. Nothing mattered more than getting to Amber as fast as he could.

George opened her car door and offered his hand to help her from the seat. Once she was standing, George drew her in close, not even waiting to get a radar check on her mood.

"I've missed you so much." He squeezed her body closer to his. "I'm so sorry; I wasn't thinking and didn't mean to hurt you." He drew away to get a look at her face, then kissed her as if his world might be coming to an end.

She returned the passion as if nothing had changed between them. George's tongue engaged in foreplay, which she also returned before trying to speak.

"I'mmm, . . . Georrrrrr . . ."

She gave him a slight push, a tell-tale sign, and George pulled back. He waited for her to say something.

"I'm sorry too," she cried. "After I calmed down and thought things through, I knew you were telling me the truth. I knew. She reached for his head and pulled him closer, kissing him again.

Kate strolled down to her Jeep with her luggage. The unlock sound from the key fob startled the couple.

"Don't mind me, y'all. I thought I'd leave and head on to Beaufort." She approached to shake Amber's hand. "My name is Kate Spaulding. I wish I would have met you under less strenuous circumstances, but I assure you, George is genuine."

When Kate spoke, Amber smiled knowing Kate was speaking the truth.

"Thank you," George said softly.

Kate turned toward Amber to offer one last word of advice. "Don't let him get away. The sooner you realize it, you will always know for sure *when it's meant to be.*"

Epilogue

Several Years Later

George turned toward Amber as he glanced at his phone. Nothing was said. He was nervous and she squeezed his knee under the table while taking his hand and lifting it to her lips for a soft kiss.

"What are you anxious about?" Amber tried to lighten his mood. "All she can do is say no to your offer. She accepted your invitation to dinner, so there should be nothing to worry about."

"I know, you're right," George said and pulled her hand toward his mouth for a similar expression of his love while twirling his tongue in small circles over the back of her hand and finishing with a kiss. He smiled. "You are always right."

George looked up to see the restaurant host guiding Kate across the room. He rose and walked around the table with his hand extended for a professional greeting. "It's good to see you again, Kate. Thank you for coming."

Amber didn't hesitate as she, too, walked toward Kate and gave her a friendly hug. "Welcome Kate, it's good to see you again. It's been a while." She pulled Kate slightly tighter in the hug and whispered in her ear. "George is a bit nervous for no reason. I've been assuring him."

The warm greetings were a noted relief for all. Standing to the side, George pulled Kate's chair to offer her a seat. Behind Kate, he held Amber's gaze across the table and blew her a kiss.

The evening was off to a start once the server brought the bottle of wine George had previously requested, poured the glasses, mentioned the specials for the evening, and said he would return once they had time to look at the menu.

"Well, Kate, tell me what you've been doing since I saw you last. Obviously, your career has been fully vetted by George, or you wouldn't be here." Amber was always the social butterfly who could get conversations started.

With Amber taking the lead, George listened while the women chatted as if they had been long-lost best friends throughout the appetizers and main course. After dinner, while they waited for dessert, George finally spoke.

"Kate, you are probably wondering why I wanted to speak with you about *Sporting Design*." George adjusted to sit straighter in his seat, took another sip of his wine, then continued to explain his company's fast-paced growth and outlook for the coming years. "I want you, Kate, to come work for *Sporting Design*, bringing your award-winning design status with you."

Kate shifted her eyes, raising her eyebrows and looking at Amber first as if silently asking, *did you know about this?*

Amber smiled at Kate, with a slight nod assuring that she did know.

George continued, "I want you to come work for *Sporting Design*. How does the vice president of Clothing Design sound to you?"

End

Kate's answer, what the future holds, and a new romance, are coming soon in the romantic novel *It Was Meant to Be*. By Danielle Gadow.

About <u>Danielle Gadow</u>

Danielle has been married 39 years to her high-school sweetheart. She is blessed with three grown children, four-grandchildren, and Cali the 16-year-old family Chihuahua. Everyone lives in Columbia, South Carolina.

She works full-time and writing has become a passion. "When It's Meant to Be" is her first attempt at writing a romance short story to be published.

Her dream for success is interpreted as anyone (outside of her family) who might read her story, love it, and encourage her to write more.

Find Danielle Online:
Facebook: <u>https://www.facebook.com/dmgadow</u>
Instagram: <u>https://www.instagram.com/dmgadow/</u>
Twitter: <u>https://twitter.com/DanielleGadow</u>

Lowcountry Romance Writers of America

Where romance writers connect, hone our craft, and create beautiful stories.

The Lowcountry Romance Writers of America is a chapter of Romance Writers of America and meets online, in Charleston, SC and Columbia, SC. Our membership includes published authors, pre-published authors, and agents from all over the Southeast. We meet every month to connect and work on improving our craft.

One hundred percent of the proceeds from all our anthologies go directly back to our chapter, thereby benefiting our members through education and connections.

http://lowcountryrwa.com

We hope you enjoyed Love in the Lowcountry.
We hope you will consider leaving a review of this anthology on
Goodreads, or the site where this anthology was purchased.

Thank you for your support!